THE METHUSELAH PROJECT

A NOVEL

THE
METHUSELAH
PROJECT

A NOVEL

RICK BARRY

Kregel Publications

The Methuselah Project
© 2015 by Rick Barry

Published by Kregel Publications, a division of Kregel, Inc., 2450 Oak Industrial Dr. NE, Grand Rapids, MI 49505.

Library of Congress Cataloging-in-Publication Data
Barry, Rick (Richard C.)
    The Methuselah project : a novel / by Rick Barry.
      pages ; cm
    I. Title.
    PS3602.A77759M48   2016   813'.6—dc23   2015019972

ISBN 978-0-8254-4387-9

Printed in the United States of America
15 16 17 18 19 20 21 22 23 24 / 5 4 3 2 1

Dedicated to Pam,
my faithful cheerleader in
so many projects

ACKNOWLEDGMENTS

I owe a debt of gratitude to a number of people for this novel. First, thank you to all the publishing professionals at Kregel who believed in *The Methuselah Project*. Especially notable among these are Dawn Anderson, Steve Barclift, Noelle Pedersen, Janyre Tromp, and Sarah Slattery. Working with all of them has been terrific.

Others who read the manuscript and helped to comb out errors or offered advice include Kari Fischer, Dr. Dennis E. Hensley, Hilarey Johnson, Darren Kehrer, Deirdre Lockhart, Carol Matthia, Patti Jo Moore, Colleen Shine Phillips, Amy Wallace, and Margaret Wolfinbarger.

Huge thanks go to my literary agent, Linda Glaz of Hartline Literary, for representing the project.

I'm indebted to the pilots of the Fourth Fighter Group, some of whose debriefing sessions proved invaluable to me long decades after their missions ended. Likewise, the writings of journalist Ernie Pyle preserve details of life in wartime England and helped to add realism.

Of course, the book would not exist without my wife, Pam, who is my first reader and constant encourager as she endures the countless hours I spend at my keyboard when I could be with her instead.

A final word of appreciation goes to people like you, who are reading this now. Without readers, no book—regardless of how diligently researched and crafted—could achieve its goal of touching hearts and minds. Many of you have asked when my next novel will be published. Here it is.

CHAPTER 1

Sitting in his cockpit, Captain Roger Greene scanned the heavens. He searched left to right, overhead, below, and behind. No sign of enemy aircraft. Just formation after formation of B-17s droning along below, plus his own umbrella of Thunderbolts providing escort cover.

Come on, you cowards. Come and defend your precious Fatherland. I dare you.

He glanced into the sun, then jerked his eyes from the blinding glare. When searching for enemy planes, he preferred his naked eyes, but his eyesight would surely suffer if he kept doing that. He probed the pocket of his flight jacket for his green aviators. Instead of sunglasses, his gloved thumb and forefinger fished up a ten-dollar bill.

Ten bucks? How the . . .

Then he noticed the message printed along the edge in blue ink: "To my good buddy, Roger Greene. On loan until I bag the next German fighter! Walt."

Roger laughed and glanced to his right, where Walt Crippen piloted his own Thunderbolt in the wingman position. Walt, too, was performing visual sweeps.

Good old Walt. He'd have to do some fancy flying if he hoped to score another kill before Roger. He found his sunglasses, then slid the ten-spot back into the pocket.

A movement below snagged his attention. The forward element of bombers altered direction, banking to the right. Behind them, the others followed the lead planes. The Initial Point already? So far, this mission was a milk run.

One after the other, he and Walt and the rest of the squadron banked their fighters to starboard, maintaining position over the four-engine bombers plodding below.

Roger pitied the poor slobs manning the B-17s. Yeah, somebody had to fly them, but . . . With his gloved hand, he patted the instrument panel and spoke to his fighter. "You're more my style, baby. You take care of me, and I'll take good care of you."

Another peek into the sun. Nothing. How long could the blue yonder remain serene?

As if on cue, Colonel Chesley Peterson's voice crackled over the radio. "Say, boys, looks like the Huns have decided to come and play. Eleven o'clock level!"

Personal thoughts vanished. Roger cocked his head slightly left. Now he saw the same thing the group commander had spotted: black pinpoints approaching. Within seconds they became unmistakable—roughly fifty bandits.

Roger's pulse quickened. This was his element: fighter against fighter, pilot against pilot, his aviation skills pitted against the very best Nazi Germany could throw at him. Never did Roger feel more alive than in a cockpit. The risk of instant death only heightened the surge of adrenaline. At moments like this, he flew instinctively, as if the controls extended his own being. The thrill defied description. He'd given up trying to explain it to the British ground pounders in the pubs of North Essex.

Following Colonel Peterson's example, Roger banked to intercept the incoming horde head-on. The black specks he'd barely detected seconds ago rapidly swelled into distinct shapes with wings and red noses. Focke-Wulf 190s. Harder to shoot down than Messerschmitts, but they'd still go down.

Another fleeting glance to the right and slightly backward revealed Walt sticking where he should be, ready to keep enemies off Roger's tail.

His gloved finger flicked the guns' arming switch. He squinted toward the onrushing planes. "I was born to fly. Were you guys?"

Whenever possible, Roger liked to hit the enemy from the high ground, diving out of the sun and pouncing on the Germans before they knew what hit them. The "zoom and boom." But at nineteen thousand pounds, a fully loaded P-47 Thunderbolt would never win awards for climbing. A Thunderbolt's redeeming quality was that its massive weight and eight .50-caliber machine guns made it a highly destructive force, especially in a dive. *No zoom and boom today, though. The Huns are swarming in from the same altitude.*

Like medieval knights on horseback charging each other with lances lowered, American and Luftwaffe fighters closed the gap at a combined air speed near eight hundred miles per hour. Roger focused on the FW 190 directly before him. To its right was another that should give Walt a clean shot. With both sides roaring head-on, split-second timing became critical.

Wait . . . Wait . . . Now.

No sooner had Roger depressed the trigger than he saw flashes from the edge of his opponent's wings. In the same instant he heard a series of rapid *wham-wham-wham*s.

"I'm hit!" he blurted into his oxygen mask.

To his right, a puff of oil and smoke erupted from an enemy plane. It slumped and careened earthward.

"Blast!" Walt had just won back his ten bucks.

The blue sky became empty as the antagonists flashed past. Some of his rounds had scored, but his target had charged on, evidently intact. His Thunderbolt still operated normally, so Roger banked tightly to the left. No time to lose if he wanted to protect those B-17s. That was the bottom line: to keep the Flying Fortresses intact so they could demolish German industry.

Roger locked onto an FW 190 beginning its dive toward the Flying Fortresses.

"No you don't, Adolf!" He rammed the stick forward and closed the gap. When the distance closed to eight hundred yards, he chopped the throttle to avoid overshooting. Seconds later, his tracers and .50-caliber rounds bored into the Focke-Wulf.

Roger matched move for move as the enemy plane broke away. Its pilot twisted sharply, first left, then right, trying to shake him. Roger expected the German's next maneuver. It was one of the enemy's favorites, but also the least effective—the Focke-Wulf nosed over and sped toward mother earth with all the speed it could muster.

Roger rammed his fighter into a dive. *Nice try, but no cigar.* No light Hun fighter could outdive the weighty Thunderbolt.

"Stick like glue to the target until you polish him off," the colonel had admonished more than once. "Many a Hun has been lost because he wasn't followed down."

I'm not losing this guy.

The enemy plane twisted every which way, desperate to stay clear of Roger's sights. But as Roger continued to trigger the guns, his rounds penetrated the target. Dark smoke billowed from the Focke-Wulf.

Roger yanked back on the stick. Using his momentum, he clawed for altitude while dodging shrapnel. Immediately remorse sickened his gut, as it did every time. Yes, he exulted in outflying another pilot. But the stark truth was that he'd just snuffed out a human being. That idiot Hitler . . . If not for him, these guys could be his friends, off flying air shows together instead of trying to blow each other to smithereens.

A swift look confirmed that Walt stuck tight, keeping Roger's six o'clock position clear. As Roger and his partner reclaimed altitude, he saw that, far from leaving the battle behind, they were drawing nearer to the dogfight as Americans and Germans wove circles in efforts to gain the upper hand.

Jumping into the thick of it, Roger stitched rounds along a Focke-Wulf that raced past him.

In the distance he spotted a Messerschmitt 109 smoking and losing altitude, probably limping for home. Should he chase the injured enemy? It would add an easy seventeenth kill to his tally. But no. Forget him. Fight as a unit, not for glory. The injured plane posed no threat. He let it go. Other enemies still prowled for blood.

Roger spotted four more Me 109s ahead, almost cutting across his path, but slightly lower and not quite as fast, in a swept-back, line-abreast formation. Without looking down, he reached for the throttle, turbo, and prop levers in succession, yanking them all the way back to slow down. No good: he was still closing fast—way too fast.

He cut a sharp right turn, then swung around to come in behind the last Messerschmitt, the one in "tail-end Charlie" position.

He swore. Still closing too fast.

Maneuvering by instinct, Roger threw in several skids to avoid over-shooting, then barrel-rolled and popped into position right on his target's tail. He narrowed the range to about 250 yards and centered the needle and ball of the bank indicator. The moment the pip of his sights aligned on the enemy, he squeezed off a long burst.

Chunks of Messerschmitt flew from the plane. The starboard wing separated, and the corpse of the aircraft crumpled earthward. The victim's three companions pulled for the sky, a maneuver Roger's heavy Thunderbolt couldn't duplicate.

He had just spared a foe's life. By sighting on the wing root instead of dead center on the cockpit, he'd given his opponent a chance to bail out. Had he been a fool? Would that pilot return to pepper him with lead someday?

"Hoosier, Hoosier!" Walt Crippen broke over the radio. "You just hit the hornets' nest. I got one on my tail. Two more on yours. Get out of here!"

Tracers flashed over Roger's left shoulder. Any enemy fighter could out-bank a Thunderbolt from behind. He needed violent evasive action—now.

Roger slammed the stick into one corner and put the rudder in the other. The result proved so instantaneous, Roger's brain couldn't picture exactly what his plane had done, but for a few seconds at least, the tracers vanished.

Inexplicably Walt's *Beautiful Betsy* roared through his path. How had he and his wingman ended up in these positions? Roger seized one thought: An enemy plane must be on Walt's tail. Forget evasive action.

Roger responded before he saw his friend's attacker. A barrage from his .50-caliber guns pierced the air. Then . . . there it was! The Me 109 hurtled straight through his stream of gunfire. The cockpit shattered. The plane tilted over and dropped from the sky.

"Gotcha!"

It was his luckiest shot ever. But now, two truths slammed home. The first was that his guns fell silent before he released the trigger switch. He was out of ammunition. Second, his own attackers were hot on his tail. Already he heard the staccato of jackhammers pummeling the Thunderbolt.

Roger jammed the stick forward, plunging earthward to outrace the two enemies. The altimeter registered only five thousand feet: not enough altitude for a speedy getaway. Worse, the P-47 responded sluggishly. Sure, he was born to fly, but even a top ace could be slaughtered if his aircraft didn't perform. Rescuing Walt had come with a price tag.

"They've shot up my rudder. This can't get any worse."

As if to prove him wrong, the fighter's engine began to cough. Steely claws of dread gripped Roger's intestines and dug in. Nothing like this had ever happened to him. In past missions, he'd always been able to out-think and outmaneuver the enemy, but with the Thunderbolt's damaged condition, he didn't stand a chance of outflying any experienced pilot.

His frustration erupted in a couple of choice words.

Roger pulled back on the stick. If he must die, it wasn't going to be from burrowing into the Third Reich. Slowly, far more lackadaisically than it should, the fighter managed to level out from the dive, but not before Roger's prop was chopping though the tips of pine trees. The engine con-tinued coughing. More tracers flashed past. Roger heard deadly rounds stabbing into his plane. As he feared, the dive had been too short to shake his pursuers.

Sweating, Roger slipped his plane up, down, left, right, hoping against hope that the two aggressors would run out of ammo before they could deliver the death blow. If only that would happen, maybe they would forfeit the chase and head home.

The hardy Thunderbolt absorbed more abuse. Roger couldn't believe he remained airborne. But the clock was ticking. He might have only seconds of life. Just one German bullet through his skull . . .

"Cripes!" he shouted over the radio. "I'm out of ammo. Rudder shot to pieces. These guys are clobbering the snot out of me. I'm not coming back. Tell 'em I shot down at least two before they got me!"

Desperate, Roger coaxed his wounded aircraft into foolhardy maneuvers. He ducked it under a bridge. He brought it up to treetop level. He barely avoided clipping the roof of a farmhouse . . . Still, the mongrels nipped at his tail with their bullets. At this low level, he couldn't even bail out. At least they weren't using their 30 mm cannons. Must've used 'em up.

Walt's voice sounded over the radio. "Hoosier, where are you? I've lost you."

"Don't know. Just passed under a bridge. Railroad tracks. They're . . ."

The fighter's engine stopped wheezing and seized up. Whether the enemies had severed an oil line or what, he had no time to guess. Willpower couldn't keep this kite aloft. A Thunderbolt's glide pattern was as efficient as a footlocker's.

Roger flashed past a road, hurtled over a snow-covered field, and dropped like a cannonball. No time for landing gear. Hydraulics were probably shot up anyway.

"Nose up! Come on, baby, nose up! Up!"

No doubt gloating in their success, the two Me 109s thundered overhead. Roger concentrated on the ground. The field was small, much shorter than a runway.

"God, help!"

The fighter smacked the earth with teeth-rattling force. It bounced off its belly, thudded down again, then skidded across the field horrifyingly fast—straight toward the tree line.

"Come on, come on . . ." Wrestling with stick and rudder, Roger fought for control. If only he could point the nose between two tree trunks instead of straight into one . . . The plane would no longer obey. Colliding with the ground must have finished whatever damage the Messerschmitts had wreaked.

Like the final scene from a nightmare, the line of trees hurtled straight toward him. Into his mind's eye sprang the image of his bloody carcass being pulled from crumpled metal.

Still wrenching the stick against the inevitable, Roger shut his eyes.

CHAPTER 2

Katherine Mueller took a deep breath and sighted along her Glock 19 a final time. She tried to ignore the sweatiness of her palm on the grip. Squinting just enough to reduce the sun's afternoon glare, she squeezed the trigger, releasing her final round.

"Yes!" All fifteen bullets had thudded home in a tight pattern on the silhouette's heart. Jubilation welled inside her chest.

"Check that out." Katherine holstered the weapon, pulled off the protective earmuffs, and turned to her uncle. A wide grin on his face rewarded her own. "It's the best I've ever done. Not bad for twenty-five yards, if I do say so myself."

"Yes, Katarina, I see. I am proud of you," Uncle Kurt said, using the German version of her name as he usually did. His gold-capped incisor glistened in the sunlight. "Superb shooting. You are becoming a true markswoman."

His approval warmed her heart. "It's taken me long enough."

"But you never gave up. You persisted. That shows tenacity, a trait sadly lacking in many young people."

"Thanks." Admiring the bullet-ridden silhouette once more, she said, "I think I'll keep that target as a souvenir. It'll be a combination of trophy and personal challenge to beat next time."

"Splendid idea. Your father would be proud, Katarina. And not only of your shooting."

The reference to her father mellowed Katherine's triumphant mood. She gazed into her uncle's steel-gray eyes. "Do you really think so? Or are you just saying that to make me happy? You know I want to live in a way that would honor them, but . . ."

Uncle Kurt laid his arm across her shoulders as they trudged across the private shooting range. "I mean every word of it. Frank had high hopes for his only daughter. He wished to see you embrace the Heritage Organization and flourish in it. It would have meant so much to him to see your progress."

"What about Mother?" Katherine pried loose the thumbtacks holding the silhouette to the weathered plywood. "Mother was a member, too, wasn't she?"

"Of course." Uncle Kurt's eyes flitted away, as if he'd noticed something among the live oaks behind the range. "Ruth worked as Frank's assistant, but she was as brilliant as he was. And not just a scientist. She excelled in psychology and other studies too. If Ruth talked less about our secret society, it was simply due to her wide range of interests." He smiled. "Your mother joked that each day was too short, that she could not learn all she wished unless she could conquer the habit of sleeping every night. Do you recall that?"

Katherine shook her head. "I don't remember many details. Mostly general things, like being cuddled on a lap or holding hands while going for walks. If it weren't for the photo album, I wouldn't even remember their faces."

Uncle Kurt paused and studied her. "You know, not until this moment did I realize how greatly you have come to resemble Ruth. Oh, you have always had the same beautiful caramel-colored hair, the same light sprinkle of freckles, and the same cute dimples when you smile. But now I see the same high cheekbones, the same confidence in your stature. What are you, about five foot five?

"Five foot six."

"About an inch taller than your mother. Blame me for giving you too many vitamins."

"I wish I hadn't been so young when they died."

She rolled the paper target into a tube.

"I know." Uncle Kurt sighed as they walked back to his BMW. "So young. Such a pity."

Katherine took her turn placing an affectionate arm around her uncle's shoulders. "What I don't understand is how such a sweet talker like you managed to stay single all his life. Surely plenty of women would've been interested in a suave European bachelor?"

He shrugged. "I suppose fate decreed it. Fortunately I have had my business and the organization to give my life meaning. Also, my wonderful niece shines her own unique ray of light into my life. You are like my private little sunbeam, Katarina."

She gave his shoulder a light shake. "Two compliments in two minutes? You're slathering it on extra thick. Either you want a favor, or you're getting sentimental."

Uncle Kurt laughed and opened her car door. "Neither. Cannot an aging old man express fondness for a niece who has become more precious than a daughter?"

Katherine's memory clicked. "Wait. We're forgetting tradition." She pulled the Glock from its brown leather holster and offered it to her uncle.

He looked at the pistol but didn't accept it. "You have already taken the target down."

"The plywood is still nailed to the post. You can put a bullet through that. Come on, at least one shot. It's tradition!"

"Oh, all right." He accepted the Glock and sized up the distance.

"Wait, you don't have to do it from the parking lot. Let's walk back to the firing line."

"What, and waste an interesting challenge?" He looked askance at the distant, bullet-riddled rectangle, then back to Katherine. Faster than she could blink, he swiveled, raised the Glock, and fired. Bits of plywood burst from the rectangle.

He slid the weapon back into its holster. "Satisfied?"

She gave him a peck on the cheek. "Satisfied. I pity the poor burglar who ever tries to break into the Mueller home." She slid onto the BMW's black leather seat and let him shut the door behind her, just as he always did in his prim, gentlemanly fashion. While Uncle Kurt circled to his side of the car, Katherine glanced down and noticed a gray object protruding from beneath his seat. She reached for it and extracted a pair of heavy binoculars.

As Uncle Kurt slipped into the driver's seat, she hefted her discovery. "These look mighty powerful. Don't tell me you've been peepin' at that curvaceous Mrs. Jansen across the street. I know she has a voluptuous figure, but really, Uncle."

For the slightest instant, her uncle's face went blank. Surely her joke hadn't struck on the truth!

"Certainly not. I am planning a vacation. A hunting expedition to Africa, actually, and I will need some good binoculars. I slipped those under there the day I bought them so no one would steal them. It seems I forgot about them."

"You're planning a trip to Africa and you didn't invite me?"

"Would you like to come? You can if you like. But I did not think you would be interested. After all, I will not be staying in a resort. This will be roughing it in the wilds. Mosquitoes. No showers or latrines." He started the engine and guided the vehicle down the gravel lane.

Katherine laughed. "You're right. I'd rather not rough it. Paris is more my speed. I wouldn't mind going back there."

"We will do Paris another time. Or maybe Rio. I have never taken you there."

He kept the car in low gear as it crept toward the road. Just another patience-demanding eccentricity Katherine had long ago stopped trying to change. Uncle wouldn't risk flinging rocks that might nick his beloved BMW's glossy black finish.

"Katherine, there is a young man I would like you to meet."

Red flags unfurled in Katherine's brain. *Here we go again.* She shut her eyes and slouched in the leather seat. "Not another nephrologist, I hope?

Geoffrey bored me stiff with his up-close descriptions of polycystic kidney disease, renal failure, vascular disorders, and kidney excretions."

"Geoffrey is a brilliant physician. He cannot resist talking about his specialty."

She opened her eyes and stared at him. "In the park? On a picnic? The man has absolutely no sense of normal social behavior, let alone romance."

Uncle Kurt braked at the asphalt road, made sure traffic was clear, then steered to the right, heading back toward Turner-McDonald Parkway. "They tell me his IQ score places him at nearly genius level. Why, if you two were to marry and have children, just imagine how extraordinary—"

"No way! I love you, but no. Not Geoffrey. Not in a million years will that walking kidney encyclopedia get close to my ring finger. Just because he's a member of the Heritage Organization doesn't mean I have to fall in love with him."

"Most unfortunate. In that case, he will probably want to return the .34-carat marquise diamond I sold him for the ring. Truly an exquisite stone."

Katherine bolted upright. "What?" Geoffrey Pullman had bought her an engagement ring after one so-called date? And her uncle had catered to this nonsense? "Tell me you're joking!"

Uncle Kurt pulled his eyes from the road long enough to grace her with a wry smile. "As you might say—*Gotcha!*" He burst into laughter. "If only I had a video of you just now. You should have seen your face."

She delivered a playful punch to his shoulder. "You and your sense of humor. I'll get you back, you know."

"Yes, I realize. In the meantime, though, would you be willing to meet a different young gentleman?"

She groaned. Could she say anything at all to get him off her case? "Uncle, I'm not a little girl anymore. Honest. Can't you just let me meet men the normal way and choose my own husband?"

The mirth disappeared from his face. "You know, your mother and father's marriage was arranged by your grandfather, and they learned to love each other deeply. This has always been the way in our branch of the Mueller family. Your contrary spirit would grieve them."

Her parents. He'd slipped the knife through the one chink in her armor. Sigh. "He's not a kidney doctor?"

"No. He's a banker."

She let out a second groan. Not that she had anything against money. But any banker who impressed Uncle Kurt as potential husband material probably came equipped with a calculator instead of a soul. The guy would be as romantic as an amortization table. "I assume he's a member of the HO?"

"Of course."

"Doesn't the organization include any swashbuckling journalists or editors or ghostwriters you can introduce me to? With someone in the publishing business, at least we'd have something mutually interesting to chat about."

"The only males I know in publishing are in their fifties or sixties, and are already married, if not already divorced."

At least Uncle Matchmaker wasn't trying to hitch her to a retiree. "All right. I'll meet your banker. But, no promises!"

"No promises needed. Still, I believe Thaddeus will impress you."

"Thaddeus?" She studied her uncle as he drove. "That's his name? No joke?"

"No joke."

Katherine's stomach grew queasy, as if she'd eaten a greasy hamburger. If only Uncle's ideas of the perfect man for her could be more normal. This conversation needed a new direction. "I've been thinking. Do you suppose it's too soon for me to try for the next level? I mean, if I'm going to be in the HO at all, I don't want to spend my whole life as a piddly little *Kadett*. I'd rather move up."

"I am pleased to hear that. I hesitated to push you. I wished it to be your decision. Yes, if you continue to shoot as well as today, that portion of the testing will be simple to pass. Of course you will need to prepare the academic and philosophical disciplines, plus hand-to-hand combat and field exercises, but those should prove no problem for a gifted and physically fit young woman. I can help train you, if you are committed."

Katherine stared straight ahead. The sunshine created a strobe-light effect as the BMW flashed through a living tunnel formed by the arching limbs of live oaks, magnolias, black walnuts, and dogwoods. She nodded. "I'm ready."

Katherine didn't voice her more private thoughts. *I'm ready for a lot of things. For life. For love. For some meaning to my existence.*

I wish he'd let me find my own husband, but who knows? Maybe the man of my dreams really is a member of the Heritage Organization, and I just haven't met him yet.

CHAPTER 3

Trembling, dazed, and damp with sweat, Roger opened his eyes. He expected to see tongues of flame licking at the cockpit. To his surprise, all he could see outside the canopy were stout tree trunks and snow-sprinkled branches. He'd plummeted from roaring aerial combat into an eerily silent world.

Roger exhaled a calming breath and willed the tightness in his stomach to relax. He'd heard of accident victims who didn't realize they were dying. He ran his hands over himself but found no broken bones. Sure, he felt a few tender spots that would turn black and blue, but nothing life-threatening.

He yanked off the slant-zipper, British-style flyer's gauntlets he'd worn since his Eagle Squadron days, removed his leather flying helmet, and ran a hand over his face. His forehead throbbed. Blood trickled from his nose. Had his head rammed the instrument panel? His flight had ended so abruptly he couldn't be sure. He rifled through each jacket pocket in search of a handkerchief. Instead, his fingers encountered the ten-dollar bill with Walt Crippen's hand-printed message.

"The joke's on you, Walt," he said aloud. "You won the bet, but you can't collect."

An unseen smolder could still ignite the fuel tank, so he needed to move. Roger slid back the canopy and climbed onto the mangled remains of the left wing. After easing to the snowy ground on unsteady legs, he surveyed the damage.

While the cockpit was nestled undamaged between two behemoth trees, the rest of the plane had not fared as well. The right wing had been shorn off completely, leaving little more than a jagged aluminum stump. Half of the left one hung, still attached, barely, but crumpled against the fuselage.

"That's one kite that will never fly again. Another eighty thousand dollars of taxpayer money down the drain."

The lower two of his four propeller blades were bent backward from gouging into the Fatherland. The underside of the P-47 was less damaged than he would have expected, though. The snow-covered field had provided little friction against the aircraft's belly, allowing it to slide like a giant toboggan.

"Well, McKenzie," he said to the absent chief mechanic, "you always claimed you'd be satisfied with any landing I could walk away from."

He gazed back between the trees, along the course the Thunderbolt had traveled to her final rest. No sign of life.

"Well, now what happens?" He pictured again the road he had shot over. At least two vehicles had been on it. Someone would show up soon enough.

The thought of Walt prompted him to survey the heavens. Empty. Neither sight nor sound of aircraft in any direction. Had Walt survived? Or had he . . .

For an instant Roger imagined *Beautiful Betsy* trailing smoke and plunging into the earth, exploding in an orange-black ball of fire. He winced. He saw no column of smoke, but that fact offered no guarantee Walt had survived the melee.

No. Walt's alive. He called over the radio. I owe him ten bucks, and he's too mulish to die before I pay up.

Chilled by the December wind, Roger tugged his flying gauntlets back on. Once he was confident the Thunderbolt no longer posed any threat of exploding, he climbed back up and retrieved his escape kit and first-aid box.

He'd received his escape kit with mixed emotions. On one hand, he was glad somebody was thinking ahead and providing them with emergency items, including a compass and a map. On the other hand, crashing or parachuting into Fortress Europe was no dream holiday. He'd never planned on using this piece of gear.

He unwound a strip of gauze and pressed it to his bleeding nose.

What to do? It didn't make much sense to go dashing through snowy woods in December, well inside the borders of the Third Reich. During those isolated moments when he'd entertained thoughts of getting stranded on enemy territory, Roger had imagined warmer seasons, when a man might scavenge farmlands for carrots and cabbages or forage apples from orchards and then sleep inside a haystack.

He turned his attention to the ground. The snow lay only a couple of inches deep, but the prints of his fleece-lined flying boots showed easily. No matter which direction he ran, Wehrmacht soldiers would have the clearest possible trail to follow. Under these conditions, he'd just be wasting valuable energy with zero hope of reaching safety.

"Well, this is lousy. Not only do I get shot down, but all the odds are stacked against me. I've got no food and no place to hide." He formulated the only possible plan to stay alive.

◆　◆　◆

Roger sat on a log and watched a squad of rifle-toting Wehrmacht soldiers approaching across the field. He enjoyed the satisfaction of knowing that, whatever they expected to find, it wasn't the sight that would meet their eyes. The Germans approached cautiously, gripping their rifles as if hunting wild lions. Then they straightened and gazed at him with puzzlement.

In front of him, a campfire merrily crackled and popped. He spread his bare palms toward the flames and soaked up their warmth even as he relished the soldiers' dumbfounded expressions. He imagined that, except for his flight jacket, in their eyes he must look as relaxed as a railroad hobo simmering a can of pork and beans.

"I see you boys finally showed up. I was starting to worry I might have to come looking for you." He beckoned them closer and patted the spot on the log next to him. "Come on over. Have a seat."

The enemy troops merely stared.

"Oh, wait. I get it. You guys forgot the hotdogs, didn't you?" Roger exaggerated a sigh. "That lousy Hermann Göring. I specifically told him to have somebody buy hot dogs in case I dropped in. And here I had the fire going and everything. That ticks me off."

The nearest German pointed his rifle at Roger, then gave a flick of his chin. *"Komm."*

"Come? You're inviting me to your place? That's a swell idea. It's chilly for barbecuing, anyway. Let's pick up some bratwurst along the way." He stood, yawned, stretched, and then stepped forward.

Immediately the soldiers tightened their grips on the rifles, as if the lone American might launch a sneak attack.

"By the way, Fritz," Roger said to the soldier who was apparently the sergeant in charge, "you might want to collect that thing over there. It'll make a dandy souvenir to show the grandchildren—if you live that long." Roger jerked a thumb toward his Colt .45, which had been lying beside him on the log.

The German barked an order, and one of his men hustled to retrieve the weapon.

Roger continued to chat amiably. "Don't expect to find any bullets. I flung 'em into the woods just to keep you guys from getting 'em."

Another grunted order from the sergeant sent a soldier forward to pat down the prisoner. The man discovered the escape kit tucked inside Roger's jacket and removed it.

Roger was certain by now that none of his captors spoke English. He smiled and nodded enthusiastically. "Sorry, no car keys, if that's what you're looking for. I left those in Indiana."

With rifles jabbing the air to indicate the desired path, the Wehrmacht band marched their prize across the field toward the road Roger had spotted during his hasty descent. He paused at the spot where his fighter had impacted the earth and studied the dark skid carved across the snow-clad field.

"That's where my plane smacked. See where the prop gouged up some of your stinking Reich? After that, it was a high-speed slide to the tree line. Then, *wham!*" He slammed a fist into the palm of his opposite hand.

The Germans exchanged remarks. One of them spat into the snow. *"Kaputt."*

"Yeah, you can say that again. She's one totally kaputt airplane."

Exerting his authority, the leader of the squad repeated his rifle jabs toward the road. Roger marched. For their part, the soldiers never slapped or struck him as Roger had anticipated. As long as he obeyed instructions, they didn't even force him to raise his hands. This was working better than he'd hoped.

At the road, a military truck with a canvas-covered bed waited by the roadside. Behind the truck idled a dark green automobile. Shadows moved inside it. The sun glared on the windshield and Roger couldn't see the car's occupants.

He glanced inside the rear of the truck. Empty. Looks like he was this group's only trophy for the day.

The doors on both sides of the automobile swung open, and out stepped two soldiers. A third figure followed from the car's back seat: an aging gentleman wearing a dark-brown herringbone overcoat and matching fedora.

A civilian? Beneath the fedora were gray hair, bushy gray eyebrows, and round, wire-rimmed spectacles that magnified his eyes. The civilian's gaze intersected Roger's. In some way Roger couldn't fathom, the older man's stare seemed to bore right into him, reading his very thoughts. Roger surprised himself by being first to look away.

The ensuing discussion between the Germans included few words Roger could figure out. But he gleaned from facial expressions and tones that the Wehrmacht troops who had captured him hadn't been expecting these others. Irritated voices competed back and forth until the civilian in spectacles produced an envelope, which he handed to "Fritz."

With an air of disdain, the sergeant extracted a single sheet of paper. He began reading aloud but then continued silently. Whatever he found written there wiped all resistance from his face and voice. Almost reverently the sergeant refolded the document, inserted it back into its envelope, and returned it to the civilian. He then stepped backward and shot off a respectful salute accompanied by, "*Heil* Hitler!"

The man in the fedora turned his attention back to Roger. He paced a circle around the pilot while scrutinizing him from head to toe. In British-accented English he finally said, "You seem to be an acceptable specimen. Well-proportioned build. Relatively light-colored skin. Brown hair. Blue eyes that reflect intelligence, despite temporary confusion. Well-defined nose bridge. Tasteful, geometric, Aryan-like attractiveness . . . I imagine you are the type that could make women swoon in your own country?"

"What is this? You're sizing me up like I'm a head of beef at market or something."

"I take it you were born in the United States, correct?"

"Yes."

"Are you Jewish?"

"Huh?"

"Do you have Jewish blood in you, or don't you? Answer quickly."

"No, I don't. Go ahead and check my dog tags if you want."

The man ignored the offer. "What is your basic ethnic background, both mother's and father's lineage?"

Roger clamped his mouth shut.

"Do not worry. The information is strictly for me personally. It will not affect the war effort, nor will it betray any vital military secrets."

Roger considered. The War Department didn't require him to state more than his name, rank, and serial number, but curiosity nibbled at him. What was the old codger up to? Was there a way to find out? Roger thought fast. He'd been reared in an orphanage and couldn't make even the vaguest guess of his family ancestry. Just to see what would happen, he concocted an answer on the spot.

"Okay. I guess it won't do any harm. My mother's maiden name was

O'Leary. Her clan immigrated to Chicago from Ireland a few generations back. My father's side of the family came from England in the 1800s, during the California gold rush. Why do you need to know?"

The civilian in the spectacles ignored Roger's question and instead posed more of his own: "You are in good health, I hope? No cold, no flu? And how about allergies? Do you have any?"

Since when did Nazis fret about the health of their prisoners?

"No. If you really want to know, my health is fantastic. I got banged around a little when my plane cracked up, but nothing serious."

"Excellent. You will do nicely."

The gent nodded and uttered something to Sergeant Fritz in German. The soldiers, in turn, dropped the tailgate of their truck and motioned for Roger to climb aboard.

"Schnell!" the sergeant barked, possibly to regain a modicum of authority in the eyes of his men. An imperious wave of his rifle needed no translation.

"Okay, I'm *schnelling* already." Roger climbed aboard and took a seat on one of the two wooden benches that lined the truck bed.

The enemy soldiers joined him, their weapons still held at the ready.

"Hey, guys, you won't need those things. People have accused me of having a hole in my head, but I won't try anything that'll tempt you to add a new one."

The grim-faced men regarded him in silence.

"Sheesh. Am I the only person here with a sense of humor?"

Through the open rear, Roger watched the civilian's dark green sedan back up, then drive around the truck. Roger's vehicle shifted into gear and jolted forward.

So, now we're following the civilian guy? Roger leaned back and shut his eyes.

What difference could his ancestry possibly make? And allergies?

I guess I'll find out soon enough.

A thought sprang into Roger's mind: this is the kind of jam that makes men pray. The notion startled his eyelids open, which caught the attention of his guards. He shut them again. Ridiculous or not, Roger's mind spanned westward across the Atlantic and touched down in the place of his earliest childhood memories, the spot he always associated with prayer: Sunshine Children's Home in Indianapolis.

He punctuated the absurd memory with a chuckle partly intended to mystify his captors. Of all the kooky things to think about at a time like this . . .

For the first time in ages he pictured those Sunday afternoons, when elderly Miss Hawkins came to visit, still wearing the prudish black or navy dress she'd worn to some church service that morning. This thin-faced matron would summon all the orphans into the activity room, where they dragged three-legged stools with chipped green paint into semicircles radiating out from her.

Even now Roger could imagine Miss Hawkins addressing the pint-sized assembly, where she would conduct her own version of a children's worship service. In her high-pitched voice, she would narrate Bible stories about Noah building the ark; about Joseph being stripped of his colorful coat and being sold into slavery; about Jesus feeding the crowds; or about the apostle Paul and his life-threatening missionary journeys throughout the Roman Empire.

As the Wehrmacht truck bounced and swayed across Hitler's back-yard, Roger continued down memory lane. Out of all the stories old Miss Hawkins had ever taught, the one that had always captivated him most was the account of how Jesus, promising to return to earth someday, ascended from the Mount of Olives and rose up to heaven.

In his mind's eye, Roger pictured himself as a child listening to that story and then craning his neck to stare skyward through the tall, streaked windows of Sunshine's activity room. The untouchable heavens. He dreamed of soaring through the air, especially on days when the clouds had resembled gigantic bunches of cauliflower solid enough for a boy to clamber up and explore.

"Children, always remember to pray," Miss Hawkins had admonished them weekly.

Roger grunted again. He hadn't thought about that wrinkled little lady for years. Surely she was long since dead. But if she were alive and could see her former pupil right now, she would no doubt waggle a bony figure and chide, "Remember to pray, Roger. Remember to pray!"

His mood turned sullen. Yeah, he'd prayed at Sunshine Children's Home. For a while. Mostly he'd prayed that his mommy and daddy—whoever they might be—would remember to come back and fetch him out of there. They never had, and his young self had lost trust in the power of prayer. Little Roger Greene had remained a ward of the state of Indiana until the age of twelve.

The unintended train of thought, spurred by the civilian's probing, reawakened the questions of his origins. Who exactly was he? He supposed that he was the result of a teenage girl's secret tryst. Or maybe the poverty of the Depression years had played a role in his abandonment. As a child, he'd wondered whether one or two women on the staff at Sunshine knew more than just his name and birthday, but the workers had remained tight-lipped. Whenever he'd asked about his family or how he'd ended up in the home, they would sigh or shrug or reply, "Hard to say, Roger," before changing the subject.

No matter how many times Roger had tried to ignore his curiosity, it eventually crept back to haunt him. Even though he'd tried to squelch it with school and sports and flying, he'd never succeeded in totally blocking the questions from his mind.

His thoughts glided forward to the Tucker years. When old man Tucker and his wife had agreed to take him home to their farm, he'd been excited that someone wanted a boy to love and appreciate. Wrong. The Tuckers already had two sons who had grown up and marched off to the Great War, never to return. Roger was just an extra pair of hands, milking the cows and bringing in the hay. That was no family. *Just a place to live and earn my keep until I was old enough to hit the road.*

Roger shook his head to throw off the gloomy memories. When he opened his eyes, his German captors were regarding him as the truck jolted and bumped along the road.

He let his eyelids drop again. Unbidden, the cracking female voice echoed down the corridor of time: "Always remember to pray."

Maybe that worked for some people, but not for him. Or did it? He recalled shouting a distress call for divine help just before his Thunderbolt had burrowed into that stand of trees. He'd been surprised to find himself alive, his cockpit relatively undamaged. Had that been an answer from the Almighty or just dumb luck? Hard to prove either way. Still, to appease the specter of wispy-haired Miss Hawkins, Roger collected his thoughts. When he'd gathered enough to string into sentences, he began.

God, I don't know if You're up there or not. Some people say You are; some say You aren't. Even if You are, I don't know if You have time to listen to an average Joe like me. I don't know if You even care. But, God, You know all I've ever really wanted to do was to fly airplanes, to serve my country, and someday to find a girl good enough to marry. Old Miss Hawkins sure believed in You, so I'm trying what she told us—I'm praying. Only I don't know exactly what to pray for in a jam like this. So if You want to help me somehow, I'd sure appreciate it.

Roger needed no theologian to tell him his unorthodox petition never would have won praise for eloquence. That task accomplished, he dismissed it from his mind. He leaned his head back and waited to see where these soldiers—and the gray-haired character with the spectacles—were taking him.

CHAPTER 4

The dark-haired technician emerged from the back room of FSC Computer Repairs bearing Katherine's laptop. "Here you go, miss," he said with some sort of Middle Eastern accent. He placed it on the counter, then sat to write up an invoice. "These older models are solid computers. You're lucky not to have one with cheap, imported parts."

"I know it's not the latest and the greatest, but it kept working, so I kept using it. What went wrong?" Katherine unsnapped her purse and extracted a credit card. She hated to add another charge to her bill, but she refused to borrow from Uncle Kurt, especially since he'd warned her against becoming a freelance editor in the first place. She could hear his voice, "There is no security, no future there. You will always be dependent on others for employment." Well, at least she could prove she wasn't dependent on her uncle.

"You had a very bad virus. Your notebook really crashed. When you tried to fix it by restoring to an earlier date and it suddenly went black . . . Well, it made my job that much harder. I had to wipe it clean and restore to factory condition."

Katherine's heart plummeted. The thought of reediting every page of Dr. Goodell's essay on robot-assisted post-stroke therapy prodded her to the brink of tears. "Back to factory settings? So you couldn't save that special document I told you about?"

34

"Oh yes, I managed to retrieve it," he assured. "Don't worry about that. I salvaged a number of other documents too. Not all of them, I'm afraid, but at least fifteen or twenty. I copied them back into your Documents folder after it was done restoring."

Blessed relief washed over Katherine. Those older documents didn't matter. Those gigs were history. But Dr. Goodell's paper was the next stepping-stone on her precarious journey to financial survival. "Thank you. You're a miracle worker. I would've screamed or cried—or both—if I had to comb through that whole manuscript from the beginning."

He shot her a smile of brilliant white teeth. "Just be sure to keep your antivirus software updated. And don't forget to back up your work. Those are the two best ways to protect yourself." He turned the invoice around and slid it across the counter. "That's $120."

She swallowed and handed him the plastic card. That figure represented a sizeable chunk of her monthly car payment. But repairing the laptop was the only way to save herself a week's worth of work, not to mention her reputation as a go-get-'em copyeditor who delivered completed jobs, not excuses.

When the technician returned her credit card, he said, "May I ask you a question?"

Feeling nearly giddy over her rescued file, she said, "Does it involve editing books?"

"Oh no, nothing like that." A nervous twitch of a smile confirmed something quite different was ready to surface. "The first time you were here, when you dropped off your notebook, I noticed what a pleasant personality you have. I also noticed you don't wear a ring on your left hand. So I couldn't help wondering if perhaps you are interested in seeing men? Socially, that is?"

The ultra-polite phrasing of his invitation struck Katherine as humorous, but with those sincere, dark brown eyes studying hers and waiting for a response, she squelched any impulse to laugh. Besides, compared to some of the crass propositions other men tossed her way, his approach might be considered chivalrous. He certainly seemed more down-to-earth than banker Thaddeus, Uncle Kurt's most recent offering.

Katherine scrounged for words. "Uh, thank you, Mr."—she glanced at the stack of business cards in their black plastic holder—"Farzeen, for your interest. I'm flattered you ask. Unfortunately my life is kind of complicated right now."

His smile shrank from hopeful to perfunctory. "It's okay. Many American women prefer not to socialize with immigrants. I understa—"

"Oh no, it's nothing like that. I'm not prejudiced against immigrants. I find people from overseas fascinating. It's just that . . ." She sighed. She really didn't care to launch into a detailed description of Uncle Kurt and the "long and honorable Mueller tradition" of the parents finding suitable spouses for the next generation. She'd endured her uncle's displeasure over unapproved encounters before. They simply weren't worth the emotional wringer. Besides, as far as the HO was concerned, she'd sworn not to mention its existence to outsiders.

"Farzeen, my life is too convoluted to explain, but at this stage of the game, I'm basically not seeing any men socially. If things change . . ."

He nodded. "My invitation remains open. You're always welcome in my shop, even without a broken computer." He broke into a good-natured grin that put her at ease.

Katherine scooped up her laptop. "Thanks for being understanding—and sweet." The moment she pushed open the shop's glass door, the day's sweltering heat enveloped her with oven-like intensity. Combined with humidity, the ninety-four-degree temperature felt even higher. It immediately popped beads of sweat onto her brow. She hurried to the protection of her car's air-conditioning.

Moments later, steering her Volkswagen Passat south on Peachtree Street with the AC blowing full blast, she let loose a rare growl of frustration. "Bless his heart, but sometimes Uncle Kurt makes me want to scream!"

It wasn't that she was attracted to the foreign technician. She wasn't. At the moment, though, he embodied all potential candidates for romance.

Why did Uncle Kurt insist on controlling a key decision in her life? Couldn't he simply forget outdated customs and trust her judgment?

As a little girl growing up with her uncle, she hadn't minded some of his old-fashioned rules. Now that she was an adult, though, she craved freedom. The social straitjacket stifled her worse than today's temperatures.

She cruised past a man and woman strolling hand in hand down the roadside. Their pace was leisurely, and the woman tilted her blonde head into the man's shoulder despite the ungodly heat. The image struck Katherine as both idyllic and torturous. She hadn't so much as touched a boy's hand since Andrei Timoshenko, back at UGA. As expected, Uncle Kurt had objected and urged her to wait for someone in the Heritage Organization if she needed companionship. In the end, Andrei had simply vanished without a word, probably back to his homeland, effectively nixing their brief relationship. She pictured the Ukrainian student's smiling face. She'd enjoyed Andrei's keen wit, and he'd always responded enthusiastically during their heart-to-heart talks. Why did he simply drop out of her life without even a goodbye?

She arrived at the intersection of Ponce de Leon Boulevard just as the traffic light switched from red to green. She flipped on her left blinker, waited for oncoming traffic to clear, then rounded the corner.

Why does my life have to be a tightrope? Lately that metaphor seemed the perfect word picture: she constantly tiptoed a slender line between the wishes of her one living relative—the man who loved her and had reared her from a toddler—and her own desires. Couldn't she figure out a way to reconcile the two?

Maybe I should just forget about men for a spell. If I focus my energy on freelance gigs and training for the HO, maybe he'll get worried I'll become a spinster and loosen up.

But even that strategy would be misery to endure. Who wanted to wait years for romance?

"Argh!" She slapped the steering wheel with her palm.

CHAPTER 5

Bumping along in the back of the troop truck, Roger could see nothing of the oncoming countryside. By gazing over the tailgate, he could at least observe the retreating terrain. Not that it made any difference. They were somewhere in Hitler's Third Reich, but no signs or landmarks helped him to gain his bearings.

The truck slowed as it swung off the main road and continued up a narrower lane. Within a minute it braked to a halt. German voices talked outside. Roger strained his ears to listen even though he didn't understand the language. Occasionally German words resembled English ones, and if he could pick out a few that might provide answers, he wanted to be alert. But the only utterance he recognized was a *Jawohl* just before the truck shifted back into first gear and lumbered forward.

Tall metal gates came into view. A uniformed soldier of the Wehrmacht was swinging one shut behind them. The two-vehicle convoy had just entered some sort of compound enclosed by a barrier of hefty stone blocks.

Not the way I pictured POW camps.

The truck halted again. This time the motor cut off. A helmeted soldier unfastened the tailgate and allowed it to drop with a metallic clank. He glared at Roger and shouted a command.

"Huh?"

The muzzle of a rifle pressing into Roger's right kidney provided a translation: jump down.

Once on the ground, he surveyed his surroundings. If his brief glimpse of the gate and wall had suggested this compound was atypical for a prisoner-of-war camp, the unhindered view clinched that impression. Stone walls about fifteen feet high surrounded him. Atop that blockade, triple strands of barbed wire glinted against the pale-blue December sky. No guard towers loomed over the complex, but large spotlights hung at intervals, guaranteeing that anyone skulking out here at night could be seen—and shot—quite easily. A couple of Wehrmacht soldiers paced muddy paths through the snow along the inner perimeter. In the center of the compound stood a two-story building of red brick. Few windows graced its exterior, and wrought-iron gratings enclosed each of those.

Roger sniffed. A peculiar, medicinal odor lingered in the chill air.

Drab and depressing. They didn't waste any Reichsmarks *decorating this place.*

Could it be a short-term holding area? If so, they'd gone to a lot of trouble for a temporary jail.

Now Gray Hair, as Roger had nicknamed the civilian in the spectacles, fired off instructions to the soldiers and led the way to the building's front entrance. One of Roger's captors motioned with his rifle. Roger marched.

Sandwiched among four soldiers, Roger followed Gray Hair over the threshold. As the entourage clumped down the black-tiled corridor, Roger glanced into open doorways on the left and right.

What is this, a prison or a hospital?

In one room, his quick eyes noted iron-frame beds, and in another, a glossy black table strewn with microscopes and test tubes. A third room offered a peek of a white-coated man examining a cage filled with white mice.

Mice?

That fleeting sight struck Roger as so incongruous he would've stopped in his tracks for a better look, except for the gun-toting defenders of the Reich behind him.

Why in blazes would they need mice? An unsettling feeling crept into his stomach.

The corridor ended at a metal door, painted blood red. About eye level in the door was a two-inch-square pane of glass. Gray Hair paid no heed to the peephole. He simply unlocked the portal and led the way inside.

When Roger stepped through, he found himself in a brick chamber divided into iron-barred cells, similar to those he'd seen in a host of Western movies. According to Hollywood, every town in the Old West included a sheriff's office with one or two jail cells to lock up bank robbers, cattle rustlers, and similar vermin. This chamber, however, featured not one but seven barred compartments. Except for the one on the far right, every cell contained a male occupant. The uniforms in the first three cells labeled the men as Royal Air Force. The other three were dressed like himself, in the flight garb of the U.S. Eighth Army Air Force.

"There he is: Number Seven," called an RAF man with a cockney accent.

"About time you showed up, Yank," joked another prisoner. "Perhaps now we can get the show on the road—whatever show that is."

"Hello, boys," Roger replied. "Looks like we're going to be roommates."

Each cell contained a toilet and an olive drab canvas cot. Obviously the place hadn't been constructed for privacy or comfort. Not a single window adorned the brick chamber. Instead, three naked lightbulbs dangling well out of the prisoners' reach provided the chamber's light. Affixed to the door of each cell was a square of tin painted yellow and sporting a black numeral ranging from 1 on the left to 7 on the final, empty cell on the right.

Roger noted the rough but clean concrete floor and the sloppy mortar job between the bricks. Somebody had slapped this building together in a hurry.

Following Gray Hair's directives, two soldiers prodded Roger toward the empty cell. No sooner had he reached its open doorway than a hard palm shoved him between the shoulder blades. Roger scarcely avoided colliding with the toilet. A clang reverberated behind him, and Roger turned in time to see Gray Hair twisting a key in the lock.

Looking extremely pleased, Gray Hair dismissed his military escort. "Gentlemen," he said to the first six prisoners, "allow me to introduce you to the last member of our ensemble. This is . . ." He paused, then turned to Roger. "Excuse me, Number Seven, but I'm afraid I never did ask your name."

"Captain Roger Greene."

"Thank you. As I was saying, Captain Greene is the final candidate. If he passes his physical examination as well as the rest of you, tomorrow, we can commence at last with the grand purpose that has united all of us in this exclusive facility."

"And what might that be, pray tell?" asked the American in the cell beside Roger's.

"The final stage in proving a theory of mine."

The more Gray Hair talked, the more animated he became. Roger noticed a peculiar gleam growing in his eyes.

"That is, on paper it's still called a theory. I, however, am convinced I have unlocked one of the deepest riddles concerning biological regeneration and molecular configuration as they pertain to the cells of the human body. In order to verify or disprove that belief, my request for suitable candidates has risen to the highest levels of authority."

"Meaning what, exactly?" asked a blond American wearing lieutenant's insignia in cell 4.

"Meaning that you have the privilege of participating in this event by the personal approval of Adolf Hitler himself!"

Like his comrades in arms, Roger burst into laughter. "Is that so? My impression was that I'm here because a couple of Me 109 pilots scored some lucky shots on my plane. I didn't realize the high and mighty Führer had summoned me."

Roger's remark sparked renewed guffaws from the other prisoners. In contrast, Gray Hair's countenance sobered.

"I will excuse your insolent remark, which is based on a lack of knowledge."

"Bloody right we suffer from a lack of knowledge," piped up the RAF man in the second cell. "We don't even know who you are or why you've brought us here."

Gray Hair snapped the heels of his brown leather shoes together and stood ramrod straight. "Then allow me to introduce myself officially. My name is Professor Heinz von Blomberg." He bowed at the waist, as if entering a dinner party for foreign dignitaries.

"Von Blomberg?" echoed one of the RAF men. "Wasn't that the name of the general who gave the order for your guys to invade the Rhineland?"

The professor beamed. "The general is a distant relative. He and I are not close, but he served to introduce me to the Führer. As a result of that conversation"—he waved his right hand in a majestic, sweeping gesture—"this entire complex has been constructed."

Roger was growing weary of Blomberg. "For what reason? Can we skip to the bottom line?"

The professor opened his mouth as if to explain, then closed it. He extracted a pocket watch and popped open the cover. "I would like to elucidate more, gentlemen, but I see that time is fleeting. I have many preparations to make. Perhaps tomorrow I will provide further details."

Blomberg turned on his heel and strode out of the chamber, despite protests of "Hey! Wait a minute" and "Come back." The red door clanged shut, followed by the clicking of a key engaging the tumblers.

Roger kicked the cell door with his bulky, fleece-lined flight boot. "Okay, clue in the new guy on the cell block. I just got shot down today, and they hustled me straight here. No explanations. Anybody know what this is all about?"

The fellow in the neighboring cell slipped his hand through the bars and shook Roger's. "I'm Bill Burgess, copilot with the Forty-fourth Bomb Group. From one through five, the other guys are Sedgewick, Rutledge, Lambright, Jamison, and Hazlitt. But to answer your question, no. Until just a minute ago, they haven't told us a stinking thing. Sedgewick down there"—Burgess jerked a thumb toward the RAF pilot in cell 1—"he understands some of their lingo. What little we do know comes from what he's overheard Blomberg telling his assistant, another professor-type named Kossler."

From down the line, Sedgewick chimed in. "They don't say much. Not in front of us, at any rate. Yesterday I heard Blomberg tell Kossler he was impatient to find a seventh candidate so they could begin, whatever that means. The moment you waltzed through the doorway, we understood you're Number Seven."

Roger grunted. "I used to claim seven as my lucky number."

"Who knows, maybe it still is," called one of the Americans, whose name Roger had already forgotten. "This place can't be any worse than a POW camp. I've been here for three days, and the grub isn't half bad. Especially compared to the Brussels sprouts they kept feeding us in Norfolk."

Roger remained unconvinced. His mind raced back to the glimpse of white mice. Now here he stood, caged exactly like a laboratory rodent. "I don't know. My gut instincts tell me I'd rather be at a regular camp. They didn't even record my name or rank or serial number. How can they report my capture to the Red Cross if they don't know who I am?"

"Say, you're right," Burgess agreed. "They didn't ask for mine, either."

"Or mine," added Lambright.

Roger put a finger to the throbbing spot on his forehead. "One more thing. That character, Blomberg. Something about him strikes me as . . ." He trailed off when no suitable description came to mind.

"Eccentric?" Burgess suggested.

"Batty?" offered one of the RAF flyers.

"I was thinking more along the lines of *abnormal*. Did you see that unnerving gleam in his eyes? If he'd introduced himself as Dr. Frankenstein, I would've believed him."

The sullen man in cell 5 spoke up. "You can bet your bottom dollar on one thing: if Hitler approves of whatever Blomberg has up his sleeve, we're not going to like it."

Roger let that thought settle in his heart. He nodded. "Roger that."

Burgess cocked his head. "I must've said 'Roger that' thousands of times, but I think this is the first time I've heard an actual Roger say it."

"Yeah, well, I've been kidded about it too many times to smile anymore. If I never hear another 'Roger' pun in my life, I'll be happy."

In cell 1, Sedgewick muttered, "Nothing's going to make me happy until we get out of here—*if* we get out of here."

CHAPTER 6

As predicted by Lieutenant Jamison, alias "Number Four," Roger had enjoyed the supper of open-faced cold-cut sandwiches and cheese on heavy rye bread, followed by steaming potato soup. What he found disquieting, though, was the realization that surely not all Allied prisoners received such appetizing meals. His mind conjured images of cannibals fattening up naive missionaries before a feast.

However, when morning dawned, no breakfast appeared. Instead, Blomberg entered the chamber alone. "Good morning, gentlemen," he said jovially. "I trust you all slept well?"

With clipboard and pencil in hand, Blomberg worked his way down the line of cells and asked each man a series of questions: Did he feel well rested? Was he still in good health, without cough, congestion, or other ailments? Had the prisoner experienced a bowel movement that morning?

Ever the outspoken one, Sedgewick stated that if the professor was so fascinated in his use of the water closet, he could "bloody well stick around and watch." Roger and the other prisoners, however, figured it couldn't do any harm to reply. If the German High Command believed it could gain a military edge by learning whether these seven had already flushed, then let it try.

When Roger, the final prisoner, had finished answering Blomberg's queries, he posed his own questions: "So what's this all about, Doc? What are we doing here?"

Blomberg responded with a resplendent smile. "What are we doing here, Number Seven? We are creating history. You have heard of Christopher Columbus? Galileo? Isaac Newton? All of them made history. If my calculations prove accurate, all those names will pale when compared to the name of Heinz von Blomberg."

"How do we figure into all that?" asked Rutledge in cell 2.

"I promise to tell you all about it," Blomberg stated. "As soon as you wake up." He turned and strode to the door.

"Wake up?" repeated Burgess. "What's that mean? We're awake already."

The professor paused. "Yes, from natural sleep. But that is not my inference."

Without further explanation, he stepped out of the chamber and pulled the heavy metal portal shut. In seconds, they heard it lock.

"He's daft," declared Sedgewick.

Roger ignored the others. Blomberg was up to something new. The thousand-dollar question was, what? Beyond the metal door he barely heard garbled voices. Even though the words were foreign, he strained to hear them, wishing for a clue to the man's meaning.

Within moments, a clunking sound drew their attention to the ceiling of the chamber. The muffled chugging of an engine or pump came to Roger's ears. An instant later, three streams of pink gas spewed into the room through overhead vents he hadn't noticed before.

"He's insane! He's going to gas us!"

Desperate to escape the gas, Roger grabbed the bars of the door and shook with all his might. Except for a rattle, nothing happened. He backed up and charged the door, impacting it with his right shoulder. The door held fast. His best effort resulted in nothing more than stabbing shoulder pain.

In the other cells, his fellow prisoners likewise shouted, banged, cursed, and kicked the bars in futile efforts to avoid the pink mist billowing toward them.

Roger's nostrils detected a sickly sweet smell. Coughing to expel the fumes from his lungs, he dropped to all fours. He looked left, then right. His mind raced, but he found no way to escape this trap.

Closer and closer, like the wispy tentacles of some unearthly octopus, crept the pink vapor. The sweet odor reached Roger where he lay on the concrete floor. Almost immediately his nostrils began tingling. In a last bid at surviving whatever toxin filled the air, he held his breath and stripped the woolen blanket from his cot. He rapidly folded the fabric to double thickness, then again into four layers. This he pressed to his face in hopes of filtering out the fumes.

But the tingling inside his nose crept farther along his nasal passages and extended down to his lungs. He pressed his crude gas mask tighter. He wanted to hold his breath, but what would that gain him? Sixty seconds? Ninety? Then what? A man must breathe.

A high-pitched whine grew in his ears. Roger was uncertain whether the sound originated inside or outside his skull. Thousands of pinpricks stabbed inside his lungs and radiated outward to all his limbs. Roger's muddled mind pictured countless fire ants crawling under his skin, inside his windpipe, through his veins, and to each blood vessel.

The shouts from the neighboring cells receded, growing fainter as Roger's grip on consciousness weakened. Still he fought to keep his breathing shallow, to limit whatever was invading his system. If he passed out, the blanket would slip from his face and expose him to the full effect of the mist. But he was fighting a losing battle. An irresistible force had clamped onto his mind and was suffocating his brain, pulling his innermost self down, down into dark oblivion.

As coherent thought ebbed from his mind, a disembodied voice came echoing to him: "Children, always remember to pray!"

God, help!

Those two words were the closest shot at a prayer he could muster. Blackness engulfed him, and Roger knew no more.

Chapter 7

Katherine Mueller did a double take at the gray-cased device mounted on her dashboard. Instead of the strong directional signal displayed just moments earlier, the miniature screen flashed two amber words: "Signal lost."

How could that be? He couldn't vanish into nothingness.

The traffic signal turned green. As soon as the last pedestrian ambled out of the crosswalk, she slid her foot to the gas pedal and continued along Ivan Allen Boulevard. Annoyed at both the lost signal and the discomfort of the clammy blouse sticking to her body, she powered down both front windows a few more inches. Why did the air-conditioning have to pick today of all days to conk out?

The increased cross-breeze swept away some of the stifling heat, but open windows also permitted an influx of everything Katherine detested about traffic in Atlanta: the noxious concentration of car exhaust and the cacophony of screeching tires, honking horns, and people talking, shouting, sometimes cursing. Worse, that MARTA bus blocking her vision was pumping reeking diesel fumes straight at her. Sitting here was like being gassed.

Katherine breathed as shallowly as possible. *Okay, girl, think. I'm not geocaching with Uncle anymore. This is the big league now. The target is mobile. What could make you lose the signal?*

Her mind conjured and discarded possibilities. She slowed her car. Her target had been extremely close when she lost him. He must be nearby. She reminded herself to stay alert, especially for a glimpse of the vehicle she stalked. She'd heard of geocachers who focused so intently on locating a hidden trinket that they stepped in front of speeding motorcycles or tumbled into ditches. If stationary targets presented danger, then tracking a moving target as cunning as her prey only ratcheted the threat level higher. She didn't want to risk her two-year-old car—or her life—on this mission. So what could make the signal disappear?

Her eyes flitted from the lumbering blue, gold, and orange-striped MARTA bus to the organization-issued homing device, or "Pigeon" as it was commonly called, mounted on her dash. *Okay, if the locator chip in his car went dead, that would cut the signal.* She ruled out that likelihood. But what if he drove through a car wash or something? She rejected that solution, too. *No, the chips are sealed against moisture. It could drop into a mud puddle, and I'd still get a signal. So what's the—*

Katherine was passing the sign for 55 Allen Plaza when the obvious answer struck her: *An underground parking garage? That's it! All those tons of concrete would smother the signal!*

Katherine mashed her brake pedal, resulting in a blaring horn from the gold Lexus behind her. *Good grief, y'all. Hold your horses.* Switching tactics, she circled the block as a safer way to approach the parking garage.

Some of these other buildings have garages too. But with the way that signal suddenly disappeared, I have a feeling . . .

Steering with her left hand, Katherine leaned to the right and picked up the pistol she'd placed on the Volkswagen's passenger seat. She laid it across the lap of her jeans. *One shot. Just one clean shot either to his windshield or his driver's side window. I can do this.*

Katherine cut her wheels and maneuvered into the parking garage. She'd never been inside this particular one, but that shouldn't make a difference. Would she be smarter to stash her car in the first available stall and proceed cautiously on foot? If she did, she might stand a better chance of catching him unawares.

Katherine drove up to the metal box and braked. Inside the garage sat row upon row of autos. A full house, even on a Saturday. Plenty of cover for him to hide in.

Katherine powered her window the rest of the way down and pressed the button on the box. With a metallic hum, half an entry ticket emerged from its slot. She plucked it out and deposited it onto the passenger seat.

Without warning, a familiar laugh echoed. Startled, Katherine looked up in time to see the black BMW—in the *exit* lane. The driver's window was down, and from inside a gleeful Uncle Kurt pointed a black pistol identical to her own straight at her.

"No, wait!" Her hand scrambled for the window button. Too late. Three squirts from Uncle Kurt's water pistol arced across the gulf and plastered Katherine's face and hair. She blinked water from her eyes to the sound of Uncle Kurt's cackling.

"Never underestimate your adversary, Katarina. I win."

"That water is freezing!"

He winked. "I kept the pistol in a cooler of ice water. Thought it would give you a brisk wakeup call."

She plucked a tissue from the packet on the dashboard and wiped her face and neck. "Just wait until next Saturday. I'll get you yet!"

"Perhaps you will. You are getting much better at cat and mouse. You figured out my subterfuge more quickly this time." He laughed again. "But my stomach says practice time is over. How about dinner? Loser picks the restaurant."

"All right. Let's head to The Varsity."

Uncle Kurt's face wrinkled.

Emphasizing a Southern drawl for fun, Katherine said, "Well, bless your little heart, how could I forget your fine, upstandin' European breedin' won't let you enjoy prime Georgian cuisine, like hot dogs, deep-fried onion rings, and all that yummy . . ."

The expression of revulsion on Uncle Kurt's face deepened.

Katherine laughed. "It was almost worth getting squirted to see that sour face. Okay, I love The Varsity, but since you don't, I'm willing to compromise. Let's make it Red Lobster. I'll circle around and follow you out."

"You have a deal!" His face disappeared as the BMW's tinted window slid up.

That man. He might be an analytical, world-travelin' jeweler most days, but sometimes he acts like an overgrown schoolboy.

Of course, she loved him despite his rules and rigid ways. Uncle Kurt was all she had left. Uncle Kurt and the HO, even though she doubted the secret society was the magnificent savior of society he painted it to be. And thanks to these mock training sessions, she felt confident she would be ready for the next round of organization promotions when the time came. Her powers of deduction were becoming sharper. She was learning to expect the unexpected—even though today's dousing demonstrated room for improvement.

But like a prowling shark, Katherine's subdued irritation with Uncle Kurt still lurked, as if waiting for something to happen. She hadn't said anything further about eligible bachelors after her miserable date with Thaddeus, the puffed-up banker, but neither had he. Was this a mute standoff, or . . .

She pondered everything he'd taught her about logic, reasoning, the power of observation, patiently biding time until just the right moment to achieve a goal. Was he playing another form of cat and mouse with her? A sneakier, stealthier, social maneuvering to control her life?

She was on his rear bumper now and exiting the shady garage into Atlanta's sun-drenched traffic. Katherine rolled the idea around her brain. Could his intentions for her love life be more than family tradition? If so, what? Maybe the old man was just afraid of being alone.

She set her jaw. It didn't matter. *Family or no family, if I decide to fall in love, that's my business. I don't want to hurt him, but this is one piece of myself I refuse to surrender. Game on!*

CHAPTER 8

Lightness. Tranquility. Floating. Before true consciousness returned, these impressions materialized within Roger Greene's being. No images presented themselves. His mind wafted higher and higher, from nether regions of shadowy nothingness to loftier, brighter levels of existence. The change was almost like a bubble rising from murky depths into increasingly lighter layers of water. But slower. Far, far slower. At last, the bubble reached the surface. Roger's eyes popped open.

A whitewashed ceiling filled his vision. Directly overhead hung a light. The harsh glare of the bulb reflected downward by a round, ceramic cover. A gradual shift of Roger's eyes revealed identical light fixtures suspended to the right and left of this one.

He was flat on his back in a chilly room. But where? And why did it feel as if he were lying in cold water?

This wasn't his quarters in Debden. Where was he? The silent question hung, unspoken and unanswered, in muddled thoughts. Perhaps an explanation would come if he were to twist his head, but for some reason his neck muscles refused to obey. All he could do was stare upward—and wonder.

Gradually his nebulous impressions crystallized into words. *Am I in a hospital?* Something about the ceiling or the antiseptic odor reminded him of hospitals and their sterile environments. *Was I in an accident? A car wreck? Maybe in a coma?*

He inhaled, then exhaled. The action reminded him of something. Something important about breathing hovered on the edge of memory. He inhaled again, more deeply this time. Fresh, incoming air expanded his chest before he forced it from his lungs. It was as if his body were purging itself of—

Roger's memory clicked. He recalled pink gas spurting through overhead vents and frantic efforts to avoid the mist with his woolen blanket.

He wanted to sit up but couldn't. Like his neck, his stomach muscles wouldn't comply. His sense of touch was working, though. Something tight constricted his chest. He willed his fingers to explore, to find out what was there, but they wouldn't move either. Some sort of restraints gripped the skin around his wrists and ankles too. Oddest of all was what his fingers detected: a peculiar layer of wet, slick substance beneath him, perhaps an inch or so deep.

"Ah," said a male voice. The sound of footsteps preceded the appearance of a face peering down at him. Brown hair and a matching mustache adorned the features. Probably Kossler, the assistant to Blomberg the others had mentioned. The fellow wore a white lab coat. Regarding Roger with interest, he spoke something in German.

Roger's handful of basic German phrases that nearly all airmen knew proved unhelpful. Whatever this fellow had uttered fell outside his limited vocabulary.

"Good morning, Number Seven," the man said, switching to heavily accented English. He placed the back of his hand against Roger's forehead and seemed satisfied with the temperature. Then he turned his head and called, "Dr. von Blomberg," before striding from the room.

Roger continued breathing as deeply as possible. If any residue of that pink gas lingered in his lungs, he wanted to rid himself of every speck. He managed to twist his head slightly. Potency was creeping back into his neck muscles.

The scene that met his eyes caused Roger to blink. Was this a nightmare? Beside him on a wheeled gurney lay Bill Burgess. He, too, reclined flat on his back but with eyes closed. A linen sheet covered Bill's body from the chest to the knees, but the man's bare shoulders showed, hinting that some—if not all—of his clothing had been removed. Atop the gurney, Bill lay in a man-sized metal tray filled with glistening gray gelatin, probably the same goop between Roger's fingers. A sturdy, three-inch-wide leather strap hugged Bill's chest. Similar straps secured his ankles and wrists.

Roger squinted at Burgess but couldn't detect the slightest movement. Was his countryman living or dead?

Struggling to lift his head, Roger discerned the remaining five prisoners stretched on identical gurneys, all in numerical order according to their jail cells and all of them unmoving. The grisly sight suggested a mortuary—or worse, Thanksgiving dinner with humans rather than turkeys on the platters.

Footsteps again sounded, and Blomberg swung into view, accompanied by the assistant. "Number Seven. I'm delighted to see you have rejoined us. Indeed, I was astonished when Dr. Kossler informed me you were already awake."

Roger made an effort to swallow but couldn't summon enough saliva. The inside of his mouth scraped like dry sandpaper. A disgusting metallic taste coated his tongue. "Water," he croaked.

Blomberg spoke something to Kossler, who nodded and walked away.

"Too much water might not be suitable just yet, Number Seven. It could induce vomiting. However, we prepared some crushed ice for this moment. You may suck on that to relieve your thirst."

Kossler reappeared and tilted a spoonful of ice chips between Roger's lips. When the airman had swirled the melting water around his mouth and swallowed, Kossler administered a second spoonful.

The muscles in his jaws and throat gradually responded enough to produce words. "What have you done to us?"

The professor offered the patronizing smile a learned astronomer might bestow on a preschool child who has just asked, "How high is up?"

"I won't attempt a complete explanation. To truly understand, you would require years of specialized training in fields related to genetics, molecular biology, synthetic regeneration, and reproduction, not to mention a dozen or so others. Even my younger colleague here hasn't received an exhaustive briefing on the procedure. There will be time for that later, if the experiment is successful."

Roger scarcely heard the final portion of Blomberg's reply. The word *reproduction* had snared his attention. Fear sprang to Roger's mind. Restricted as he was by leather restraints, he had no way to investigate what they had done to him. No pain radiated from between his legs, but had this crazy scientist performed surgery down there? "Reproduction? Can I still have kids, or what?"

Blomberg looked confused. "Young goats?" Then his eyes lit with comprehension, and he placed both hands on his stomach as if about to laugh, but he restrained himself. "Ah, sorry to have alarmed you, Number Seven. I didn't mean to imply that I've tampered with your reproductive system. I know of another doctor, a man by the name of Mengele—at least, he considers himself a doctor, though he is more of a barbarian in my opinion. With him, the more intimate portions of your anatomy might have been at risk, but I have no such interests."

Roger noted again that Blomberg was one of those individuals who could dole out a great many words and still communicate very little specific meaning.

"What, then?"

"I will tell you and your flying comrades more details after they have regained consciousness. Oh yes, they're alive. Just asleep. Probably you would still be asleep, too, if you had not managed to filter some of the gas before passing out. Do you recall starting to revive in the middle of my procedure?"

The question gave birth to a hazy memory. Roger pictured a brief, blurry moment: Blomberg's face, his nose and mouth obscured by a white mask, shouted commands. Something rubbery descending over his face . . .

"A little. It's fuzzy."

"Interesting. Probably not significant, though. Your friends should not sleep much longer. When they become alert, I shall share an announcement with all of you."

The two scientists exited the room, Blomberg speaking in German as they departed.

What kind of loony bin have I landed in? Roger recalled his earlier comment about Blomberg reminding him of Dr. Frankenstein. *Maybe my guess wasn't far off the mark.*

◆ ◆ ◆

Within an hour, the six other Allied airmen began to stir. Roger shared the few details he'd gleaned from Blomberg. Then Blomberg himself and two soldiers bearing Luger pistols appeared. One at a time they wheeled the men back to their barred cells.

When Roger's turn came, the soldiers leveled their weapons at him as Blomberg unfastened the restraints. They needn't have bothered. Throughout Roger's body, every muscle ached. Even his eyebrow and scalp muscles hurt. It was as if he'd spent the past month pulverizing rocks with a sledgehammer twenty-four hours a day. He couldn't have rallied enough energy to swat a mosquito, let alone to throw a punch.

The linen sheet he clutched around his nude body provided scant protection against the frigid air of the cell. All he could do was shuffle his bare feet across the frosty concrete floor. Even his military dog tags had disappeared from his neck.

Roger noticed his clothing lying at the foot of the cot, but he had no energy to dress. Like the others, he eased onto the cot and tugged the woolen blankets up to his neck. Was the chamber truly colder than before, or was the coldness inside him?

When Roger, the seventh and last prisoner, lay securely in his cell with his door locked, Blomberg dismissed the soldiers. Moments later, Kossler showed up bearing a clipboard, which he handed to Blomberg.

Blomberg examined and then returned the clipboard to Kossler. "Gentlemen, I understand you feel somewhat lethargic. Not to worry. Based upon my earlier experiments, that's to be expected. The weakness should pass relatively quickly."

"What have you done to us?" Sedgewick demanded.

Blomberg paid no heed to the RAF man's curt tone. "I was about to explain that, Number One. During the past forty-eight hours, your bodies have undergone more than thirty separate injections of various preparations, each of you receiving slightly different applications. Equally critical, however, was the phase gas, which you inhaled, plus a powerful electromagnetic field through which your bodies have passed."

"Phase gas?" Burgess repeated from his cot.

"Excuse my crude abbreviation. Even if I pronounced the full name in German, you wouldn't recognize it, as it's my own invention. I translate it 'phase gas' for the sake of brevity. Possibly you assumed the pink fog was simply to render you unconscious? That's merely a helpful side effect. My phase gas is an airborne, highly potent array of compounds and catalysts. When administered through the lungs, these components quickly disburse throughout the body, preparing the blood and cell tissue for alteration."

Despite his aching muscles, Roger hung on every word. Was this character a crackpot, a demon, or a genius?

"What kind of alteration?" Rutledge asked.

"An alteration for the better, I assure you. In fact, what I have done for you should be considered an honor. Many men will someday desire what you now possess. Let me give you a complete overview—"

Roger shook his head. "Let's skip to the bottom line." Left to his own way of explaining things, Blomberg might take days trying to explain the chemistry and every scientific detail behind his experiment, not to mention why they should be giddy with delight about it. "You've done something to us. We want to know what it is—without the scientific mumbo jumbo."

"Right," said Lambright from cell 3. "Heaven help you if you've injected us with monkey brains or some such muck just to see what happens."

Blomberg sighed. "As you wish. Although I would have enjoyed recounting details about the process, even if only in a rudimentary outline. The whole concept is fascinating!" He paused, as if contemplating how to summarize. "Perhaps you have heard of Methuselah?"

The word meant nothing to Roger, but Hazlitt raised himself onto one elbow. "Methuselah? The Bible-time character?"

"Exactly." Blomberg grew enthusiastic again. "The man who lived the longest life in recorded history. According to the ancient record, Methuselah lived 969 years. He must have been a genetically perfect specimen—the perfect Aryan prototype!"

"The old boy's off his rocker," a British voice commented in an undertone.

Roger focused on Blomberg's eyes. As before, he saw the animated glint that might signal the light of brilliance—or of lunacy.

"Since when do Nazis care about the Bible?" Burgess spat out. "The Bible also says, 'Thou shalt not kill,' but you Nazis have murder down to a regular science."

As if interrupted by an impudent child, Blomberg replied, "In the opinion of the Führer, most of the Bible is a collection of myths fabricated by an inferior race. But that didn't stop nomadic tribes from adopting and plagiarizing earlier recorded histories, such as the Genesis genealogies. Without a doubt, some earlier humans once lived extraordinarily long lives. Not until they mingled with lesser races did their life span become corrupted and diminish to the present norms."

The professor paused, as if expecting a reaction. When none occurred, he puffed up his chest as if to make the announcement of the century. "Gentlemen, the ultimate purpose of this facility is to restore a human life span to that of Methuselah's day. Man can live for hundreds of years. With your help, I plan to demonstrate that truth."

Burgess caught Roger's eye and tapped a finger to his temple. "He really is nuts."

Kossler, the assistant, stepped forward with a glower. "Show respect. Dr. von Blomberg is one of the most brilliant intellectuals of our time. You wouldn't speak so rashly had you been here to observe our experiments with the mice."

Roger shook his head. "How did you ever talk Hitler into financing this half-baked scheme?"

Blomberg paced to the end of the chamber and stood directly in front of Roger's cell. "Militarily, the benefit is priceless. A soldier with physiology enhanced by my procedure will heal rapidly from wounds. Too fast, in fact, even for infection to set in. However, to answer your question more specifically, the Führer has personal reasons to support this research. Have you never heard our leader describe this country as 'the Thousand-year Reich'?"

"Sure. It's in all the propaganda. What of it?"

"For your information, Number Seven, the Führer has never intended to pass control of the Fatherland to a successor. Our Third Reich *will* endure a thousand years, and the Führer wishes to lead us for the full millennium."

CHAPTER 9

Although Roger wasn't familiar with German cuisine, he believed he detected a slight bitterness in some of the meat dishes. Was Blomberg sneaking more chemicals into the chow? He considered a hunger strike, but by the time each meal tray arrived, an uncontrollable craving for food overpowered all self-restraint. The other prisoners exhibited the same urges.

The soreness in the men's muscles dissipated gradually. For the next five days—a period in which Christmas came and went without celebration—regardless of how much they rested or how well they ate, all of them experienced physical exhaustion and confined themselves to their cots.

"Totally normal," Blomberg assured. "Your body cells are rejuvenating themselves, restructuring and realigning according to ancient genetic blueprints. This process taxes the organism's energy reserves. It will pass."

"It bloody well better pass," the ever-defiant Sedgewick threatened. "Germany signed the Geneva Convention, you know. You've got no right to use Allied prisoners for your filthy experiments."

Blomberg's voice gained an almost compassionate timbre. "You still don't understand. Explorers like Ponce de Leon have expended vast amounts of time and capital roaming the globe in search of a fountain of youth. What price would be too high for multiplying one's life span by ten or fifteen times? Yet you have received this golden opportunity for free, Number One."

"We would have appreciated being asked first."

Blomberg shrugged off the complaint and departed. Did he assume their grumpiness would fade once his patients better understood the "adjustments" he'd performed on their bodies?

By the sixth day after Blomberg's experiment, Roger's body ached much less. By the tenth day, the extreme muscular soreness passed. But each night the men slept more deeply than ever before, and they continued to experience maddening hunger pangs throughout the following week.

One day while Blomberg made his morning rounds, Roger seized the opportunity to pose unanswered questions. "Why us, Doc? Why were we chosen? There were plenty of other warm bodies in Germany before we got shot from the sky."

"Quite so. The specific decision was the result of medical, social, and political considerations. Not to mention fortuitous timing."

Hot frustration ballooned inside Roger's chest. Why couldn't this man who commanded such an impressive array of English words give a straight answer? "I don't suppose you could clue us in on these considerations?"

"Primarily I proceeded through a process of elimination." Blomberg appeared gratified to have an attentive audience, even if it was only one individual. "At first, I considered using Jews from one of the internment camps, but we quickly ruled out that option. As I've already mentioned, you participants of the Methuselah Project receive a priceless honor. Although I don't necessarily concur from a scientific viewpoint, the leadership of the Third Reich views Jewry as inferior stock. Thus, bestowing such an honor on people with Jewish ancestry was out of the question.

"Next, I weighed the possibility of utilizing subjects from Poland, Russia, or other Slavic lands. However, the Führer overruled. His viewpoint is that these people groups are undeserving in a biological sense. The same holds true for gypsies and similar subgroups within our grasp."

In the next cell, Burgess sniffed. "Oh, naturally. After all, you can't go around bestowing such a significant honor on just anyone."

"Precisely," Blomberg replied, either not detecting or ignoring the sarcasm. "Of course, I would have been willing to use French candidates, but again, the Führer adamantly opposed. Our Wehrmacht blitzed through France like a hot scalpel through butter. The Führer interprets their capitulation as a sign of weakness and inferiority. The French disqualified themselves for Methuselah."

"Why didn't you just use one of your own German citizens?" asked Lambright. "Surely your beloved Führer couldn't object to a purebred Aryan?"

Blomberg stepped backward to better address his growing crowd of listeners. "Actually he did. Despite the honor and privilege involved, Methuselah is still an experimental procedure. If anything were to go wrong . . . Well, the Führer would not subject citizens of the Reich to that possibility. No, we required healthy, suitable, admirable specimens from outside our own nation."

"So, that left the Brits and the Americans," Roger said.

"Correct. Despite the losses from your aerial bombardments, Adolf Hitler holds a grudging respect for you airmen. General Göring was the one who recommended captured Anglo-Saxon flyers. Your fortitude and tenacity have quite impressed him, as well, although he can't admit it publicly. As soon as this facility was equipped, Göring issued documents authorizing the redirection of seven Allied prisoners into my care. Your timing and good fortune at being shot down in this vicinity were highly opportune. Or to quote your own slang, you got a lucky break."

Jamison sat up on his cot. "Are you saying we can't die anymore?"

The professor shook his head. "You misunderstand. If you were stabbed through the heart or if your head were chopped off, you would perish as quickly as any man. But if your bodies don't suffer mortal trauma, they should function quite well for hundreds of years. In fact, better than before. If you receive nonlethal injuries, I theorize that your cells will regenerate ten times faster than before. Possibly faster. Of course, only the coming weeks will tell. We must observe you and maintain detailed records of all pertinent information." The professor jotted a final note onto his ever-present clipboard. "Good day, gentlemen." He departed through the metal door.

Clang.

When Blomberg was gone, Burgess shook his head. "No day is going to be good until we get out of here. How can a guy who looks so normal be so whacko?"

Sedgewick agreed. "If you ask me, whatever that madman injected into us is more likely to shorten our lives than extend them. From now on, I plan to drink as much water as I can. Maybe it will flush out some of the chemicals."

Roger latched onto Sedgewick's idea. The sooner his body could rid itself of Blomberg's lunacy, the better. The question was, would drinking extra water actually help? Or was it possible the seven had already been poisoned? If so, their bodies might already be slowly dying.

CHAPTER 10

Ignoring the sweat beading her brow, Katherine tightened the belt of her white cotton *gi*. Without warning, she whirled and squinted contempt at the dummy before her—or rather, half a dummy. Instead of legs, the lower portion of the mannequin was just a thick support pole rising from its round, heavy base. From the upper thighs to the head, the figure represented the fairly realistic torso and head of a man molded from soft, skin-toned rubber.

What did you say you're gonna to do to me, jerk-face?

With a shout of "Hai!" she circled her left foot forward and snapped the first two knuckles of her right fist into the lower end of her opponent's rubber sternum. Her blow landed precisely, even though she maintained eye contact with the dummy to avoid telegraphing her punch. If this had been an actual attacker, her offensive would've broken off the small bone and driven it inward, puncturing the diaphragm.

Katherine started to turn away, but next imagined her foe making a last-ditch attack. She cocked her right leg, and then drove her bare heel into the dummy's crotch with the force of a battering ram. The mannequin rocked from her blow. "You never should've eaten lead paint chips as a kid, dimwit."

The staccato of clapping erupted behind her. "Very good, Mueller. Looks like you've really mastered that kick."

Despite the mirrors lining the dojo's walls, Katherine hadn't noticed her instructor's return. He'd already exchanged his black *gi* for Wrangler jeans and a purple muscle shirt that emphasized his beefy physique. Frank Lawson's build resembled that of the dummy she'd just defeated.

Katherine wiped the back of her hand across her sweaty brow. "Thanks, Sensei. But aren't y'all supposed to say something like, 'Very good, Grasshopper. You have learned well'?"

He chortled. "I used to watch those reruns when I was a kid. But practice your Chinese accent before you try out for a martial arts movie."

She tugged at the hair band that confined her ponytail and shook her hair free. "I'll keep that in mind—if I ever decide to try out for Hollywood. For now, I have other plans for my life."

He crossed his arms, possibly as a natural gesture, but maybe to show off the girth of his biceps. "You're really committed to driving a taxi for a living?"

She laughed. He must have seen her drive up in Charlie Taggart's taxicab, which was even now parked out front. "Heavens, no. I didn't work my tail off at the University of Georgia just to drive a cab. I've started a freelance-editing business I'm trying to get off the ground. I could apply to a newspaper, do the typical journalism thing, but going freelance allows me more control of my hours and my assignments. At least it will as soon as I build up a stable clientele. Right now, jobs are like karate: hit and miss."

Lawson pressed his lips together and nodded. He sniffed and jerked a thumb toward the front window. "So what's with the cab then? If you don't mind my asking. Kind of unusual for a pretty gal to be driving one."

There he went again, trying to be nonchalant while slipping in a compliment. "It belongs to a really close friend. Whenever I'm running low on cash, he lets me borrow it to do a little moonlighting." What she didn't mention was that Charlie Taggart, the "close friend," was in his sixties, sported an enormous beer belly, and was married. Let Sensei draw his own conclusions.

"I see." Lawson picked up a rag and a plastic squirt bottle of Lysol to wipe down the practice dummy. "I had the impression your family was pretty well off. I mean, sometimes I see that rich-looking guy in the BMW drop you off and pick you up. Figured it must be your dad."

Uh-oh. Gone from chatting to fishing.

She wouldn't have minded the curiosity if Frank Lawson were the least bit attractive to her, but she needed a man with more depth. She wanted somebody who could hold an intelligent conversation on a variety of topics rather than ramble eternally about the advantages of free weights over machines and cables. "I don't accept money from my uncle. We believe in people earning their own keep. If that means driving a cab until I get my business going, then that's what I'll do."

She strolled to the corner of the karate studio, where she slipped on her new running shoes without wasting time on socks. She scooped up her handbag and slid the strap over her shoulder. "Time for me to hit the road. See you, Sensei."

Lawson unfolded his arms. "You're not going like that? In your *gi*, in January? It's only twenty-eight degrees out there." He paused. "I wouldn't mind sticking around if you want to shower and change before I lock up." Katherine forced a polite smile but shook her head. Lawson licked his lips, and Katherine had the sudden impression of a big, hungry cat.

Uneasiness prickled the back of her neck. No way was she going to strip and shower if Lawson was the only other person in the dojo. "Uh, thanks, but it's not far to my house. I don't mind driving like this."

"Yeah, but"—he searched for words—"I just thought you and me . . . you know. Might stop at Mitch's or someplace and grab a beer together?"

This was the kind of invitation Katherine hated—from a guy who might be fine for some other woman but definitely not for her. On top of the fact that he and she were a mismatch, up close Frank Lawson's breath suggested the odor of stale gym socks. She absolutely didn't want to sit and chitchat at one of those microscopic tables inside Mitch's. "Gee, Sensei, thanks, but I don't think so. It's getting late. I still need to catch up with paperwork. You know, the business." She padded across the mat toward the door.

"Yeah, I understand. Maybe some other time. By the way, you don't have to call me Sensei outside of class. You can call me Frank."

Pushing open the door, Katherine gave a halfhearted smile, followed by a goodbye nod. *And you can keep on calling me Mueller.*

Dusk was already deepening as she walked to the taxi, unlocked it, and then relocked the door the moment she was inside. Karate or no, she didn't like being on the street alone after dark. Uncle Kurt was right: if she was going to drive the cab, she did need to master self-defense. Besides, the organization required martial arts training. It was all part of their grand design that each member be well rounded in education, physical fitness, problem solving, and other qualities.

Maybe she should switch to another karate studio. She would hate doing that, especially now that she'd bonded with Robyn, Amy, and some of the other female students. *If he keeps hittin' on me, I won't have a choice.*

She started the engine, popped on the headlights, and pulled away from the curb. Once on the road, Katherine sighed. *Why does this always happen to me? I can attract all kinds of men I don't care about. Isn't there just one man in the world who's my type? Surely just one?*

Slowing at an intersection, she flipped on her signal and turned onto Autry Lane. Yes, in her heart she was confident that somewhere on the planet Mr. Perfect was out there waiting, maybe even searching for her at that precise moment. But, where was he hiding?

I hope I don't have to wait a lifetime.

CHAPTER 11

SUNDAY, JANUARY 2, 1944
THE METHUSELAH FACILITY, GERMANY

Gripping the handle of his aluminum spoon, Roger scratched his six-teenth tally onto the brick wall of "Blomberg's House of Horrors." *January 2. What a joyous New Year.* Listening to the banter of the men behind him, he was startled to hear Burgess seeking a silver lining on the dark cloud of captivity.

"You know," Burgess said, "except for that pink gas and whatever they did while we were unconscious, this place has to be a lot more tolerable than a regular POW camp. At least here we get three squares a day. Plus, it's a comfortable shelter for the winter."

"I've been thinking the same thing," Lambright said. "If we have to be caged up, at least the cage is halfway gilded."

Roger stopped scratching the brick wall and wheeled around. "You've got to be kidding. Good grub or no, I'd rather be in a regular POW camp. Then we would be with our own guys and away from Dr. Jekyll."

"Don't get me wrong," Burgess said. "If I had my choice, I'd rather be with a bunch of our guys too. I just meant that, as long as we're stuck here, we might as well eat their home cooking and enjoy the ride while it lasts, since it could be worse."

Roger shook his head. "Don't forget, nobody on the Allied side even knows we're here. This place is Blomberg's secret, and it's a safe bet he's not going to let the Red Cross or anyone else without Nazi credentials find out the stunts he's been up to. When his ridiculous experiment doesn't produce the results he expects, it'll only be a matter of time before Hitler cuts the funding and shuts this place down."

"So we'll end up in a regular POW camp after all," Burgess concluded with a shrug.

Roger stepped the few paces across his bit of concrete floor and grasped the bars separating him from Burgess. "You actually believe we'll end up in a regular camp? Where we can tell hundreds of our guys that they've been treating Americans and Brits like throwaway rats in lab experiments? Don't buy that garbage."

"Right you are, Roger boy," Sedgewick called from the far end of the chamber. "More than likely, someday seven unidentified corpses will end up in unmarked graves. That's how they'll shut our mouths."

Burgess and the others grew thoughtful. It was the last time any of them referred to their cage as gilded.

Meanwhile, one word constantly pushed forward in Roger's mind: *escape*. Even while he lay aching on his cot that first week, his eyes had studied the walls, the ceiling, the floor, the bars, the hinges of the doors. Although the House of Horrors was a basic, no-nonsense structure, its very simplicity provided challenges to would-be escapees.

Except for the single toilet built into each cell, the concrete floor was a solid slab, without so much as a crack to mar its surface. Even if Roger had a better tool than a tablespoon for tunneling, how could he penetrate that concrete to begin one? If he did get past the concrete floor, how could he camouflage the entry to a tunnel? His cot was the only movable object in the room, and it did nothing to conceal the floor beneath it. An additional problem: where could he dispose of excavated dirt? Down the toilet? Just a single bucketful of dirt would require countless flushes to get rid of the soil without clogging the drain and inviting closer inspection.

I've got more questions than answers.

He looked at the two-inch-square peephole in the metal door that separated this chamber from the corridor. Guards on the other side could observe the prisoners any time, day or night. At least one incandescent bulb illuminated the chamber at all times.

On top of these challenges, even if he managed the miraculous and escaped this building undetected, he had no way to scale the sheer wall and the barbed wire that enclosed the entire complex.

During a quiet conversation, Burgess nodded. "I've been wondering the same things. I always come up blank. Even if one of us could manage an escape hole, only that one man could use it. The goons weren't stupid when they built separate cells."

"Looks like we'll have to bide our time and keep our eyes peeled for opportunities," Hazlitt said from cell 5.

This was a glum conclusion but, under the circumstances, waiting and watching seemed realistic.

Unbidden by Roger, Old Miss Hawkins's words from Sunshine repeated themselves in his brain: "Children, always remember to pray!" Roger had been amused when the admonition resurfaced in his mind the day he was captured. But the words weren't funny anymore. They seemed to invade his thoughts at least once every twenty-four hours.

Are Blomberg's chemicals messing up my brain? I hadn't thought about Miss Hawkins and her Bible pictures for years. Now she's haunting me.

Even that concept gave the pilot pause. By now Miss Hawkins must be dead and moldering in some churchyard back in Indiana. Could her ghost be floating around earth and visiting all those who'd once listened to her at Sunshine?

"Knock it off," he berated himself. *Keep thinking like that, Greene, and you'll end up nuttier than Blomberg.*

"Knock what off?" Burgess said from the next cell.

Roger wasn't about to tell his neighbor about elderly Miss Hawkins. "Nothing. Forget it."

But Burgess didn't forget it. Occasionally Roger caught his neighbor casting sideways glances at him.

He's wondering if I'm coming unhinged. Who's to say I'm not?

Maybe if he yielded to Miss Hawkins's directive, she would go away and leave him alone. *Okay, God, don't let me go off my rocker. In memory of Old Lady Hawkins, I'm asking You to keep me in my right mind, no matter what Blomberg does. And if there's a way out of here—any way at all—I'd like You to point it out, because I'm coming up empty. I guess that's everything. This is Roger Greene, out.*

After the prayer, Roger lay on his cot, staring upward. He craved a glimpse of azure sky, of clouds, of luxurious sunshine—everything he relished when airborne. Instead, gray concrete and ash-colored bricks blocked his vision. "They could've at least given us a window. Even a window with bars would be better than none at all. Don't they realize it's torture for pilots not to see the sky?"

"Try not to think about it, Rog," Jamison said. "Instead of dwelling on everything you want to do but can't, do what I do. Be free in your brain. Think about cities, parks, restaurants, and other places you've visited, and then try to recall every minuscule detail. Blomberg can lock our bodies behind bars, but he can't lock up our imaginations."

Be free in my brain?

Roger lay down and buried his face in his pillow. Within a few moments, he was back at Station 156 in Debden, sitting in the cockpit of his P-47. Step by step, he mentally closed the canopy, fired up the engine, taxied away from the hardstand and out to the runway. He could imagine the increasing vibration of the airframe and the roar of the engine as the aircraft picked up speed. Free as an eagle, he lifted from the tarmac, raised his landing gear, and soared above the English countryside. *No doubt about it, I was born to fly . . .*

When Roger opened his eyes, he realized he'd drifted off to sleep. Only one of the three light bulbs in the chamber glowed, dimming the light but not extinguishing it. His six companions slept. Someone breathed heavily, although not quite snoring. It must be nighttime.

Faint and distant, muffled by the brick walls, Roger heard something: a drawn-out, wailing sound. He quickly guessed what the siren must mean. As if in confirmation, another distant noise steadily grew into a distinct droning. Aircraft. Lots of them.

"Hey, you guys, wake up. I think it's an air raid!"

Roger's words performed magic. Each of his companions rolled over and cocked an ear.

Sedgewick bolted upright. "Night bombers! That's the RAF about to give Adolf another kick in the rear."

"Go get 'em, lads," Lambright shouted toward the ceiling. "Teach Jerry a lesson for us!"

The siren also roused the guards. Through the metal door, guttural shouts sounded, followed by the rapid clomping of jackbooted feet pounding along the corridor. The single lightbulb winked out.

Burgess's voice cut through the darkness. "It's a blackout. They've cut the juice to all the lights."

"This would've been the perfect time for an escape hole," Roger said. "Right when all the outside lights are off and the guards are scampering away to cower in a bomb shelter."

Even as he finished his sentence, the thunder of an aerial bombardment reverberated in the chamber. He lay motionless on his canvas cot, where even from a distance he could feel the vibrations as tons of high explosives ravaged whatever target lay beneath them. The concussions were marching closer, closer . . .

Above the din of explosions, Roger heard Burgess rattling the door of his cell and shouting. "Blomberg! Kossler! You idiots! Unlock the doors before we're blown to bits!"

Although Roger couldn't see them in the darkness, he heard the other prisoners following Burgess's example. The inky blackness echoed with a cacophony of rattling bars, frantic cries, curses, and deafening booms that literally bounced men to their knees on the concrete floor.

Roger half-crawled, half-stumbled to his cell door to join in the shouting. "Nazi cowards! Get in here. Save us!" He prepared to ram the barred door with his full force, but he stopped. *Don't panic—think!* He'd tried ramming that door once before, and the effort had produced nothing more than a black-and-blue shoulder. What defensive measures could he take?

Unbidden, the haunting refrain popped into his mind: "Children, always remember to—"

"Shut up!"

The concussions marched on top of them. Surely his eardrums would burst! In grave-like darkness, he scrambled to his cot, where he fell to his knees, but not to pray. He flattened his flight jacket to cushion the floor under the cot, then crawled underneath to join it. Feeling above him, he grabbed his pillow and pulled that down too. Covering his head with the pillow and clamping it tightly around his ears, he lay there under the cot, hoping against hope to ride out the bombing. His makeshift shelter offered ridiculously pitiful protection, but no other options existed.

Jumbled with the horrified screams of his comrades, two more near-deafening detonations rocked the earth. Roger Greene's blackened world exploded with inhuman might. Like a concrete bronco, the floor bucked him into his cot and slammed him back down, even as ear-shattering detonations pummeled his brain. From all directions, flying chunks of brick battered and buried him under their incredible weight. His lungs fought for breath.

As consciousness ebbed, a final conclusion penetrated his mind: *This is it. I'm going to die.*

CHAPTER 12

"Herr Doktor! Ich habe einen Flieger gefunden!"

Deep inside Roger Greene's mind, some flicker of life sensed spoken syllables but attached no meaning to them. His world had gone cold and dark, and something within the core of his being expected the situation to remain that way. But other sounds—scrapes and clanks—forced their way into reality, tugging him back from the suffocating blackness. Bit by bit, sections of the crushing weight lifted from his body. Not until dust-laden air whooshed into his lungs and ignited a coughing fit did the full truth dawn upon him: *I'm alive.*

Several pairs of hands clamped onto Roger's arms, his legs, even the back of his belt, and dragged his body from the debris of what had been cell 7. As they did, a jagged finger of broken brick gouged into the skin of his right cheek. He winced, but couldn't summon energy to protest. In that moment, a rag doll could protect itself better than he.

Roger coughed again, his reflexes trying to rid him of the grit lining his throat. When his nose detected the steaming aroma of ersatz coffee, he opened his eyes and gratefully parted his lips. The hot liquid he gulped solidified the truth. Yes, he really was alive.

Stupefied and still blinking eyes that felt caked with cement dust, Roger swept his gaze left and right in the predawn grayness. The carnage astounded him. Blomberg's Methuselah facility had become a heap of blasted rubble and twisted steel. Here and there, wisps of smoke curled upward to mingle with the unnatural pall that hung over the entire area.

No one could live through that. Yet he'd just done it. Barely. For the second time in recent days, the possibility of God's existence flitted through his mind. Had the Almighty personally intervened to spare him? True, Roger hadn't taken time to pray actual words as the bombs were falling, but part of him—his soul?—had cried out for protection from such a death.

Roger pulled himself to a sitting posture. Shivering, he crossed his arms against the biting cold of January.

"Einen Augenblick." A soldier reached into the cavity where Roger had lain and tugged loose the leather flight jacket, which he draped over the airman's shoulders.

Roger's dry throat could manage only a croak. "Where are the others?"

They regarded him with uncomprehending eyes.

"Where are my friends?" Anger pushing him to rise on wobbly legs, he stood now and motioned at the heap of wreckage. "Where . . . are . . . my . . . friends?"

From behind him came the accented voice of Blomberg's assistant, Dr. Kossler. "We're still digging for them. So far, we've uncovered only three others: Number One, Number Two, and Number Three. All dead."

Roger turned and glared at Kossler's serene features. Not one spec of dust marred the man's face or wool greatcoat. More frustrating than the deaths of his fellow airmen was the fact that this Nazi, who bore part of the blame, could stand here and clinically speak about their demise as if they hadn't been men, as if they'd merely been so many expendable rodents.

"You dirty, stinking, good-for-nothing—" Roger hurled himself at Kossler, ready to pummel the man's face to a pulp. Immediately soldiers grappled him, holding him back. "You and Blomberg should rot in hell for this! You left us locked up during an air raid. Here we were, getting blown to bits, while you and your men cringed in some cozy bomb shelter."

With eyes sadder than Roger would have expected, Kossler shook his head. "No, Captain. None of us here were in a bomb shelter. Unfortunately a shelter was not included in the facility's design. Since we are three kilometers from the nearest industries, it was assumed we wouldn't need one. Every man you see here was in the barracks, in the forest off in that direction." He waved his hand toward the paler sky to the east. "So if it is any consolation, we lost more of our men than you did."

"Yeah? Well, cry me a river. Get that old geezer Blomberg out here. I want to tell him exactly what I think of him and his precious facility."

Kossler's head drooped. "Your request is impossible. Do you see that crater?"

The German tilted his head, and Roger followed the man's gaze. Just past what must have been the outer wall of the building was a blackened pit, undoubtedly the impact point of the bomb that had destroyed the House of Horrors.

"Dr. von Blomberg never slept in the barracks. He kept a bed in his office, beside the laboratory. If the hell you mentioned truly exists, then Dr. von Blomberg just spent his first night in it. No corpse will be found."

Roger stared at the blast site, then back at Kossler. He was prepared to spout, "Good riddance," but something in Kossler's demeanor sapped the heat from Roger's words.

Kossler withdrew a white handkerchief from his overcoat pocket and offered it to Roger. "Here. You're bleeding. Under your right eye."

Without a word, Roger snatched the cloth and pressed it to the spot. He remembered something sharp and painful scraping his cheek when the soldiers had hauled him loose. When he drew the handkerchief from his face, it bore a red stain mixed with grime.

"I will have you taken to the barracks to rest."

"Not yet. I want to stay here until my friends are found."

Kossler offered no argument, so Roger remained. With thirty or forty soldiers on the scene, no one seemed to fear the American would bolt for freedom.

Wrapped in his leather flight jacket and a dusty woolen blanket pulled from the rubble of his cell, Roger watched the diggers excavate for his comrades. Before long, however, their slow progress gave rise to a swelling tide of impatience. He stood and tossed the blanket aside.

"What are you doing?" Kossler picked up the blanket. "You need rest. You've been through an ordeal."

"No, I want to help. The more hands, the better." Not waiting for the German's reply, Roger joined the brigade of men passing broken chunks of brick and twisted steel bars from hand to hand.

Within two hours, the last Allied body appeared. On hands and knees, Roger stumbled forward to feel Hazlitt's neck. No pulse under the chilly skin. Roger was the sole survivor.

If I'd been standing up like the others, I'd be dead too. Guilt swamped his soul. *What right do I have to survive when they didn't?*

As the diggers wrapped Hazlitt's corpse in a drab green blanket, Roger turned away. He wouldn't let the enemy see the tears welling in his eyes.

From behind, footsteps crunched closer over the debris. Kossler's voice said, "My condolences, Captain Greene."

Roger held his gaze in the opposite direction. "Tell me they won't end up in some unmarked grave. Promise me they'll get a decent burial."

Kossler stepped beside Roger, both men gazing into the distance yet regarding nothing in particular. The German removed a cigarette from a silvery case, almost inserted it between his lips, but then offered it to Roger instead. Roger didn't smoke. This time, however, he accepted the gesture. If nothing else, the burning tobacco would provide warm air for his lungs. Kossler lit the cigarette, then a second one for himself.

"You have my word. Their identification tags will be replaced around their necks. Their bodies will be transported to the nearest prisoner of war camp. They will be buried alongside their countrymen."

Roger exhaled a long stream of smoke. No need to thank the man. It was the very least they could do.

"You lead a charmed life, Captain. First you survived being shot down. Now you have survived a bombing. Perhaps somebody 'up there' is looking out for you, as they say."

He took another drag on the cigarette. "Yeah. Maybe. So what happens now?"

The German stomped his feet against the cold. "Unfortunately Dr. von Blomberg was an eccentric genius. He allowed no one to copy his documentation. He stored all the records in his personal office, where he slept and ate. He allowed me to sit and read his notes when I had time, but only in his presence. His documentation and resource material were voluminous. As of yesterday, I had read only about 25 or 30 percent of the material."

"You mean everything Blomberg knew and accomplished here just got blasted to kingdom come?"

Kossler took another puff on his cigarette. "Correct. We were within one hair's breadth of achieving our goal. But now it's gone. Wiped out. We who remain don't possess one shred of evidence that the Methuselah Project would have been successful."

"Tough break, Doc. Looks like you need a new job. So where does that leave me?" Even though Blomberg had perished, whatever government bureaucracy oversaw this experiment wouldn't merely ship him to a POW camp as if nothing had happened.

Kossler looked him in the eye. "That depends entirely on—" The German halted mid-sentence and studied the American's face. Next he stepped backward and inspected Roger from head to foot. "How do you feel, Captain?"

Roger took a last drag on the cigarette and tossed away the glowing butt. "How do I feel? Angry beyond words. How do you want me to feel, when six buddies just got snuffed out through no fault of their own?"

Excitement grew in Kossler's eyes and voice. "No, no. I mean, how do you feel physically after your trauma? Are you in pain? Sore? Stiff?"

"No. I feel fine. Why?"

Kossler placed an index finger on Roger's right cheek. "When my men pulled you from the rubble, your cheek was bleeding. I gave you a handkerchief. Now the wound is gone. Not even a scratch remains. In little more than two hours, your body has regenerated new cells and completely healed the injury. Remarkable!"

Roger explored the spot with his fingertips. Kossler was right. Not only had the blood disappeared, but instead of feeling a throbbing gash, his fingers encountered only smooth, normal skin, as if the injury had never occurred. "How can that be?"

His head held high and proud, Kossler seized Roger's hand and pumped it in uncharacteristic glee. "Evidence! We now have tangible, indisputable proof that the Methuselah Project is a success. Congratulations, Captain Greene. You are the Third Reich's first Methuselah man!"

CHAPTER 13

Katherine raised a hand to knock on the ornately carved ebony doors. She paused. Through those heavy double portals wafted the muffled notes of *The Ring of the Nibelung,* Wagner's famous opera and Uncle Kurt's all-time favorite. The music, however, wasn't what stayed her hand.

This is idiotic. I should've outgrown this feeling when I gave away my dolls.

But she hadn't outgrown it. She could never explain to herself why the image of those foreboding doors evoked trepidation. Perhaps she'd describe the emotion more like . . . awe? Apprehension? No. What was wrong with her? The English language formed her editor's toolbox. Why should a description for this eerie feeling prove so hidden?

Hidden. Her brain parked on the word. Inexplicably that simple adjective struck closer to the bull's-eye. Katherine considered various synonyms for the word *hidden*—concealed, veiled, clandestine, unknown, unseen, buried . . .

No, no, no. Maybe the etymology? Occult. A shivery tingle danced up Katherine's spine. *Occult?* Why should that word affect her in this spot?

"Oh, don't be silly." She refused to let wooden doors intimidate her. She stepped forward and knocked. When no response came, she rapped louder.

"Come in, Katarina."

She slid open the twin doors, glad to be shoving them into their recesses in both walls, and strode into her uncle's den.

Uncle Kurt—whom she'd expected to find sitting behind the massive baroque table he used as a desk—rose from the black leather davenport where he'd been reclining and lifted the tone arm of the record player. Wagner's masterpiece evaporated in mid-note. "I hope the music didn't disturb you. I closed the doors. But Wagner is so invigorating. I can rarely resist the temptation to turn up the volume."

"No, you didn't disturb me. I couldn't even hear the music up in my room. I just have some questions about the HO."

"Ah, questions!" He rubbed his hands as a hungry man might do at the mention of roast beef. He crossed to the leather seat behind his desk. "Please, sit down, and ask all the questions you wish."

Katherine perched on the edge of Uncle Kurt's wooden chair, feet flat on the floor. "Well, I've been reading this pamphlet you gave me."

"And?"

Katherine tucked a strand of hair behind her ear and then smoothed the pamphlet on her lap. "It raises more questions than it answers. I was wondering if you could help me understand it better. For instance, the objectives of the organization. The pamphlet includes lots of rosy talk about 'improving the world' and 'choreographing improvements in society from behind the scenes,' and 'leaving behind a richer heritage.' Yet it's all so vague. Why doesn't the organization say straight out exactly how it benefits society?"

Kurt Mueller placed both palms on his desk. Contrary to what she feared, he didn't evidence any offense. "An excellent question, Katarina. To be truthful, I've been waiting for you to ask. Think of it like this. A selfish man does not act for the sake of others. He won't do anything philanthropic unless he can receive some credit, a little glory at the very least."

"I suppose."

"In the Heritage Organization, that's not our way. We swim against the stream, race against the odds. We discipline the inner self to reject self-centered glory-seeking and unite with our fellow HO members to function in concert with one another in quest of positive goals that will serve us as an association and society as a whole." Uncle Kurt was donning the impassioned voice he used to sermonize on topics close to his heart. The HO topped that list.

Katherine studied the gold-and-burgundy patterns in the imported Middle Eastern rug hanging behind Uncle Kurt. "That still doesn't explain exactly what the HO accomplishes."

"Correct, Katarina. But it does explain why we don't boast of our achievements and why we don't even mention the organization to outsiders. The Christian religion declares, 'The meek shall inherit the earth.' The HO replies, 'Rubbish.' The only way the meek can inherit a better world will be if a global confederacy of individuals unites to strive for the common good."

Katherine straightened. "Confederacy?"

"A poor choice of word, especially considering where we live. Think of it more like an amalgamation of bright, concerned minds. Noble souls who benefit a world that doesn't know they exist! And if protocol dictates that inexperienced ranks are not made privy to the wonderful string of advances in medicine, science, industry, and business, all I can ask is that you trust us. The more you learn and train, the more valuable you'll become to yourself and to the world around you."

This explanation wasn't the revelation Katherine had hoped to hear. "But you trust me, too, don't you? Can't you crack the window just a little so I see what accomplishments you're talking about?"

He stood and laughed. "You possess a keen, inquisitive mind. That's admirable. But all in due time. Be patient and faithful to the HO. I promise—you'll be glad you did. Now, any more questions as you study?"

"I guess not."

He accompanied her to the doorway. "I guarantee, the longer you are in the HO, the more you will trust and appreciate it."

"That's encouraging to hear."

"I have full confidence in you. You are an intelligent, ambitious girl with a gift for researching and understanding the heart of an issue. May you rise to the highest ranks of the organization, where new vistas will open and all your questions will receive answers." That said, he slid shut the double doors to his den. Moments later, the majestic strains of "The Ride of the Valkyries" resumed from the beginning.

CHAPTER 14

Blindfolded, Roger descended the steps, feeling his way with his flight boots. He still hadn't decided how much he bought into Kossler's claim that he was a "Methuselah man," but fast healer or no, he didn't care to tumble headlong down concrete stairs with his hands cuffed behind his back.

After he reached the bottom, strong fingers clamped onto his elbow and maneuvered him forward. When the guiding force stopped, someone removed the handcuffs.

"Don't remove the blindfold until you're told." It was Kossler's voice. "No need to get beaten unnecessarily."

A moment later, Roger heard the all-too-familiar clang of steel on steel.

"You may uncover your eyes."

Roger jerked off the blindfold and surveyed his new surroundings.

"No holiday resort, but certainly more comfortable than your cell at the Methuselah facility and your temporary cell upstairs."

Once more, Roger found himself behind bars, but this place was much roomier than his previous cage.

"You may go," Kossler told the two guards.

To Roger's surprise, he found not a cot, but a genuine, civilian-style bed, complete with a plush pillow and a thick comforter. To the left of the bed stood a wooden table and an armchair flanked by a floor lamp.

Beyond those was a set of bookcases reaching from the floor to the ceiling. The shelves contained hundreds of volumes. Maybe thousands. He
stepped closer and saw most of the books were in English, mostly classic
literature, but also textbooks. Many books brandished titles in German,
which he dismissed as useless. Others appeared to be in Dutch, French,
Russian, and various other European languages. To the right of the bed
was a wooden door. Most depressing of all was the wall: large steel plates
bolted to it created an impenetrable barrier.

It'll take more than a soup spoon to dig my way through that.

With the toe of his boot, Roger folded back a corner of the Persian
rug beneath his feet. Steel deck plating likewise shielded the floor against
tunneling attempts. He let the rug flop back into place and swore under
his breath.

Outside the bars, Kossler watched him like a zookeeper with a new
specimen.

Roger ignored him. Instead, he surveyed the rest of this lower level.
Against a backdrop of whitewashed concrete walls stood two desks, two
lab tables with microscopes, bank after bank of file cabinets, and an
assortment of scientific apparatuses Roger couldn't identify. The solitary
exit was a battleship-gray door, heavy-gauge steel. No need to ask why
there were no windows. The number of steps he'd descended made it obvious he was deep underground.

Kossler spread his arms wide. "Captain Greene, welcome to your new
home. These quarters replace your temporary place of confinement upstairs,
in my ancestral home. Now I shall be able to live in familiar surroundings
while continuing my scientific work down here, where you will live."

"Do all Kosslers build dungeons in their basements?"

"You've been asking about the construction noises. Now you see the
fruit of our labor. We call it the Methuselah bunker."

Kossler swept his gaze around the underground chamber, obviously
pleased. "Fortunately my great-grandfather was a successful businessman
and built a large residence. If he hadn't, your accommodations would be
much more humble."

Roger slipped off the flight jacket he'd been wearing while handcuffed and tossed it on the bed. "Why am I here?"

"Three reasons: speed, safety, and secrecy. When the Führer received my report on the amazing results of the project, he authorized me to continue Dr. von Blomberg's work at once. Or rather to labor backward, attempting to piece together the countless missing fragments of the puzzle that altered your physiology. I needed a private place to work, an invisible location that could withstand future bombings. Constructing this bunker solved all three needs."

"But you don't need me anymore. If you think you can recreate Blomberg's technique, go ahead. But ship me to a regular POW camp."

Kossler gripped his sides and laughed as if Roger had just told a hilarious joke. "Impossible. You're the key to the entire Methuselah Project. By observing you, we can determine with certainty whether the process produces unfortunate side effects. Also, from time to time I will require samples of your blood, urine, epidermis, and hair. So you see, your role is nonnegotiable. You are essential."

Roger resisted the urge to spit at the man. "I'm touched to the core." He jerked a thumb toward the unvarnished pine door beyond his bed. "What's in there?"

"One water closet and one sink. I'm afraid you'll have to bathe from the sink. Oh, and you'll find a mirror of polished metal. I'll obtain a safety razor so you can shave your whiskers."

Once more, Roger's eyes roamed the new cage. Bolted to one wall was a scratched and dented hunk of tin: a yellow square with a black numeral 7 stenciled onto it. From his cell at the House of Horrors. A silent tribute to Dr. von Blomberg.

Roger stepped over to the armchair and dropped into it. He kicked off his bulky flight boots and crossed his ankles on the bed, using it as a footstool.

"You know, Doc, when I was walking down those steps, I had a bad feeling. Like maybe I was going to be executed and buried underground."

"I assure you, Captain Greene, we have no such intentions."

"Nice to know." Roger reflected on the washroom. "No tub or shower, huh? What about these clothes I'm wearing? They already smell pretty ripe."

"We took measurements while you slept. We'll provide civilian clothing so you may wash these and hang them to dry." Kossler looked at the fleece flight boots. "Just to prove we aren't the monsters you believe, we'll even provide civilian shoes."

"So you really think you can recreate whatever hocus-pocus old Blomberg pulled off? How long will it take?"

"Respectively my replies are 'Perhaps' and 'I don't know.' Dr. von Blomberg was a genius. He had much more formal education than I, and he possessed uncanny intuition regarding multiple fields of science, some of which don't yet have names. We have no guarantee that I, or anyone else, can duplicate his results. I, however, am the only scientist who read any portion of his records before they were destroyed. How much time will it take? That's anyone's guess. Months? Years? Never? Who knows?"

"And you're going to tackle this all by your lonesome self?"

Kossler strolled to a mantel clock sitting on a shelf behind one of the two desks. He picked up a key and began winding it. "No, not alone. I've requested an assistant to help me."

"Say, make it a female assistant. Somebody who looks like Rita Hayworth. Or maybe Betty Grable. Sure would be nice to have a face prettier than yours to admire."

Kossler laughed lightly and swung shut the glass plate of the clock. "You Americans. The fountain of your humor never runs dry. Unfortunately for your fantasies, the chosen assistant is male. Werner Neumann is his name. They tell me he is bright and insightful. Equally important, he is fully dedicated to the party."

Roger reached for his jacket, unsnapped one of the front pockets, and retrieved his green aviator sunglasses. "Another heel-clicking Hitler fanatic? I can hardly stand the suspense."

Kossler's face clouded. "A little humor can be admirable, Captain. Misguided jesting becomes insolence. I warn you, although we want you alive, I can still punish impertinence."

"Yeah? Well, mairzy doats and dozy doats."

Kossler's eyebrows lowered. "What is that supposed to mean?"

"Maybe I expressed my opinion in secret code, developed by the U.S. Army Signal Corps to protect top-secret information. Don't expect me to translate." He held up the sunglasses, then straightened a bend in one of the temples.

Kossler sniffed. "You may keep your precious code. I guarantee your U.S. Army won't receive any messages from this bunker."

Through the bars, Roger observed Kossler's crossed arms with satisfaction. His words had struck the target of opportunity. "Thanks for the warning, Doc. Now if you don't mind, I think I'll get a little shuteye. You know how moving to a new prison cell always wears me out." He slipped on the sunglasses and settled into the armchair, which felt cozier than he wanted to admit. Would Kossler feel indignant that it was he, the prisoner, rather than himself, who had signaled the end of their conversation? Who cared? Let the mad scientist feel snubbed. For now, fatigue was tugging Roger's brain toward dreamland.

CHAPTER 15

Standing in the salon of his home, Dr. Otto Kossler stared into the ice-blue eyes of SS Colonel Heinrich Wolf. Kossler struggled to absorb the information the colonel had just told him.

"Surely you cannot be serious? The government—"

"Dr. Kossler, I'm not a man endowed with an overly active sense of humor." Judging from Wolf's inhumanly frigid gaze, the colonel was also not a man blessed with a soul, if such a thing existed. "The Third Reich's future can now be numbered in months, if not weeks. Germany is dying, shriveling on the vine, and the military can do little to prevent it. You would have foreseen the same truth had you not been so preoccupied with your test tubes and microscopes."

"But the news reports. What about the secret weapons being developed? The Führer has promised—"

"Propaganda for the masses. Those weapons are too little, too late. Even if we had more time for research and development—which we don't—the Allies have obliterated most of our means of manufacturing them. Like a steamroller, they are crushing the life out of Germany."

Kossler's eyes dropped to the polished Black Forest oak floor of his study. "So it has come to this." He sighed with resignation. "What am I to do concerning the project? Destroy the evidence?"

"The project is why I'm here. Methuselah must continue at all costs.

But no information concerning this research must fall into Allied hands. Do you hear me? None of it! From this point onward, even high-ranking party members are not to be trusted without authorization."

"Methuselah is to continue? But how? If the Allies overrun us, then all is lost."

"First, we will send you several faithful engineers who are skilled in construction and camouflage techniques. This house and your estate will remain, but the entrance to the underground bunker will be disguised. Do not speak to the engineers about Captain Greene or the nature of your work. Do not name the Methuselah Project. Permit them to conceal the entrance to the bunker, and then dismiss them."

A wave of confusion crashed over Kossler's brain. "How will the research be financed if the Allies are victorious? After all, the end of Germany means the liquidation of the very government that sponsors the project."

Heinrich Wolf squinted at him. Almost as a chess player sizing up his opponent, he stared until Kossler decided to study the rug instead of looking into those eyes. Wolf removed a leather-bound notebook from an inner pocket and flipped it open. He ran a finger down a column, turned the page, and continued halfway down another column before he found what he was looking for. He grunted.

"Dr. Kossler, I see here that your allegiance to the party is deemed impeccable. You have the leadership's utmost confidence. Your security clearance is higher than Blomberg's was, nearly as high as my own. How can it be that a man of your standing knows so little of the Consortium and of the plans being laid for the postwar struggle?"

Kossler waved his hands, palms up. "My experiments. The project. Over and over, Berlin has stressed to me how vital Methuselah is to our cause. I leave military and political matters to more experienced hands in order to concentrate on my own assignment."

"I see," Colonel Wolf said, as if pondering some unspoken matter. "Your eye truly has focused on the microscopic rather than on the wider screen of human affairs unfolding around us." Wolf drummed his fingers on Kossler's desktop. "All right. I will bring you up to date. This is information you need. Mark my words: the Reich will soon die. But the Nazi faithful, certain key men with the wits to survive, will live on. If we maintain allegiance to each other—and if we refuse the option of defeat—then like puppet masters, we shall exist behind the scenes and manipulate the strings of world events in our own ways. But at least temporarily we must play the role of silent chameleons. We will soon doff our insignia, our uniforms, and our salutes. We will assume new identities and the role of innocent German citizens swept along by the tide of a war we never wanted. Do you understand?"

Kossler nodded, even though the scenario Wolf painted left a multitude of squirming, unanswered questions. "Yes, I understand. The principle, but not the practice. If everything you say is true, then the clock works against us. Little time remains for covert preparations."

"Much groundwork has already been laid, although I won't take time to explain it in detail. Do you know General Reinhard Gehlen?"

"Not personally."

"General Gehlen is one of those already coordinating a network to survive after surrender. Others include Borman, Eichmann, Brunner, Skorzeny, and many other worthy comrades—some whose names you might recognize, some not. But all these men know how to keep their mouths shut even if captured. When the time comes, our top men will be secreted to Geneva, Cairo, Lisbon, Buenos Aires, Sydney, Washington, and other strategic cities. Each man will receive a new identity and become a phantom, a genuine member of an invisible international consortium. *The* Consortium, to those of us in it. Following the war, we will occupy seemingly peaceful positions scattered around the globe. But away from the spotlight of public attention, our purpose will be to manipulate world politics and economies to suit our own purposes. Make no mistake, Dr. Kossler: the ship of the Fatherland is sinking. It will soon founder beneath the waves. But the unseen Consortium—code-named the Heritage Organization—is our life raft. Why go down with the ship, when we can live and choose another day to resurrect our goals?"

Kossler pondered those words as he scrutinized the cuff title adorning

Colonel Wolf's left jacket sleeve. Anyone would recognize the elite SS Viking as a famed combat force. If a ranking officer in such a division foresaw no hope for Germany, then it must be true. It struck Kossler that "Viking" was an apt adjective for this determined warrior who wouldn't accept defeat. "What of me? Do I rate the status of a 'key man' to be smuggled to Buenos Aires too?"

A smile that smacked of tolerance formed on Colonel Wolf's face. He lowered a hand onto Kossler's shoulder. "My dear doctor, I would not be rehearsing these details if we did not consider you an essential cog in our machinery. The sooner you unlock whatever secret is at work in the American's body, the sooner you can duplicate the process for those of us in the Heritage Organization. I don't need to explain the advantages if each of our members could live for a millennium. The possibilities are absolutely staggering."

Wolf extracted a silver cigarette case from his tunic pocket and pressed a button. The case popped open. "Care for a Lucky Strike? Courtesy of an American prisoner."

In recent years, Kossler had come to prefer smoking with a pipe, but in the spirit of camaraderie, he joined Wolf in selecting a cigarette.

A lighter emblazoned with an American-style eagle appeared in the colonel's hand, and he lit both their cigarettes. After blowing a stream of smoke out of the corner of his mouth, Wolf continued. "As I was saying, we are laying escape lines to sneak our most faithful men out of the Reich. In your circumstance, however, such recourse isn't realistic. You need your equipment, your notes, your files. Most of all, you need this Captain Greene alive, intact, and permanently confined. Attempting to smuggle you, plus him and your entire laboratory, out of the country would be lunacy. Foolishly hazardous. Methuselah is vital to the Consortium. We won't risk losing you—and it. Therefore, you will receive new identity papers, but you must remain here. Of course, we will protect you and finance your operations. When things cool down politically, perhaps even during the occupation, we will try to recruit additional assistants to work under you."

Hearing such praise heaped upon his role, Kossler's back straightened. The Aryan pride of National Socialism swelled inside his chest. "Thank you, Colonel Wolf. I understand, and I will cooperate fully. I'm grateful for your confidence. But if I may be so bold, you never answered my question about how the project will be funded. You remember what happened to the economy after the last war."

Wolf took another casual draw of his Lucky Strike. "I remember too well. That's why our organization has already amassed much of the financial backing we shall require—and I'm not referring to *Reichsmarks*. Does the name Martin Weiss mean anything to you?"

Kossler probed his memory. "No, I don't believe so."

"I thought not. Weiss is currently acting commandant of the concentration camp at Dachau. Under strict orders of silence, Weiss's officers have stockpiled an enormous quantity of gold, international currency, and other valuables confiscated from his Jewish population." Wolf paused to relish yet another leisurely lungful of his cigarette. "These truly are excellent. I'll have to acquire more of them. But back to financing. In the past, this wealth accumulated at Dachau was shipped to Berlin. Now, however, Weiss agrees with our group that, at this juncture in history, our Consortium has greater need of gold than Berlin.

"In addition, the Wehrmacht has been plundering every museum and estate from the English Channel to the Balkans. They have, shall we say, appropriated choice works of art to be found in France, Belgium, the Netherlands, and all other occupied countries. We in the SS have found it expedient to siphon off and reroute untold treasures. We are stockpiling them in hidden underground vaults scattered around Europe. In due season, they can be sold to private collectors to further expand the Consortium's coffers."

Kossler nodded. "I see. If that is the case, you must have access to enough money to fund the Methuselah Project for several years."

For the first time, Wolf threw his head back and chortled in unrestrained humor. "If only you knew your gift for understatement, Doctor. In gold and silver alone, the Consortium already commands enough wealth to purchase a small nation. On top of that are mountains of international currencies. We will continue to squirrel away jewels and precious metals right up to the end. Yes, we can afford to finance Methuselah—plus many other worldwide activities that I won't discuss. Of course, no postwar authorities will be able to trace these funds. We have concealed our tracks with utmost care."

Kossler turned toward the hearth, where wedges of split oak popped and crackled, radiating warmth. The Kossler family home featured steam radiators, of course, but he enjoyed the smoky smell of a fireplace and had lit it today in anticipation of Wolf's arrival. Should he voice his final nagging question? He turned away from the flames. "Colonel, I'm extremely grateful. But tell me: if Germany is going to lose the war, why is the Führer going to such lengths? Surely he must realize he will never benefit from the research? He can no longer hope to become the thousand-year Führer of a thousand-year Reich. With his well-known face, he can't hope to hide—"

"Hitler will not profit. The Allies will hang him or shoot him—if our side doesn't kill him first. The Führer knows nothing of our plan. We can't save him, so we excluded him. Our Consortium can't afford the risk of him ruining Methuselah through some sort of eleventh-hour madness."

Again, Kossler peered into those eerily pale eyes. Despite the compliments, this SS officer unnerved him. With his cutthroat SS tactics, he might be capable of anything. Kossler wouldn't want the man for an enemy. "Thank you, Colonel Wolf. I'm honored."

"One more thing. When the Allies arrive, hang white sheets from your front gate and windows. Better yet, hang out homemade American and British flags. Be receptive. Be friendly. Welcome the swine as liberators. Even permit their soldiers to sleep here if they wish. You can halt your research for a time. Simply do whatever is necessary to protect the Methuselah Project." Colonel Wolf didn't wait for a reply. He flicked the butt of his cigarette into the fireplace. "We'll be in touch." With that, he pivoted and strode out the door, the heels of his glossy boots clacking noisily across the hardwood floor.

Kossler sank onto the divan and reviewed the entire conversation. When defeat for Germany arrived, should he inform the American? No. From a psychological standpoint, that would be counterproductive. Let the captain believe the war was still raging. Otherwise he might become combative—or worse, suicidal—in prolonged postwar confinement. Better if he didn't know.

CHAPTER 16

Seated at the banquet table, Katherine Mueller glanced left and right before feeling for the edge of the burgundy tablecloth that hung to her lap. Beneath the protective cover of the table, she wiped both palms on the dry linen. Why was she so nervous? It was just an award and promotion ceremony. No big deal.

Her eyes swept the rented hall again. Of the three hundred or so members of the organization finishing their chicken cordon bleu, at least twenty or thirty men looked young enough to be potential candidates for romance. Surely some of them were bachelors. Several weren't bad looking at all. Of course that wasn't her main reason for being here, but why not check out the territory? It wasn't every day the HO held a regional promotion ceremony.

She stole another glance at the two athletic specimens seated four tables away. The men were so similar in appearance that they were obviously twins. Katherine loved their untamed, tousled blond curls. Sure, they were older than her by six or seven years, but she liked older men. Guys in their early twenties could be so immature.

"Nervous, Katarina?"

Katherine broke off guy-watching. Uncle Kurt observed her with a half-proud, half-amused expression.

Her voice dropped to an undertone. "A little bit. I dread the part on stage."

Uncle Kurt's smile wilted. He leaned to her ear. "Is it the salute? Is that what's bothering you? As I explained, it's not the same salute the Nazis used. In the organization—"

Katherine shook her head. "It's not that. I just don't like being the center of attention, even among friends. I'm more of a behind-the-scenes kind of person."

Uncle Kurt's good humor rekindled. He massaged her back just below the neck, the way he'd always done to soothe her. "I understand. Don't worry. Your role in the ceremony will be brief. Besides," he added with a wink, "being a 'behind-the-scenes kind of person' isn't a bad trait. Very often, people behind the scenes accomplish far more than those who revel in the limelight."

Katherine let his statement slide by unexplained. Just another "Uncle Kurt-ism" that she no longer dwelt on for long. She simply smiled, feigned understanding, and nodded, which usually put him at ease. Uncle Kurt radiated approval, and for her, that was enough. Right now his glowing pride for her trumped any personal wish to snare the interest of suitors.

A middle-aged man with salt-and-pepper hair mounted the steps to the stage and approached the podium.

Here we go. The after-dinner festivities. Katherine risked yet another peek at the twin Adonises whom she'd been ogling. She couldn't be sure but, as far as she could tell, neither had looked her way, not even once.

Might they already be married? *Maybe I'm not pretty enough for them. Or maybe they're like Uncle Kurt—too involved with business and the organization to get serious about romance.*

The man at the microphone extended his right arm, holding it parallel with the floor but cocking his hand upward from the wrist. He packed his greeting into one word: "Heritage!"

"Heritage!" Many in the crowd returned the salute from their seats.

The man at the mic, whom Katherine knew only as some sort of business tycoon introduced earlier as Mr. Schneider, launched into a speech praising family, cultural heritage, and lineage. In no hurry whatsoever, he waxed on about the higher calling for individuals from well-bred back-grounds to become guiding forces in a misguided world.

Katherine had heard such lectures before and had practically memo-rized pamphlets on the subject provided by Uncle Kurt. Evidently such propaganda formed a vital foundation for indoctrination into the Heritage Organization. Even though the speaker and those who nodded during his talk obviously harbored strong sentiments on the subject, Katherine allowed much of the discourse to flow past without paying attention. Even now, she stifled a yawn for fear of hurting Uncle Kurt's feelings.

Would I even be here if my father and mother hadn't been HO supporters? She didn't normally pose such blunt questions to herself, but as soon as she had, she knew the answer. No. In fact, some aspects of the HO struck her as bordering on cultish, even though they shunned all connections to religion.

Fragments of childhood memories rushed back: Mom filling her tiny palms with bread crumbs to feed pigeons in the park, swinging her legs on a counter stool beside Daddy in a restaurant, a family trip to the zoo with Uncle Kurt . . . This last memory was clearest, since her nightstand still bore a framed photograph of Uncle Kurt holding her beside her parents with giraffes towering behind them. For each precious memory, Uncle Kurt had regaled her with stories of her scientist parents and how much they had wanted to see her join the HO and continue their legacy.

Mom and Dad loved me. That much I remember. I can't thank them for loving me, but I can fulfill their one wish for my life. When I rise higher in the ranks, I'll get a better appreciation of how the HO improves the world.

Katherine thought about the homeless women she often passed while driving the taxi, shuffling down the street with stringy hair and sad eyes. *I certainly would love to help them.*

"And now," continued Mr. Schneider, "it gives me great pleasure to preside over this year's regional promotions. We shall begin with those advancing from Kadett to the rank of *Leutnant*. When I call your name, please step forward and join me onstage."

Nervousness fluttered inside Katherine's stomach.

"Katherine Mueller," read Mr. Schneider from his list.

Katherine swallowed. With a surname beginning with "M," she hadn't expected to hear hers first.

A hand touched her shoulder. Uncle Kurt spoke into her ear. "Highest score goes first. Well done!"

She scooted her chair back, then walked forward, accompanied by the loud staccato of applause.

As prescribed by organization protocol, Katherine mounted the steps, took a position behind the speaker, pulled her heels together, and raised her right arm parallel to the floor, the hand cocked to an upward angle as the speaker had done earlier. She glued her eyes to the back wall. Even without peeking at Uncle Kurt, she knew he brimmed with joy for his niece. Imagining how she must look from his vantage point was simple, since she'd modeled her appearance from an old black-and-white photograph of her mother: a smart-looking black beret, a matching black skirt, plus a white button-down silk blouse. Even though she was reared in Georgia, Katherine liked how the outfit emphasized her Germanic lineage. It had certainly elicited compliments from senior Heritage members all evening.

Maybe now those two blond studs will notice me.

At the microphone, Mr. Schneider continued reading names, summoning forward eleven other young men and women. In her peripheral vision, Katherine saw each one in turn climb the steps and take a stance in a line abreast of her. Their bodies stood at stiff attention, their right arms held rigidly in the organization salute. An unnamed brunette woman—some sort of organization functionary—proceeded down the line and pinned a pewter star with sunrise emblem onto their shirts. The twin symbols of a "new day dawning" and the stellar future awaiting them.

When the last new Leutnant had received the insignia, Mr. Schneider stepped aside and addressed Katherine and the others. "Leutnants of the organization, do you vow faithfulness to our heritage?"

"We vow," Katherine chorused with the others.

"Do you recognize your higher calling?"

"We recognize the calling." ·

"What will halt you from this lifelong duty?"

"Only death!"

On cue, everyone in the banquet room rose and returned the salute. "Only death," they echoed.

Even though it broke protocol, Katherine flicked her eyes to her own table. Uncle Kurt stood like a ramrod, his arm extended in the prescribed posture, his eyes sparkling with emotion.

Schneider initiated applause, and the assembly joined in. Katherine led the others from the stage, and they returned to their tables.

Mr. Schneider folded over the top sheet to continue with page two. "Now for the higher promotions. Rising from the rank of Leutnant to Defenders . . ."

Relieved that her portion of the ceremony was over, Katherine rejoined Uncle Kurt. Never before today had she seen tears in the man's eyes, and never before had she seen him struggle so hard just to choke out a few words.

"So proud. I am so proud of you, my Katarina."

Internally Katherine struggled too, but with self-accusations of hypocrisy. Perhaps devout members of the Masons, the Elks, and Veterans of Foreign Wars nurtured affectionate bonds for their societies. For her, the ritual was nothing but an outward formality, fulfilling an expectation of Mueller clan history embodied in her sole surviving relative, Uncle Kurt.

"Family and tradition are paramount," she chastised herself, parroting a line from one of Uncle's pamphlets. *I might chafe under some of his demands, but this is the best way I can honor my parents. I won't let them down. No matter what, I'll stick with the organization.*

CHAPTER 17

Inside the cage beneath Kossler's residence, Roger closed Dostoevsky's *Crime and Punishment* and placed it atop the four-foot stack of volumes beside his armchair.

Lacing his fingers behind his head, he watched Kossler peer into a microscope for a long moment before inking a notation into his logbook.

"Hey, Doc."

Still writing, the German replied, *"Was wollen Sie?"*

"Was will ich? I want a lot of things. For starters, I want to speak in my own language today, not German."

The doctor shifted his gaze to meet Roger's eyes and readjusted the glasses perched on his nose. "But why?" Kossler's Germanic accent persisted, but his English had grown much better over the past ten years. "You've made such marvelous strides in German. In fact, your vocabulary now surpasses that of many citizens of the Reich. Your accent is superb. Much better than my English pronunciation."

"Maybe so. But English is still my mother tongue, and I want to use it. If I don't, I won't know how to talk to my own people when the war is over. I'll end up sounding like a goose-stepping Kraut."

"Goose-stepping?" Kossler laid down his pen and crossed his arms. "That's hardly an appropriate adjective. Geese walk with a . . ." His eyes strayed toward the concrete ceiling as he searched for a suitable description. "Widdle?"

"Waddle. But it doesn't matter whether the word is appropriate or not. I don't want to end up sounding like one of your precious Führer's buddies."

Kossler shrugged. "As you wish. For today, we will speak English."

"I was also going to ask if you've ever read this book, *Crime and Punishment*."

"No. As a man of science, I haven't indulged in fiction since my school-boy days. Besides, Dostoevsky is a Russian author. As you may have heard, Russian literature isn't highly esteemed in the Third Reich. Much of it was burned. Don't think it's easy finding English-language reading material for you."

Roger sat up straighter and crossed his legs. He picked up the novel. "I'm surprised you don't know this one. Adolf Hitler has a lot in common with the main character of the story."

Kossler's eyebrows lifted. "In what way?"

"You see, this young guy named Rodion dreamed up a theory. He suggested that some people who commit crimes deserve to be caught and punished because they're stupid. They make mistakes. But he also surmised other people are so smart that they can rise above ordinary law and commit crimes—even murder—because of their superior intel-lect. That strikes me as a lot like Hitler. He figures he can wage war, murder innocent people, do anything he wants to do because he has delusions of Aryan grandeur. But when you boil it all down, he's still just a petty little two-bit crook who's too big for his britches. In the end, he'll be punished for his crimes." Roger had phrased his words calmly, unemotionally; however, his barb was intentional. He studied Kossler's face to see whether the verbal attack had scored any damage to the target.

"Am I supposed to become indignant or outraged, Captain Greene? Do you hope to see me fly into red-faced rage for your amusement?"

"Nope. I'm just telling you how I see things. In Dostoevsky's book, Rodion got what was coming to him. Someday Adolf will too. It's just a matter of time."

"Not the most profound philosophy I've ever heard." The doctor picked up his pen and carried on with his writing.

It was Roger's turn to shrug, even if the doctor wasn't looking. "I just call 'em like I see 'em. Sorry if it's not deep enough to challenge vast mental resources like yours."

The doctor paused and returned his attention to Roger, another miniature victory in the airman's ongoing war to slow Nazi progress on the Methuselah Project. "Are you aware of the change in your own mental resources since you arrived here?"

The question caught him off guard. He considered it. Had there been any particular change in his thinking? Sure, he could speak fluent German. He'd mastered grammar books for several European languages. Trigonometry and calculus had become enjoyable distractions to while away the hours. Classic literature had become part of his life—

"I thought not," Kossler said. "The fact is, your years with me have greatly deepened your own education. The Methuselah process might also deserve credit for enhancing your mental faculties and your memory since you came here. The same way it enhances and preserves your biological systems. Yet the incredible amount of reading you have done certainly broadened your mental horizons. Based on our conversations, I daresay you could easily teach university graduate-level courses even without formal academic training."

"Maybe so, but I'm still the same guy. Still a pilot."

"You mean, you *were* a pilot."

Roger shook his head. "Wrong tense. I *am* a pilot, Doc. Ever since I was a little tyke looking up at every airplane that flew over the orphanage playground, I've wanted to be a pilot. As soon as I grew old enough to get a job, I signed up for flying lessons. Flying is in my blood. You can cram a canary into a cage, but it's still a bird. And you can lock me behind bars in this private zoo of yours, but you can't change my nature. I, Captain Roger Greene, am a pilot."

During Roger's brief monologue, Kossler once again put his eye to his microscope. The man was ignoring him. How to get his mind off his work? Shifting strategies, Roger broached a new topic. "So how's the war going? I haven't heard bombs falling in eons."

Kossler flipped the notebook to a clean page. "Captain Greene, as I've repeatedly told you, I'm not permitted to discuss military topics with a prisoner. I sympathize with your curiosity, but my orders from my superiors—"

"Doc, those simpletons are not your superiors. They are inferior to you. The pompous officials who strut in here to see me and inspect your work don't possess one iota of your intelligence. Their eyes practically glaze over when you begin discussing the most basic physiology. Think logically: Is giving me a hint about whose side is winning going to send the Reich swirling down the toilet? Besides, who am I going to blab to in this dungeon?"

"Blab?" Kossler peered into the cage and straightened his spectacles as he did nearly every time he looked up. "What's *blab*?"

"It's one of those quaint American slang expressions I don't want to forget. It means to talk too much, to spill the beans."

"Ah. Spill the beans. I recall the phrase from my undergraduate studies in Tübingen. Quite a colorful expression."

"Well, how about it? Surely you can give me just a little inkling on the course of the war? Just the most interesting headlines from the newspapers. That would be no secret."

Kossler hesitated, as if debating within himself. He glanced across the lab to where Werner Neumann increased the blue flame under a boiling beaker of liquid.

"Aw, don't let Werner stop you. He won't tell anybody."

Finally Kossler seemed to reach a decision. He set the pen on his notebook and looked Roger in the eye. "As a civilian man of science, I won't pretend that I follow the military situation closely. But perhaps I can give enough information to quench your general curiosity so that I may concentrate on my work."

"Hallelujah! Now you're talking, Doc!" Roger sprang from the bed and grasped the cool steel bars, ready to hang on Kossler's every word.

The attempt to divert the old boy from his work had paid off better than expected.

The scientist called to his associate. "Werner, perhaps we do an injustice in keeping our guest totally uninformed. Even if it's against policy, I believe it should be permissible to share a few insignificant details."

"That is your prerogative, Herr Doktor. In this laboratory, you are the authority."

Kossler stood and circled his desk, on which he sat to address Roger more directly. Arms crossed, he said, "I must warn you, when my superiors come to visit—whether they are in military or civilian clothing—you are not to breathe a word of what I am about to tell you. It wouldn't be good for me, but it would be worse for you. Our National Socialist leadership doesn't appreciate having their instructions cast aside, even when they affect only one prisoner."

The long preamble stretched Roger's annoyance to the breaking point. "Okay, okay. Scout's honor. Now tell me, who's winning?"

Kossler sighed. "Winning? Well, that's difficult to say. Both the Allies and the Axis powers have experienced gains and losses."

"Such as?"

"Well, as you may have guessed, England has fallen. Wehrmacht troops now occupy England, Wales, Scotland, and Ireland. Oh, and Iceland too. That was the latest island our side acquired, although I don't see any practical use for such a place."

Roger felt his jaw drop before he could stop it. He'd never imagined such a nightmare. The Allies had been planning to invade Europe when he crashed. "How's that possible?"

Kossler shrugged. "The tides of war. They come in, they go out. When our Japanese comrades convinced the Chinese to attack the Eastern Soviet Union, Moscow realized it couldn't survive an onslaught of powerful armies on both the east and west. To preserve what was left of his nation, Stalin made concessions and sued for peace."

Roger gripped the bars more firmly even as his legs went rubbery. "Concessions?"

"Basically Ukraine, Byelorussia, Moldavia, and some Central Asian regions that end with -*stan* were ceded to the Third Reich. Also, large tracts of Eastern Siberia were yielded to the Empire of Japan. In exchange for these lands, new treaties were signed, and Germany is now at peace with the Soviet Union, which is much smaller than when you arrived. Our new territories comprise what you might call a nonmilitary buffer zone."

Roger groaned from his heart. "So all those German troops and aircraft that used to be on the Russian front—"

"Were reassigned to France and the Netherlands. From there, they invaded the British Isles. That battle occurred in 1949. Or was it 1950? As I said, I prefer to concentrate on science."

"What about our American guys? The United States had air bases scattered all over England."

Kossler cleared his throat, as if embarrassed at what he must confess. "I hear they fought gallantly, both in the air and on the ground. But when the Luftwaffe unleashed new, technologically superior fighter airplanes and bombers, England no longer stood a serious chance of resisting. The blitz ended almost as soon as it began."

Roger's head sagged. Bile churned in his stomach. For once, no snappy retort came to mind. Should he step into the bathroom? He feared he might vomit.

"Of course, not all of the British and American military personnel died. Many of them survive in prisoner-of-war camps. As I understand it, however, conditions are not so enjoyable. Unlike here, they suffer from inadequate diet, poor sanitation. Still, thousands of them are alive."

"And Churchill?"

"Rumor has it Mr. Churchill perished in one of the V-5 rocket attacks on London, but I don't believe his body was ever identified." He turned his head. "Werner, did you ever hear whether Churchill's body was recovered?"

Werner gave his colleague a long, silent look before replying. "No, I never heard."

Roger stared down at the threadbare patch he'd worn in this corner of the Persian rug. He almost regretted having asked. Eventually his gaze met Kossler's blinking owl eyes behind their spectacles. "You admitted both sides experienced gains and losses. So far it sounds like all the losses have been on the Allied side. What did Germany lose?"

The scientist returned Roger's gaze with sadness. "Lives, Captain Greene. The lives of untold numbers of citizens. War is such a horrible business, and even the innocent pay. Between those lost in battle and those sent to occupy newly acquired territories, the population of the Fatherland has been quite sharpened down."

"Sharpened down? Do you mean 'whittled down'?"

"Excuse me. Whittled down."

Roger pumped for more information before the flow ran dry. "So where's the worst of the fighting happening right now?"

"At the moment, hostilities have cooled quite a bit, even though our two countries are technically at war. The main problem seems to be the Atlantic and Pacific Oceans. Without all those aerodromes in England and northern Africa, your American forces can't reach us. Neither can our Luftwaffe bombers or Japanese airplanes reach American soil. Stalemate."

"You mean, nobody is fighting anyplace?"

"I didn't say that. At the moment, both sides are dueling on the high seas with ships and U-boats until more effective long-range weapons can carry the battle farther. And the Japanese are still skirmishing in southern Australia. Pockets of resistance remain there."

Roger ran a trembling hand through his hair. The nightmare grew worse with every sentence. "But surely Germany must run out of soldiers one of these days. I mean, even with the Atlantic separating us, the United States and Canada are a lot bigger than Germany. We've got a larger population. It has to be only a matter of time before we overpower your military through populace alone."

Kossler paused, as if debating whether to express something else on his mind.

"You're hiding something, Doc. I see it in your eyes. Go ahead, say what's on your mind while you've got my attention."

Kossler once more cleared his throat. His face bore all the signs of a schoolboy who must make an embarrassing admission. "All right, but remember that you're the one who asked me to—how did you say it?—blab the beans. You're quite correct about our limited population. The many years of warfare seriously eroded our civilian and military forces. But you're not the first person to foresee this predicament. If steps had not been taken early on, there might have come a day when we simply ran out of men."

"Steps were taken? I don't think I'm going to like whatever you're about to say."

Kossler looked to Werner Neumann, who had ceased working to listen. "Werner, it's so degrading. Would you like to be the one to tell him?"

Evidently surprised by the offer, Werner uncrossed his arms and coughed. "*Nein,* Herr Doktor. You should continue. This is your laboratory."

Kossler sighed. "A solution had to be found. The Führer decided it was time to take drastic measures."

Roger felt his impatience reaching the boiling point. He rattled the barred door of his cell. "Come on, Kossler! Quit dragging it out, will you? This is torture. Just tell me what they're doing, for Pete's sake."

Kossler repeated his sigh. "Farming, Captain Greene. The Führer issued orders to begin planting seeds on behalf of the Third Reich."

"Farming?" What in blazes was that supposed to mean?

"It's quite simple, really. The procedure first began in France, but is now common practice in all occupied territories. Our military units surround a town, and all females from age thirteen through forty are herded into a, shall we say, processing center. Soldiers then line up to receive female carriers and then impregnate them with Aryan seed. The troops then proceed to the next occupied town or village and repeat the process.

"A year later, mobile medical units return to collect the abundant harvest. Even as we speak, millions of children are growing up in National Socialist orphanages. Instead of attending traditional schools, they receive political indoctrination and begin training for the military. Even the females. I should think the oldest children must be about nine already, so they will soon be bearing arms for the Fatherland. Quite a rich boon to the military."

If Roger had felt like vomiting before, the gut feeling resurged stronger than ever. He backed away in revulsion. "That's the sickest, most disgusting, most demented thing I've ever heard! Only perverted Nazi minds could reduce innocent little girls to breeding stock. And then, treating their offspring like nothing more than brainless little puppets to throw into battle . . ."

Kossler shrugged. "For what it is worth, Captain, I agree. But what can I do? I'm just one tiny grain of sand on a vast seashore. Ironically only you and the secret inside your body give my own existence any meaning right now."

Roger placed a hand over his stomach to quell the nausea. "Sorry I asked."

Kossler half-turned and closed the notebook on his desk. "As long as you've interrupted me, I believe I'll halt for lunch. What can I bring you, Captain Greene?"

"Nothing. I lost my appetite."

"As you wish. Will you me join me, Werner?"

"*Ja*," the assistant replied, slipping back into their native tongue.

✦ ✦ ✦

Together the two white-coated scientists passed through the massive metal exit. As soon as it clanged shut behind them, Werner reached for Kossler's forearm to stop him.

"Herr Doktor, why in heaven's name did you fabricate such a complicated fairytale for Greene? Why not just tell him Hitler committed suicide years ago and that the war is over? And that twisted description of the children in the *Lebensborn* program. What purpose could you have for such a ridiculous farce?"

Kossler grinned as they mounted the steps. "The main reason is to keep the prisoner happy. He's been here a long while, Werner, and unless you and I stumble upon an unexpected breakthrough, he's likely to remain in that cell for a very long time to come."

"You believe all of your convoluted nonsense made the prisoner *happy*? Didn't you see his face?"

"Psychology, Werner. Think long term. At this moment, no, Captain Greene isn't pleased at all. But by believing the Axis powers and the Allies are still at war, he has hope. Now he can ponder the wonders of American industrial ingenuity and hope his countrymen will develop new, long-range weapons to defeat the Nazis someday. Not anytime soon, though. No. To wage actual war across the Atlantic with the technology he remembers from 1943 would take much time. Possibly decades."

"And if you were to tell him the war ended within two years of his capture?"

"Despondency. Complete, utter depression. What a crushing weight such knowledge would be on a man who has been imprisoned for nearly a decade—and with no end to captivity in sight. In normal prisons, criminals receive a specific release date, something to which they look forward. Not so with the good captain. As long as he believes battles are raging somewhere, anywhere, he has an understandable reason for remaining behind bars.

"At best, knowing he's been held prisoner during peacetime would make him angry, aggressive, and dangerously violent. At worst, he might take his own life just to end his pitiful existence and to thwart our efforts. We can't allow either to happen."

Werner rubbed his chin. "We definitely need him alive. He's our only source for blood and tissue samples."

At the top of the steps, Werner pushed open the camouflage cover to the main level and allowed his superior to exit first. "Now we draw close to a question I've wondered about, but no one ever mentions. What if we are successful, Herr Doktor? What happens if we duplicate the original process by which Greene's aging process was suspended? Will you simply tell him the whole history you concocted was a web of lies to keep him docile? Will you show him the door and say, 'Good luck, Greene. Have a nice life'?"

Kossler burst into laughter. Once Werner had stepped clear, he swung shut the bookcase that concealed the bunker entrance. "*Nein, nein.* Of course not. That would be ludicrous. Inconceivable."

"Then what will be done with Greene if we succeed?"

Kossler clasped his hands together into a single fist, as if success were already assured. "When we reach such a time, my dear Werner, Captain Greene will finally become expendable. He may safely be eliminated."

CHAPTER 18

Roger allowed his eyes to remain closed. He didn't need to see the dusty mantel clock that perpetually ticked off the hours from its shelf behind Kossler's desk. During his twenty-five years of confinement, some inner timepiece had engaged, waking Roger at precisely six o'clock each morning. Ever since his first day in the underground bunker, he'd disciplined himself to perform morning calisthenics while waiting for breakfast. Lately, however, dredging enough willpower simply to rise from bed was becoming a struggle. He rolled onto his stomach and buried his bearded face in the pillow. *What a stinking, lousy, rotten, downright worthless way to spend a life.* He pounded a fist into the mattress.

Over the course of recent months, Roger's mood had drooped deeper into depression. Whenever Kossler shared a tidbit concerning the war, Roger's spirits would rise if Kossler's news reported the American forces had achieved some victory, however slight. But when it became obvious he was still far from liberation, the leaden shroud of gloom would descend to smother him once more. The pilot who yearned for the heavens was inexorably suffocating beneath the concrete sky of his dungeon. For years his practice of "being free in his mind" had provided a release valve, a way to keep a grip on sanity by mentally revisiting every house, store, park, airport, and hangar he'd ever been inside. Yet even that strategy was wearing thinner than the threadbare Persian rug in his cell.

I'd give a million bucks for five minutes in a P-47. Even a crop duster. Just five minutes to soar above the clouds. To see the sky and feel real sunshine, not just a sunlamp under a concrete ceiling!

In response to Roger's pleas, Kossler had cut photographs of sunsets, clouds, forests, rainbows, and even pictures of pretty girls from old magazines and allowed the prisoner to paste them onto the wall of his cell. Yet paper-and-ink images of the outside world were cheap, two-dimensional counterfeits. The sunlamp prevented Roger from rivaling the linen sheets for paleness, but it could never simulate the beauty of dawn, nor the reds, pinks, oranges, and purples of a glorious sunset.

Greene, you're going to go stark raving mad if you don't get out of here. Somehow or other, even if the guards gun you down, it would be worth seeing the sky one last time.

Kossler's aging face materialized in his mind. Over time, he'd noticed how Otto Kossler had developed crow's feet at the corners of his eyes, wrinkles about the mouth. The doctor's hair had gradually thinned as it developed gray streaks. Although Werner Neumann was just a few years older than Roger, his receding hairline and bags under his eyes evidenced time taking its toll on him, as well.

Not so with Roger. Each time he used the bathroom, he studied his face. Yeah, at first he'd dismissed all of Kossler's talk about him being a "Methuselah man" as a bunch of bunk. But his reflection never showed the slightest sign of a wrinkle, not a single strand of gray. To his own eyes, he looked exactly as he had the day he'd crash-landed.

Almost like being in limbo. As if time in the outside world flows past without realizing I'm here, hidden deep underground.

Roger hadn't lost any physical stamina, either. Since his main pastimes had become reading, daydreaming, and exercising, he had become more fit now than in freedom. He could crank out a hundred pushups without breaking a sweat, run in place for an hour without becoming winded. Fifty chin-ups on the water pipe that ran through the top of his cell? No problem.

He scowled. "What point is there in physical fitness when you're cooped up like an animal?"

Once or twice a year, some sort of officials visited the laboratory-bunker to speak with Kossler and to eyeball the prisoner personally. Early on, such visitors had worn uniforms emblazoned with the lightning-bolt SS on their collar. For a long while, however, Kossler's visitors had been showing up wearing civilian suits and ties even though they conducted themselves with military bearing.

On these occasions, Kossler would typically retrieve black-and-white photographs of the prisoner from a file cabinet and point out how his facial features had remained virtually unchanged since December 1943.

"You do not dye his hair? You have not performed cosmetic surgery?" some guests questioned in their native German.

Although Roger refused to speak to the visiting bigwigs, he now comprehended every German syllable. Kossler realized this, of course, and reminded his guests not to mention certain subjects in the American's presence, particularly topics concerning the outside world.

Various visitors had reappeared multiple times over the decades. Roger reviewed their faces in his mind in case he should ever need to identify them after the war. Each time they had seemed duly impressed with Roger's youthful complexion. Inevitably these officials—whoever they were—would shake Kossler's hand and promise him their utmost support in his "vital scientific endeavor."

I'm sick of it. Of this whole futile existence. Wouldn't he be better off dead than living a pointless, artificially prolonged life with zero purpose for him or his country?

Who knows? Maybe my best duty for the United States would be to file my spoon to a sharp edge and slit my wrists. If samples of my hair and blood ever do help Hitler to extend Nazi life spans, I could be considered a traitor for letting them use me.

Somehow, though, he could never summon the willpower to end his life. In part, he was unconvinced that Kossler would succeed in replicating Blomberg's technique, which would make suicide the crowning irony of a futile existence. In addition, Roger clung to hope. If he could just hold on to his sanity one day at a time, perhaps some morning, some year, he might walk out of this scientific dungeon a free man once again. Sooner or later, American forces and the side of justice must crush Hitler and everything the lunatic was trying to accomplish. Mustn't they?

He grunted at the scheme of slashing his wrists. *It might not even work. The skin and veins might heal too fast. To really knock myself off might take something with more oomph, like a grenade or a bayonet through the heart.*

Even though he never attempted the act, the knowledge that he could try to end his life whenever he wished provided glum comfort. The Huns were holding most of the cards, but he had one ace tucked up his sleeve. If he decided to play it.

More than one night he'd dreamed of mounting the concealed steps behind that steel door, stepping out of this building—which he'd never seen from the outside—and finding his old P-47 repaired and waiting to wing his way home forever. Such pipedreams were ridiculous, but every time he relived the vision, his spirit gained a slight bit of altitude. He pictured hope as the parachute that kept him safely dangling above total anguish and self-destruction.

One additional idea encouraged Roger to remain among the living. From time to time, Miss Hawkins's voice would wheeze out from his memory and remind him that he could petition the Almighty for help. This particular morning he lay in bed feeling lethargic, and for the first time in weeks those words pierced the gloom in his mind.

Finally motivated to action, Roger threw back the bedclothes. In desperation, he sank to his knees beside the bed and folded his hands. "God, I need help. I'm going nuts. Save me from this dungeon. Please, help America to whip these insane Nazis and restore peace to the world. I don't care about living a long life, but if You get me out of here, I'll do whatever You want. I swear it. I'll even go and preach to orphans like Miss Hawkins did if that's what You tell me to do. Please, please just get me out of here before I go totally mad."

Even as Roger breathed an "Amen," a startlingly simple inspiration flashed into his brain: ask Kossler for a Bible. Why hadn't he ever thought of that before? Despite the doctor's fanatical devotion to the Nazi Party, he'd never objected to the American's reading books. Sometimes, when Kossler could find some old English hardbacks for sale, he would unexpectedly show up with a paper sack filled with yellowing volumes in English, French, Dutch, or other European languages to puzzle over, in order to keep the prisoner occupied and quiet. Was it possible that an English-language Bible could've survived somewhere in the Third Reich?

"A Bible?" Kossler slid the breakfast tray through the slot in the bars. "Have you turned religious overnight, Captain Greene? Perhaps I should check your temperature."

"I'm fine." Roger nearly growled the words. He was sick of Kossler interpreting every comment as a possible side effect of Methuselah. "I haven't suddenly turned religious. I just want a Bible."

Kossler stood, contemplating his captive with crossed arms.

"I'd also like it to be in English, please. Even though I can read German, it's still not the same as reading in my own language."

Kossler circled his desk and eased into his leather chair. "A Bible in English . . . It might be possible. I know of quite a few used-book shops. But I can't promise. I've never searched for such a thing. I don't even own a Bible."

"Why is that so easy for me to believe?"

Kossler's gaze locked on Roger. "What an extraordinary mood you're in this morning, Captain. But tell me, do you believe in the Bible, or do you simply want to read it as a pastime, similar to Norse myths of Odin, Freya, and Thor?"

Except for isolated verses Miss Hawkins had printed on large squares of pasteboard, Roger had never read the Bible. He'd feel uncomfortable saying he definitely believed it. But he radiated irritability this morning and wouldn't yield one inch of territory to the enemy.

"Oh, I have proof that at least some portions of the Bible are true."

"Indeed? Such as?"

"Well, the Bible mentions a place called hell, doesn't it? I have to believe that much, since I've been living in one for the past quarter century."

Kossler erupted into laughter. "Touché, Captain Greene!" He applauded. "But honestly, I had hoped that my family's estate would rate a little higher in your estimation."

"Maybe the upstairs where you live isn't so crummy, but just try living behind these bars for a couple of decades. You'll figure out what I mean."

"Personally I follow Friedrich Nietzsche's philosophy on such topics. I have no time for God, nor for investigating whether such a being exists." Kossler withdrew a pocket notebook from his lab coat and picked up an ink pen. He jotted a reminder: "One Bible. English." He flipped the booklet shut. "Very well. I'll try. Is there anything else you desire?"

Roger's eyes landed on the locked cell door.

"I mean anything else, barring the obvious. No pun intended."

"Yeah. I need more ways to pass the time. I want to learn how to play a musical instrument. Could you order a piano for me?"

Kossler scoffed. "Request the planet Jupiter, why don't you? I have no funds for extravagant luxuries. Furthermore, you don't have enough room in your apartment for a piano."

"My apartment? Ha! That's rich. Just call it what it is: my cage. Okay, if not a piano, how about something smaller? I'm willing to negotiate."

"How much smaller?"

"I'm reasonable. Say, a guitar?"

Kossler looked upward and heaved a sigh. "Really, Captain Greene—"

"Hey, I could've asked for a trumpet. Or a screechy violin. Or bagpipes. I could even drive you batty drumming on these steel bars all day with my spoon. You have to admit, a guitar is pretty tame. Not too hard on the nerves, and it would help me to while away the hours. What do you say, Doc? Have a heart."

"I see your tactics, Captain. You're like the boy who begs his father for an elephant, only to accept a compromise in the form of the puppy he wanted all along." Kossler sighed again, then retrieved his pocket notebook. "One guitar. But only if I can find a used one at a bargain price. No guarantees."

"No need to promise." Roger lifted his mug of coffee to his lips. *I wouldn't trust your promises anyway. Not in a million years.*

CHAPTER 19

As he did on every Christmas in the cell, Roger backed to the far wall when the pistol-toting guard in a black turtleneck waved him away from the bars.

While the unnamed guard held his pistol ready, Kossler unlocked the barred door. With his traditional Christmas greeting of *"Fröhliche Weihnachten!"* the aging doctor completed the ritual by placing a miniature, brightly decorated fir tree inside the cell. Then Kossler retreated and relocked the door. He dismissed the man in black with, *"Danke. Das ist alles."*

With a reverence akin to awe, Roger approached the three-foot evergreen. He sank to his knees and pressed his cheek against a prickly, needle-laden branch. Eyes closed, he inhaled the delicate scent of forest until his lungs neared bursting. He exhaled and drew another huge lungful. How he yearned to be outdoors, standing in a grove of such trees! He could soak up this wonderful, natural fragrance all day and not tire of it.

Kossler broke the silence. "I'm always gratified to see how you enjoy my little peace offerings. Not that I celebrate Christmas personally."

Roger heard the words but let them pass without response. The fir tree—this random sample from God's creation—had completely filled the grounded pilot's steel-bound universe. He drew back to gaze at it, to stroke the pliable, green needles, to touch the slightly sticky roughness of its narrow trunk, to drink in the whole intoxicating vision.

The woody scent fetched back memories of hikes through forests in Indiana, of Christmases in the past. Even without the silver garland Kossler had draped over its boughs, Roger would've come to the same conclusion: "It's beautiful."

Kossler settled onto the leather sofa he'd installed in the basement a decade earlier and proceeded to fill his pipe with tobacco. After lighting it, he leaned back and crossed his legs. Dedicated though he was, the German had never worked on holidays, including December 25. Today there would be no glowing Bunsen burners, no bubbling test tubes, no odor of sulfur or other chemicals, no injections into white mice. "Would you like to smoke, Captain? I don't have a spare pipe, but I believe Werner kept some cigarettes in his desk."

Roger pulled his eyes from the Christmas tree and regarded his captor. What was left of Kossler's hair had turned Santa Claus white, just a sparse thatch that allowed quite a bit of scalp to peek through. The decades had etched deep lines into his forehead, under his eyes, around his mouth. How old would Kossler be by now? At least seventy-five. Probably older.

The airman shook his head. "No thanks. You should give up smoking, Doc. I don't think it's good for you. After all, look at me. I don't smoke, and I'm the spitting image of good health. You're always lighting up that chimney of yours, and look what it's done to you. You look old enough to be my great-grandfather."

Kossler laughed, coughing out smoke in little puffs. "Yes, I do look old, Captain. But tobacco isn't the culprit. Your body can shake off years as a duck shakes water from its back, but mine can't. My time is running out." Something in the man's voice suggested he'd raided a liquor cabinet before descending the steps this evening. His words were coming out slightly slurred.

Roger jerked his head toward Werner's desk. Dust had accumulated on its once-glossy surface. "You never told me—how was his funeral?"

Kossler twisted the pipe sideways in his mouth, an idiosyncrasy that signaled he was willing to converse while enjoying his smoke. He shrugged. "It was a funeral. A couple of old schoolmates. A handful of cousins, nieces, and nephews."

"I would've gone, but no one invited me."

Mirthful twinkles appeared in Kossler's eyes, as if the prisoner had shared something enormously amusing.

Studying his aging captor, Roger pondered his emotions toward the man. Part of the airman's heart despised this creature who played the role of warden, guard, and mad scientist. Yet now, watching the wrinkled man puffing on his pipe, pity welled inside him. Although it was true that the past fifty-two years of Roger Greene's life had been fruitless, the same could be said of Otto Kossler's. For all these decades, the scientist had dedicated himself to chasing a persistently elusive goal. Did the man still clutch hopes of success?

Somewhere over the past half century, the line between captor and companion had blurred. Certainly Roger harbored no love for Kossler and would often draw him into verbal sparring matches. On the other hand, this enemy scientist had become his main source of conversation. During evening hours, Kossler had increasingly descended the steps simply to relax on the sofa and to banter with his prisoner.

Thanks to Roger's growing collection of books, which overflowed the cell into stacks just outside the bars, the airman could discuss world literature all day and never repeat himself. The German scientist wasn't nearly so widely read, but he enjoyed waxing eloquent on the mysteries of science, especially in the realm of biology. Occasionally he would discuss the specific experiments he was conducting and what he hoped to accomplish. In recent days, the man seemed to prefer relaxing his brain and discussing lighter topics.

"So why didn't you ever get married?" Roger asked.

Kossler gave his characteristic shrug. "Marlene Dietrich wouldn't have me."

The German's uncharacteristic humor startled a laugh out of Roger. Along with the 78 rpm records of classical German composers, Kossler had frequently played records of Dietrich's songs. When he did, Roger would listen, enthralled, to one of the few female voices he'd heard since leaving England.

After a few more puffs on his pipe, Kossler provided a more serious explanation: "I've always been married, Captain Greene, but unfortunately, never to a woman. In school days, I was married to my studies. Later, I married the Nazi Party and its ideals. For the remainder of my life, I've been married to my research. So you see, circumstances left no time or energy to seek female companionship."

Roger grunted understanding. But if his own presence had kept romance from the German's life, he didn't feel one shred of guilt.

"How about you?" Kossler questioned. "Have you ever pursued a romantic interest, Captain?"

"Oh, I dated a few girls in high school. We had fun, but I knew they weren't the ones for me. Besides, back then, I mostly wanted to fly airplanes. Got my first couple of lessons from the man who crop-dusted our cornfields. As soon as I got out of school, I ran off to Canada, and from there volunteered to fly for the RAF."

"Didn't you tell me you were an orphan?"

"I was, but when I turned twelve, a farmer and his wife took me in. Not for love of children or anything. He just needed some extra hands milking his cows and plowing the fields. His wife might've felt a tiny bit sorry for me, but even she didn't act like a real mom."

Kossler absorbed these details with a thoughtful nod.

"If I could have the girl of my dreams," Roger continued, "she probably wouldn't look like some glamour-girl screen star. I figure those kind are fun for looking at, but not for marrying. I'd rather have a girl-next-door kind. She'd be pretty, sure, but her head wouldn't swell up over it. And she would look natural whether she was wearing satin and lace or faded dungarees. She would be soft as moonlight, but with real spunk and backbone to her. Of course, she would like airplanes. And children. I always thought it would be fun to have at least three or four someday."

Kossler lowered his pipe and leaned forward, as if struck by a fresh revelation.

Roger squinted back. "What's that look in your eyes?"

"It's incredible. How could I have such tunnel vision? Until this moment, I never stopped to consider what kind of offspring might result if you mated. I mean, with the Methuselah effect in your body, who can guess?"

Indignation churned Roger's gut. "Don't even think about it. If your bosses want to repopulate the Fatherland, they'll have to do it without my help."

Kossler leaned back and took another puff. "My apologies. Just my scientific curiosity getting the better of me."

Roger stared at the man. It was the first time Roger could recall Kossler truly apologizing to him for anything. Maybe he really had been drinking?

"I see you created a new decoration for your quarters." With the stem of his pipe, Kossler pointed to the wall of the cell.

Roger looked up to admire his own handiwork—an imperfect but unmistakable flag consisting of thirteen red and white stripes, plus forty-eight stars on a blue field. His heart filled with pride and love of the country he'd left so long ago. "Yup. I wondered when you would notice. I'm no whiz with a needle and thread, but I thought it turned out pretty swell."

"Of course, I should take it down. This is Germany, after all."

"Correction. That's Germany out there where you're sitting. I've decided to colonize this humble little square on behalf of the United States of America. Right now, it's only a territory. But when I get around to holding an election, I'm confident this spot will become our forty-ninth state."

The bemused twinkle reappeared in Kossler's eyes. "And if I come in there with an armed escort and remove the flag from your colony?"

Roger shook his head. "Sorry, Doc. I can't let you do that. You see, this is U.S. territory, and you happen to be a foreigner. Nobody from the outside gets in without an approved passport."

"What leads you to conclude I don't own an approved passport?"

"Because in addition to serving as governor of this territory, I'm also in charge of customs and immigration. I promise, no passport with your photograph on it will be accepted in here."

Kossler didn't exactly smile, but deepening crinkles in the crow's feet at his eyes signaled approval of the game. "What of your own passport? Hasn't it expired by this time?"

"I don't need one. I've lived most of my life here. I'm a naturalized citizen."

"I see. And what is the name of this newly declared territory?"

"Well, I considered calling it Greene Land, but that smacked of plagiarism. Instead, I settled on Rogervania."

Kossler raised his chin. "A pity that Rogervania is landlocked. It's totally dependent on the Third Reich for all its food and water, not to mention electricity."

"Minor details. Maybe some year I'll solve that issue by annexing all of Germany. You know, like you guys did to the Sudetenland."

The airman again leaned into the fir tree and inhaled its freshness. When he shut his eyes, he could almost imagine himself standing in a forest glade. But when he opened them, the reality of his drab prison existence hemmed him in all the more closely. If not for the comfort and hope he'd found in the Bible Kossler had brought years ago, he would've gone insane. "I can't believe the war has dragged out this long."

Kossler cupped a hand behind one ear. "What did you say?"

Roger kept forgetting the man had become hard of hearing. He spoke louder. "The war. It's hard to believe they haven't found a way to end it by now."

Just as Roger knew he would, Kossler shrugged. "It isn't the first time a war has lasted so long. Have you never heard of England's Hundred Years' War with France?"

"Yeah, I've heard of it. That was six or seven hundred years ago. Buried somewhere in my stacks is a history book that tells all about it. You would think with modern weapons—"

"Ah, but if both sides modernize their weapons, a stalemate is still possible. Like the Hundred Years' War, this one has degenerated into a series of miscellaneous conflicts. Neither side wins. Neither side concedes defeat. The struggle continues, even when blood isn't flowing."

Roger didn't want to ruin Christmas by asking his next question, but as long as his captor had broached the subject, he pressed for information. "So what's happening in the war, anyway?"

Kossler took a long pull on his pipe. These days, he no longer refused to speak about the subject, but he always seemed to require a moment of contemplation before deciding how much news to reveal.

"I told you Greenland is now under German control, did I not?"

"Yes, yes, a long time ago. What's the scoop since then?"

"At the moment, the German High Command seems to be avoiding direct confrontation with the United States. The current strategy is apparently to steer clear of openly assaulting the strongest enemy and instead to deal with weaker ones. For that reason, Germany and her comrades are solidifying their hold on the African continent."

"Aha! That sounds like smokescreen propaganda to say they're licking their wounds and have backed off to pick on littler guys. What part of Africa are they fighting in?"

"The real battles are over. Africa and all the Middle East are in Axis hands. Our troops met our Japanese comrades on the eastern border of Afghanistan. Only minor skirmishes with ragtag rebels continue in the mountain regions."

"You've got to be kidding."

Falling back on his all-time favorite gesture once again, Kossler shrugged. "Don't believe me, if you so choose, but if not, please don't inquire for news. These topics are most depressing."

"You're telling me."

"At least you can take comfort that you're not Canadian, Captain. So far, no part of the United States has been occupied by the Wehrmacht."

Instantly Roger was on his feet. Admiration for the fir tree forgotten, he nearly knocked it over in his rush to reach the bars. "Wait a minute! Are you telling me the Nazis have invaded Canada?"

"Not all of it, of course. Just some northeastern provinces. What are they called?" He scratched his head. "Newfoundland. Nova Scotia. Prince Edward Island, I think. Surely I've already mentioned that?"

Anger welled inside Roger. He punctuated each word with impatience: "No, you have not already mentioned that."

"Indeed? I didn't intend to perturb you. Not on your Christmas holiday. If it's a consolation, not many Canadian or German lives were lost. The Canadians no longer exhibit the same aggressiveness as you Americans. For the sake of saving lives, they were ready to negotiate a separate peace."

Roger seethed. "Turncoats! How could they? I would've expected better from our best neighbors."

"They say the occupation has proceeded with minimal bloodshed. Not even a traditional occupation. In exchange for military bases on Canadian territory, we permit them to continue governing their own country. They hold their own elections, just as before. The yoke imposed by the modern Reich is not unduly heavy."

Roger gazed in disgust as the doctor took several puffs. From the scientist's relaxed demeanor, he might just as easily have announced some minor annoyance, such as thunderstorms in the forecast or a broken pencil lead. Roger could hate this man when he talked of Axis victories in such a tone. "Is there any news that would make me happy?"

Casually the doctor emitted another puff of smoke. "Adolf Hitler died."

Before he realized it, Roger had his face pressed between the bars. "Blast you, Kossler! You sit there puffing away like a smokestack and making idle chitchat while sitting on the story of the century! Spit it out already. Give me some details."

"There isn't much to add. His death isn't such an important event as you imagine. The Führer's health had been declining for some time. He passed away blissfully, in his sleep. The Unterführer, a man whose name you wouldn't recognize, had already accepted most of Hitler's responsibilities, so it was a smooth transition. Do you take pleasure from this news?"

Roger weighed the question. At one time, he would've been ecstatic to hear of Hitler's demise. Evidently, though, it had struck no major blow to the government or its military agenda. No doubt, an evil man had passed from the stage of world events. Hell was brimming with evil people, and another soul had crashed in flames.

"No. He deserved to die more than anybody I know of, but it doesn't make me happy that he did. The world would've been better if he'd never been born."

Kossler set his pipe on its desktop holder. "Enough talk of war and death. This is your Christmas, a holiday of light. Let's have some music! Will you play your guitar, or shall I get out some records?"

Roger barely heard the question. He mentally digested the details Kossler had revealed.

Kossler crossed the room to a wooden cabinet. He selected a record, blew a few specks of dust from it, and placed it on the phonograph. The tender notes of "Stille Nacht"—"Silent Night"—wafted throughout the bunker.

Roger sat on his bed. Before long, he was humming along. From his leather sofa, Kossler swayed his head.

When the record ended, the scientist cleared his throat. "I have an announcement to make. In light of my advancing age and my lack of success at reproducing Dr. von Blomberg's work, my superiors are taking full control of the research. To be frank, I've expected it for quite a while."

Roger cocked an eyebrow. "What's going to happen?"

"My role will change to that of caretaker. They're bringing in three or four younger scientists. I will inform them of everything Werner and I have learned thus far, and they will continue the project. With Werner gone and my own health declining, this is the best way to ensure the future of Methuselah."

Did that glint of moisture in the old man's eyes reveal a tear?

"Because I leave no heirs, I have willed my estate to those who will continue Methuselah. I will still live here, of course, but after the New Year, you will see new faces in the building. Faces nearly as youthful as your own."

Words escaped Roger. Despite his loathing for the Nazi doctor and everything he represented, the American pitied the man's empty life, an existence in which he constantly searched for, but never achieved, his dream of reproducing Blomberg's breakthrough. Perhaps Roger, with his own pointless existence, could empathize better than Kossler's own people.

In fact, the airman had immediately thought of Kossler when he'd first discovered Jesus' words in the gospel of Matthew: "But I say unto you, Love your enemies, bless them that curse you, do good to them that hate you, and pray for them which despitefully use you, and persecute you." At the time, he hadn't believed he could ever pray for this jailer, but eventually, Roger had learned to do it. After all, who needed his prayers more than this hateful creature?

Had his prayers made any difference? Kossler certainly cared nothing about God. Yet the man's attitude had softened. His fanaticism had mellowed. Was that change wrought by prayer or from old age?

More importantly, would the "new management" bring any positive changes for Roger? Or maybe changes for the worse?

Time would tell.

CHAPTER 20

Stretched on the bed, with her laptop providing the only illumination in her darkened bedroom, Katherine clicked shut the last of the Internet pages she'd opened for the topic "codependency."

"Robyn was right," she whispered to herself. "I'm codependent on Uncle Kurt."

Who would've thought psychologists had actually fabricated a name for her weird need to please him even when he bugged her? Katherine had scoffed when her friend from the karate studio had suggested she research codependence. She certainly didn't feel mentally ill. However, Robyn's gentle persistence over Greek salad at Panera had piqued curiosity. Without knowing about the HO, Robyn had pieced together enough telltale clues to suspect the unhealthy nature of Katherine's constant need to win Uncle's praise—even at the cost of her own happiness. The question now became, what would she do about it?

"What'll I do? For starters, I'm going to grow some backbone. I'll do whatever I want, even if Uncle doesn't approve. This is *my* life. I need to live it for me, not for him."

Her fingers typed "Georgia dating sites" into the Google search engine. Bingo. A full page of hits.

Katherine paused. A swift peek assured the bedroom door remained locked. Good grief, how ironic. Even with index finger poised to spark a revolution, she still had to make sure he couldn't catch her? *Get on with it!*

She clicked the first link.

Instantly the screen transported Katherine to the welcome page for Peachtree State Match & Mingles. "Love is in the air!" shouted the inch-high Arial banner scrolling across the top. "Let us help you find your Southern soul mate."

Despite her resolution, Katherine's eyes flew once more to the lock on her doorknob. *Oh, stop. It's not like I plan to marry these guys. I just want to check out the fish in that big ol' sea.*

"Sign up now!" urged Peachtree State Match & Mingles.

She tapped to register. The first three login names Katherine concocted for herself were rejected as already taken. Finally the system accepted "Paperdoll777." Unlike the others, this moniker conveyed no direct connection with writing or editing, but at least it involved paper, which elicited a giggle. That, plus her favorite number in triplicate, should be impossible to forget.

Ha! I'm in.

She proceeded to fill registration blanks with her age, marital status, interests . . . "Headline for your profile?" asked the next line. What could she say? Seeking inspiration, Katherine reviewed sample headers: "I'm Your Fantasy Come True." "One Hot Tamale!" "The Golden Haired Godiva of Your Dreams."

Oh, good grief. Don't make me throw up.

She lowered her fingertips to the keyboard and typed simply, "Trying Something New."

Yeah, that sounded about right. Nothing wild or exotic. No promises. Just a down-to-earth girl crawling out from under her uncle's thumb to breathe fresh air in a nice, controlled atmosphere.

Visiting a dating website wouldn't fit most people's definition of rebellion. But it was an option she'd never pursued before. She powered off the laptop. Would anything promising develop?

Time would tell.

CHAPTER 21

Roger had long ago grown accustomed to the comings and goings of the three young scientists—Hans, Gerhard, and Martin—who had been assigned to the Methuselah Project nine years earlier. At first the trio, who looked to be in their late twenties, stared into Roger's cage with awe when Kossler introduced them and pulled open the first drawer of bulging, photo-stuffed binders on Subject 7. As the months yielded to years, however, the new men took less interest in the prisoner. When they did acknowledge him, they regarded the American with almost mocking contempt. Although they never spoke of the war or the Nazi Party, each of them oozed the haughty ego that Roger concluded must be genetic among their breed.

Unlike Kossler, who now descended the steps primarily to bring meals or to chat in the evenings, the others rarely appeared after working hours. Evidently the younger men's dedication to Methuselah screeched to a halt at 5:00 p.m.

Of course, the newcomers occasionally entered the bunker to track down some needed information—*data*, they called it—in one of the file cabinets lining a full wall. Usually, though, they confined themselves to laboring upstairs with whatever equipment had been installed there.

Judging by their appalled expressions, rolling eyes, and the snide remarks they dropped to each other, the younger men clearly regarded much of Kossler's methodology to be as archaic as stone knives and bear skins. On the other hand, various aspects of Kossler's findings prompted large eyes, exclamations, or fingers tapping on some particular page.

"Absolutely incredible," Hans said to himself one day as he sat at Kossler's desk and pored over a stack of hand-typed reports.

On rare occasions, one or two of the men would descend merely to spend a few minutes of conversation with "the subject." Such conversations usually revolved around his sleeping habits or other biological functions. In these moments, Roger tried to pump them for information about the war and the outside world, but the new managers only grinned and shook their heads.

"Forbidden topics, Captain Greene."

Roger had been tempted to boast that he already knew about the Nazi invasion of eastern Canada, the occupation of Africa, the Middle East, and other notable events. In the end, though, he'd decided to bite his tongue. After all, the trickle of information he received from Kossler might dry up completely if these others mentioned the American's knowledge to their bosses in Berlin.

Still, through them Roger gained glimpses of changes in the outside world. The day the leader of the new team, the arrogant Hans, lugged several cardboard cartons downstairs and set to work assembling an apparatus on Werner's old desk, Roger watched in fascination. What could it be?

Each of the components came with electrical cords, plus other wires Hans connected to the rear of a black rectangle on a stand. The rectangle sported a dark window to nowhere, and this, too, Hans connected to the box by a cable.

"What are those things?"

Hans smirked. "Watch." He pressed a button, and soon the blackness of the little window yielded to words and pictures. Hans sat and began tapping a flattish typewriter. Roger watched in bewilderment as his own name appeared on the screen in bold, scarlet letters.

"This is a desktop computer," Hans explained. "With it, we can do calculations and perform experiments without actually going through all of the physical motions. We ran out of room upstairs. Extra equipment comes down here now."

Roger emitted an impressed whistle. "I suppose that's another invention of your Nazi scientists?"

An especially peculiar grin stretched across Hans's face. "Of course. Germany now uses computers for everything—in stores, businesses, the military, even in private homes. German technology on the march!"

Roger cast a fishhook to see if he could snare some *data* of his own: "I wonder if my side has anything like that."

Hans permitted himself an indulgent smile. "Oh, I suppose it's possible America has a few computers by now." He reached into the desk drawer and withdrew a small, rectangular object. "Did Dr. Kossler ever show you this?"

"He didn't specifically show it to me, but I've seen him poke on it with his fingers. What is it?"

"We call it a calculator. Catch."

Reaching between the bars of his cell, Roger caught the object Hans tossed to him. Rows of buttons with numbers and mathematical symbols filled its surface. "What does it do?"

"Press the On button. You can perform mathematical equations much faster than with pencil and paper."

Roger multiplied two times two, then twelve times twelve, then larger and larger figures. Again, he whistled in admiration. "This thing is all right!"

He turned the object over and noticed miniature words stamped on the back: *Made in China*. The Japanese had occupied China. "This isn't German technology. Your Axis friends in Japan must have dreamed this up."

Hans grinned in an odd way that made Roger wonder what joke he'd missed, then nodded. "You are quite astute, Captain Greene. I can't fool you, can I? Our Japanese partners invented that calculator. They are clever inventors, those Japanese."

"Very slick. But I don't need to perform much arithmetic in here." Roger tossed the device back to Hans.

Out of nowhere, musical notes began playing a tune, the German national anthem. From his shirt pocket, Hans extracted another device, one even smaller than the calculator. "Hans here." A pause. "Speak louder. The reception is very bad where I am." A moment later, "I don't care what her lawyer says. It's all lies. The sooner this divorce is over, the better."

The conversation continued, giving Roger his first peek inside Hans's personal life. Since Hans wore no wedding band, Roger hadn't realized the scientist had a wife. Even more surprising was the portable pocket telephone. Kossler had never used such a thing.

"Trouble on the home front?" Roger asked after Hans slid the portable phone back into his pocket.

Hans glared. "My personal life is no concern of yours." He turned off the computer and stalked out the door.

Now that was an interesting glimpse of changes in the outside world.

But as Roger lay down to reread *The Story of the Wright Brothers*, he couldn't shake one basic question: Why was *Made in China* printed in English instead of Japanese or Chinese? Even printing it in German would make more sense than using English, the language of an enemy nation. No amount of puzzling produced a satisfactory explanation.

That evening, when Kossler's shaking hands slid the supper tray into the cell, Roger mentioned his conversation with Hans about the calculator. "Why would *Made in China* be in English, Doc?"

Otto Kossler evaded his eyes. His expression resembled that of a child caught with one hand in a cookie jar. Instead of answering, he turned and walked stiffly back to the exit. His arthritis must be getting worse. Over his shoulder he said, "It's all very complicated. Politics, expediency, science . . . I haven't tried to educate you concerning all that happens around the globe, Captain Greene." He half opened the door. "You know, it's possible that if you were suddenly to leave this place you would find modern society so confusing that you would end your own life. Please don't concern yourself about such things. You will be cared for."

The door clanged shut. He'd never seen Kossler react so oddly. Whatever it meant, Roger had stumbled onto a topic the man preferred to avoid. But why?

◆ ◆ ◆

The next day, Roger still puzzled over Kossler's reaction. And why hadn't the old boy showed up with breakfast? The dusty mantel clock showed 10:37 a.m. Kossler often tottered in late, but never this late. When Hans, Gerhard, and Martin—the Three Musketeers, as Roger dubbed them—entered the bunker, Roger sensed something fishy. Rather than going about their work as usual, the three approached his cage with untranslatable expressions of amusement pasted across their faces.

Roger shifted his gaze from one pair of eyes to the next. "Okay. Something's up. Spill it."

"We have heard a colorful expression from your country," said Martin in stilted English. "It is 'red-blooded American.' Would you consider yourself a normal, red-blooded American, Captain Greene?"

Of all the questions his German captors had ever asked, this won the prize for the screwiest. Was it a joke, or a threat? Were they planning to kill him after all these years?

Roger cleared his throat. "If you mean, am I a normal American male, the answer is yes. I might not look my real age, but that's the only unusual thing about me. Why?"

The three exchanged schoolboy glances. Gerhard literally giggled. Hans strolled back to the steel entry door and placed his hand on the knob. "We just wanted to make sure before we introduce you to the newest member of the Methuselah Project."

Hans cracked open the door and addressed some unseen person: "You may come in now."

When the latest addition to the Methuselah team stepped through the doorway, Roger had no idea what emotion his face registered, but the reaction ignited a chorus of laughter from his three German captors. Roger simply stared. For the first time in seventy years, he found himself gazing into the lovely eyes of a living, breathing woman.

CHAPTER 22

Hans led the woman into the bunker as if he were the host at a dinner party. "Captain Greene, allow me to introduce Sophie Gottschalk. I'm delighted to announce that *Fräulein* Gottschalk has received clearance to participate in our project. She's now a permanent member of our elite Methuselah family."

Roger realized he was staring, but he couldn't help himself. To a starving dog, even a rubber bone must look appetizing, and Sophie Gottschalk was definitely no rubber bone. For a man who had spent decades in captivity, the shapely figure before him radiated pure femininity. At about five feet, seven inches tall, Sophie was blessed with waves of luxurious chestnut-colored hair that cascaded over her shoulders and disappeared behind her back. Unlike the men, she didn't wear a white lab coat. Not yet, anyway. Instead she sported a navy-blue skirt and a silky, pastel-blue blouse that accentuated her slender waist. A single gold chain adorned her dainty neck. To Roger, her face evoked memories of Hollywood actress Hedy Lamarr.

Cutely uncomfortable under Roger's intense gaze, Sophie directed her eyes back to Hans. "Who is this man? What's he doing here behind bars?"

"Allow me to introduce our guest officially. This is Captain Roger Greene of the United States Air Force."

Roger shook his head but kept his eyes nailed to Miss Gottschalk. "You mess that up every time. It's United States Army Air Corps, Eighth Army Air Force, Fourth Fighter Group. You don't need the squadron number."

"My mistake. U.S. Army Air Corps. You see, Fräulein Gottschalk, the captain's fighter plane was shot down. He was brought here, where he has provided invaluable data for the Methuselah Project."

Sophie's eyes darted back and forth between her three new colleagues. "Shot down? Where? In the Middle East?"

Roger yearned to lure those luminous green eyes back to himself, so he hurried to provide the answer. "No. I've never been anywhere near Egypt, Persia, or any of those places. I was flying cover for a group of B-17s, but my wingman and I ran into trouble with some of your German fighters. Two Messerschmitt 109s latched onto my tail and kept blasting until I crashed in the Third Reich."

Sophie's eyes were undeniably on him now. But the emotions in those eyes ranged from confusion to resentment. "Whoever you are, I don't appreciate being mocked."

Roger basked in her presence. "You're gorgeous, even when you're angry. Did they tell you that you're the first woman I've laid eyes on in seven decades?"

Her eyes flashed, and she turned to Hans, Gerhard, and Martin. Clearly they were enjoying their sport.

"Who is this person, and why is he babbling like an imbecile?"

Hans crossed his arms and sat down on Kossler's desk. "He told you the truth. Captain Greene was participating in a bombing raid over the Third Reich when one—excuse me, two—of our faithful Nazi pilots shot him down in the year 1943. He has been a guest here ever since that time. So you see, we have living confirmation of Methuselah's viability. Our project is not a theoretical one. The task is to reconstruct the genetic signature and physiological realignment process that we achieved in 1943, but which was destroyed in an Allied bombing."

Astonishment washed over Sophie's face. She eyed Roger the way a scientist might scrutinize a living dinosaur. Her gaze transformed into one of fascination.

Hans caught Gerhard's eye and snapped his fingers. "Show her a file."

Gerhard approached the bank of file cabinets and opened the top-left drawer of the first column. He removed a bulging folder, which he handed to Sophie.

"Your orientation assignment will be those file drawers," Hans said. "Study the material thoroughly. The one you're holding contains a general overview on Captain Greene. Become familiar with every minute detail. These files, coupled with Captain Greene's presence, provide indisputable proof that artificially enhanced physiology resulting in scientifically extended human life is definitely possible."

Roger relished every graceful movement as Sophie opened the folder and leafed through its contents. For the first time, he could glimpse the yellowing, black-and-white photographs of himself as a freshly captured airman. He hadn't been aware some of those images existed. One was a group shot of him with the other six airmen who had died in the bombing. A second pictured him lying unconscious in a tray of soupy liquid. Another showed him standing behind the bars of cell 7 back in Blomberg's facility, a Nazi flag with a black swastika hanging on the wall just outside his reach. He recalled how much he'd wanted to rip that rag to shreds.

Sophie held up one of the photographs, comparing the picture to Roger, who stood watching her. He had witnessed similar comparisons countless times. She was trying to decide whether the face beneath his beard and mustache was indeed identical to the one in the image. For her sake, he wished he hadn't stopped shaving. He must look like a Neanderthal. "Yes, it's me. Your people have kept me a prisoner all these years."

"It's utterly extraordinary. All during the time of the DDR? Why, if the Soviets had ever suspected that—"

Hans bolted off Kossler's desk. "Hush! No politics or current events in front of the subject."

Too late. Roger's mind was racing. "The DDR? What's that? And what about the Soviets? Is the Red Army advancing?"

Gerhard put a finger to his lips. "Not one word. There is a standing policy. We do not discuss politics in his presence."

Sophie nodded. "I understand." Again she studied the face in the photographs and then scrutinized Roger like a rare zoological specimen.

He, in turn, gazed back, relishing her feminine curves from her head to her toes. She stepped closer, and his nose detected a heavenly floral fragrance. Perfume. Combined with Sophie's natural loveliness, the experience bordered on intoxication.

She leafed through more pages. "Inconceivable. All accomplished with 1940s technology? I have so many questions."

Hans motioned toward the exit. "That's the problem. We do too. The material in your hands will answer some questions while sparking others. You will help us to find the missing puzzle pieces."

Before they departed, Roger seized his chance to ask about breakfast. "Hey, what's keeping old Kossler with breakfast? I'm starving."

Martin glanced at Hans and raised one hand in a gesture of innocence. "I forgot. So many things have happened today."

Hans addressed Roger. "Dr. Kossler won't be back. He died in his sleep last night. Interesting timing, isn't it?"

"A nice change for you, perhaps?" Gerhard suggested with a crass grin.

Kossler dead? Roger regarded the men's faces. He was unsure whether to rejoice or to grieve. During all these long years, Otto Kossler had practically embodied Germany, captivity, and the evil of so-called "Nazi ideals." Often Roger had loathed the man's presence and had refused to speak to him for days at a time. That self-imposed solitary confinement, however, always proved too heavy a burden. Then Roger would resume conversing with Kossler for the sake of being in touch with a fellow human. Somewhere during those perpetual empty decades, the German scientist had become either an enemy Roger cared about, or else the companion he loved to hate. Suddenly he was dead. An inexplicable sense of loss descended over Roger's heart.

Hans jerked Roger out of his musing. "Never mind. We will supply your meals now. Each of us four will take turns bringing breakfast, lunch, and dinner. Now excuse us. Changes are coming, Captain Greene."

CHAPTER 23

In the weeks following Sophie Gottschalk's arrival, her face, the musical timbre of her voice, and the fragrance of her lilac-scented perfume consumed Roger's thoughts. At night atop his bed, he relived every glimpse of her and every word she uttered. During the day, he tried to pass time as he had for years, by reading, exercising, strumming the guitar, or playing solitaire. But self-distraction failed him. The printed pages of *The Count of Monte Cristo* would fade, only to be replaced by smiling visions of Sophie and her luminous green eyes.

What are you doing, admiring one of the enemy? She's a German, a Nazi. Then again, he'd never known a Nazi could be so enchanting. After such a sterile existence without female companionship, this daughter of the Third Reich emotionally overwhelmed him. He yearned for her appearances with his supper tray.

For decades, Roger had incorporated Bible reading into his daily regimen. Back when his spirits had sunk into the nether regions of depression and he had been near suicide, only the leather-bound Bible had stabilized his mind. It had lifted his sinking soul from bottomless pits of despair. He clung to his Bible to maintain sanity. Because of this spiritual nourishment, he strove to obey the Scriptures' admonitions against lust, to keep his mind off Sophie's body and to concentrate on her face. But the years of isolation and what the male scientists labeled

his "red-blooded" qualities sometimes overruled and lured his eyes elsewhere.

Well, I'm human. What fellow in my shoes wouldn't admire a girl for being a girl?

Occasionally Sophie would descend to the bunker, not to bring supper, but to retrieve a piece of equipment or the next file from the bank of cabinets lining the walls. Each time she departed, it was as if murky clouds had scudded over the sky and blocked out life-giving sunshine.

For years, he hadn't bothered much about his appearance. If he grew shaggy and resembled an aborigine, so what? Now he diligently shaved each morning. He would spend hours in front of the mirror as he meticulously groomed his hair with the round-tipped scissors supplied by Kossler.

One morning, right in the middle of trimming his sideburns, he scolded his reflection. "You shouldn't be doing this. She's the enemy." Within seconds, he returned to fussing over his appearance like a high schooler preparing for his first date.

Was she really so gorgeous? Or would even a plain Jane come across like a living doll to a guy in his shoes? He wasn't sure. He also grew tired of philosophizing.

At first, whenever Roger spoke to Sophie, she appeared both intrigued and intimidated. Heeding Hans's warnings, she never stepped within reach of the bars. Before she slid his supper tray through the rectangular slot in the bars, she placed the key ring on Kossler's desk. This had been the drill from the beginning of his bunker existence. Even if Roger had succeeded in grabbing a caretaker through the bars, the effort couldn't reap those priceless keys.

But gradually Sophie Gottschalk warmed to his attempts at conversation. Beginning with a few awkward questions, she asked where he grew up. Which states he had visited. What had been his interests and hobbies. The day Roger launched into a passionate description of the joys of piloting single-engine aircraft and of weaving in and out of towering

cloudbanks, her rapt eyes never left his. He could see that, in her imagination at least, she was up there with him, soaring in freedom.

But even his most velvety-soft attempts to squeeze her for news about
the outside world proved fruitless. Apparently Hans had thoroughly
lectured her. Each time Roger tried to glean a nugget of information,
she stiffened. Her demeanor became formal. "I must go," she would say
before retreating through the detested metal barrier.

One day Roger gave his mirrored reflection a pep talk. "Okay, if asking
about world affairs drives her away, then stop asking. Instead, talk about
your past. Give her compliments. Just don't give that girl an excuse to
walk away."

On another occasion Sophie actually sat and marveled at his description of how the two Messerschmitt fighters had shot him down after he'd
run out of ammunition by rescuing Walt Crippen. He believed she literally held her breath as he recounted how his Thunderbolt had skidded
across a farm field and careened into the trees.

"Weren't you hurt?"

"That's the amazing thing. My plane was busted up all around me, but
the cockpit slipped right between two massive oak trees." He held out his
arms to show the girth of the trunks. "When I climbed out of the wreck,
I had nothing worse than bruises and a bloody nose. Maybe God was
looking out for me. I don't know."

The memory of Walt Crippen's ten-dollar bill popped into his mind.
Roger considered showing it to her, explaining how he and Walt had a
running bet about who could flame the next enemy plane. On the other
hand, maybe a Nazi girl would be angry if she learned how many of her
countrymen he'd blasted from the sky. He left the bill in his flight jacket.

Sophie's air turned wistful. "I've flown before, but only on passenger
airplanes. Never in a single-engine one."

"Maybe I'll take you up for a spin someday." With a frustrated shake of
the barred door, he added, "Sorry. That probably won't be anytime soon.
I don't get outside much."

The conversation ended. With a quiet *"auf Wiedersehen,"* Sophie turned and disappeared through the metal barrier to the steps beyond. But what was that emotion peeking through her eyes just now?

Did I see a tear? Has somebody in this God-forsaken country actually shed a tear for me?

He wasn't positive. Part of him hoped it was true. Some corner of his soul yearned to believe that, after nearly a lifetime, a fellow human cared about him personally. Especially if that person bore the face of an angel. Then, like a shaft of sunlight piercing storm clouds, inspiration shot through Roger's mind. The concept struck him as so thrilling, so staggering, that the full magnitude of the scheme pressed him down into his armchair.

What a tantalizing idea. If I play my cards just right, is there a chance—any chance at all—that Sophie might care enough that she would help me to escape?

He could already picture himself stepping through that despicable barrier and bounding up the steps he'd never laid eyes on. The very thought of bursting through the outside door and seeing genuine sunshine, green grass, and trees swaying in the wind set his heart pumping.

I wonder.

Even with this turning point in Roger's thinking, Sophie Gottschalk lost none of her feminine beauty. However, a craving that overpowered even his longing for female companionship latched onto his heart and wouldn't let go: the hunger for freedom.

In the course of the past seven decades, Roger had developed mental tricks to distract himself from the yen to be free when no way of breaking out of the bunker presented itself. But the mere concept of recruiting an accomplice released the genie from the bottle. Now that he'd finally found a strategy to follow, escape gained more urgency than ever before.

Yet was it proper to manipulate a girl's heart for his personal goals?

Why shouldn't I use her? I'm a prisoner of war. It's my duty to escape. If I can coax one of the enemy to lend a hand, then why not?

Like a jeweler twisting a diamond in his fingers, Roger paced his cell and studied each facet of this new strategy, calculating his odds of winning Sophie to his cause.

They don't let just anybody work on Methuselah. They have to be indoctrinated, totally loyal. Is it possible I can override her brainwashing?

He plumbed his memory, sifting for every fragment of information Kossler had ever let fall about Methuselah. *Sophie must have passed a test of Aryan integrity or some such hogwash. But she's still a woman. Hopefully her female instincts run deeper than her fascist education.*

On the other hand, wasn't there a real danger of falling in love with this enemy scientist? The question halted his pacing. Yes, that was a danger. After all, she truly looked like a Hollywood starlet. He did relish opportunities to chat with her. Roger stood and probed his own soul for a long while. In the end, he dredged up one word: no. If he could get her to care for him, that would be helpful, but somehow—in a way he himself didn't understand—he was positive Sophie wasn't the girl next door he'd always dreamed of. He would be friendly, even charming, but he would keep his heart securely locked.

From that point on, Roger warmed to every opportunity for establishing a one-on-one friendship with Sophie. His social skills creaked with rust, but he dusted them off and played the role of the dashing-but-humble soldier. His chief fear was of overplaying the part, of pushing too hard in his eagerness to establish a relationship. This snail's pace required all the self-restraint he could muster.

Roger devoted hours of evening mirror time to practicing his most becoming smiles. Later, during conversations with Sophie, he would flash the expressions he considered most endearing. Another tactic was to avoid all talk of escape. *Don't be transparent. It'll be better if she thinks that springing you out of here is her idea, not yours. Otherwise, the whole scheme will crash and burn.*

Bit by bit, as the days dragged past, Sophie truly did pay more than casual attention to him. One day he was sitting in his armchair and daydreaming. The green-tinted aviators rested on his nose, but his eyes were closed. In his mind, he explored the sky, circling puffy cumulus clouds in his repaired Thunderbolt. He was so deep in fanciful flight that Sophie's voice startled him.

"What are you doing, Captain Greene?"

Roger opened his eyes and sat up straighter. Through green tint he saw her standing just outside the bars, a coquettish expression gracing her face. He grinned and pulled off the aviators.

"Sorry. I didn't hear you come in. To answer your question, though, I was piloting a P-47 high over the English Channel. It was an incredibly resplendent afternoon. Brilliant sunshine flooded my cockpit, so I had to put on my sunglasses. I had the entire sky to myself, and I could zoom as far as I wanted in any direction. It was magnificent."

A delightful giggle escaped her lips. "Do you often pilot your arm-chair?"

"At least once a week. It's part of my routine. A way of being free on the inside, even if not on the outside. I mentally run through all the preflight checks, and then the actual flights as I adjust the flaps and rudder and check the instrument panel. I never want to forget how to fly. Besides, it gets me out of this place and into the sunshine. It's only a fantasy, of course, but everyone needs a castle in the sky. Without dreams . . . well, a person without dreams might as well be dead, I suppose."

Even as the words spilled from his mouth, Roger berated himself. He'd cautioned his reflection against talk of freedom. Sophie might guess how an American prisoner would do absolutely anything—including manipulating her—to break free of this dungeon existence. Instead of backfiring, though, the comment enticed Sophie closer. She stepped within inches of the bars, an action she'd never done before.

Roger remained seated. The spell might pop if he budged. In a voice close to a whisper, Sophie said, "When was the last time you felt sunshine—genuine sunshine—on your face, Roger?"

Electricity streaked up his spine. One of the enemy had just tiptoed over an invisible threshold: she'd called him by his first name. Equally significant, it was the first time she'd openly shown sympathy for his plight.

He cleared his throat. Was this his chance? He couched his reply in the softest of tones: "The last time I saw sunshine, Sophie? Bona fide, natural sunshine from the sun in the sky and not from a sunlamp? By my best guess, I would say that happened at least thirty years before you were born."

He scrounged the recesses of his mind for additional comments he might tack on. True things, like how sometimes he believed he would go insane if he remained cooped up much longer. About how torturous life became without even a glimpse of the blue heavens he longed to roar through. Instead of speaking, Roger bit his tongue. He gambled that a few well-chosen words would deliver more impact than a ramble.

A shadow of sorrow mingled with guilt passed over her face. Her head drooped. "I'm sorry you have to stay here."

Roger longed to stand, to hug this woman right through the bars for her simple confession. But he didn't dare. "Me too. I've been sorry about that for a long, long time. I'm the innocent victim of circumstances."

A shadow flitted over her countenance.

"I can't stay. Martin asked me to reanalyze some data. He's expecting me."

She crossed to the bank of file cabinets on the far wall, but not before Roger observed a motion that might have been her fingers wiping away a tear.

That's sure what it looked like.

He studied the burgundy Persian rug under his feet while his mind replayed everything they had said to each other. He regretted nothing. To the contrary, the exchange had occurred more subtly than he could've scripted.

Sophie pushed shut the file drawer. "I'll be going."

"And I'd better get back to my airplane. Wouldn't want it to spin into the English Channel. But thank you for the conversation. Thank you, too, for an inspiration you've given me."

She paused at the metal exit. "An inspiration I gave you?"

He nodded and allowed a half-smile to slip onto his face. "You see, until today I always imagined myself flying alone. That daydream has worn itself threadbare. Now I'll trade in my imaginary Thunderbolt for some kind of two-seater. Maybe an old Stearman biplane. It'll be more fun to imagine myself giving my friend Sophie her very first ride in a single-engine airplane."

With a barely perceptible nod of her head, she opened the door, then disappeared. This time, Roger definitely glimpsed a drop on her cheek.

Initial Point reached! Banking toward target.

CHAPTER 24

Katherine reached the top of the stairway in the Muellers' Tudor revival home just as Uncle Kurt emerged from his bedroom. Slung over his right shoulder was a bulging black-leather travel bag. His other arm pulled a two-wheeled travel case. In contrast to his usual business attire, he wore brand-new jeans topped with a khaki shirt and a green polyester bomber-style jacket barely thick enough to deflect the February chill.

"There you are!" Katherine said. "I was starting to think you had fallen asleep up here."

"Just tying up last-minute details. I can't go on holiday without clearing my schedule."

"Let me help." She took the handle of his rolling bag. "Say, this isn't very heavy. Especially considering that you'll be in Africa for three weeks. And where's your rifle?" She hoisted the bag and followed him down.

"I shipped my supplies ahead so I can travel light. An old acquaintance of mine lives in Botswana. He offered to receive my crates and let me spend a night at his villa, provided I take him hunting with me."

"A friend in Botswana? Now why doesn't that surprise me? Is there any corner in the world where you don't know an old friend?" By the time she reached the bottom step, Uncle Kurt had the front door open.

"You exaggerate, Katarina. I can think of many places where I don't have acquaintances: Antarctica, the North Pole, the Himalayan Mountains, the Gobi—"

Katherine raised a palm to cut him off. She'd accidentally sparked his routine. Every time Uncle Kurt stood on the verge of a new safari, his subdued excitement manifested itself in a ridiculously playful vein—at least, as playful as his straitlaced personality would permit. While he held the front door, she rolled the bag down the front walk to her sky-blue Passat and popped the trunk.

"This old friend of yours in Botswana, is he a business associate or a friend in the organization?"

Uncle Kurt lowered his shoulder bag into the trunk, then hefted in the rolling bag. "Both. No reason not to mix business and pleasure. Doubles the profits, doubles the fun." He shot her a wink before heading to the passenger door.

Katherine slid into her seat behind the steering wheel. As soon as she had the Passat up to speed, her uncle said, "Speaking of the HO, have you heard anything from them lately?"

"Not a word. Why?" She glanced at his face. Her uncle didn't ask idle questions for the sake of chitchat. As she expected, his bushy, gray eyebrows were lowered and protruding, the way they always did when he pondered some matter.

"Your field exercises. I would've expected the HO to contact you about them before now."

At the stop sign, Katherine braked briefly, then rounded the corner and headed toward Buford Highway. Her eyes jumped to the digital clock on the dashboard. If traffic wasn't too heavy, she could still drop him at the airport by the advised two-hours-before-flight time for international flights. "Maybe the HO leadership has more important things than field exercises on their plate. I'm pretty small taters, you know." She offered a reassuring smile, but found him looking the other way.

"Yes, I suppose the exercises aren't high on the priority list. Still, I can't help wishing they had called before my trip overseas. I'm not superstitious, you know, but I still would've liked to wish you good luck on whatever assignment they give you."

She stretched out an arm and patted his back. "I'll take that last statement as a good-luck wish right now, you sweet ol' uncle. Who knows? Maybe by the time you come home, you'll have dangerous jungle-safari stories to wow me with, and I'll get to tell you how I aced all the HO exercises with flying colors."

This elicited a smile. "Do you think you're up to it? No doubts? No fears?"

She laughed. "No doubts, no fears. After all, I was raised by Kurt Mueller himself. I have such a great heritage and training that I can handle any assessment test they throw my way."

"That's the spirit, Katarina. Show them what you can do. Make me even prouder!"

"I'll sure try," she replied in a chipper voice. Uncle Kurt probably wouldn't leave the country if he had any idea of her personal plans.

CHAPTER 25

As the passing weeks merged into months, Sophie had found various creative excuses to descend into the bunker for a few minutes, even when not bringing Roger's supper tray. She couldn't pay a social visit every day, but whenever she did, she made a point of sharing a few minutes of conversation.

In the beginning, she would mention whichever flimsy reason she'd invented for coming downstairs—to fetch a new box of test tubes, or to replace a file, or to pose a few questions: Did he ever experience headaches? Did his memory retain crisp, clear images from his youth? Or did his memory fade like any elderly person's?

If Hans or Martin or Gerhard accompanied her, she ignored Roger, and he did the same in return. If it was necessary to ask "the subject" a question in their presence, she addressed him formally as Captain Greene. But whenever she arrived alone, she called him Roger and chatted. He looked forward to the visits, but kept a tight rein on his emotions.

Throttle back, buddy boy. Don't get carried away by this German gal. Keep your sights on the target: escape. You've got to get out of this madhouse, no matter what it takes.

At last, on the day when Roger calculated he and Sophie had become friendly enough to take the risk, he gazed into her eyes and said, "You'll never know how much I wish we'd met under different circumstances, Sophie."

Like a tuning fork, she responded in perfect pitch. "I wish we'd met under different circumstances too. You're brilliant as a college professor, witty, charming . . ."

He delivered a smile intended to look wistful. "If I'm well-educated, maybe I have this bunker to thank. I've had more time to read than most people get in a lifetime. I've practically memorized scores of classic novels. Trigonometry and calculus while away my hours. But forget academics. You have a pretty impressive list of wonderful qualities too."

She blushed but smiled. "I've heard American men are flatterers. You reinforce the stereotype. Would you mind if I perform a private experiment with you?"

He blinked. "Experiment?"

Before Roger realized what she was doing, Sophie had her right hand inside the bars. She intertwined her soft fingers with his. Against his will, genuine tears welled in his eyes. A warm, living girl trusted him enough to reach out despite warnings to avoid him. Her fingers gave him his first female touch after nearly a lifetime.

Roger accepted her hand in both of his and, raising it to his lips, kissed the back of it. He closed his eyes and pressed her fingers to his cheek. No, he did not love her, but her gift provided something no man or woman should live without—human touch.

"Now the second half of the experiment."

The fingers of her free hand circled to the back of his head, drawing him closer to the bars. When her lips met his, no amount of self-discipline could stop the tidal wave of emotions that washed over him. Just that fast, he no longer felt like a specimen in a cage. Once again, he became a man.

Sooner than he would have liked, Sophie pulled away. "You make a wonderful laboratory partner, Roger Greene. The experiment is a success."

He needed a moment to find his voice. Finally, "A success? What did we find out?"

"A couple of things. First, that kiss persuaded my heart that, even though you're a fascinating man—and a magnificent kisser—you're still not the one I'm waiting for. My ideal husband will be a scientific wonder—both intelligent and humble—someone I can partner with both in and out of the laboratory. When I kiss him, there will be magic in the air."

Roger deflated. Sophie was a woman he could not manipulate.

"Second, kissing you assured me that, if you were a free man, you would make some American woman deeply happy to have you. You're not the kiss and grope kind. You're a true gentleman, Roger. One with a noble heart."

Despite the compliments, Roger felt empty. He'd failed. He'd tried to persuade her to love him, to help him escape, and the plan hadn't worked.

"So what do you plan to do with this information? Add a footnote to one of those bulging file folders about me?" He didn't hide the bitterness in his voice.

She picked up a glass beaker. "Please don't be angry. We're still friends. My experiment had nothing to do with Methuselah. It had everything to do with me and my role in the human race."

"I'm not following you."

"Your touch gave me the backbone I need to do something. You see, as a scientist I tried to accept your captivity as necessary for scientific progress. Yet as we got acquainted, my personal principles have been warring with my scientific side. This place—it isn't right. There is no justification for keeping you locked down here all these years. I don't want to sound like a coward, but I needed to kiss you—to feel you as a man instead of an experiment—in order to strengthen my resolve to help you."

Roger's heart lurched. "Help me? What do you mean?"

Beaker in hand, she strolled to the door. "For now, let's just say my colleagues aren't as clever as they believe." With that statement, she was gone.

Alone, Roger stared at the gray metal exit. Did she mean what he hoped she meant?

He thought through the kiss. Relived it. Sure, he'd enjoyed it. But all in all, it was only a kiss. No zing. No "magic" for him, either.

Would he ever meet the girl of his destiny?

CHAPTER 26

"Escape?" Roger tried to downplay his eagerness. "Is such a thing possible?"

"Anything is possible. The organization has security, yes, but no security system is foolproof."

"The organization?"

"The group that oversees Methuselah, plus other worldwide activities even I don't know about. I've been observing the guards. They're lax. After years of just going through the motions with no real threats, they've grown casual."

He didn't want to ask the next question. According to the old saying, he wasn't supposed to check the teeth of a horse someone presented as a gift. Still, he had to know her heart. "Helping me out of here will jeopardize your career. Why would you do that for me, a foreigner?"

"Some things are more valuable than careers. Oh, I'll admit, my scientific side is fascinated by this entire Methuselah Project. Knowing that it works makes me want to dedicate myself to rediscovering the process. But you should not be held here. It is simply wrong. Who knows? Maybe freeing you will be the one truly remarkable act I will do in my life."

A dying man's vision of an oasis in the Sahara wouldn't have elicited more euphoria than this news sparked in Roger. She would help, and he didn't need to manipulate her affection after all. "Do you have a plan?"

"Not yet. But I'm sure there must be a way to get you out of here."

"If I can get myself past that metal door, is there anyone watching the opposite side?"

"No, not there. Just steps leading up to the ground floor. Two other men are stationed at a guardhouse outdoors, beside the main gate. They check vehicles in and out, and one of them does regular foot patrols around the property."

"Could they be bribed to turn a blind eye?"

Sophie shook her head. "Everyone who works anywhere near Methuselah must pass an allegiance test. Any attempt to bribe a guard would end in disaster."

"Is the property fenced?"

"Not fenced, but walled. A tall stone wall encloses the entire perimeter. On top of that is barbed wire."

Roger's mind raced. As if on the tail of an enemy Messerschmitt, he was closing the distance on a bid for freedom. "How do you arrive each day? On foot, or—"

"I drive my own car. Why?"

"I have an idea. Can you get your hands on a key to this cell?"

She shook her head. "Hans carries the only copy I've seen. The keys I bring down here open only the front door to the building and this metal one behind me. I don't believe even the guards outside have the cell key. In fact, I'm not convinced that all our security people know you're down here. At least, not the regular guards at the gate. They might be oblivious of you."

"Hmm. That's a complication, but maybe we can overcome it. If I report that I sometimes get chilly, could you get permission to bring me a wool sweater?"

Sophie's eyebrows shot up. "A sweater?"

"Yes, I think I can use it to get out of here. You see, every Monday morning Hans has been coming downstairs for a couple of hours."

"I've noticed. I assumed it was to do research or to interrogate you."

Roger shook his head. "Hardly. Hans barely notices me. To him, I'm a lab rat. The reason he comes is to take a nap on that couch. My guess is that Hans enjoys his weekend parties. Maybe overdoing the Schnapps. Whatever he does, he slips in here to sleep and recover."

"If that is so, Hans could lose his position, both in Methuselah and in the organization."

"Don't utter a word to anyone. This could work to our favor. You see, when Hans arrives on Mondays, he drops his keys on the desk, then stretches out and drifts off to dreamland. If you can bring me a sweater, I can unravel it for the yarn and make a long string out of it—"

"You think you can fashion a hook and catch his keychain?"

"Exactly."

"What if you fail?"

"If I fail, only I will be to blame. Who could predict I might use a sweater that way? That's why I'm not asking for a ball of string and a fish-hook. Those would incriminate you. If my yarn idea doesn't work, what are they going to do to me? Put me in jail?"

Sophie's lips puckered into the adorable smile Roger never tired of seeing. "I'll buy the sweater. They keep petty cash for little purchases. If you can sneak out while Hans is asleep, I'm sure you could hurry out the front door before anyone stops you. If I meet you at my car, the orange Volkswagen, we—"

"An orange car?" Roger laughed. "I've never seen such a thing."

"You've been out of circulation too long, Captain Greene. It's about time we change that situation."

"I love the way you think."

"Leave it to me. I'm sure Hans will grant permission for the sweater."

+   +   +

Exactly one week later, Monday, February 2, 2015, found Roger sitting in his armchair and reading the Bible. His pent-up excitement over escaping had drawn his thoughts to Exodus, the story of the Jews' getaway from Egyptian captivity. For years he'd disciplined himself to ignore clocks. Now he waited impatiently for the minutes to tick past. Instead of the sweater, which he'd unraveled, he wore his leather flying jacket. Sophie had reminded him it was winter in the outside world.

At 9:31 a.m., as if on cue, the metal door swung open. Roger lifted his eyes from the thin pages of Scripture and observed Hans stepping through the doorway.

Ignoring Roger's presence, Hans pushed the door shut until it clicked. He tossed his key ring onto the desk with a clatter, emitted a long sigh, then settled into his customary spot on the leather sofa.

Snooze while you can. When your precious Nazi bosses find out how I escaped on your watch—with you right in the room—that might be the last good sleep you get for a long time. Unless hanging counts.

Despite the tension drawing his muscles as taut as bowstrings, Roger forced himself to lower his eyes to the Bible again. *Don't tip your hand. Don't do anything you don't normally do. Lull him to sleep with normalcy.*

Despite these admonitions, he couldn't concentrate on the printed words. He dragged his eyes over the lines, but he was no longer reading about the ten plagues or pharaoh's hard heart. He merely play-acted while he waited for the heavy breathing that would signal his opportunity. But for once Hans didn't doze off quickly. Every few moments he coughed lightly or shifted position.

Come on, fall asleep already!

Another cough. Hans sat up, cleared his throat, then lay back down.

Oh, great. A ticklish throat is keeping him awake today, of all days?

The minutes crept past. In the end, however, Roger rejoiced to hear the sound that quickened his heartbeat: the soft, rhythmic pattern of heavy breathing.

Praise the Lord and pass the ammunition! Noiseless as a snowflake, he stood and pulled out his "ammunition," a ball of yarn tied to a hook fashioned from his belt buckle. He floated to the bars, straining his ears to make sure the heavy breathing continued uninterrupted. This had to work.

Roger paid out the line, then pushed the hook through the bars and began swinging it, just as he'd rehearsed the night before. Back and forth, back and forth—*Now!*

As he intended, the hook sailed well over the desk and plopped into the padded seat beyond. He wanted no clanks or clunks to disturb Hans.

Steady now. He pulled the yarn and continued drawing it back. He could feel the weight of the hook rising up the far side of the desk . . .

Hans snorted. The heavy breathing stopped. He shifted position.

Roger froze. It was too late to dash back to his armchair and act nonchalant. He simply locked his eyes on the reclining man, willing him not to sit up.

A few seconds later the sound of breathing resumed, and Roger continued reeling in his line. When the hook crested the far edge of the desk, his fingers trembled with anticipation. He tried to steady them, but he could nearly taste freedom.

Not too fast. Slowly, slowly . . .

The hook inched across the desk, but not directly toward the keys. Roger paused, then repositioned, moving to the right and extending his arms between different bars to guarantee the yarn crossed directly over the keychain.

Come on, baby, just a little farther.

The hook reached the keychain, slid up onto it, and—as Roger held his breath—proceeded to slide off again without snagging the prize.

No! He yanked the yarn and caught the flying hook before it collided with the steel bars. He glanced at Hans. Still asleep, but for how long?

Unsure how many more minutes he might have, Roger repeated the attempt, but more rapidly this time. The hook sailed over the desk, landed, appeared on top of the desk, slid toward the key ring . . .

Roger's palms were sweating. He didn't dare take time to wipe them. He studied Hans—still no movement. This was taking too long. Would Sophie's excuse for going out to her car thirty minutes after Hans descended be plausible enough to let her remain outside so long?

The hook snuggled up to the key ring. *Good, good, good . . .* Through the bars, he raised his hands as high as he could reach. The open end of the hook twisted and *bingo!* For the first time, Roger had a direct link to the key that could release him. He reeled his catch across the desk. A deft flick of the wrist had the keys arcing through the air directly toward him. With his left hand, he reached to grab them—and missed.

Clink. The keys bumped a metal bar near Roger's knee. The sound wasn't loud, but to him it carried the report of a rifle blast.

Hans's breathing altered, but he didn't move. Working feverishly Roger seized the ring. He selected the one out of six keys that would open the portal. He reached through the bars of the door, and inserted it into the keyhole. *Snick.*

Freedom was his! Heart thudding, Roger pushed open the cell door.

Creak. The rusty hinges had betrayed him!

"Greene!" Hans leaped to his feet.

Roger sprinted to the metal barrier. Just as his fingers inserted the next key, a punch walloped his left kidney. He turned in time to dodge a second blow. He caught the man's arm, twisted it behind his back, and heaved.

Hans collided with the steel bars, bounced off, and collapsed onto the floor. To his credit, the panting scientist struggled to rise. "Martin! Call security!"

Roger jerked the exit door open and removed the key before slamming it shut. He doubted the shouts could be heard upstairs, but he didn't know for sure. He had charged up only three-quarters of the steps when the harsh blare of an alarm erupted.

Hang that Hans! There must an alarm button down there.

Alarm or no, retreat wasn't an option. He had to move faster! Roger reached the top and flung open the bookcase camouflage Sophie had described. Half a dozen people stared at him with wide eyes. Martin and Gerhard were the only faces he recognized.

"Who's that?" shouted a man Roger had never seen before.

"The prisoner—he's loose!"

A barrel-chested bruiser with close-cropped hair and a black shirt lunged at him. Thanks to Sophie, Roger already knew security personnel at this facility didn't wear uniforms with patches or badges, just black shirts and matching trousers. Faster than even he would have believed possible, Roger sidestepped the leap and delivered a kick that sent the muscleman sprawling.

Martin hefted a wooden chair over his head, but Roger slammed a fist into the man's stomach. Martin and chair crumpled. Another man, whom Roger recognized as an occasional visiting official, shot a hand into his suit jacket. A shoulder holster!

Even without a black outfit, anyone wearing a weapon deserved attention. Before the man could withdraw his hand, Roger rammed a knee into the man's groin and shoved him to the floor. He whirled toward the only visible exit just in time to see Sophie entering, flanked by two burly men in black.

"Get him!" someone ordered.

With a shout, the men scrambled past Sophie in a beeline for Roger.

Roger's bid for escape was crumbling fast, but he spotted a glimmer of hope. If these were the two guards from the gate, then no one was manning the outdoor barrier. If only he could reach the outside, he might still escape. He could run away, hide, sneak by night to the address Sophie had given him.

He darted forward, hoping speed alone would enable him to slip between the two attackers before they drew weapons or took a swing. But unlike Hans, these goons knew how to fight. One drove a sledgehammer fist into Roger's ribcage. The other cracked his knuckles into Roger's jaw with a blow that nearly twisted his head off.

Before Roger knew it, his knees hit the carpeted floor. Out of the corner of his eye, he glimpsed a hand pulling a gun from a holster. Just before him was the outside door—still standing wide open and admitting brisk, wintry air as if begging him to make a final effort.

Roger sprang. He staked everything on the hope that if a bullet only wounded him, the miraculous recuperative power Blomberg had bestowed would enable him to recover once he found a hiding place.

"Don't kill him," Gerhard's voice commanded. "Just stop him. Knock him out!"

Adrenaline coursing through his veins, Roger leaped through the door, where the full force of blinding sunlight reflected from the snow, forcing his eyes down to slits. By squinting and shading his eyes with one hand, he saw that he stood on a wide brick veranda. In front of him were eight or nine parked cars. Beyond, he glimpsed a gate with a red-and-white bar lowered across it. No one was visible in the guardhouse window. Still shading his eyes with a hand, he flew down the steps. He was nearly free!

Roger had barely reached the ground when a heavy body tackled him from behind. The collision knocked him down, exploded the wind from his lungs, and ground his chin into the snow and gravel of the parking lot.

He struggled to rise, and then something rock-solid cracked over his skull. Pain erupted in his head. He collapsed. Mustn't stay down. Get up! With a groan, he rolled over. High-pitched whining filled his ears. Black dots swirled before his eyes. In his confusion, he almost imagined the dots to be a swarm of distant enemy fighters.

Then, far above everything else, he saw it—the thing he'd longed to see for so long: the sky. Genuine, brilliant, azure sky. The place he belonged. High overhead droned one small, single-engine airplane. The sight was so blissful that he groaned again, not out of pain, but out of envy for the unseen pilot.

Gray mist engulfed his vision. Roger sank into blackness.

CHAPTER 27

When consciousness returned, it arrived in a rush. One moment, Roger was oblivious, aware of nothing. The next moment, he realized his eyes were shut and that something was wrong. He opened them, blinked, and saw once more the ugly concrete ceiling over his bed in the cage. Like a newsreel in a movie theater, his mind replayed the ill-fated escape scene, the fight upstairs, and his short-lived taste of chill, fresh air.

The sensation of goose bumps prickled his skin. Sitting up, he found himself nearly naked, with only his boxer shorts on.

"Ah, Captain Greene. You have rejoined the waking world."

Hans sat on the leather sofa, his legs crossed and a glowing cigarette pinched between his fingers.

"Why are my clothes gone?"

"Not gone. They are folded, there on the chair. While you were unconscious, we redeemed the time by performing a long overdue surgical procedure. Do you have a scar on your left bicep?"

Roger noticed a patch of white gauze taped to the spot. He ripped it off.

"No. Just a pink spot. Why?"

"Truly amazing." Cigarette smoke escaped Hans's mouth. "In a few short hours you have healed faster than most men would in days, maybe weeks."

Roger rubbed the spot. His fingertips detected something new and hard embedded inside his arm.

"For quite a while, we've foreseen that someday you might attempt to escape. Perhaps it's more noteworthy you didn't try decades ago. A lack of testosterone, perhaps?"

"If you want to discuss testosterone, maybe we should review how long you lasted in a boxing match with me. As far as escape goes, your predecessor built a pretty solid mousetrap."

Hans glared, then flicked the glowing cigarette butt at Roger's face. Roger backhanded the butt right back. Hans tried to duck. Too late. The glowing missile lodged in his hair. By the time Hans's frantic efforts succeeded in raking it to the floor, an odor of singed hair was spreading.

Roger chuckled. "I'd forgotten how bad burnt hair smells."

"You think you're very funny, don't you, American? See how funny you think this is: lest you ever try another escape, we've inserted a special device inside your arm. I won't attempt to explain twenty-first-century technology to a Neanderthal. But with what is inside you, our people can track you down anywhere on the globe."

"A homing beacon?"

"You wouldn't comprehend global positioning, nor a thousand other modern marvels of the outside world. Besides, for you such explanations are forbidden."

The lump was so tiny, Hans's claim seemed absurd. Roger stood and reached for his trousers. "Why forbidden? Am I such a frightening risk in this bunker that you're scared to let me know what's happening in the world?"

Hans tapped a fresh cigarette from his pack and lit it. "To me personally, no. But that's the policy. And if this rule frustrates you, then I'm happy to obey it."

"And sleeping on the job every Monday morning demonstrates faithfulness to your puppet masters?"

Hans's eyebrows knit together. He crushed the remains of his cigarette into the ashtray. Approaching the cell, he enunciated each word slowly and deliberately: "That is the last time you will mention such incidents, Captain Greene. Why? Because you are under my heel. You're a cockroach. You think you're living in misery? Just wait. I can make your existence more hellish than you can imagine. Shall I inject venereal disease into your veins to see what happens? Or we could strap you down and break your legs with an iron bar to time how fast they heal. Believe me, my mind can devise many other painful experiments for your body. Do we understand each other?"

Roger finished buttoning his shirt and sat down. "Hansie, I've understood you for a long time now. The question is, do you truly understand me?"

The German glared. "I warn you. Keep silent, and life can be tolerable. If you cause more trouble, then I guarantee payback a hundred times over." Hans pulled the key ring from his pocket—evidently he no longer trusted the desktop—and exited the bunker.

Now that the adversary was gone, Roger dropped his antagonism. He rested his elbows on his knees and buried his face in his hands. *So close. We came so close!*

We? The word reminded him that he still knew nothing of Sophie's fate. Had the security men been marching her into the building when Roger escaped from the bunker? Or had they noticed her fiddling with something under her car hood and simply come over to lend a hand to a damsel in distress?

With her shapely figure, how could they not notice her lingering in the parking lot? They might even have convinced themselves she was trying to win their attention. He sighed and shook his head. *We went about it all wrong. I was too eager. Shouldn't have depended so much on chance and perfect timing.*

He considered what Hans had told him about the thumbnail-size bump inside his left arm. Could such a tiny object actually reveal his position even if he went to Argentina? To New Zealand? How about the North Pole? *Impossible. Such an apparatus would need gigantic batteries. Radio equipment. A tall antenna. Hans is trying to frighten me into submission.*

No Sophie descended to the bunker with an evening meal. The only sound came from the clock, ticking through the evening. Apprehension tightened Roger's gut. He couldn't imagine any clue that might tip off Hans or the guards about her. Sure, she'd bought the sweater, but Hans had approved it. Kossler used to bring him clothing, too, when necessary.

The prospect of life in the cage without Sophie's visits oppressed his soul more than any threat Hans could snarl. On impulse, Roger jumped from the chair and gave the barred door a savage shake.

◆   ◆   ◆

Gerhard arrived with breakfast—if dark bread and water qualified as a meal.

"Punishment rations?"

"Hans's orders. Behave yourself. His anger will subside. You have no idea what a predicament your antics put him in."

Roger ran a finger along one of the steel bars separating the two men. "Considering the pickle Hans has kept me in for so long, excuse me if I don't shed any tears."

A faint smile that may have been admiration graced the scientist's lips. "American humor. Like rubber. So resilient, even after so long."

"If I have a choice between laughing or crying, yeah, I choose laughing."

Without another word, Gerhard exited the bunker.

Lunch, the meal normally brought by Hans, didn't arrive at all that day. But just before the wall clock reached five o'clock, Roger heard the metal door opening. He leaped to his feet when Sophie strolled in balancing a supper tray. The door clanged shut behind her.

"Thank God. I thought they arrested you or something."

"No. I believe they suspect nothing about me. The overseers for

Methuselah blame you—and Hans—for what happened." She slid the tray through its opening, then hurried back to the door and cracked it for a furtive peek up the stairs. "I can stay only a moment. Hans is waiting for me to report on your attitude."

"Hans can drop dead, for all I care."

"That's how I feel, but he's still my supervisor. One disrespectful word from me, and he can banish me from Methuselah."

"Sophie, I'm sorry I got you involved. We shouldn't have done anything that might endanger you."

"Don't be sorry. We just got impatient, made mistakes. Next time, we'll be more careful."

Roger couldn't hold back the grin that sprang to his face. "Next time? You don't intimidate easily, do you?"

"I might not be a fighter pilot, Captain Greene, but when I set my sights on a target, I keep shooting until I get what I want."

His grin grew wider. "Girl, you're talking my language. All right, hurry upstairs and tell Hans I'm down here pouting and looking all meek and deflated. That's probably what he wants to hear."

She winked. "That's the spirit. Soon I'll tell you about a new escape plan I'm developing."

"Another plan? Already? Hey, I'm all ears."

"Not now." With that, Sophie disappeared.

His spirits restored, Roger settled into the armchair with the supper tray on his lap. "Thank You, God, for a friend who doesn't give up."

CHAPTER 28

"So was I right? Isn't Fiona's the greatest?"

Katherine met Jason's sparkling eyes. His unquenchable smile warmed her heart. "Jason, you were more than right. This place is out-of-this-world crazy fabulous! I've heard of murder mystery dinner theaters before, but I never knew what I was missing. I've never had so much fun!"

"You lucked out. Your first time here, and you get to play the murderer. I've been here a dozen times for five different plays. I still haven't gotten to kill a single person."

She laughed. "If we talked like this anywhere else in town, people would think we're psychopathic serial killers or something."

Jason drained his wine goblet, leaned back, and crossed his legs. "Want to know a secret?"

Katherine leaned in. "A good secret or a bad secret?" she asked conspiratorially. The incredible five-course dinner, topped with her participation in the mystery, plus attractive male company had lifted Katherine's spirits to a bubbly mood. This could likely be considered flirting. Uncle Kurt would be aghast.

"Oh, this is a wonderful nonsecret type secret," Jason replied. "I know. I'll let you guess."

Most of the other patrons were already on their way out the door. Jason paid no heed. "Look around you. The walls of Fiona's are famous for their collection of Hollywood actors and actresses."

Katherine took a last sip of wine and swept the dining room again with her gaze. She'd already enjoyed picking out classic performers such as Audrey Hepburn, Marlon Brando, Greta Garbo, Rock Hudson, James Dean, and Humphrey Bogart. Now that other patrons no longer blocked the view, she could spot even more famous figures. "Yes. I see them. Now what?"

"Out of all the faces around you, guess which person is the author of tonight's dinner theater."

She scanned the movie stills. Which actor also wrote plays? Then the truth dawned. "Is it you?"

Grinning, Jason stood and bowed low. "You guessed it. So you see, I had an ulterior motive for inviting you here. I didn't want to say anything earlier because I didn't want to spoil the show."

Katherine stood too. "Spoil it? Just the opposite. I'm impressed. Knowing would've made me appreciate the performance even more." She allowed her new friend from the Peachtree State Mix & Mingle site to help her with her jacket.

"Shall we go, my dear?" He held out his arm dramatically, as Carey Grant might do in an old black-and-white movie.

Katherine hesitated. Tonight's dinner was their first face-to-face meeting. Even though she hadn't told Jason, this evening was her first genuine date in ages with anyone not connected with the Heritage Organization. She didn't normally walk arm in arm with any male. The gesture seemed harmless enough, but something caused hesitation. Into her mind sprang the forbidding image of Uncle Kurt.

"No fleas. I promise," Jason said with a laugh. "I got fumigated just yesterday."

Katherine laughed, too, and forced Uncle Kurt from her mind. She accepted Jason's arm. Together they strolled out the door of Fiona's and along the fifty feet of sidewalk to the parking garage. Katherine shivered. After the crowded warmth of a dinner theater, the March evening breeze chilled her legs under her dress.

By the time they reached her blue Passat and the silver Honda Accord parked beside it, theirs were the last two cars in the garage. Jason lowered his arm, taking Katherine's hand in one swift motion. The movement struck her as choreographed. Had he seized other women's hands the same way? Or was she just being overly suspicious?

"Hey, this evening has been too great to end so early. How about coming over to my place for a few drinks?"

"It's not that early, good sir. Don't forget, I have work to do in the morning."

His smile diminished by a degree, but still clung. "All right. How about I follow you to your place, then? When it's bedtime, you can feel free to nudge me out the door—or invite me to join you, if I get lucky." He winked. Still holding her hand, he took an intimate step closer and circled an arm around her waist.

Katherine pulled away and flipped through her car keys even as she fumbled for words. "Uh, not tonight, Jason. I had fun. But the timing isn't good."

She found the key and inserted it in the car door.

She felt his breath on her neck as he leaned in. "Come on," he said, drawing out the words. His voice had shifted to deep and husky. "We've had such a good time together; I just don't want it to end." He ran his palm down her arm then cupped it around her hand as she unlocked the door. "Hold on, girl."

"No, really. I need to get home."

Swiftly his hands found her shoulders and spun her around with her back against the car. He caged her with his arms and planted a fast kiss on her lips. "There, you like that, don't you, Katherine? The night's been fun, but the game isn't over. You're just playing hard to get, aren't you?"

Confusion clouded Katherine's mind. Jason had acted gallant all evening. Where had this come from?

He pressed close to kiss her again, but she twisted her head. His lips landed hard on her ear. "Stop, you're hurting me!"

His face darkened. "You're not getting away that easy. I just paid sixty bucks apiece for this evening. That's not chicken feed, girl. After a night on the town, a guy's entitled to some female comfort." His hands slid to her dress front.

Katherine trembled. If Jason really did write the play, wouldn't they let the author in free? Had he lied to seduce her? Was Jason even his real name?

All at once, her training clicked, and Katherine drove her knuckles into Jason's stomach. He reeled back, providing enough distance for her to deliver a kick to his ribs. His face contorted in shock and pain.

Seizing her chance, Katherine jerked open the car door, leaped inside, then mashed the lock button.

"Oh, I get it," Jason said, approaching the car, his fingers opening and closing into fists. "You advertise online and give guys the impression they can get some nighttime action. But then you just take advantage of their wallet and run home with a full stomach. Is that your little game?" Jason raised a fist and slammed it onto the hood of her car.

With hands shaking and blood pounding in her ears, she started the engine, threw the car into reverse, then roared toward the garage exit.

Her mind raced. Had she let slip any information he could use to track her? Fortunately she'd given him her pen name—Katherine McNeil— and certainly not her address or phone number. Her fingers trembled at the thought.

"What's wrong with you?" She berated herself aloud. "Uncle Kurt can't find the perfect match, and you can't, either. After a week of trading e-mails, how'd you miss the poignant detail that the guy was a savage miscreant? Or worse, a rapist. Did you do your homework? And you call yourself an editor. Are you hopeless, or what?" The sound of her own voice was beginning to ease the shock. "No way he wrote that play! Probably stole the real author's name."

Of course, not all men visiting dating websites would turn into berserk nutcases like Jason Carmichael, but just one was enough to sour her interest. She hated that Uncle Kurt might be right.

CHAPTER 29

In the days following the botched escape, Sophie had never dared to spend more than a few moments downstairs, and even then only when she brought Roger his supper. "I want Hans to think I'm frightened of you. He's already warned me that you'll murder me if I step too close while delivering meals." Concerning whatever plan she was concocting, Sophie would say nothing except, "Stop shaving. Let your beard grow again."

"Not a bad idea. It'll make Hans think I'm drowning in depression. Good way to lull him into relaxing his guard."

As days passed, life resumed as before. The one exception being that Hans no longer descended for Monday-morning naps.

Roger tried to allay any concerns by returning to his own patterns of behavior. Once more, he whiled away the days by reading, strumming his guitar, running in place, and performing calisthenics. He refined the blueprints he had created for a cable-stayed bridge using engineering textbooks on bridge construction. In the past his goal had been to distract himself and keep physically fit. Now, pacifying his captors until the next escape figured largely in his strategy. On the rare occasions when the male scientists descended for any reason other than to deliver meals, Roger ignored them and played the role of a sulking child.

At last, the day came when Sophie said she could lengthen her visits a little. "Are you ready to hear my new escape idea?"

"Let me guess. You're going to bake me a machine gun in a cake?"

She giggled. "Nothing so dramatic. Besides, if you had killed anyone on the first try, you wouldn't be alive today. I've heard them say that."

"Lucky me. So what's your scheme?"

"You're going to walk out of here in full daylight disguised as Hans. I'll drive you straight to the airport in Frankfurt. I will personally escort you to a safe place."

Roger was skeptical, yet intrigued. "I don't look like Hans. The guards would nab me in two seconds."

"We can make you look like Hans. Your hair color is very close. Hans has a goatee, and your beard is growing out nicely. On the morning of escape day, you'll trim it to look exactly like his. Add a pair of sunglasses, maybe a hat, and we can fool them."

Roger rubbed the new growth covering his chin. "Having you beside me and acting casual would tip the scale in our favor. They wouldn't expect that."

"Right. Also, shortly after the last incident, Hans and I started sharing rides to work. The guards are accustomed to seeing us arrive and leave in one car."

The revelation jarred Roger. "Don't tell me you and that egomaniac are getting cozy."

"He believes he's winning my affection. Just the opposite. The better I know Hans, the more I detest him. But he trusts me. After all, I have clearance from the organization. I've even been to his apartment after a date. When he opened a desk drawer, I spotted his passport. Now all I need is the right moment to steal his keys and some of his clothing."

Roger stepped back. "You're dating him?"

"Only to trick him. To get you out of here."

"You realize that snake wants to take you to bed?"

"Of course, I realize it. And he believes he can do it. I told him I won't go to bed with any man until my wedding night. He smirked and said, 'We shall see.' It's sickening."

"Be careful, Sophie. Hans is a serpent—only more lethal."

She nodded. "I'll be careful. And you must, as well. Don't do anything that might arouse suspicion."

"You bet. Meanwhile, if you need me, you know where to find me."

◆　◆　◆

A week later, on Friday night, Sophie radiated excitement when she slid the supper tray to Roger.

"Has something happened?"

She beamed. "Tonight I'm going to dinner and dancing with Hans. Tomorrow I'm leaving the country with you!"

Roger nearly dropped the tray. "Are you serious? But how?"

"I have it all worked out. I'll ply him with wine all night but only pretend to drink my own. By the time we reach his apartment, if he's still functioning, I'll smash a vase over his head and knock him out."

"I wish I could handle that vase part for you. I'd like to even the score."

"Here, take this." Between the bars, she handed him a plastic bag she'd carried tucked under her arm. "I bought you new clothing that looks like Hans's. Tonight, trim your beard and hair. Make yourself resemble Hans as best you can. That's all I have time for. Have to go."

She hurried to the metal door.

"Say, you still haven't told me where we're headed. Where's the final destination?"

She paused with her fingers on the door handle. "I bought airline tickets. We're traveling to your country. America!" On that note, she disappeared around the door and let it clank shut.

Roger's skin crawled with goose bumps. "To America? Just like that, we're heading to the United States?" He nearly burst with exhilaration. He wanted to shout. To clap. To run a hundred miles. To do anything wild to celebrate those magnificent words. He leaped onto the bed, bounced off the other side, then sank to his knees and clapped both hands together. "Oh, God, I beg You a thousand times . . . please let this work!"

His hasty prayer completed, Roger dashed to the washroom and tugged the pull-chain for the bulb over the sink. He picked up his razor and, examining his beard in the mirror, pictured Hans's goatee and mustache. *I have to imitate that guy's ugly mug? Well, anything for a good cause.*

Chapter 30

When the wall clock verified Saturday morning had dawned in the outside world, Roger was amazed he still hadn't slept. Pent-up tension had apparently staved off the Methuselah forces that normally plunged him into deep sleep each night.

What a night. I'm as restless as a willow in a windstorm. Let's get the show on the road!

At seven o'clock, Sophie still hadn't arrived. Myriads of disastrous scenarios crowded into his imagination. He considered opening his Bible, as its pages had often calmed his heart and passed time. Not this morning. He couldn't even pretend to read. He could do nothing but pace and worry.

Please, Lord, help Sophie. Don't let anything go wrong.

At 7:41 a.m., he finally heard the familiar clunk of someone pushing the release bar on the far side of the gray door. Roger dove onto the bed to hide the navy shirt and khaki pants Sophie had brought him. He feigned sleep but left his eyes slit open enough to see who entered.

When Sophie appeared and shut the door behind her, he threw off the covers and flew to the bars. "I was worried about you!"

"I had to wait. If I arrived too early on a Saturday morning, the guards would wonder." From her handbag she extracted Hans's key ring.

"You got them! The long silvery one opens the cell door."

Roger watched as Sophie's trembling fingers inserted the key and turned it. He shoved the door open and stepped out. "What a glorious feeling. Hold still. I need a celebration hug."

She'd been holding a brown leather briefcase, but when he embraced her, she winced and dropped it. "Ouch."

"You're hurt! What happened?"

"Hans doesn't get drunk as easily as I hoped. At his apartment I realized I would have to club him over the head after all. He spotted me in a mirror just as I swung. He dodged. We fought. He . . . he struck me many times before I knocked him out. I think I have a cracked rib. Luckily the organization requires us to train in martial arts."

"He hit you? I'll murder him!"

"No, forget Hans. I tied him up. We must flee. Here, take these sunglasses. And this." She fitted a hat onto Roger's head. "Hans likes this one. He believes it makes him look—what is the English word—debonair?"

"Hans? Debonair? What a lost cause."

"Oh, and I brought this for you." She retrieved the briefcase from the floor. "If you want to take any personal possessions, they must fit in Hans's briefcase."

Roger had already considered the matter. "I'm taking only four things: my razor, my Bible, my Air Corps sunglasses, and"—he carefully folded his leather A-2—"my flight jacket."

When he opened the briefcase, he found a blue booklet: a United States passport. Inside the front cover, a photo of Hans Heinkel stared back at Roger. "How can that creep have American citizenship?"

"I don't know. In his desk drawer, I found three different passports: one German, one Ukrainian, one American. I grabbed this one for the easiest border crossing."

He compressed his belongings into the briefcase and snapped it shut. "Okay. Let's go."

The old manse that had once belonged to the Kossler family exuded eerie silence as Sophie led Roger past the bookcase that concealed the bunker's upper entrance. This portion of the building contained desks and file cabinets divided into cubicles by five-foot barriers.

"On weekends no guards enter the building. They just watch the gate and the grounds. An alarm system keeps the main building secure."

Roger peeked out the window. He spotted five vehicles: an orange car, which he knew to be Sophie's, plus four others of various hues and odd stylings. Two must belong to the guards at the gate, but whose were those other two?

Sophie joined him at the window. "At eight o'clock the guards change shifts. Let's wait until the first two leave. Since they saw me come in alone, I don't want them to see two of us exit."

Roger spotted a flaw in Sophie's scheme. "Surely they keep a record of who comes and goes? It will be logged in a blotter."

"I'll shrug and tell the new guards that whoever wrote it down made a mistake. I have the passenger seat tilted all the way back. It wouldn't be hard to overlook a resting person that way."

"I hope so." Roger dried his palms against his pants.

Shortly after eight, two laughing, black-shirted men stepped out of the guardhouse. One waved his *auf Wiedersehen*. Each climbed into a vehicle and drove out the gate. Once the second vehicle cleared, the gate pulled shut again.

Relief flooded Roger's mind. "The coast is clear."

Sophie eyed him up and down. "You're a little taller than Hans, but that shouldn't matter." She adjusted the hat on his head. "There. That's how Hans wears it. With the hat and sunglasses, you make a good Hans."

"No need to insult me. Well, it's now or never."

With his heart pounding inside his ribs, he stepped out the door behind Sophie. She'd already reset the security system but, as they'd agreed, Roger was the one who relocked the exterior door, just as the genuine Hans would do.

As they sauntered to her orange Volkswagen, he sneaked a peek at the sky with its few cumulus clouds. Fabulous weather for flying. Just as quickly, he set aside such thoughts. Escape first. Fly later.

It occurred to Roger that the arrogant Hans might insist on driving, even if it wasn't his car. He whispered, "Who should drive? You or me?"

She glanced sidewise. "When was the last time you drove a car?"

"In 1942. A Desoto."

Despite the tension of the moment, she giggled. "You're not driving me anywhere until you get a new license."

The car wasn't locked. Roger casually opened the passenger door. Now he understood what she meant about tilting the seat back. Cars in his day never looked like this. He slid in, shut the door, and reclined as if drowsy.

Sophie took her seat and started the engine. "I'm so nervous."

"You're doing terrific. Keep it up."

At the exit, a red-and-white-striped arm that could have barred the way pointed straight up—no problem there. But a section of chain-link gate blocked their way. Through his new sunglasses, Roger watched as Sophie slowed the car and gave a casual wave to the black-garbed man in the window. Instead of opening the gate, he squinted with a puzzled frown.

Sophie faked a grin and motioned toward the gate, as if it should be obvious what she wanted.

One of the two guards inside pulled on a jacket and stepped out of the guardhouse. He peered first at Sophie, then at the reclining figure beyond her. He motioned for her to roll down the window. "Two of you? The record shows only one person arrived."

She giggled. "How can that be? Dr. Heinkel and I arrived together just twenty minutes ago." She glanced toward the relaxed figure in sunglasses. "Ah, with the seat back, the other guard must not have noticed Dr. Heinkel. We had a late night last night."

When the guard hesitated, Sophie placed an arm on Roger's knee. "Hans, at least wave so security will know I'm not transporting a corpse."

Roger wiggled his fingers in a way he hoped would dovetail with Hans's sarcastic personality.

The guard straightened. *"Auf Wiedersehen."* Still looking perplexed, he stepped back to the guardhouse and reached inside the door, where he evidently pushed a button. With a hum, the chain-link gate crept open.

Inside the guardhouse, a telephone rang. Watching, Roger saw the second guard answer. In a flash, the man holding the receiver jumped to his feet. In German the man blurted, *"Was? Dr. Heinkel?"* A pause, then an expression of shock. His eyes bore into Roger.

The gate slid in slow motion.

Come on . . . faster!

The man holding the telephone mashed an unseen button. The gate shuddered to a halt.

"Go!" Roger hissed.

"But the gate. It's not all the way—"

The man with the telephone made a motion that telegraphed one meaning: he was reaching for his holster.

"Sophie, go—he's got a gun!"

Sophie stomped down the gas pedal. The Volkswagen shot through the opening, scraping its right side along the gate as it began closing again.

"I'll bet that was Hans on the telephone. He must have worked loose from your knots."

Sophie swore.

Roger glanced back in time to see both guards taking aim with handguns. "Duck!"

In the next instant, the rear windshield shattered. The vehicle swerved, but Sophie kept the gas pedal floored. "This isn't how I wanted it. They'll sound an alarm. The organization has agents all over Germany."

"Get off the main road. Don't take the shortest way to the airport. If you can, use any cow path where they'll least expect to find you. Keep 'em guessing."

She nodded. "Yes, we can travel by smaller roads. But don't underestimate this organization. They know my car and license number."

"Is it far to the airport?"

"It's not close. Nearly an hour away. They'll have time to pursue us." She turned to look him in the eye. "And I guarantee, Roger, they definitely will give chase."

◆   ◆   ◆

For more than a half hour, neither Roger nor Sophie said much. She sped along, frequently turning, changing directions in case an agent had observed their passing. Meanwhile, Roger's glimpses of twenty-first-century Germany flabbergasted him. This "Autobahn," the architecture, the gleaming automobiles straight out of Flash Gordon adventure stories—all of these threatened to overwhelm him. He'd never moved so fast along the ground in his life. It was dizzying to watch the world flash past.

"When we get to the airport," Sophie explained, "we have to check in. Then we'll walk through a security area, but don't worry. With your beard and new haircut, you resemble the passport enough to get through. Airport security isn't connected with the organization. They mainly want to ensure no one is sneaking weapons or bombs aboard."

"Sounds like they're afraid of partisans. I'll act casual."

She flashed him a confused look, but fished a plastic sack from the floor of the back seat and handed it to him. "Here. These are some of Hans's belongings. His watch, reading glasses, and an envelope of cash from his office at Methuselah."

"Good girl!" He slid the watch onto his wrist, then pocketed the other items.

Roger had noticed that every few miles on this Autobahn, special exit points allowed motorists to stop and buy gasoline. As Sophie passed one such place, Roger spotted a maroon car parked alongside the ramp that funneled cars back onto the highway. Both of the car's male occupants reacted as the orange Volkswagen sped past. The maroon car leaped into motion, pulling onto the highway behind them.

"Trouble, Sophie. We've got company."

Her face revealed concern but also determination. Whatever training this mysterious "organization" had given her was paying off. She might be a female scientist, but she was no pushover. Knocking out Hans had proven that.

Twisting in his seat, Roger watched as the passenger in the pursuing car stuck his hand out the window.

"He's going to shoot!"

Sophie cranked the steering wheel hard left, then right, jockeying to present a difficult target. Roger heard no gunfire, but the mirror outside his window shattered. Like Sophie, he hunkered low in the seat. "If only we had a gun!"

"A pistol? I have one. The organization issued it." She reached under her seat, pulled out a leather case, and shoved it at Roger.

Inside, Roger found a pistol in pristine condition. Not the Colt .45 he had carried as an airman, but nothing so complicated he couldn't figure it out.

"The magazine is already in place. Fully loaded. Fifteen rounds."

"Baby, I love you!"

"Who, me or the Beretta?" Sophie yanked the wheel left again.

"Both!"

In a flash, he spotted the safety, about two inches higher than on his Colt, on the slide instead of the frame.

"Pull the hammer back if you want to take it from double action to single. Single action is easier to take that first shot."

Roger aimed the weapon out the smashed rear window. "Eat this!" He squeezed off a round. Then another.

The windshield of the trailing car didn't shatter, but glistening spider-webs appeared in the glass. The driver backed off, but his companion still held his own weapon out the side window.

Roger drew a bead on the gunman, then squeezed. *Crack!* A new hole appeared in the pursuers' windshield. The gunman slumped as his weapon tumbled to the roadside.

"One down!" Roger waved a fist at the pursuer.

The organization car dropped back but didn't stop.

"He'll be radioing our location and direction," Sophie said.

"Think you can shake him?"

In response, Sophie swerved onto an exit, whisking them off the Autobahn and toward Frankfurt's city center. Saturday morning traffic grew thicker. She passed slower vehicles, weaving in and out of gaps between cars, ignoring blaring horns. Behind them, the determined pursuer duplicated each maneuver.

A traffic light turned red.

Sophie jammed the gas pedal to the floorboard. "Hang on!" They roared through the intersection, barely darting between two cars. Roger watched as the car behind them imitated her gamble. It braked violently, swung sideways, and then got T-boned by a delivery van.

"Girl, you can fly in my squadron anytime!" With the immediate threat diminished, the mere mention of flying lured Roger's eyes to the sky. What he saw gripped his attention: "Wow, look at the size of that bomber!"

"Bomber? What?"

He pointed toward the descending aircraft.

"That's no military airplane. It's a normal airliner. Just like the one we're taking to America."

"An airliner? You said we're traveling to America, but I didn't know you meant directly. All the way from Frankfurt?"

She grinned. "Now you've got it. To Atlanta. I wanted New York, but all the seats were booked. The main thing is, you're going home."

The realization that such long-range flights had become routine passenger trips staggered his imagination. Roger had realized that life didn't stand still outside the Methuselah bunker, but this revelation dumbfounded him. "I have a lot of catching up to do. How can we fly in a civilian aircraft straight to the States with a war going on?"

Sophie slowed to a less conspicuous speed. "What war?"

How could she not understand? The fighting had been going on all her life. "*The* war. You know . . . between the Allies and the Axis powers. Kossler didn't spill everything, but I know that the Third Reich invaded—"

"Roger, I don't know what nonsense Dr. Kossler fed you, but that war is over."

Her statement smacked him between the eyes like a baseball bat. "Over? For how long?"

"A long time. Years. The States and Germany are best of friends."

Each new chunk of information challenged his understanding. He had no reason to doubt Sophie, but these claims contradicted the picture Kossler had painted. If the States and Germany were such great pals, then why was Captain Roger Greene still a prisoner of the Nazis? Who were the men chasing them?

Sophie forced a smile, but the stress showed through. "This isn't the time to discuss it. We have to change tactics. Get rid of this car."

"What do you suggest?"

She screeched to a halt behind a taxi. "You have the cash. Here's the information on our flight." She shoved a folded sheet of paper into his hand. "Jump into that taxi. Tell him to take you to the airport. Lufthansa is the airline. Check in and follow the signs to whatever gate number they tell you at registration. It's easy. Copy what everybody else does."

"Why don't you come with me?"

"There's a chance they're tracking my car by GPS. If we just leave it here and they find it, they'll guess where we're headed. But if I drive away from the airport and park where they can't get a signal, that should buy some time."

GPS? Roger didn't understand, but said, "You won't take unnecessary chances?"

She grinned. "We already have. Now hurry. I'll meet you at the gate to the airplane."

Clutching Hans's briefcase, Roger hopped out and trotted to the cab. Sophie's orange VW sped around the corner. The moment it was gone, he stopped short. Those initials—GPS. Did they stand for a homing device? Hans had bragged about the object he'd surgically implanted inside Roger being some sort of homing beacon. At the time, the claim seemed absurd—that tiny bump, dangerous? Surely Hans had been bluffing to intimidate him.

He reached for the taxi door. *Thank God for you, Sophie. See you soon!*

CHAPTER 31

The modern, bustling mosaic of humanity at the airport jarred his brain. He was rubbing shoulders with bodies from unfathomable numbers of nations, some Oriental, others wearing turbans or sarongs as if from India or the Middle East. The mixture of languages astonished him. He'd expected to hear only German. Instead, a veritable babel of tongues assailed his ears from every direction. It was as though he'd taken a spin on H. G. Wells's time machine.

He spotted a sign for Lufthansa and joined those standing in line. When Roger's turn came, the brown-skinned woman at the counter asked for his passport. She shot him only a cursory glance before typing on the device Roger recognized as a computer.

"Here's your boarding pass, Mr. Heinkel. Enjoy your flight." With one glance at Hans's American passport, she had switched from German to English, even though her darker skin suggested Turkey or some other exotic upbringing. How long had minorities been acceptable employees in the Third Reich—or Germany, or whatever they called this baffling country?

"Thank you." He accepted the boarding pass and strolled away. Amidst a medley of voices, public address announcements, and foreign faces, Roger ambled in the direction the woman at the counter had pointed.

The spectacle of a gaunt male walking past snagged Roger's eyes. The man's head was shaven, except for an upside-down triangle of hair above his forehead. Lining the outer edge of both ears were a dozen shiny rings. Another metal ring pierced one of his eyebrows, yet another his lower lip. Roger realized too late he was cringing in horror.

Poor devil. The stinking Nazis must have experimented on him, too, before the war ended.

His steps slowed as he approached the security area with its uniformed personnel. Nobody paid him particular attention, but he feared looking conspicuous. He recalled Sophie's hurried assurance that airport police searched only for weapons, not for escaped Americans. What if she'd miscalculated?

Pinpricks of sweat beaded his brow. As casually as he could, he wiped them away with the back of his hand. The whole process mystified him, but he placed his briefcase on the conveyer belt as everyone else did and let it slide into some kind of gizmo. Following other passengers' examples, he stepped through the opening, where another uniformed man studied each individual.

"*Gut.*" The man gave him a business-like nod.

Roger exhaled the breath he hadn't realized he was holding. He picked up the briefcase and continued walking. He paused at a floor-to-ceiling window and gaped at the behemoth parked outside. Beyond it, similar monsters landed and took off. Unbelievable. All that weight, and not a single propeller. Jules Verne's imagination had sprung to life.

A tantalizing aroma wafted his way. Then he saw it—an eatery named simply "China Restaurant." He wasn't positive what Chinese food tasted like, but German cuisine was all he'd received in the bunker. The delectable smells of Oriental dishes beckoned him closer. He swallowed, then glanced at his wristwatch. Why not? Plenty of time before their flight. Sophie couldn't be here yet.

He retrieved the envelope of cash in his pocket. Instead of the Reichmarks he'd expected, the envelope contained bills the taxi driver had called Euros. It was another question for Sophie. He crossed to the restaurant and placed an order for "their most delicious chicken dinner."

Soon Roger entered gastronomic paradise, savoring the smell and spicy flavor of a dish he'd never encountered. With his back to a wall and an eye on the people churning by, he devoured his meal quickly.

Sophie could easily have walked right by without him spotting her. He'd not seen so many people in one place in his life, even before his capture. He continued on to his gate, following sign after sign, until at last he found the proper waiting area and took a seat among the crowd.

Where are you? Still no Sophie. *You're making me nervous. Ditch that car and grab a cab over here.*

As the minutes crawled past, Roger watched other passengers. The sight of children especially delighted him. During his captivity he'd seen adults, even if in limited numbers. But youngsters provided a welcome sight. A lot of living had been happening while he languished underground. More people with piercings all over their faces, bare midrifts, unnatural hair colors, bold tattoos—it appeared that nothing was *verboten* anymore. He hardly knew where it was safe to look. Women didn't cover themselves as they used to. In some cases, it was hard to know if he was looking at a man or a woman. He had to force himself not to stare.

From the ceiling of the waiting area hung a device that fascinated him. Like a miniature movie theater, it apparently showed colorful newsreel after newsreel about global events. He glanced around, searching for the projector. He saw none. Apparently this device was similar to Hans's computer, with the pictures and sound originating inside.

Roger divided his attention between keeping an eye out for Sophie, watching for hostile pursuers, and trying to absorb the torrent of news flowing from the curious machine. Strange craters appearing in Siberia, some sort of military conflict in the Ukraine, incomprehensible political and religious strife in the Middle East, the final moments of a golfing competition . . . For ages Roger had longed to hear about events in the outside world. Now that he could, the flood gushed too quickly for his sleep-starved brain. His head began to ache.

A woman's voice sounded over the public address system: "Ladies and gentlemen, we will now begin boarding Flight 444 to Atlanta." Most of the throng stood and shuffled toward a woman accepting boarding passes.

Come on, Sophie! What on earth is taking so long?

Then the news device launched into "a dramatic piece of news," as the announcer called it: "In a dramatic clash, members of rival organized crime syndicates evidently engaged in a violent cat-and-mouse automobile race through the suburbs of Frankfurt this morning. The chase ended in disaster for at least one of the participants . . ."

In horror, Roger watched as the picture flashed to the demolished guardrail of a bridge. Below, half-submerged in water, was a crumpled orange automobile with no rear windshield.

"Witnesses to the crash agree no one emerged from the vehicle after it broke through the guardrail. Even if any occupants survived the reported gunfire from a pursuing automobile, it's difficult to conceive of anyone surviving the plunge off the bridge. Many questions in the case remain unanswered. One policeman who asked to remain anonymous suggested competing crime bosses may have staged an old-fashioned execution . . ."

Roger fought to keep down his Chinese meal. *Sophie's dead? That organization killed her? And now they're blaming a gang of criminals?*

The news flowed on to economic growth in India, but Roger stopped listening. In shock, he pictured Sophie's face, the flowery scent of her perfume—then imagined the terrible, painful death she must have suffered when the mysterious organization attacked her. This time, her copilot hadn't been aboard to shoot back. Sophie had died alone.

Guilt washed over him. *I shouldn't have left her. I should've stayed no matter what.*

"Final boarding call for Flight 444 to Atlanta."

He stood up. Part of him wanted to walk away from the airport, to stay in Germany and personally beat the tar out of the people responsible for Sophie's death. He could already picture himself ringing Hans's scrawny neck. Then saner thoughts prevailed. He had nowhere to live, no idea how to get back to where he started that morning, and he stood on German territory. Here, the enemy held the best cards. Besides, Sophie had risked everything to get him to the United States. The least he could do was finish the trip and give her sacrifice some meaning.

For her sake, he must go. Roger stoically picked up his briefcase and joined the last few passengers at the gate. Imitating those ahead of him with a confidence he didn't feel, he strode down the carpeted walkway to the waiting airliner.

CHAPTER 32

Roger had yearned for nothing more than to be in the air again, to soar above the clouds and admire the earth from lofty heights. Now that it was happening, the horizons outside his miniature window had lost their appeal. Escaping and being airborne couldn't ease the pain of Sophie's death. He shouldn't have left her. With him, she might have stood a fighting chance.

"Are you feeling ill?" a voice asked in German.

Roger turned. Although the seat beside him—Sophie's—was empty, on the other side of it a gray-haired, grandmotherly type peered through thick glasses. She eyed him with concern, then placed her plump hand atop his.

"Pardon me for asking, but you look so pale. Is this your first time in an airplane?"

Under other circumstances Roger might have howled with laughter. This matron couldn't imagine the gutsy stunts Roger had performed in a cockpit. She suspected he was ill merely from sitting on this airborne bus?

"I'm fine. I've flown before. It's just been a long time."

"There's an airsickness bag in the seat pocket, if you need one."

"Thanks."

He jammed the miniscule airline pillow between his head and the window and closed his eyes. Roger felt in no mood for small talk. He didn't want to see the other passengers. He cared even less about the screens showing motion pictures to passengers wearing pitifully tiny headphones. The modern world had engulfed him too hard, too fast. He just wanted to block everything out.

The image of Sophie's smiling face materialized. His one and only friend—murdered for helping him. The fact that they hadn't loved each other did nothing to lessen the pain. She had cared—and paid the ultimate price.

God, is my life cursed? Or is this some sort of test? What's the use of staying young and healthy if it brings misery, especially to innocent people like Sophie?

Emotional and physical weariness descended over him. When sleep came, he yielded willingly, welcoming the oblivion.

◆   ◆   ◆

When Roger awoke, he clicked into full alertness. Something had altered. The cabin full of chattering passengers still surrounded him. They provided living evidence that his escape hadn't been just another dream. Then he realized what had startled him. It was the old sensation he'd nearly forgotten but could now feel in his gut—the aircraft was descending.

A crackly voice sounded overhead: "Ladies and gentlemen, we are now making our descent into Hartsfield-Jackson Atlanta International Airport. The temperature on the ground is six degrees Celsius, or about forty-four degrees Fahrenheit. The local time is 2:00 p.m. On behalf of the captain and flight crew, let me thank you once again for flying Lufthansa."

Mixed emotions wrestled for dominance. Although anger, remorse, and guilt concerning Sophie's death still churned inside him, outside his window for as far as his eye could see was land. His land. The United States of America.

The aircraft descended lower. A shudder and a hum surprised Roger before he realized what it must be: hydraulic landing gear. Through his window, he saw the aircraft was racing over a broad ribbon of concrete runway. Off in the distance fluttered an unexpected bit of color that captured his attention as nothing else could: a red, white, and blue banner snapping and flapping atop a flagpole.

Roger swallowed. Manly or no, tears welled in his eyes. *After all these years, I'm really back. Thank You, God—and Sophie.*

But what kind of country had he returned to? For whatever reason, old Kossler had fed him a bunch of malarkey. Sophie had said the war was over, that it had been over for years. How long? Two years? Twenty years? Was any portion of what Kossler shared true?

If he hoped to fit into twenty-first-century America, Roger needed answers. His first priority would be to get a fast overview of the war's real outcome in order to set his chronological bearings. But quietly. He remembered the object embedded in his arm. Part of his brain wanted to believe Hans had simply been trying to intimidate him into submission with his claim that they could find him anywhere on earth. After all, the thing was so small. It seemed absurd to believe they could actually find him, say, in the Sahara Desert, or Antartica, or on some Pacific island. Yet, here he was, looking like a young man when he should be in an old folks' home. He'd be foolish not to give grudging respect to their technology. Even if they couldn't use it to find him literally anywhere, it was still possible they could somehow hone in on him once they got in the area. They would be watching those endless news stories, like at the airport. He would have to lie low until he figured out his options.

One thing he couldn't do was tell anyone who he really was or how old. They'd lock him up as a lunatic. *And nobody, but nobody, is going to lock me up again. I'm through with cages forever! I'll die before I step into another one.*

In the Atlanta airport, he followed the other passengers shuffling along to the gray-and-pink carpeted Passport Control area. When the uniformed agent accepted Hans's passport and scrutinized it, Roger suppressed the urge to blurt, "That isn't me. That's the passport of a Nazi scientist. I commandeered it to escape back to the States."

Regardless of how much Roger longed to reassert his own name and nationality, this wasn't the time or place. Even in the 1940s, only a fool would show up at a border crossing and confess to a stolen passport. Add to that the insane-sounding story of the Methuselah Project, and his own countrymen would toss him into a booby hatch.

Playing the role of a returning tourist, Roger answered the agent's questions with a smile, as if he'd enjoyed a pleasant holiday in the old country.

"Have a good day," the agent replied, handing back the passport.

With no baggage except his briefcase, Roger slipped into the first men's room he saw to shave off the Hans-style goatee and mustache. He had to watch another man in order to coax water from the faucet with no handle. Liquid soap sufficed for shaving cream. Soon he was clean-shaven and feeling refreshed. Enough of imitating Hans. From now on, he would be Roger Greene, playing on his home field.

When he strolled out the airport's double-glass doors to the curb, he spotted a taxi. Roger walked over to the partially open window. "Hi. Take me into town?"

"Sure, *amigo*. Hop in. Where to?"

Roger climbed into the rear seat. He hoped his request wouldn't sound too abnormal. "Do you know where the nearest library is?"

"Library?" The cabbie scratched his head.

For half a second, Roger feared that libraries had become outmoded and been bulldozed. Then, in the rearview mirror he saw the cabbie's eyes brighten.

"You mean the one on Main Street, over in College Park?"

Relieved, Roger feigned knowledge of the place. "Yes. Take me there, please."

"No sweat, amigo. Five minutes away." The cabbie started his meter, and they were off. Along the way, the driver bobbed his head to noises blaring from the radio. The endlessly repeated beat and nonsense rhymes grated Roger's nerves, but he bit his tongue. For now he wanted to soak up American scenery. His first culture shock came at the library, when the cabbie announced the fare.

"Six dollars and fifty cents? I just wanted to ride in a taxi, not make a down payment on one."

"That's the fare, amigo."

Roger peeled off seven of the dollars he'd received in exchange for his Euros in the airport. He'd supposed five hundred dollars would last maybe a year. Gross miscalculation.

Behind the desk sat a woman with silver hair. In the manner of helpful librarians everywhere, she offered a polite smile. "May I help you?"

"Could you point me toward the history section? Specifically, military history. Anything about the war between America and Nazi Germany."

Oblivious to time, Roger pored over volume after volume, noting dates, maps, details concerning troop movements, everything leading up to D-Day in Europe and V-J Day in Japan. Particularly interesting were the accounts of a long-range fighter plane that had enabled American bombers to wing all over Germany under protective escort. He admired the photographs. *P-51 Mustangs, huh? That's one sleek-looking bird.*

By contrast, the accounts of an atom bomb that pulverized Nagasaki and Hiroshima in Japan flabbergasted him.

That Kossler . . . All those years, he was feeding me a pack of lies. And I swallowed it. Wasn't it bad enough keeping me imprisoned without duping—

In a flash, the truth illuminated Roger's understanding.

He was stringing me along for my own sake. He knew I'd go insane if I had no hope. He spun those tales as a life preserver.

The unexpected insight gave Roger a new appreciation for Kossler he'd never had while the scientist was alive. Compared to Hans, Kossler was practically a humanitarian.

Someone cleared her throat. "I'm sorry, but we're closing now," interrupted the woman from the checkout desk. "Actually you were so engrossed in your research we let you stay a little longer. Did you find everything you needed?"

Roger closed the volume. "Not everything. Enough for today, though. I have a special interest in the air war over Europe back in the 1940s."

"Have you checked the Eighth Air Force Museum in Pooler? I understand they offer both displays and extensive archival material."

"Pooler?"

She smiled. "Judging by your accent, you're not from around here. Pooler is just outside Savannah."

"You're right, I haven't been in Georgia very long. Thanks for the tip."

When Roger stepped outside, nighttime was descending. The temperature had dropped to somewhere in the thirties, he guessed, and the wind sliced through his shirt and ruffled his hair. Into his mind sprang two lines from a depressing French poem by Paul Verlaine he had translated back in the 1980s: *It rains in my heart, Like it rains on the town.* . . .

So much for his first day back in the States. Of course he hadn't expected a brass band or a welcoming committee, but he'd expected something—anything—more exhilarating than a jaunt to the library and frigid wind. Sophie had been his one link with reality. Without her, he was an aircraft with a busted rudder and no airfield to land on.

"Now what do I do? Saturday night with no date and no place to go."

The wind gusted again, harder this time. It felt like an icy blade knifing through the cotton shirt and khaki trousers Sophie had bought him. *Georgia might be on the verge of springtime, but winter isn't quite whipped.*

The flight jacket lay folded inside the briefcase. Should he put it on? He didn't want to attract attention, but it was his only protection from the cold. Organization or no, he'd look like an idiot standing outside in just shirtsleeves. He opened the briefcase and extracted the flight jacket. When he did, he again spotted the Bible tucked beneath it. The sight caused him to glance heavenward, where the first stars already glittered against the blackening dome. He stood and stared at their delicate twinkling. Truly the heavens declared the handiwork of God. How had he never realized that before his capture?

Lord, I have no idea where I'm headed or what to do. I'd appreciate it if You would guide my steps.

He slipped on the jacket and began walking. Now that he was aware of the pricey taxi fares, he didn't even consider this option. Better to find a motel or something if he didn't want to sleep on the street.

Clutching the briefcase, Roger wandered the streets for well over an hour. When he spotted a box truck with an open rear pulling away from a curb, he sprinted to catch up, then jumped into the back. Although he relished his newfound freedom to walk, the chilly wind had spoiled his first evening back. Also, his stomach was growling.

Could the sudden time difference explain the fuzzy feeling in his head? Who would've imagined flying straight from Frankfurt all the way to Atlanta in only ten hours?

Eventually the truck halted at an intersection. Across the street, Roger spotted an aging motel with a faded green-and-white sign: The Shamrock Paradise Inn. Next door glowed the sign for an equally run-down establishment pegged as Slick's Bar and Grill. *Shamrock Paradise Inn, eh? Is that a sign my luck is changing?*

Roger hopped off the truck and jogged toward the warmth of the motel. Inside, the woman behind the counter surprised him by not looking or sounding Irish at all. Instead, she appeared to hail from India or some other exotic land. She frowned when she learned he carried no identification.

"But I have cash. The sign says $29 a night, right?"

When he spread three crisp, ten-dollar bills on the counter, she brightened. "All right. I'll get your key."

In his room, Roger examined his surroundings. The wallpaper sported four-leaf clovers on a yellowing background. Appropriate. By the looks of things, this place just might be older than he.

After enjoying a luxuriously long and hot shower, Roger dressed and stepped back outside, where he walked next door to Slick's for supper. Despite the late hour, a boisterous crowd populated the bar and grill. Roger settled into the last empty booth in a corner. Even after so many decades overseas, he recognized Slick's as a greasy spoon. At least it would offer all-American grease.

"What'll it be, hon?" drawled a jeans-clad waitress with oily brunette hair. "We got a special on the BLT basket. Only five bucks."

"BLT? You mean you serve bacon, lettuce, and tomato sandwiches?" Just hearing those forgotten initials prompted Roger to salivate.

The waitress laughed and cracked her chewing gum. "Yeah, sure. You want just the sandwich, or the whole basket? Comes with fries and a Coke."

Roger savored the memory of bubbling, ice-cold Coca-Cola. "Give me the whole show."

When his meal arrived, Roger lost interest in watching Slick's other patrons and devoted his full attention to the BLT basket. With eyes closed, he relished the tantalizing American flavors dancing across his taste buds.

Ketchup, pickles, French fries, and Coca-Cola. Could freedom get better than this? With the next thought he answered his own question: It sure could. An airplane of his own to fly whenever he wanted would make the picture perfect.

A female voice interrupted his reverie: "Hey, handsome."

Roger opened his eyes to find a twenty-something brunette with large, silver circles for earrings standing beside his table. Despite the dropping temperature outside, she wore a low-cut yellow blouse over a scandalously short plaid skirt.

"Mind if I sit down?"

Roger swallowed the bite of sandwich in his mouth and hurried to stand. "Please do."

A brilliant white row of teeth that looked too large to be real illuminated her face as she slid into the seat across from his. She didn't bother to close her mouth while chewing her gum. "Ain't you the gentleman? Ya know, I been watchin' you from the other side of the room. You're cute."

Roger hesitated. What did modern etiquette demand he say after such a statement? Then again, he would've been unsure how to respond even in 1943. "Uh, thanks. So are you."

The woman smiled a mouthful of teeth. "I'm Ginger. Ya know, I'm not the pushy type, but if I'm gonna have fun, I'd rather do it with a good-lookin' one like you. Know what I mean?"

Words fled from Roger's mind. Was she suggesting . . .

Ginger reached for his paper napkin and jotted a series of numbers with an ink pen. "This is my cell number. You can reach me there. Day or night, handsome."

Roger glanced at the napkin, then back at Ginger's coy smile. "Let me get this straight. This is your cell number? Your very own cell?"

"None other, sugar." She stood and ran a forefinger along his cheek. "Don't spread it around, 'kay? I don't share my cell with just any man." She winked and sashayed away.

Incredulous, Roger stared again at the napkin. Undoubtedly Miss Ginger was the most blatant floozy he'd ever encountered, but her brazen invitation threw a negative light on the whole nation. *My word, what has the United States come to? Female convicts out roaming the streets, inviting men to spend the night in their prison cell? How does she do it, buy off the warden?* Judging by the length of the number, the Atlanta prison must be gargantuan. He wadded the napkin in his fist. The whole encounter sickened him. He left his fries unfinished.

Roger paid for his meal and retraced his steps to the Shamrock Paradise Inn. When he unlocked the door to his room, the temperature inside felt surprisingly cool—much chillier than when he'd left. Then he noticed the moss-green curtain fluttering in the breeze. Behind it, the window stood wide open. He glanced left and right for the briefcase—gone.

"Robbed!" Roger wheeled and gave the bed a vicious kick. "What a stinking way to end my first day back in the States. Why didn't I think of checking the window lock?"

Of course, in his old life Roger would've been savvy enough to lock up his belongings, but he was out of practice. He paused to calculate his losses. The briefcase contained Hans's passport. He hadn't planned on using it again for traveling, but it would've helped to corroborate his story of being held prisoner in Germany. Also gone was the Bible that had buoyed up his spirits through dreary years in the Methuselah bunker. He could buy a replacement, but he hated to lose the one in which he'd underlined so many passages and jotted personal notes in the margins.

About half of his five hundred dollars had been in the briefcase too. If only he hadn't asked for small denominations of bills, they wouldn't have formed such a thick wad when he folded them. Then he would have kept all the money on him. He emptied his pockets. "Two hundred thirty-nine bucks left. Nowadays that's chickenfeed."

From the pocket of his jacket, he extracted the folded $10 bill he'd received from his wingman Walt Crippen decades earlier. Should he add it to his little stash? "Nope. I'm not spending you. Ten bucks might not be worth much anymore, but you're one souvenir I'm not giving up."

After locking the window, Roger consoled himself with another long, hot shower. After decades of sponge-washing from a sink, he'd never take showers for granted again. When at last he'd had his fill of cascading streams of steaming water, he toweled himself dry and then crawled into bed.

What did the future hold? He wished he knew. In the meantime, he wasn't so sure he was going to like the changes in his homeland. And poor Sophie. He'd planned on exploring America with her.

I never even got to tell her goodbye.

There was no dodging the truth. If not for him, she would be alive today. Resolution stiffened Roger's heart: no matter who he made friends with, he must not reveal anything that would endanger anyone else.

CHAPTER 33

SATURDAY EVENING, MARCH 7, 2015

KRESCHATIK STREET, KIEV, UKRAINE

"*Gott im Himmel,* Jaeger!" exclaimed the middle-aged man in the pin-striped navy suit. He stepped from behind his polished mahogany desk and paced toward the bookcases lining the far wall. "What an abomi-nable case of bungling. Do you realize what an unprecedented security breach this whole affair presents? Has the organization inducted a crew of imbeciles to staff our protective services?"

"I agree about a security breach, Herr General," Jaeger said. "But I object to the accusation of idiots in the security section. You might recall how I opposed keeping Greene alive after his first escape attempt? Every cage has its weak points. It was only a matter of time before a clever mind would exploit a weakness and flee."

The man in the pinstriped suit whirled and pointed an accusing fin-ger. "This wasn't a simple escape! Greene had help—from a woman who passed your own fidelity test with no hint of suspicion. Now Greene is gone, and the woman's bullet-riddled automobile was broadcast on tele-vision. Meanwhile, the American boards an airliner and slips out of Germany like a common tourist? I want the men who let him get away punished—in the most permanent manner possible."

"I understand. It will be done, Herr General."

"See that it is. Preferably before more tongues wag. Now what is the latest intelligence on the American?"

"Fortunately our people had enough foresight to order a locator implant for him. Elimination was my recommendation after his first escape, but the implant became my backup—"

The general in the civilian suit slashed the air with his hand. "*Ach*, cut the praise for your hindsight and foresight, Jaeger. Get to the point. Can we determine Greene's location? Or at least in which direction he's headed?"

"Absolutely. To the United States. To Atlanta, to be exact. Once my people realized he was at the airport, they penetrated the major airlines' computers and scanned the passenger names. They got a hit. Hans Heinkel. He will be landing soon."

The senior man looked toward the ceiling and took a deep breath before speaking. "He's in the United States? Already? Please tell me we have an elimination agent based somewhere near Atlanta."

Jaeger hedged. "Yes and no. As it turns out, we do have an elimination agent near Atlanta. A no-nonsense businessman who goes by the code name of the Jeweler."

"That's right! Mueller the Jeweler. Top security clearance, and he's one man who has never fumbled an assignment." The general's words provided a verbal cuff at Jaeger. "His eyesight isn't what it used to be. I hear Mueller has taken to tracking his quarry with binoculars, but no matter. Have you gotten in touch with him?"

Jaeger cleared his throat. "Unfortunately Mueller is not in the United States at the moment. He fancies himself a big-game hunter and is currently on holiday. He's on safari in Namibia."

"Namibia?"

"In the south of Africa. The Jeweler is somewhere in the bush."

The thick eyebrows sagged, and the general grimaced as if in physical pain. "Raw sewage would smell sweeter than the news you bring, Jaeger. Have we no other elimination agents who can reach Greene and terminate him before he compromises us? No one at all?"

"At this moment, we have only one organization member in that immediate vicinity. A Fräulein named Katarina Mueller. She is the Jeweler's niece. Unfortunately she is not yet fully trained or indoctrinated."

"Please don't tell me she's an unrefined Kadett."

"No, Herr General, she's not a Kadett. But she's not much higher. She recently received the promotion from Kadett to Leutnant."

With a sigh, the general closed his eyes in an expression that, under other circumstances, might have signified the death of a comrade. He shook his head, settled himself into his espresso-brown executive chair of full-grain leather, and clasped his hands together with both elbows propped on the desktop. "Recommendations?"

Jaeger sank onto the high-backed chair in front of his superior's desk. "Here is my proposition. Obviously a freshly promoted Leutnant is unsuitable for a termination assignment. Most likely she would balk and become a security risk herself. But perhaps we can still put her to use until we maneuver an experienced eliminator into position."

"Put her to use?"

Jaeger spoke quickly but with passion: "Being a newly promoted Leutnant, Katarina Mueller will expect field training at any time. If her uncle hasn't revealed the nature of typical training assignments— and there's no reason to believe he broke protocol—Fräulein Mueller will suspect nothing if we confer on her a mission that is extremely unorthodox."

"Go on."

"Imagine that we transmit Greene's photograph and approximate coordinates to the Fräulein. We could explain that her field exercise is to locate and observe the subject, whom we pretend is an organization member simply acting out a role for the sake of her field exercises. Obviously her uncle possesses organization-issued equipment, including a Pigeon that can trace Greene's GPS implant. The Jeweler's most recent reports say he has trained her in the efficient use of basic equipment. As often as prudent, she should report Greene's location and activities to us. That way, when we move an elimination agent into position, he'll have full knowledge of Greene's movements. He'll know whether he needs to liquidate others too. That would contain the damage. Case closed."

The general squinted at Jaeger, as if so doing would aid in seeing the recommendation more clearly. "What if this Katarina Mueller communicates with Greene, even accidentally? If we tell her that he's simply an organization controller playing a role, won't contact with him contaminate the scenario you propose? The man might even confide in her."

"Not a problem, Herr General. We simply fabricate a cover story and feed it to her in advance. For example, we could advise her that our man might pretend to be a person of some importance. Or we could suggest he is at liberty to concoct a preposterous cover story for the sake of her training. As long as we tell her to expect something possibly bizarre, she will trail him carefully but will not believe a word, even if he babbles the absolute truth about himself and Methuselah."

The general's eyes narrowed even more, but a devilish grin played about his lips. He stroked his chin. "Yes. If she believes the whole episode to be a fantasy fabricated and controlled by the organization, she will suspect nothing. Excellent, Jaeger. Who knows? Maybe we should consider such exercises for future Leutnants. It would add an intriguing dimension to their training."

Pleased with the general's praise, Jaeger parted his thin lips, revealing two rows of slightly yellowed teeth. "Then you authorize the order?"

"*Ja.* Make the assignment, exactly as discussed. I can't stress enough that Katarina Mueller must suspect nothing. She's young in our ways. Her fidelity is untested. Meanwhile, we need to position a man capable of removing Greene. Where's the Griffin?"

"The Griffin? He just arrived in Cork, Ireland. He's on another assign—"

"Cancel the other assignment! This Greene muddle just became top priority. Get the Griffin on a plane to Atlanta immediately. Don't wait for a commercial airline. Requisition one of our Lear jets. The Griffin can return to Cork and hit the other target after Greene is out of the picture."

Jaeger stood. "Right away, sir."

"One more thing, Jaeger. I want to oversee this Greene affair personally. Forward copies of all reports directly to my attention. Especially the final notation—the one in which you describe the details of Captain Greene's untimely demise."

"As you wish, General Wolf." Jaeger strode across the wine-colored carpet and paused at the oaken door. When the general depressed a button on his desktop, a buzz sounded. Jaeger twisted the handle and exited, shutting the door behind him.

Once again, General Wolf sucked in a deep breath, which he exhaled slowly. Jaeger's scheme sounded plausible, the best course under foul circumstances. Still, it was a shame to shut down Methuselah. He'd dreamed of its eventual success ever since his grandfather had briefed him on the project. Even though the team hadn't yet achieved its goal, they had ruled out thousands of variations, thus advancing the Methuselah Project that much closer to a breakthrough. Of course, not every officer in the organization knew of Methuselah, but each one who did had shared his hope the procedure would be rediscovered and perfected during his own lifetime.

The general tilted back in his chair. "To live a thousand years," he murmured aloud. "What would it be like?"

On impulse, he rose and strode to the collage of photographs decorating one of his office's four walls. There he admired the portrait of his grandfather as a younger man, resplendent in his spotless SS uniform, the left arm cocked just enough to brandish the proud Viking cuff title on his tunic's sleeve. Although only black-and-white, the photograph still conveyed some of the ice-blue eye color so common among the Wolf family.

As he'd often done before, the general pictured a cadre of comrades who lived without graying, who manipulated politics, industries, international banks, the media, public opinion . . . At first, they might have to assume new identities every few decades, but a corps of Methuselah leaders could literally rule the world without the world realizing it.

General Wolf returned to his chair and swiveled to open the doors of the liquor cabinet behind it. His hand hesitated in front of the old bottle of cognac his cousin had given to congratulate him on the promotion to general. Certainly tempting, but no. He would save that bottle for the celebration after Greene became history. Instead, he selected the newer bottle he himself had purchased in Bordeaux and poured a glass. As always, before sipping he relished the combined aromas of warm caramel, dried apple, cocoa, and spice. He tipped the glass to his lips and savored its mellow richness on his tongue.

Might it be possible to continue Methuselah even after Greene was dispatched? He would decide later, after he could ascertain the full extent of the damage. For the moment, though, so many foolish blunders rendered clear concentration difficult.

He swallowed the silky-smooth blend of spirits. *Perhaps the experiment can proceed without him. I'll be able to think more clearly once Captain Greene is dead.*

CHAPTER 34

Stepping up to the full-length mirror, Katherine repositioned her hair on her shoulders. Satisfied, she stepped back again to take in the whole effect.

Not bad. The extra volume the stylist had given her hair really looked good. Who knew? Maybe she and Robyn would bump into a couple of handsome bachelors, either at the cinema or afterward, while they sipped their traditional cappuccinos at Panera Bread. The image of Jason Carmichael came to mind. No, she didn't want to see that face again. She would share that misadventure with Robyn tonight. It should provide a laugh while proving that Katherine had made strides against codependence.

The thought of good-looking men resurrected the memory of the blond twins she'd observed at her promotion ceremony back in Tampa. Their Hollywood-quality cheekbones and dimples remained etched in her memory, and their higher ranking in the organization promised intelligence. Unlike her former karate sensei, Frank Lawson, those two were probably proficient at conversation. Sadly, though, neither man had requested her name or phone number. They hadn't taken notice of her at all. Would she meet them at some future ceremony?

Keep your hook in the water, girl. The ocean is full of fish, and Saturday night is prime time for fishing. She regarded her reflection again. Sure, the ocean teemed with fish, but maybe they spotted something unattractive about her bait? No woman could see herself through others' eyes. Did those few freckles turn men away?

A digitized version of the Beatles' classic "I Want to Hold Your Hand" broke the silence. Katherine reached for her cell phone. Probably Robyn calling to say she was running late. "Hello?"

"Katherine Mueller?" The caller pronounced her name with zero trace of the Southern twang she normally heard from Georgians. The voice sounded European, similar to Uncle Kurt's.

"Yes. What can I do for you?"

"My organization has been intending to contact you."

The caller placed extra emphasis on the word *organization*. No doubt about the origin now.

Field exercises. Please don't let them start tonight, not before the movie.

"Now that we are sure you are home, we are dispatching an electronic communiqué to you. We know you've been anxiously awaiting field training. The exercise begins now, this minute. I suggest you check the message and start your assignment without delay."

"This minute? But I had plans for tonight. I was about to—"

"Miss Mueller, I cannot make up your mind for you. But part of the exercise is to assess your resourcefulness, to gauge your creativity and your ability to adapt to shifting challenges. If you hope to rise within our ranks, you might want to postpone your personal plans until a later date."

Katherine forced herself not to sigh. A groan might even cost valuable points on the evaluation. "Okay. I'm on it. I'll check my e-mail right away."

"Excellent. I'll inform my superiors you are beginning the hunt."

"The hunt?"

"Read the communiqué. It explains everything."

The line went dead. Peeved at the infringement on her personal time, Katherine pushed open the carved ebony doors of Uncle Kurt's study and tapped the keyboard of his computer. Within moments she was reading the incoming message from an address she'd never seen before.

When she finished wading through the screen of information about her quarry for the exercise, Katherine clicked open the attachment and studied the subject's photos. The man in the first image wasn't smiling. He looked resentful, almost rebellious, with his chin tipped up a bit, accentuating a strong jawline. In the next photo, the man sported a full beard and mustache, but something about his eyes caught her attention. Their independent, defiant glint struck a harmonious chord inside her. This man bore an expression she'd never seen on an HO member.

"You're a handsome devil, aren't you?" she said to the photo. "I suppose they could give me worse jobs than tracking down a gorgeous guy with great eyes." Of course, the chase would be more fun if it were the other way around.

The unexpected twist of events brought a smile to her lips. "Okay, girl, you've been wanting a handsome, intelligent guy that Uncle Kurt's never mentioned. Since this man's in the HO, I can spread my wings a little, and even Uncle won't have an excuse to object."

Katherine reread the final lines of the message: "The quarry's true name is irrelevant. In previous field exercises, this HO member has occasionally assumed false identities, sometimes American, sometimes German or other nationalities. Part of your assignment in locating and trailing him will be to learn his current alias and to penetrate any disguises he may use for lodging, transportation, etc. Create a written log detailing all persons with whom the individual has significant contact. All organization-issued equipment in your uncle's keeping is at your disposal for this assignment. Good luck."

Katherine ran her fingers through her hair as she often did when pondering unforeseen developments. The assignment struck her as peculiar, but not particularly challenging unless the guy could sprout wings and fly. The HO expected her to employ creativity and resourcefulness. She must keep close tabs on this man's movements and report all significant activities and contacts.

I'm no state trooper. Without a badge, I'll need a cover story before I poke around asking people if they've seen the man in the photo. Katherine ran various scenarios through her mind while her fingers tapped out a text message, telling Robyn she'd be late. *I know. If I say he got my sister pregnant and then ran out without paying child support, that would provide a plausible backstory. And a sympathetic one. Who wouldn't want to help out in that situation? It's perfect!*

Slipping into her scrutinizing-editor mode, she reviewed the instructions, noting both the overt mandates as well as the liberties left to her discretion. The seed of a plan took root. "Okay, Mystery Man, the hunt is on. Ready or not, here I come."

CHAPTER 35

The next morning when Roger stepped out of the Shamrock Paradise's cramped lobby, the dreary sky reflected his mood. Not only had the foreign woman at the check-in desk been unsympathetic about his stolen money, she'd even acted as if his own carelessness was to blame.

Forget her. You'll never see her again. Just like you'll never see that dough again.

His sense of justice still wished he could submit a police report. That option was out. Complaints to the police would involve questions and answers he didn't want to give. Not yet, anyway. Whoever had sneaked through his window last night had found the perfect victim: a man who didn't dare call the cops. He zipped up his flight jacket to block out the morning chill. March or not, winter definitely hadn't removed its fingers from Atlanta.

Well, Greene, where to now? You're kind of stuck, aren't you, old boy? In the back of his mind, he clung to a vague desire to return to Indiana, to see again the west Indianapolis area and the nearby town of Plainfield, where he'd spent his teenage years. That yearning made little sense. Most people he'd known would likely be either dead or so elderly he wouldn't recognize them. Still, his roots lay there. Was it possible some elderly geezer back in Hendricks County might remember him—and help him?

How could he get to Indianapolis from Georgia? He didn't want to sacrifice a big chunk of his money on a train ticket, but neither did he want to wear out his shoe leather hiking all the way. He needed to earn some cash until he could figure out where to go, what to do. Underlying everything else lingered the number one question: how could he regain his identity and lead a normal life again?

I can't just strut into the War Department in Washington and shout, "Hey, everybody, it's me, Captain Roger Greene. I just flew home from World War II!"

He lifted his eyes to the sunny sky. *Sorry, God. I didn't read any of the Bible today. You know why—it got stolen too. So if You're paying any attention to this grounded airman, please help me to take the right next step. I'm just playing this by ear.*

The quandary about transportation drew his attention to a taxi parked up the street. Instead of the male driver Roger expected, the figure reading a newspaper behind the steering wheel looked like a woman. Female cabbies? That was a new sight. But it was just one more in a string of countless new sights and sounds. On a whim, he stepped off the curb and strode straight toward the cab.

Noticing his approach, the driver cracked her window. "Need a ride, sir?"

A double surprise: Not only was the cabbie a girl, she was an attractive one. Something about her honey-colored hair and the sprinkling of freckles across her nose struck him as refreshing. Here was the kind of American gal he'd pictured whenever he dreamed of coming back to America. She seemed pure, more wholesome, than the women he'd encountered at Slick's.

"No, can't afford it. I'm kind of new around here. I figured, who would know the area better than a taxi driver? Okay if I ask for some advice?"

She set aside the newspaper. "Okay, shoot. Tell you what, I won't even start the meter."

He flashed a grin. "Great. My motel room was robbed last night. I'm short on cash right now."

The cute smile that had blossomed on her face wilted. "Are you serious?"

"Unfortunately, yes. So my first question is, do you have any suggestions on where an out-of-town guy could get some money?"

She jerked her thumb backward. "There's a bank a few blocks up the street. Too early to be open, but it should have an ATM."

The initials ATM meant nothing to Roger, but thank goodness people still used banks. "I don't mean withdrawing money from an account. I mean, would you happen to know of anyplace that needs temporary help? Maybe a warehouse? I'll dig ditches if I have to. I just need to earn enough money to get back home."

The woman in the taxi looked him straight in the eyes, as if deeply interested. She shook her head slowly. "I don't know of anyplace hiring. To tell the truth, I'm not even a full-time driver. I'm just moonlighting to make both ends meet."

"Oh. I see. Well, sorry to bother you." He turned to leave.

"Say, wait a second. I just had a thought. Have you eaten breakfast?"

"No."

She practically pinned him in place with her penetrating gaze. "Okay, here's an offer for you. Even if I do need the income, taxi driving isn't the safest career, especially for a woman. You strike me as a decent guy. How about I buy you a couple breakfast biscuits and a coffee if you'll ride shotgun for a while and make sure my male passengers behave? It won't help you much, but it'll give you a warm meal while you decide where you want to go."

"You're on. I'm not likely to get a better offer in the next few minutes."

"All right, then. Hop in."

A few blocks later, the female cabbie, who introduced herself as Katherine, surprised Roger when she wheeled behind a building, then began talking out her window.

"Still want the breakfast biscuits? Or maybe some other meal?"

"Uh, biscuits and coffee will be fine."

"Breakfast combo #2," Katherine said to the air.

A disembodied female voice told her to pull around to a window. Roger watched with interest as the female cabbie drove around the building and handed several dollars to a young girl in a window. Seconds later, Katherine passed Roger his biscuits and coffee.

"Cream or sugar for your coffee?"

"Uh, no thanks. I'll drink it black."

Katherine handed him a cup and a paper sack, then pulled away and maneuvered back onto the street. "Bon appétit!"

"Thank you." Roger unwrapped a biscuit stuffed with sausage, still amazed at how quickly a hot meal had appeared in a window. Maintaining a personal tradition he'd begun years earlier, he interlaced his fingers, bowed his head, and shot a mental prayer of thanks heavenward. He opened his eyes in time to see Katherine glance away.

She braked for a traffic light. "That's nice. Sort of quaint."

"What, the food?"

"No. Your praying before eating. Except on TV, I don't think I've ever seen anybody do that."

He swallowed the bite he'd been chewing. "Maybe the world would be a better place if everyone took time to thank God for things they have, instead of coveting everything they don't."

She studied him with a look Roger couldn't interpret. "Maybe so."

◆　◆　◆

For the next several hours, Katherine and the man she'd accepted as a fellow member of the Heritage Organization wove in and out of Atlanta's traffic. She halted the cab whenever a pedestrian waved a hand to flag her down, then delivered the passenger to the requested address. Whenever customers occupied the rear seat, the man who had introduced himself as Roger Greene studied Katherine's *Atlanta Journal-Constitution*. By all appearances he seemed more engrossed in the day's headlines than in her—which seemed odd, since she knew she was the main reason he was in town. Whenever the rear seat was empty, she exchanged small talk with the clandestine HO man.

Katherine had hoped her subterfuge of borrowing a cab to trail the quarry in this field exercise would score points for creativity with the HO. But when she'd seen the unexpected opportunity to invite the man to "help" by riding shotgun, she'd given the idea a try. For this morning, at least, she would have no trouble at all trailing her target—he was seated only two feet away.

But what now? Her instructions were to note anyone with whom the HO man interacted. But Roger—or whatever his real name was—appeared in no hurry to contact anyone whatsoever. In fact, if not for the organization photos, she might have doubted he was the right man. So from time to time between customers, Katherine subtly tried to pry information from him, or at least about the person he pretended to be. "Have you been in town very long?" or "Do you have family in Atlanta?" She posed questions broad enough to sound genuine, but which might provide clues concerning how to continue this peculiar game.

As expected, Roger answered her queries vaguely, not revealing specific details, but also speaking in a casual way that wouldn't arouse suspicion to the average listener. Occasionally he fired a question back. Under normal circumstances, his responses might pass as polite conversation. But she recognized his questions as providing a subterfuge. The man tactfully diverted attention away from himself by posing questions in return. The game of cat and mouse all over again, but this time with words.

By lunchtime, Katherine had tired of this apparently purposeless sport. Was she missing an unspoken point to the exercise? Instead of probing about Roger, she switched gears and talked about recent movies she and Robyn had seen. How strange that each time Roger responded that, no, he hadn't yet seen the film she mentioned. She chuckled. "You must not watch many movies."

A grin began to form before he turned his head toward his window. "Let's just say I've been concentrating more on reading lately."

Books. Bingo. A subject close to her editor's heart. "Really? Tell me what you've been reading."

"Mostly the classics. For instance . . ."

Katherine was pleasantly astonished when her passenger began dissecting the plots of classic novels, many of which she'd read. Books like *Jane Eyre*, *Crime and Punishment*, *The Count of Monte Cristo*, *Don Quixote*, *Silas Marner*, *Tess of the d'Urbervilles*, and *The Invisible Man* all fell within his repertoire. As he discussed them, his demeanor lost its guarded tone. His eyes actually lit up. Like no literature professor she'd ever heard, Roger launched into fascinating recollections of the characters, subplots, and techniques each author had used to lure readers deeper into the stories. There was no trace of Frank Lawson in this HO man. Quite the opposite, she found him highly articulate—and intriguing. The fact that he was even more handsome in person than in his photos didn't hurt, either.

"Excuse me," she interrupted. "You look too young to be a college prof, but I've never met a man my age who knows so much about classic literature. Are you a graduate assistant or something?"

The question elicited another amused smile. "What makes you think I'm your age?"

"Well, maybe not exactly my age, but close enough. I mean, you can't be in your thirties, right?"

A playful twinkle gleamed in his eye. "Nope, I'm definitely not in my thirties. But to answer your first question, no, I never attended college. I've just read tons of books. Many of them more than once."

She braked for a traffic light. "I'm getting a whole new perspective on you. When I picked you up outside that seedy motel, I never expected such a well-educated Yankee gentleman."

After this ridiculous field exercise ended, might there be a chance of getting better acquainted with him?

"I guarantee that's the first time I've stayed in a lowlife place like Shamrock Paradise Inn. I'm down on my luck, but I'm planning to bounce back. Once I find a job and earn a few bucks, I'll be on my way."

"Will work for food, huh? Right now, good jobs are as scarce as hen's teeth."

He was parroting some sort of script written by the HO. So how could she manipulate this job angle he kept mentioning? A gear clicked. Would he change his tune if she found him a job? "Roger, you look like you have a good build."

Even before his lips curved up, she realized her Freudian slip. She ignored the warm glow in her cheeks.

"I mean, you're in good health, right? A strong back? You can do physical labor?"

"My health? It's fine. Why?"

"Is there any reason you need to stay in Atlanta, or could you work in another city?" She didn't know how far to push this training-exercise business, but Roger—or whoever he was—fascinated her. She resolved to stay in contact while fulfilling the organization's requirements.

Evidently caught off guard by the flurry of questions, her passenger shook his head with raised eyebrows. "No, I don't have any ties to Atlanta. I just don't have money for traveling back to Indianapolis."

"I've got this friend named Woody, short for Woodrow, which he can't stand. He dropped out of the University of Georgia to start his own tree-trimming business in Savannah. He once told me he's always on the lookout for men with strong backs and a will to work. If you're interested, Woody would be happier than a tornado in a trailer park. It wouldn't be a cushy desk job, and there won't be any health insurance or benefits, but it would be good pay. Cash at the end of each workday."

Instead of grappling for excuses to decline as she half expected, Roger sat up straight. "That sounds perfect."

Perfect? Really? What was he up to now? Okay, two could play this charade as well as one. She pulled her cell phone from her purse and scrolled to the correct number while steering the taxi with her left knee. Within moments she had Woody on the line and learned he definitely could use a worker.

"Terrific. He'll be there tomorrow morning." She shoved the phone back into her purse.

"Whoa, I don't have any way to get to Savannah."

Still feeling impulsive, she nodded. "Oh, yes you do. This will be off the meter, my good deed for the week. If you'll agree to split the cost of gas with me, I'll trust you to pay me back out of your wages from Woody. Besides, I've been wishing for an excuse to get out of Atlanta. For me, cruisin' down to Savannah will be a nice little escape."

He flashed a smile she was beginning to recognize as his trademark. "Believe me, I understand. Nothing in the world is quite so satisfying as a nice escape. I can't thank you enough."

"Then it's all settled. We can hit the highway at the end of the workday. But right now, I'm famished. Let's grab a quick lunch." She switched on her turn signal and wheeled into a parking lot. "I'm craving a Big Mac combo with Dr Pepper. How about you?"

Roger paused, giving her a stare. "You know, Katherine, there's a certain kind of hot sandwich I've been dying to eat for a long time. Is there any chance this restaurant might serve hamburgers?"

Now it was Katherine's turn to stare blankly into his earnest-looking eyes. Then she exploded with laughter. "You crack me up. Yes, I'm pretty sure we can rustle up a hamburger at McDonald's!"

CHAPTER 36

The next morning, Katherine was still toweling her damp hair when, for the fifth time, she paused to part the curtain of her Budget Inn window. This time Roger was not only awake but outside the cab and stretching. She giggled when he began a series of old-fashioned jumping jacks right in the parking lot. *If it was me who slept in the car, I'd need more than jumping jacks to work the kinks out of my back.*

Katherine tossed away the towel and proceeded to brush her hair, which had lost most of its waves and hung nearly straight. She reflected back on the previous night's drive down from Atlanta. By this morning's light, the memory seemed bizarre. Almost surreal.

She hadn't intended for the mention of a hotel to sound suggestive, but when she could barely keep her eyes open on the interstate, she'd had to confess she couldn't stay awake all the way to Woody's place. It had been either stop and get a room, or risk falling asleep at the wheel. Based on previous experience with wolves in men's clothing, she'd expected this organization man to try finagling his way into the room, if not her bed. If he had, she would've protested, volunteered to pay for a second room, whatever. Instead, he'd simply asked to borrow the second pillow so he could sleep in the car. Case closed. No chance for her to flaunt Victorian principles.

"I'm afraid that seat won't be very cozy." She'd surprised herself by uttering the words.

"I've slept in worse places." Then he'd disappeared out the door and climbed into the taxi for the night.

The memory left her—what? Wishing he'd expressed at least a hint of carnal lust for her, some romantic interest? She couldn't resist wondering how his arms would feel around her waist. Maybe her freckles turned him off. She yanked the brush through her hair. Then again, this trip wasn't real life.

Perhaps Roger, the Yankee gentleman, was a set-up specially designed to make her interested in a relationship with her dream guy so she'd let down her guard and make some kind of mistake. In reality Roger was probably some boring HO banker. She let out a puff of air. The point of this whole charade wasn't to find a date.

The HO had set into motion some sort of field exercise to assess her strengths and weaknesses. That's the only reason she'd dared to drive an unknown male to Savannah in the first place. But where on earth was this escapade headed? Instead of trailing so-called Roger Greene and keeping tabs on him, she'd ended up chauffeuring him and then offering him a job—which he'd accepted?

"What can the HO possibly see in this exercise?" she asked her reflection.

She unhooked the hair dryer from its cradle beside the sink and caressed her locks with warm air from the Low setting to avoid split ends.

True, Roger showed intelligence and owned a dazzling smile. He'd also been a perfect gentleman. Other than Uncle Kurt, she couldn't remember the last man who had held the door for her and stood when she did.

On the other hand, he could irritate her. Like why did he pay such rapt attention to how she drove? Surely the organization didn't award or sub-tract points for driving habits? Good grief, she wasn't a sixteen-year-old taking a driver's test.

"And another thing." She turned off the hair dryer and waved it at her reflection. "That antique military jacket . . . is it supposed to be some kind of puzzle piece to figure out? He's got to be wearing that old thing for a reason."

Oh, great. The organization. They'd told her to check in when prudent, but she'd crawled into bed and forgotten. That probably cost her some points.

After punching the long-distance telephone number into her cell phone, she heard a male voice. "Yes?"

"This is Katherine Mueller. I'm on training exercises. Reporting in that I have had my quarry under observation for nearly twenty-four hours. The subject has been in contact with me, but he hasn't attempted communication with anyone else during this time."

Even as she spoke the words, she realized they might not be accurate. After all, Greene could have sneaked out of the car during the night, and she wouldn't have known it.

The voice didn't question her statement. "Understood. Another organization member will rendezvous today. He will take over the case from there." Click.

What on earth? What was there to "take over"? Besides, how could another HO member meet up since she hadn't even mentioned her location? Oh, of course. The same way she found Roger in the first place. The locator chip. He must carry it in a pocket, maybe in that old jacket.

A knock on the motel door interrupted her musings. Katherine donned the oatmeal-colored sweater Uncle Kurt had brought her from Ireland and opened the door. Outside stood Roger, looking well-rested and cheerful as ever.

"Good morning. Okay if I wash up?"

"Of course." She stepped aside and let him enter, noting that even first thing in the morning Roger Greene cut an impressive profile of masculine good looks and physical fitness. She swallowed. Unlike many men, however, he didn't behave as though he realized it.

◆   ◆   ◆

Before long, the two had finished breakfast at a nearby Waffle House and were back on Interstate 16. Roger sneaked a look at Katherine. In the restaurant she'd barely touched her fried eggs and hash browns. A quieter mood had settled over his benefactor this morning. *She's thinking something she's not saying. I guess that makes two of us.*

"Much farther to your friend Woody's?"

"We'll hit I-95 soon. From there we head north. He lives just outside of Savannah."

He nodded, then resumed staring at the passing scenery. A large airplane glided overhead, apparently descending for a landing. He craned his neck to study this modern flying behemoth. Must be an airport nearby. When he noticed Katherine wordlessly observing him, he leaned back, then froze.

"Stop the car!"

"What? Are you going to be sick?"

"Just stop. Please!"

She angled the taxi onto the asphalt shoulder and braked to a halt.

He pointed. "Katherine, that sign . . ."

She followed his eyes and read aloud the brown-and-white road sign: "'Mighty Eighth Air Force Heritage Museum and Memorial Garden, Exit 102.' So what?"

"The Eighth Air Force . . ." This must be the same museum the librarian back in Atlanta had mentioned. He hadn't realized they were heading anywhere near it.

"Doesn't mean a thing to me," she remarked. "None of my family was in the military. Or if they were, no one admitted it. My family lived in Germany back then."

Roger stiffened. He studied her in a new light. *This cute southern girl is German?*

"I still don't get what's so fascinating about the sign. Did you serve in the Air Force?"

Of course, her branch of Germans wouldn't be the same as those he'd encountered in captivity. Besides, for her the war must be ancient history. He relaxed and nodded. "Yeah. A long time ago."

"Aw, it couldn't have been all that long ago. You're what, about twenty-three, twenty-four?"

He couldn't restrain the smile that grew on his face. "You're a good guesser."

"Were you ground crew, an air-traffic controller, or what?"

He hesitated. How much more could he reveal safely?

"A pilot."

"Okay, mystery man, I can see you're hiding something. But I've decided one thing: you're no chainsaw massacre freak or anything like that. Tell you what, if that museum strikes you as so breathtaking, I can drive you there, if you want. It's early, but they might be unlocking the door about now."

Her suggestion lifted his spirits like a firm wind under an airplane's wings. "Could you? I mean, I already owe you for the ride and meals. But if you have the time before going to Woody's, that would be swell."

She laughed. "It would be *swell*?"

Roger searched her face for a clue to the joke.

"Sorry. It's just that I haven't heard anyone say that word in real life. You might be a brave military vet, but sometimes you talk like Beaver Cleaver. Okay, let's go check out the museum, then we'll hightail it to Woody's place. We need to get you working so you can pay me back!"

✦   ✦   ✦

When Roger stepped out of the taxi, he couldn't stop staring at the museum's white exterior. Would anything inside give closure to the life he'd left behind? Behind him, Katherine was saying something, probably idle chitchat. At the moment, the building before him commanded his full attention. The glass doors practically beckoned.

Tall, slender sentries, a dozen flagpoles stood vigil out front. Atop each fluttered a blue flag bearing a golden numeral "8" with wings sprouting from each side. Except for the patch on the left sleeve of his flight jacket, it was the first he'd seen that beloved symbol in well over half a century.

The Eighth Air Force. Finally something real, something I can understand.

A walk through the museum would provide a welcome retreat from the nightmare he'd been living since escaping. Since escaping? Since 1943.

"Hey, are you listening?"

Roger snapped back to the present. "Sorry, Katherine. Did you say something?"

"Yes, I did. In fact, I said several somethings. For a moment, you were in zombie land. I said it's a little nippy out. You might want your jacket. Besides, if there's one place where that antique will look appropriate, this museum is it."

"Oh. Yeah." Roger reached into the taxi's rear seat and snatched up his Air Corps jacket. The russet-brown leather felt slightly stiff to touch, dryer than he'd noticed before. He pulled it on.

"Come on, Mr. Top Gun. Let's go in. Just to prove what a softie I am, I'll even treat you on the admission price."

Despite the early hour, the middle-aged man tending the visitor desk offered a robust greeting. "Mornin', folks. You two are the first guests of the day."

Katherine set her purse on the counter. "Two, please."

"That'll be twenty dollars."

Katherine opened her purse, but Roger slid two tens across the counter. "Let me pay this time. It's tough for a guy to get treated by a girl too often."

Before they moved on, Roger examined the vestibule. Mounted on the wall were dozens of brass plaques and flags. To the left, he noted the entrance to an eatery called—of all things—Miss Sophie's. The coincidence put a lump in his throat. To the right, a sign pointed the way to a gift shop.

"Nice lookin' A-2 you got there, mister."

Roger turned to see the attendant eyeing the Air Corps jacket.

"Once in a while we get visitors wearing reproductions, but that's the best original I've seen in a long spell. Even better'n what we've got on display. Bet it would fetch a pretty penny on eBay."

Roger blinked. *E-bay?* "Uh, yeah. It's been in the family a long time. Kind of a souvenir."

The museum employee handed Katherine two maps. She held one out to Roger. "Come on, ace. We're in."

Roger's heart skipped. "How did you know?"

"Know what?"

"That I—" Roger mentally kicked himself. He'd allowed the museum to distract him. Mistakes would invite trouble.

"Forget it. I misunderstood. Let's see what's in here."

The two strolled into the main museum. As they walked from one gallery to the next, Roger still saw no other visitors milling about. He preferred it this way. If he'd purposely planned a stop at the museum, he couldn't have chosen a better moment to arrive than opening time.

Glass cases contained a treasure trove of memories from World War II: a Norden bombsight from a B-17, .50-caliber machine-gun shells, an oxygen mask, fleece-lined gloves, flying goggles, bits of flak extracted from aircraft, plus uniforms of Air Corps personnel who'd served in England. Black-and-white photographs also adorned the galleries. Some showed grainy enlargements of Flying Fortresses and Liberator bombers. Others featured more agile fighter planes. Still other pictures depicted airmen in various slices of life. Wafting from overhead speakers, big-band music from the war years overwhelmed his heart with nostalgia.

Roger stopped and looked around, soaking in the atmosphere. He shook his head. "You know, it's almost comical. Objects people use every day eventually end up in museums for others to gawk at. Just imagine people oohing and ahhing over your toothbrush fifty years from now."

"I never thought about it that way. From now on, I'll keep my toothbrush clean."

A sharper edge had crept into Katherine's voice. Had he said something wrong? He hoped he hadn't offended her, but right now his excitement at being here prodded him onward. He cocked his head as a new tune began. "Just listen to that music." He nodded his head in time. "Know what this song is?"

She crossed her arms. "I don't have a clue. It's a little before my time." Again, impatience tinged her voice. Why?

"Then you don't know what you're missing. That's 'String of Pearls' by Glenn Miller and his orchestra." He stood still and relished the flowing notes of his favorite big band. Even before the song ended, another glass case caught his eye, and he strolled over to see what it contained.

◆ ◆ ◆

Katherine studied her passenger as he scrutinized glass cases of outdated Air Force gear. Clearly the organization had sent him. He *must* be the right guy. The photos in her purse proved as much. Plus, he carried the locator chip. But this whole field exercise had degenerated into a pointless detour. Cute or not, this man didn't behave like a member of the HO. If he wasn't what they said—and even the HO leadership must make mistakes—then who was Roger Greene?

Once again she took in Roger's old jacket. She considered the stenciled "Greene" nametag over the left chest. He'd claimed the jacket had been in his family for years, but that didn't explain why he would wear an heirloom every day. The jacket presented yet another riddle she couldn't answer. What did the HO expect her to do?

Even as questions swirled through her mind, one truth pierced Katherine's confusion: she hated charades. Yes, Roger was attractive, but what had begun sounding like a fun diversion had deteriorated into this unplanned detour to the Mighty Eighth, a World War II museum light-years away from her own existence. She had better things to do, a life of her own outside the HO. How could she attract editing gigs when she was gallivanting around Georgia, wasting time?

She yawned and brushed an unruly strand of hair out of her eyes. In contrast to her boredom, mystery man now stood squinting at every individual face in a series of old, black-and-white photographs. From the intensity in his gaze, she concluded that he wasn't faking. The photos literally fascinated the man. Roger behaved as if he'd forgotten her. How could that be, when the organization specifically stated that *she* was the reason this handsome Yankee had traveled to Georgia in the first place?

The HO isn't testing any skills of mine. The only thing getting tested is my patience.

She chided herself for proposing the unscheduled detour. She wished Roger hadn't even spotted that road sign. If she hadn't suggested stopping, she could've delivered him to Woody and been on the highway heading home by now. Katherine glanced at her wristwatch: ten thirty. Half the morning shot, and no end to this game in sight. Could she sneak away and just leave him? No, the organization might interpret that as noncompliance. Maybe even defiance. Worse, Uncle Kurt would view her action as an insult. She must handle this in some other way. Firmly, but still within the parameters of a field exercise.

"Look, flyboy—"

Roger's head snapped in her direction. He appeared genuinely startled. If he was role-playing, then he was the slickest actor she'd ever seen.

"Just call me Roger, will you?"

"Okay. Roger. I'll admit you have me more than a little curious. Most of the men I meet in that taxi think only about cars, beer, basketball, football, and sex—not necessarily in that order. Yesterday I meet you—a nice guy who seems down on his luck—so like a good Girl Scout I volunteered to drive you to my friend, who offered you a job, sight unseen. Suddenly the only things you care about are old-fashioned music and antique airplanes. I know you said you served in the Air Force, but . . . this is weird. What's with you?"

The hurt in those blue eyes caught her off guard. She immediately regretted her harshness. But mingled with the sadness she glimpsed something else. Not for the first time. Her degree might be in English, but she'd lived long enough to recognize conflicting emotions. Roger bore all the signs of a man stretched in opposite directions. His gaze dropped to the polished terrazzo floor. What secret hid inside that handsome head? Did he want out of the HO or something?

Halfway hating herself for caving in, Katherine broke the silence. "Oh, never mind. Let's look around. You paid for us to see this place. We might as well get your money's worth. As soon as you're done, though, we have an appointment with Woody."

"You bet."

"C'mon, Mom," called a young voice.

Katherine turned. A redheaded boy of ten or eleven sauntered in. Behind the boy followed a woman whose matching red hair pegged her as "Mom." The boy cocked his head. "What's that song, Mom?"

The woman looked upward, as if the answer might be posted overhead. "I'm not sure. It sounds familiar, though."

Roger stepped closer to the boy. "That's called 'Don't Sit Under the Apple Tree.' You see, during the war boyfriends and husbands were shipping out for duty overseas. They didn't know how many years they might be gone. So the idea was for sweethearts to wait for each other until the war ended."

The mother nodded. "Were there words to go with the music?"

Roger picked up the tune: *"Don't sit under the apple tree with anyone else but me . . ."* Both mother and boy glanced at each other, all smiles for this impromptu performance. Despite her earlier irritation, Katherine realized she was smiling too. Roger might be different, but he possessed a great singing voice. Almost too great. With his good looks and that voice, why wasn't this guy in Las Vegas?

Mother and boy broke into applause, and Roger bowed.

"Will you sing another?" the woman asked, her gaze locked on Roger's eyes.

Katherine noted the woman's left hand. No wedding band.

Roger cleared his throat. "Well, I don't know—"

Katherine sidled over and linked an arm around Roger's. "Sorry, end of concert. We're on a tight schedule." As she tugged Roger away, disappointment registered on the mother's face. The sight somehow pleased Katherine.

◆   ◆   ◆

In the adjoining gallery, a display highlighting fighter planes immediately drove all thoughts of Woody and the temporary job from Roger's mind. No complaints from his female driver could deflate his thrill at spotting a sleek, life-sized aircraft hanging from the ceiling. Was it the one he most wanted to see? He strode straight toward it.

"So that's a P-51 Mustang. It's even more impressive than the photos. I'd give anything for chance to climb inside the—"

Katherine's expression stopped him in mid-sentence. She stared at him in open-mouthed alarm.

"What's wrong?"

Katherine pointed.

Roger spun and came face to face with a poster-sized photo of a brash fighter pilot—himself—standing by the propeller of his war bird. In a flash, he recalled posing for a photographer from *Yank* magazine back in Debden. Decades ago. How could he explain it?

"It's just a wild coincidence . . ."

He looked again. The name tag on the jacket was clearly visible: Greene.

Katherine began stuttering a reply. She backed away. The photo had spooked her. He needed an explanation fast, or his sole helper on earth might vanish.

"Katherine, that's a photo of my father. I mean my grandfather. Yeah, Grandpa flew in World War II. This is his jacket I'm wearing. You don't think I'm a ghost, do you?"

Katherine hesitated. Was she buying it? He hated lying to her, but it was the only way.

"So!" interrupted a new voice. "Captain Roger Greene. What a pleasure to meet you at last."

A swarthy man with short, dark hair swaggered into the gallery. His right hand pointed a pistol straight at Roger's chest. The man's other hand held something too. A modern grenade?

"Tsk, tsk, Captain Greene. You have caused a lot trouble. You should have stayed where you were."

"Who are you?" Roger's mind raced. Should he run? Risk a bullet in the back? Not with Katherine here.

Katherine continued to stare. He couldn't tell if her face reflected more fear or confusion.

"Some people call me the Griffin. I think you can guess for whom I work. But that's irrelevant. What's important is who *you* are."

After a smug glance at Katherine, the Griffin returned his attention to Roger. "You know, it's truly amazing. When they informed my section about you, my associates and I could scarcely believe the report. In certain circles you sparked quite an uproar when you departed Europe."

"You're not taking me back."

"Correct. I'm not taking you back. The chase is over."

"Meaning what?"

"Meaning the organization has come to a decision. Normally I would have killed you and been on my way. But in your case I couldn't resist exchanging a few words. Also, I'm to confiscate that jacket, along with any other objects or documents on your person. I love a good mystery, and that's exactly what I'm going to leave behind—another mystery that the inept American police will never unravel."

Roger's mind raced. Was there nothing he could do?

"Come. You are out of time, Captain Greene." The gunman twisted his mouth into a sneer, as if relishing a private joke. Then his jaw clenched. "Remove that jacket and toss it to me. Now. Or I'll make your end much more painful and gruesome than it needs to be."

Keeping his eyes on the gunman's, Roger obeyed, but in slow motion. *Gotta stall! How can I surprise him?*

At that moment, a youthful voice called, "I'll be in the next one, Mom!" Into the room jogged the redheaded boy. He was well into the gallery before the sight of a pistol pointing at Roger stopped him in his tracks. The boy's eyes bulged.

"Bad timing, boy. No witnesses." With that, the Griffin pointed the pistol at the youth and shot two silenced bullets. The boy crumpled.

"Danny!"

In the gallery entrance stood the boy's mother.

"Silence!" The gunman targeted the mother and fired again. Blood spurted from her chest. Her scream died even before her body thumped to the floor.

Wielding his jacket like a whip, Roger lashed the Griffin's hand. The pistol clattered away. Roger's left fist smashed an uppercut to the gunman's chin, sending him sprawling backward into a heap.

The Griffin tried to roll—too late. As if acting on its own, a display case tilted toward him, then toppled, crashing onto him and his weapon.

Roger blinked. Surprise of all surprises, there stood Katherine, the one who had shoved the display onto his attacker. He wouldn't have believed this light-hearted girl with the cute laugh had the gumption.

Only then did Roger sweep around to assess the damage. Both mother and child lay motionless in scarlet puddles. Two innocents dead, simply because they stood in the same room with him!

He wheeled back. Praise God, Katherine was alive, not even bleeding. But did this guy have partners in the building? He had to protect her!

He seized her hand. "Katherine, we have to run! There might be more of them!"

◆   ◆   ◆

As if released from a spell by Roger's touch, Katherine sprinted hand in hand with him, back the way they had come. Despite her aerobics classes, she struggled to keep up with his fast pace. When the pair reached the front lobby, no one manned the desk. Running at full throttle, Roger half-led, half-dragged her across the parking lot to the taxi.

"Give me the key."

She fumbled through her purse with trembling fingers. "Here!"

Roger slammed the passenger door shut behind her, then ran to the opposite side. He scrambled behind the steering wheel. A second later, he gunned the vehicle out of the lot and raced back toward the interstate.

Roger drove jerkily, stomping too hard on the brakes and over-steering on corners. Hadn't this guy ever driven a car before? She screamed when he nearly broadsided another car. However, the ramp to I-95 was only a block away, and soon he had the car roaring back in the direction of Atlanta.

"They found me. They threatened they could find me anywhere in the world. I didn't believe they could actually do it."

"Who found you?"

"Hard to explain. I don't totally understand it myself. I think their headquarters are in Germany."

Katherine's mind raced. The kaleidoscope of events outpaced her brain. Clearly, though, a man who respected bullets and could punch a gunman to the floor was no ghost. For the moment, she set aside the unexplainable poster in the museum. "Roger, what have you done? Why would anyone want to kill you?"

He rocketed the taxi around a lumbering gravel truck, then spared her a fleeting look. "I haven't done anything. I'm just a normal American serviceman who loves to fly airplanes and signed up to serve his country. But these guys . . . they're like Hitler's grandchildren. They want to kill me because I was their prisoner. I escaped, and now they want to shut my mouth for good."

"Hitler's grandchildren?"

His eyes flicked to the rearview mirror, then back to her. "It's a long story. Like I said, it's hard to explain. Especially while barreling down the road. First let's put some distance between us and that Griffin guy. I'll explain the whole deal. I warn you, though, this story won't be easy to swallow."

CHAPTER 37

The green-and-white road sign announced Atlanta lay only sixty miles away when Roger finally wound up his life's story. Guiding the taxi through the orange barrels of a construction zone, he looked askance at Katherine. She remained silent. He couldn't tell what she thought of him.

"So that's my whole bizarre life. I've been back in the States for only a couple of days, and already they've figured out where I am. Now, what do you say? That I'm off my rocker? An escapee from a loony bin?"

"I honestly don't know what to think. You must realize that story sounds like a plot hatched in the mind of a Hollywood screenwriter."

"Every word is true, whether you believe me or not. Don't those bullets and bodies count for proof?"

"They prove one man wanted to shoot you, or at least threaten you. For all I know, you might have double-crossed a bunch of drug dealers who want revenge. Look at it this way. Pretend we're back in the year 1940. You and I are eating in a restaurant when, all of a sudden, a young man bursts through the door and claims he's an officer from a Union Army cavalry outfit that fought in the Civil War. He claims Confederate scientists captured him and performed complicated experiments and extended his life. He shouts that he just now escaped from a deep cave in Tuscaloosa. Would you believe him?"

The hairs on the back of his neck bristled. Was she mocking him?

"That's different, and you know it. This kind of science didn't exist in Civil War days."

"Roger, ask any medical doctor. He'll tell you the kind of science you describe doesn't exist nowadays, either. The one fact I know for sure is that a man at the museum shot real bullets and murdered two people."

"These guys play for keeps. If you have any way to check news reports for Frankfurt, Germany, you'll find a story about Sophie's shot-up car being hauled out of a river. They killed her for helping me. Now two more civilians are dead, and I've gotten you involved. I'm sorry." He took a swig from the plastic bottle of Coke purchased at the last filling station.

"Let me postpone my verdict on your story. I want to know what you're planning to do next."

"That's the million-dollar question. I keep wondering if it might be possible to find some old-timers who remember me from my Indiana days. Then maybe the authorities would believe me instead of trying to cart me off to a nuthouse. As far as the future goes, I can guarantee only one thing: I'll never let anybody lock me behind bars again. I'd go insane if I ever ended up in another cage."

"So you still don't want me to phone the police?"

"Please don't. Not yet, at least."

"We're witnesses, Roger. We need to tell the authorities what we saw."

"The police won't believe me. They'll lock me up for sure. Besides, we don't know where that shooter came from. Cops will want solid information, and we don't have any they'll buy."

"Then let's go back to the beginning. Start with the orphanage you mentioned. What was the name of it?"

"Sunshine Children's Home."

Katherine reached into her purse for her wireless telephone. She clicked several digits. A pause, then she lowered it again. "No such orphanage is listed for Indianapolis."

He tipped the Coke bottle for another swallow. "No surprise. That place should've been torn down when I was there. Next, you'll want the name of the farm couple who took me in when I was twelve. It was

Tucker. But don't bother trying to contact them. They would've died long ago."

He veered halfway into the left lane to avoid the carcass of a dead deer. "As soon as we get back to Atlanta, I'll get out of your hair, Katherine. I'll buy a road map and set out for Indy on foot. Maybe I can hop a train, travel like a hobo."

"That's crazy. If somebody is really out to murder you, you'd be easy pickin's. I say we get rid of the taxi and take my car to Indianapolis."

His Coke stopped in midair. "We?"

"Yes, we. Either your cockamamie story is true, or it's false. If it's true—which is hard to believe—then you need a friend big time. If it's false and you're covering up something . . . Well in that case it will be interesting to tag along and see how this whole drama plays out."

For the first time since the escape, his spirits lifted. "You're sure? This trip might not be a milk run. I mean, no easy mission."

"Sign me aboard anyway, Captain. Let's see what happens."

He set down the Coke and shot her a playful salute. "Katherine, for a girl, you're turning into a pretty good wingman!"

"Yeah? Well, for a young guy who claims to be an old coot, you're pretty interestin' company yourself."

◆ ◆ ◆

In the northern Atlanta suburb of Norcross, Roger and Katherine dropped off the taxi at its owner's house. There they picked up her less-obvious sky-blue Passat.

"Let's swing by my place so I can pack some clothing," Katherine said.

Red flags sprouted in Roger's mind. "Please, let's not. It's too risky. I mean, even though we've been on the road four hours, that Griffin guy or his pals could be on our trail. I'd feel better if we hit the highway this very moment."

"If you say so. But this is already my second day in these same clothes. Don't blame me if I look like a wrinkled mess."

"I won't say a word if you don't. For me it's the third day in these pants and shirt."

Roger wondered—should he tell her about the object inside his arm? Unless there was some other technology at work, that object was the only explanation for how that Griffin guy found him. Katherine already thought his story sounded hokey. If she'd never heard of inserting tiny homing equipment inside people, it would be one more nutty yarn to swallow. He definitely needed to get the thing out of him, but decided not to mention it right now. Could he find a doctor, somebody who knew the position of veins and arteries, willing to do the job without asking questions? If not, he'd need to risk it and slice his own arm open. Until then, speed and constant movement would be his best protection.

Now that Roger had mastered the use of power steering and power brakes, his driving skills were much improved. Squinting against the sun's glare, he slipped thumb and forefinger into his shirt pocket for the green aviators and put them on. "Driving a car isn't half as fun as flying a fighter, but it's better than being a passenger. By the way, I don't suppose you would know anything about an airplane called a P-51 Mustang? The one hanging in the museum?"

"Sorry, no. I'm a landlubber."

He shook his head. "Landlubber is naval talk. In the U.S. Air Corps, we'd say you're a ground pounder. It's not important. Just interesting to a pilot. How about you bring me up to date on life in the modern world instead? I have tons of catching up to do."

"What do you want to know?"

"Anything. Everything. I'm a blank slate. While you talk, I'll keep an eye on the rear view to make sure no one is tailing us."

As mile after mile passed along northbound I-75, Katherine described modern life. Roger often posed questions that veered the conversation into new directions. He tried to stretch his brain to comprehend Katherine's answers, but many of her explanations defied understanding. He jumped from topic to topic: "What are those little gadgets clipped to some people's ears?" "Since when do women get tattooed like sailors and men sport

The Methuselah Project

earrings like girls?" "Those dinky records you called CDs—is it possible to buy them with any kind of music, or only new-fangled songs?" "Do they still make Nehi orange and grape soda pops?"

Katherine didn't pretend to be an avid student of politics. However, her sketchy overviews of the Korean War, the Cold War, and Vietnam all fascinated him and sparked yet other questions. Hearing that Dwight Eisenhower had been elected president, he let out a whoop of excitement as if the election had happened yesterday. On the other hand, her description of the Nixon years and the Watergate scandal left him shaking his head.

"Washington politics." He crinkled his nose.

When Katherine casually mentioned Neil Armstrong landing a space-craft on the moon, Roger stared at her with disbelief. "People fly to the moon?"

"Roger, look out!"

He swerved to avoid sideswiping a guardrail.

"People visiting the moon? Shades of Jules Verne. So what did this Armstrong fellow do before he started buzzing around outer space?"

"Um, I think he was a pilot. Probably for the Navy or the Air Force."

"A pilot, eh?" Roger nodded in satisfaction. "Sounds like my kind of guy." He paused. "Say, you wouldn't be slipping the new guy a gallon of propwash, would you?"

"Propwash?"

"Propwash—you know, like sending somebody to fetch a yard of flight line? Never mind. It's a pilot thing. Ground pounders wouldn't understand."

In the discussions that followed, Roger found the dismantling of the Soviet Union simple enough to understand, but he couldn't decipher the hostilities revolving around the Middle East. Oil . . . terrorists . . . missiles . . . suicide bombers . . . perpetual murders of innocent civilians . . .

"I don't understand it all, either. That corner of the world never stays peaceful for long."

He nodded. "I'll have to pick up a Bible and compare your information to what it predicts about future events."

She offered no reply. He didn't expect her to. He understood. Until he started reading a Bible in the Methuselah bunker, he'd always shied away from religious topics too. Maybe in time, Katherine would be willing to swap thoughts about God and faith and deeper issues of the universe.

Katherine twisted sideways to face him more directly. "Now, let me ask you some questions. You claim you were stationed in England, that you flew with the RAF even before America entered World War II. If that's true, what memories from those days stand out especially in your mind?"

Roger said the first word that popped into his mind. "Coventry."

"Coventry? What's that?"

"It's a city in England. In November of 1940, the Luftwaffe staged an all-night blitz on Coventry. I wasn't there, but I happened to be nearby at the time. An RAF buddy and I—Ballard was his name—we drove over the next morning. The sight was appalling. Beyond anything I'd ever imagined."

Katherine's voice softened. "How so?"

Roger fixed his eyes on the strip of highway in front of him, but the screen of his mind returned to sights and sounds he'd witnessed all those years ago. "At dawn, we encountered droves of people pouring away from the city any way they could: in overloaded cars, on bicycles, by oxcart, on foot. Sometimes parents limped along carrying little bawling babies. To this day, I still picture the horror etched in those faces. A bunch of 'em shuffled along in a stupor. Others just stood by the roadside staring nowhere, as if their brains got clicked off or something."

"How horrible."

"You haven't heard the half of it. Ballard and I were like salmon swimming upstream in his car. When we finally reached the city, the place was a smoking rubble heap. In one spot, Ballard told me we were standing at a downtown corner, but in three directions I saw nothing but pulverized mounds of wasteland. Places that were once streets were nothing but ankle-deep mud. He pointed out a smoking ruin he said used to be a newspaper office. All that was left were broken bricks, twisted girders, and smashed-up linotype machines. I still recall the taste of powdered brick and ashes on my tongue. I heard later only five hundred people died in that city, since most hid themselves in shelters. But I saw bodies. Some had been covered with sheets to keep the crows from pecking at them."

Katherine's head drooped. "No wonder people would be stunned. Just hearing your description is turning my stomach."

Roger's own stomach agreed, even after all these decades. "For me, Coventry became the dividing line. When I sailed to England with a bunch of Canadian boys, I went as a wet-behind-the-ears Hoosier hoping for adventure and a chance to get paid flying airplanes. At Coventry my naïve sense of adventure died. My new goal became to stop the Nazi war machine. Or at least part of it."

"What about London? Did you visit there?"

"Sure. Londoners lived through more than their share of blitzes. How can I describe it? Sandbags everywhere. Barrage balloons tethered over every neighborhood. Nighttime blackouts so dark you couldn't see the nose on the face beside you. Sirens. Searchlights. Strangers in pajamas and overcoats all crammed into musty bomb shelters. Stirrup pumps positioned all over town—"

"Stirrup pumps?"

"Yeah, it was something the Brits invented. A stirrup pump was a few feet of hose, a manual pump, and buckets of water. Incendiary bombs started lots of fires. With stirrup pumps, ordinary citizens could squelch small fires before they grew into big blazes."

Roger glanced from the road to see Katherine's face. Her intent eyes studied him. Was she convinced he'd really experienced the Battle of Britain? He couldn't tell. Would he have believed such a story if their situations had been reversed? No answer for that one, either.

After hours of asking Katherine questions and struggling to comprehend her answers, Roger needed time for the ocean of new information to soak into his brain. "Okay if we ride in silence a while? I need to digest all this stuff."

Katherine nodded. She, too, looked weary from the marathon discussion. "Six hours down, and possibly six to go before we hit Indianapolis.

I'm going to rest my eyes." She slumped down in her seat. Before long, her even breathing signaled she was asleep.

Roger considered. Would this trip turn into a wild goose chase? Would driving to Indy achieve anything he couldn't accomplish in Georgia? Maybe not. Even so, remaining on the move should buy some time. He needed to plan. How could he reclaim his identity as a normal American citizen? According to Katherine, the Social Security system FDR had created back in the 1930s still functioned. Except for short, temporary work, nobody could legally hold a job without a Social Security number. How might he use his old number, even if he could recall it? Or how could he get a new number?

And computers. If everything Katherine described was on the level, a public computer—say, in a library—should be able to tap into the system she called "the Enter Net." He could learn things. Look up old acquaintances.

I can't stay on the run from the Methuselah people forever. I'm going to need sleep. When I do . . . He rubbed the lump inside his arm. Eight hours—even six hours—might be plenty of time for one of Hans's cronies to plug him while he slept.

He pondered their destination. *Okay, so what if I just go to the Indianapolis police for protection? Maybe I wouldn't have to tell the whole story about the war and Nazis.* Would they believe him if he simply said that he was homeless and that somebody was trying to murder him?

What a laugh. Even before the war, policemen had required details before getting involved. They would ask questions he couldn't answer without convincing them he was a crackpot.

He compiled a mental inventory of classmates from Plainfield High, faces he hadn't pictured in ages: Lloyd Mason, Agnes Appling, Leon Vetter, Edith Hendershot . . . Even as he dredged up names and images, his hope of locating them sank.

Probably a lot of fellows died in the war. Others must've moved away. The girls would've married and lost their maiden names. But what if a few old classmates survived? Memories fade. *Would any elderly person swear on a Bible I'm the same Roger Greene they sat beside in math class?*

The likelihood seemed microscopic. Still, he resolved to give it a shot. Even one testimony would carry more weight than his flimsy solo story. *Maybe I could run an ad in the newspaper? I could list the people I remember.*

On second thought, maybe not. The organization had murdered Sophie for helping. He'd never forgive himself if anything happened to Katherine. Once more, he admired the girl slumbering in the passenger seat. She was cute when awake. Asleep, she was cuter. Gutsy, too, since she'd stuck with him and even helped despite obvious danger. He smiled, imagining them sitting arm in arm in front of a crackling fireplace, her head resting on his shoulder. He couldn't resist another glance at her lips. *How would it feel to be kissing—?*

That's when Roger noticed Katherine's purse had tipped over, spilling her portable telephone, ink pens, a pack of Juicy Fruit, and several other items onto the floor. One object in particular snared his attention. He pulled off the green aviators, then reached down and hefted the gray-cased gadget.

Exactly like the gizmo Griffin was holding when he found me. The exact same thing! Must be some kind of tracking device. He examined Katherine's sleeping face with fresh interest. Sleepy Beauty was hiding something.

CHAPTER 38

Daylight faded into dusk when Roger stopped to refuel. He thought again about the tracking device. They still had several hours' drive ahead. It made sense to get the device out before they reached their destination, but if Katherine was in cahoots with Griffin and others like him, it was a moot point. Katherine awoke under his gaze, realized where they were, and handed him several tens to pay for the gasoline.

She yawned. "Want me to take another stint driving?"

"Not quite yet." He started the engine and angled back to the interstate. "I've been mulling over a lot of stuff. I need you to explain one item."

She rubbed her eyes and groaned. "I've already reviewed half of human history with you. What's left?"

"This." Roger held up the gray device he'd discovered. "It tumbled out of your bag. I want to know what it is, how it works, and why you—the one person in Atlanta who just happened to offer me a free ride—are carrying a device exactly like one that assassin at the museum was holding."

Shock registered on Katherine's face. *So it was true—she didn't mean for me to see this gadget.*

"It's not mine. It belongs to my uncle Kurt. He's the one who adopted me after my parents died."

"Go on."

For a fleeting moment, the look of a cornered animal sprang into

239

Katherine's eyes. Just as quickly, she exhaled in exasperation and slumped against the headrest. "Okay, I confess. I really, honestly don't know if this whole thing is a super elaborate HO field exercise, or if I'm trapped in the *Twilight Zone,* or what. But if it's a field exercise, then I'm calling it quits right here, right now. The game is over."

Roger heard the words, but understood nothing. "What are you talking about? What's an HO? Or a field exercise?"

Inexplicably tears sprang into Katherine's eyes. "You know good and well we're not supposed to talk about it. I swore an oath. Don't try to trick me."

Roger grew more confused. "Look, Katherine, I don't know beans about any oath or about exercising in a field. All I know is that yesterday a guy holding one of these gray thingamajigs tried to nail me into a coffin. You carry one too. That makes you look like you're on his side, not mine."

She snatched a tissue from the holder on the car's dashboard and dabbed both eyes. "Okay, I'll talk. But if this is some sort of trap, then spare me the grief and kick me out of the HO this minute."

"I'm not tricking you."

"The HO—it's a kind of secret society. Sort of like Masons or Shriners, but it's all behind the scenes, aimed at improving individuals and society in general. The goal is to raise the level of achievement, morals, and ethics in each country where members live."

"So what does 'HO' actually stand for?"

"The full name is Heritage Organization, but hardly anybody says the whole thing. Sometimes we say, 'HO,' sometimes just 'the organization.'"

At the word *organization*, a chill gripped Roger's heart. Sophie had said the same thing about the Methuselah controllers. "And you're a member of this organization?"

She nodded and dabbed her eyes again. "I'm just a newbie. Barely above Kadett, which is a first-level beginner. Ever since I was old enough to keep a secret, Uncle Kurt has told me story after story about the HO and how much my parents cherished it. In fact, my dad headed up a team of HO scientists working on a cure for diabetes. Mom was his assistant. The Heritage Organization funded the whole project. Uncle Kurt says the team felt close to success when a terrible fire broke out, killing them all. When Uncle invited me to continue the family tradition and enlist, it seemed the right thing to do. I mean, the HO funded my parents' life's work, and after the fire, they gave Uncle a huge sum of money to raise me, all in memory of my parents. I felt obligated."

"How much do you know about this organization?"

She shook her head. "Nobody gets in without an invitation, usually from a higher-ranking friend or family member. Quite a few seem to come from a Germanic ancestry, but not all of them."

"I mean, what do you know about their specific activities, their projects?"

"That part is fuzzy in my mind. Like I said, it's a behind-the-scenes type of society. The lower ranks don't know exactly what happens at upper levels. It's all aimed at challenging individuals to higher levels of achievement, improving the world with inventions and positive influences, then passing on a stronger heritage to the next generation."

He hefted the gray device. "Is this some sort of tracking mechanism?" Even as he spoke, he gave the rearview mirror a glance. No one trailed them.

"It's nicknamed a Pigeon. I recently received a promotion. In light of my new rank, some sort of field exercise was next on my agenda. It's a challenging experience to heighten intuition and problem-solving skills. I'll show you what they sent me." She dug to the bottom of her handbag and pulled out the printout of her assignment, complete with photos of Roger.

Listening while she read the instructions to locate and trail the "HO member," Roger felt a tide of anger rising in his chest. "What a devil's pack of lies! In other words, they needed some innocent patsy to keep tabs on me until their killer could move in. They used you as a chump to do their dirty work."

Roger began connecting the dots for her, explaining that "higher levels" of the group who'd sent the Griffin after him were the ones who had imprisoned him for so many decades. They financed the Methuselah Project. Even Sophie had referred to them as "the organization." He also recounted his first escape attempt, but this time elaborating on the conversation in which Hans claimed to have planted some sort of homing device in his arm to track him down, evidently with one of these same gizmos.

"A locator chip inside your arm? I figured you had one, but I assumed you carried it in your pocket to let me find you as part of the exercise. Still, my uncle would never get tangled up with the kind of people you describe. Neither would my parents. I don't have all the answers, but—"

"I tell you, this organization is wormy to the core."

"But Uncle Kurt—"

"Look, I don't know your uncle, and I have nothing against him. Maybe he's a jolly good fellow who doesn't realize what the uppity-ups do. But don't you think it's a little fishy he just happens to own one of those Pigeon gadgets? What do you think he uses it for?"

"We treated it like a sport, a mental challenge. He would plant a locator chip somewhere around Atlanta, and then I had to find it. When I got better, he made the game more challenging by becoming a mobile target. It was all in fun."

Roger appreciated Katherine too much to argue. But the impression of Uncle Kurt developing in his mind was less than stellar. He grunted. "Some games can be practice for real life. Even the army stages war games."

"Roger, my uncle isn't a Nazi ogre with some psychotic obsession about racial purity and superiority. He's got his shortcomings. He's too strict, for one thing. But he's a respectable businessman. He uses the Pigeon to track jewelry shipments, among other things."

"I didn't say he's not a nice guy, but evil minds can manipulate nice people. Including nice girls," he said, with a significant glance in her direction. "Maybe he got sucked into something he doesn't understand. They could be using him like they used you."

Instead of retorting, she jumped to a different topic. "If you have a GPS chip embedded in your body, someone could be tracking you this very minute."

"No fooling? Even while we're driving down the highway?"

"Moving objects are harder to trace, but a hunter could get a general fix on the direction and travel the same way."

"All right, I believe you're innocent. I need surgery. The sooner, the better. Do you have a knife?"

"A knife? No, not with me. We might be able to find a store—"

Roger shook his head and pulled the car to the side of the expressway. "No time for shopping. Because of the experiment, I drop into a deep sleep every night. Almost like a coma. Flying in from Europe has messed up my sleep patterns, but I can tell I'm on the verge of conking out. My thinking gets fuzzy, and I hear a little whine in my head. You have to drive. In the morning, we'll buy something sharp and cut this thing out of me. If you spot any bandits on our six, try to wake me up."

"Bandits on our six? Wait, let me guess. It's a pilot thing. Ground pounders wouldn't understand, right?"

He patted her shoulder. "Sorry. Air Corps jargon. It means hostiles on your tail. If you see danger, punch me or kick me, whatever it takes to wake me up. If I'm going to get shot, I want to be awake when it happens."

✦ ✦ ✦

Roger's cockpit was shaking. The P-47 he piloted was disintegrating, spinning, tumbling out of control. *Bail out!*

He jerked upright and popped open his eyes. His airplane, the sky, and the Focke-Wulfs vanished. Instead, Katherine gripped his shoulder, worry etched into her features.

"Roger, are you all right?"

He rubbed his eyes. "Yeah, I'm fine. What's wrong?"

"Nothing's wrong. You've been asleep all night. You weren't exaggerating about being a sound sleeper. When I tried to wake you, it was like you were drugged or something."

He nodded and blinked his eyes again. Morning sunlight bathed the car. "Yeah. I used to be a light sleeper, but Methuselah changed that. Doc Kossler noticed right away. He theorized that whatever biological process keeps my body young and in good repair shifts into super high gear when I sleep. Maybe it uses those hours to fix and refresh every cell."

He glanced around to get his bearings. The Passat sat in the large parking lot of some sort of shopping complex. Katherine had parked in a distant corner, far from all other vehicles.

"You stopped?"

"The sign said we're in a place called Greenwood, just south of Indianapolis. I've been driving every which way to give you more time to rest, but my eyes are tired. I had to stop."

The pair traded seats. Roger continued the drive north, but found himself rubbing his eyes. "I don't know if it's the stress or what, but I'm just not thinking straight. I don't usually need this long to perk up."

Katherine spoke with closed eyes. "Want to stop for a coffee?"

"Not yet. We've already been stationary too long. I want to move, blend in with the thousands of people in the big city."

When they reached Indianapolis, he followed the exit from I-65 onto Market Street and toward the downtown district. Even without coffee, the sight of his old stomping grounds filled Roger with fresh excitement. "A lot of new buildings, but I recognize some of the old ones. Feels bizarre being here again—but it's a good kind of bizarre, you know?"

Katherine sat up and took in their surroundings.

At the heart of the city, he maneuvered the Passat onto the red bricks of the Monument Circle roundabout, where traffic revolved around the towering Soldiers and Sailors Monument. Rather than exiting into a side street, Roger circled several times while admiring the two-hundred-foot obelisk rising from the center of Monument Circle.

"Boy, is that a sight for sore eyes. They built the monument back at the start of the twentieth century in honor of all Hoosiers who had died in wars. Every time I think of Indianapolis, I picture this spot. I nearly gave up hope of seeing it again." Then, as an afterthought, he said, "Ironic thing is, in school they taught us the monument was designed by a German. Bruno somebody. Funny how little details can stick in a person's brain."

"I see a door in the base."

"Yeah, it's hollow. There used to be steps and an elevator going up to observation windows." On a whim, he turned and braked at the curb. "Come on. I know we should keep moving, but let's spare ten minutes. I want to celebrate my homecoming. We can look out the top, if they still allow tourists."

A couple of minutes later, they were rising in the cramped elevator. When the doors slid open, Roger and Katherine exited to a narrow, enclosed platform, then mounted a twisting metal stairway the rest of the way up. At last they reached the glass-enclosed walkway encircling the peak.

"Not exactly roomy up here," Katherine said. "It's stuffy."

Roger slipped off his flight jacket and draped it over a forearm. "It's more cramped than I remember. But it's home. I used to love coming up here when I was in high school."

They walked around the four sides of the monument, gazing down on the surrounding streets and buildings. "Plenty of changes, but it's still good old Indy," Roger said when they had seen the fourth side. "Okay, my holiday is over. Let's head down and figure out our next course of action." They clumped back down the metal steps to the elevator landing.

Katherine pushed the elevator button, but the doors remained closed. Evidently it had been summoned to the bottom by more sightseers. "Where do you suggest we try first? It's your hometown."

"I've been thinking. This might sound like a harebrained idea, but I'd like to head for the closest newspaper and—"

The clunk of the returning elevator interrupted him.

Roger stepped in front of the opening door just in time to see the Griffin leveling a pistol at him. "No!" Roger tried to dodge, but the leering killer pulled the trigger at pointblank range.

The silencer muffled the blast, but not the bullet's effect. Roger staggered back, struck his head against the limestone wall, and collapsed even before the white-hot pain erupted in his chest.

CHAPTER 39

Katherine froze in horror. A splotch of crimson blossomed on Roger's shirt. The grinning gunman pointed his weapon straight at Roger's head.

Katherine's karate instincts took over. Despite the confined space, she snapped a kick using the *Isshin-Ryu* she'd learned in the dojo of Sensei Frank Lawson. The pistol sailed from the man's hand. Before she could move in for a jab, the assassin counterattacked by snapping a kick of his own.

Katherine had absorbed blows from sparring partners before, but this was no mere strike for points. The Griffin's black leather street shoe exploded into her stomach with the force of a battering ram. Air gushed from her lungs. She staggered backward. Nearly fell. Somehow she stayed on her feet, but she gasped for breath and couldn't straighten up.

"Fool, I have orders not to hurt you, but I will if you get in the way."

Doubled over from the intense ache radiating from her midsection, Katherine couldn't speak. She wanted to say something. Distract him from Roger. All she could manage was to shake her head at this man she suddenly hated.

"As you wish, then."

This time Katherine read his body language quick enough to dodge the kick. Instantly she drove forward with a punch to the man's Adam's apple. To her surprise, he didn't fall. Not hard enough! Performed properly, the blow could incapacitate a human. Instead of stopping her opponent, she succeeded only in kindling wrath in his eyes. Katherine shifted her feet. Could she deliver a kick to his groin? She tensed her leg, kicked . . . Too late!

The older and obviously more experienced adversary evaded her foot, then sprang. Iron-hard knuckles slammed into her already-throbbing midsection.

Reeling with agony unlike any she'd ever imagined, Katherine gasped and dropped to her knees. She couldn't fight anymore. Couldn't lift her head. The torturous pain in her stomach . . .

Another muffled report from a pistol! The shock jerked her head up. A second gun?

The smugness had disappeared from the gunman's face. He clutched his right side, where crimson rivulets trickled between his fingers.

Still lying on his back and grimacing, Roger gripped the gunman's pistol. "Didn't you ever learn your manners? Never hit a lady, fat-head."

With a roar, the killer leaped onto Roger, wrestling for the weapon. Katherine wanted to help, to deliver a kick or a punch. But the two men thrashed and rolled together in the tight space. She could do nothing without risking hurting Roger.

Another gunshot. Their thrashing stopped.

Unsure of what had happened, Katherine stared in trepidation. Roger shoved away the limp body of the gunman.

"Don't move, Roger. I'll call for an ambulance." She struggled upright, gasping for breath.

"No. No ambulance." He eased into a sitting position and clamped a hand over the crimson stain on his shirt. "Just let me rest a minute."

"Rest? You're wounded!"

"I think it'll be okay."

"Don't be insane! You've got a bullet in you. You need a doctor."

"You're forgetting about Methuselah. Not only does it keep my body young, but it regenerates damaged tissue extra fast. If he'd shot me in the head or the heart, I'd be a goner. But if the bullet lodged in a nonvital area, my body will heal around it. At least, I think it will."

"What if you're wrong?"

He forced a grin. "Then you can say, 'I told him so,' for the rest of your life."

"You're the only man I know who would sit around joking with a bullet in him."

He pulled his hand away from the wound and unbuttoned his shirt for closer inspection. Meanwhile, Katherine retrieved the pistol and examined it: a Ruger .22. Not a powerful weapon, but in tight quarters a bullet to the head or the heart wouldn't need to be powerful. A .22 would also reduce the likelihood of telltale blood splattering the assassin. She stuffed the Ruger into her purse. Today was the second time they had been caught weaponless. There wouldn't be a third time.

"The bleeding has just about stopped. Help me to the elevator."

Despite her aching stomach, Katherine slipped an arm around Roger and assisted him to his feet. Her hands broke into a sweat, and her breathing hitched as his hand slipped to her waist. She'd dreamed of having him in her arms, but not like this.

He turned to look her in the eye. "Say, where did you become such a fancy fighter? Those moves you pulled were better than Jiu-Jitsu."

"It's *Isshin-Ryu*. A style of karate from Okinawa."

He stared at her. "Okinawa? In Japan? Sheesh, Katherine. German and Japanese too? You're a regular Axis bombshell!"

Through his grimace, she detected a glimmer of his signature grin. "If you weren't wounded . . ." She let her statement trail off as they stepped into the elevator. "So the bullet doesn't hurt anymore?"

"I didn't say that. At first, it felt like King Kong whacked me with a pickaxe. Now it just hurts like the dickens. Here, let me zip up my jacket to hide the blood." That done, he looked at Katherine with concern. "Are you okay? That guy was trying to take you down for keeps."

She couldn't hide the ache radiating from her torso. "I feel like a ramblin' wreck from Georgia Tech."

"Like a what?"

She managed a wink. "It's a Georgia thing. Yankee pilots wouldn't understand."

When the elevator halted at the bottom, Roger shocked Katherine by straightening and rushing out the door as if he were fine. "Call the police—and an ambulance!" he shouted to the man at the desk. "Some crazy idiot shot himself up there. I tried to stop him, but I was too late. He's lying there bleeding."

The attendant's eyes shot wide. "I'm on it!" He snatched the telephone from its cradle and began punching numbers.

"We'll watch for the cops outside. They'll want witnesses."

The attendant nodded, then began speaking into the phone.

Outside, Roger winced and placed his good arm around Katherine again. "Let's scram. We're not sticking around for any cops."

Within moments, they were safely inside her Passat and driving away from Monument Circle, this time with Katherine at the wheel. "Which way?"

"Any direction. For now, just put distance between us and the monument."

A wailing police car careened down the street toward them. Like every other driver, Katherine eased her vehicle to the right and let it pass.

"'Atta girl. No panic. Nice and normal."

"Do you think there might be another gunman nearby?"

"I doubt it. Not yet, anyway. If that guy had a partner anywhere in Indy, they probably would've teamed up to come after me together. This little incident may have bought us some time to think and plan before the organization moves another thug into position."

"Good. We need a motel or someplace where we can clean your wound and let you rest in peace." Out of the corner of her eye she saw him give her a double take.

"Rest in peace? I wish you'd worded that a little differently."

"Sorry."

"But no motel. I need to cut that transmitter thing out of my arm right now. Too bad we don't have a gun for you to stand guard while I'm performing the operation."

"Who says we don't?" Katherine pulled open the top of her handbag to reveal the Ruger .22 nestled inside. "Mr. Griffin didn't need it anymore."

He whistled. "I was right, Katherine. For a girl, you make a terrific wingman. Only—"

"Only what?"

"Only now it will be obvious to the cops that that Griffin guy didn't commit suicide. The organization might not be the only ones hunting us."

✦ ✦ ✦

Katherine hopped into the car gripping a white plastic bag, which she passed to Roger. "Drug stores don't carry scalpels or kitchen knives, but I found a Swiss Army knife. Feels pretty sharp. Plus rubbing alcohol to sanitize the spot, antibiotic ointment for afterward, and cotton bandages with surgical tape."

"Aunty *who* ointment? Never mind. I assume it's like sulfa powder. First"—he opened his own door, then climbed into the back seat—"drive. Anyplace. We've been sitting still too long."

She started the motor and pulled back onto the street. In the rearview mirror, she could see Roger already had his shirt off. "I still wish you would let me get you a motel room. At least a gas station restroom. First you get shot, now you're about to slice your arm open."

"Nothing doing. This thing is coming out."

His eyes met hers in the mirror. Unexpectedly his took on that smiley face look with crinkles at the edges. He held the pocketknife up where she could see it. "If you're interested in medicine, I guess you could park long enough to assist with the procedure."

The mental picture of the knife piercing his arm and blood running out sent a shiver down her spine. "No thank you. I'll just watch the road and keep an eye on our six, as you put it. But please don't make a mess of my back seat."

The sound of his chuckling reached her about the same time as the odor of rubbing alcohol.

"Katherine, do me a favor?"

"One more on top of the other hundred? What is it?"

"I've never done anything like this. Please don't think I'm a weakling if I say ouch or something."

"I promise I won't—"

"Ow!"

A series of grunts and groans painful even to hear encouraged her to concentrate on traffic. Would she have the courage to gouge into her own body without anesthetic? She hoped never to find out.

After an eternity, Roger said. "It was deeper than I expected."

The sound of rushing air announced he'd opened the rear window. After the sound stopped, he said, "Done. I tossed it out. With all this traffic, that thing will be crushed to bits in no time."

"Good. What's our next stop, Doctor?"

"I have some people I'd like to look for. Let me explain, then tell me if there's some fancy twenty-first-century way of doing this . . ."

CHAPTER 40

Seated in front of a computer terminal, Katherine sighed. She continued clicking the object she called a mouse. "No trace of a Walter Quentin Crippen. I checked the entire United States."

Her words dragged Roger's mood downward like lead anchors. Pencil in hand, he crossed off the last name on his list of his Fourth Fighter Group buddies. "I was saving Walt for last. He was the best wingman a pilot could want, and my closest American pal in England. I guess he's dead if you can't find him."

"Not necessarily. He could be alive and using an unlisted number. Or he might use a cell phone instead of a landline."

"Cell phone? You mean those pocket-sized telephones are called cell phones?"

"Sure. Or iPhone. Or Android. Or even just 'cell.' Is that important?"

He couldn't help grinning. "Not important, but it clears up a little misunderstanding of mine. I'll explain later."

"Back to your friend Walt. He might also be alive and live with family. I see plenty of Crippens all across the country, just not Walter Quentin Crippen."

"In which case, searching for the right family might take forever. Even if he's alive—which he probably isn't—he could pass away before we stumble across a relative." For the hundredth time, he scanned the library with his eyes. "Watching for Luftwaffe fighters was a piece of cake compared to constantly checking people to see if anybody looks like a killer. I could spot Messerschmitts a long way off, but an assassin on foot could walk right up to us before he pulls a gun or a knife."

"I know. I'm trying to hurry."

While Katherine continued scanning the computer screen, Roger gingerly touched his chest. It no longer throbbed. The sensation had downgraded to a cross between a dull ache and itchiness, but at least he could use his right arm without wincing now. As a bonus, the quickly healing wound had finally convinced Katherine that at least part of his story was on the level.

"Do you want to check out more local listings for old Indiana friends?" Katherine asked. "Even though we struck out on those first dozen classmates, there might still be someone in the area who remembers you. Maybe a student who was a year or two younger?"

Roger shook his head. "I'm feeling too antsy here. Let's switch to Plan B, placing an ad in the *Indianapolis Star*. If anybody has a grandpa who attended Plainfield High in the late '30s, a big ad might spark their curiosity."

The two walked toward the library exit, but then Katherine abruptly stopped. She pointed to a bulletin board of community events. "Roger, look."

He read aloud: "Award Ceremony for Military Veterans. Overdue medals for valiant actions to be awarded to Hoosier vets of WWII, Korea, and Vietnam who never received proper recognition—"

"Roger, the ceremony will be right here in Indianapolis. If you were to attend wearing that flight jacket, it's just possible some elderly veteran might see you."

He rubbed his chin. "Talk about a long shot. But long shots might be all I have left." His eyes cut to the bottom line. "We're shaving it close. Tomorrow morning at ten o'clock, Pershing Auditorium, Indiana World War Memorial."

"Do you know where that is?"

"I never heard of Pershing Auditorium, but they were building the War Memorial when I left for Canada. You and I saw it from the top of the Soldiers and Sailors Monument." He nodded. "Okay, we'll go. Meanwhile, let's place that classified ad in the newspaper and then buzz out of town. If the organization has any more clowns hunting for me, let's give 'em a run for their money."

The pair strode back to the car. On the way Katherine explained they didn't need to drive to the *Indianapolis Star* in person to place an ad. "I can call the paper on my cell phone and pay by credit card. Their number is here in today's newspaper."

Roger whistled in amazement. "Just that easy?"

"Just that easy."

Katherine powered up her cell phone. The moment it was ready for service, it emitted a ring tone. "I missed a call." She grew animated when she saw the caller's number. "It's from Uncle Kurt! He must be home from Africa early." She punched several buttons and listened to whatever message had been left—a process that still boggled Roger's mind. Katherine's face transformed from excited to perplexed.

"What was the message?"

"All he said was there had been some kind of terrible, horrible mistake and that he'll be headed to Indiana as soon as possible to set things straight."

Roger's stomach tightened. "When did you tell him you're in Indiana?"

She shook her head. "I didn't. I never had a chance. Besides, we left Atlanta so fast I didn't bring my phone charger. I've kept it off to stretch the battery."

"Well, somebody clued him in. Three guesses which organization might have done that."

Katherine's face clouded. A moment later, she brightened. "The communiqué, the one they sent me with your picture. I received it on Uncle Kurt's computer. If he's home, that would be the last e-mail I'd opened, and it has all the details he would need to trace that GPS chip, same as I did. Of course, that would have been before you threw it into traffic."

She keyed in a number, then waited for a reply. "No answer. His phone is turned off."

"Why do I have a bad feeling about this?"

"Roger, no matter what happens in the HO, I assure you Uncle Kurt will be on our side. Like you said, he probably doesn't even know what the upper levels are doing—*if* it's even the same group."

"I hope so. Meanwhile, go ahead and call in the newspaper ad. By the way, let's take the battery out of that portable phone when you're done. Call me suspicious, but these days I just don't trust gadgets I don't understand."

Katherine froze, then stared at him. "You're right. I've been so stupid. I'm not sure how it's done, but rescue workers can ping a cell phone if someone is missing or unconscious. I'm so used to carrying one, it just never occurred to me."

The pitiful look in her eyes broke Roger's heart. He placed a comforting hand on her shoulder. "Forget it. We're both facing challenges we've never dealt with before. Just make the call, then cut the power to the phone."

Once those tasks were done, Roger asked Katherine to drive any which way to confuse would-be trackers, but then to head out of the city in a generally westward direction. It was anybody's guess whether the Griffin reported Roger's last known position before closing in. Still, some inner urge wouldn't let him come this far without at least a quick glimpse of the small town of Plainfield where he'd lived and worked for the Tuckers. When he spotted the sign for Washington Street, he instructed her to turn west onto it.

Twenty-five minutes later, Washington Street became Main Street in the suburb of Plainfield. Roger pointed out old, familiar landmarks from the more abundant newer homes and businesses. Downtown Plainfield retained a quaint appearance, but it wasn't the scene fixed in his memory.

"Well? Is it what you expected?"

"I honestly didn't know what to expect. These older two- and three-story buildings are the same ones I remember, only now they have fancy modern windows, and the names on the signs are different. Even the bricks look different, as if someone gave all these buildings new, modern fronts. Along this street, there used to be Morris Café, Symons Hardware, Beacham's Dry Goods, Wilson's Grocery, Plainfield Variety Store, Grimes Café and Hotel. Being here feels like going to see an old friend, only to find a stranger living in the house." He studied the pedestrians, but none of them looked the least bit familiar.

He tried to dredge up sufficient words to describe the feeling of emptiness evoked by these surroundings. No words he could muster conveyed the peculiar emotions sparked by simultaneously being "home," yet not.

When Katherine reached the far limits of town, she swung the Passat in a U-turn and cruised back the way they had come.

"Pull over to the curb a second, will you?"

When Katherine obliged, Roger read aloud the sign on their right. "Central Elementary School? That building used to be Plainfield High. They must've built a new high school somewhere else."

"Do you want to find the new one?"

He shook his head. His eyes were still on the two-story schoolhouse of dark brick. "No. A new building won't hold any attraction for me. This is the place that overflows with memories."

Like him, she was glancing around, looking for suspicious observers. Good girl. She stayed on the alert. "Describe it, Roger. What was life at Plainfield High like in those days?"

To Roger's surprise, Katherine's request pleased him, even if she might be testing him. "For one thing, the school didn't have a gymnasium when I went here. Mr. Girard—the principal—was always trying to improve the place, even when money was tight. I heard he finally managed to get a gym built in 1939, after I was gone."

"Did you go out for sports?"

"You bet. I played football and baseball. We didn't have our own field, though. The Quaker football squad played home games in the city park. We had a swell coach, Mr. Armstrong."

"I assume you had a lot of girlfriends in school?" Her smiled puckered in a cute way when she teased.

He smiled back and shook his head. "My heart was elsewhere. This might sound funny, but back then I still had a schoolboy crush on Vilma Banky."

Instead of smiling or laughing as he expected, Katherine stared blankly. Was she kidding?

"You know, Vilma Banky? The famous movie starlet? 'The Hungarian Rhapsody.' She costarred with leading men like Rudolph Valentino."

Katherine shook her head. "Never heard of her."

Discouragement washed over Roger. "Incredible. If the world has forgotten a gorgeous bombshell like Vilma Banky, how can I hope anyone will remember a nobody like me?"

Katherine changed the subject. "Which school course was your favorite? Literature?"

"Not in those days. For me, shop class ranked tops, but only because they didn't teach aviation." He laughed. "Someday I'll tell you stories about how we used to scare freshmen spitless at the Haunted Bridge."

Katherine reached for the door handle and popped it open. "Come on."

"Wait, where are you going?" Roger glanced around. Still no one suspicious in sight, but they'd already lingered longer than he'd intended. They should leave.

"Humor me for two minutes. I've got a lot of time and gasoline invested in you. I want to double-check something."

Not understanding why she cared but gratified to see she took along her handbag containing the pistol, Roger hopped out and joined her. Merely walking up the school sidewalk resurrected countless ghostly memories.

Katherine followed the signs to the school office, and Roger trailed her, furtively looking left and right. When they entered the office, two women looked up.

"Hello," Katherine greeted. "This might sound strange, but we're doing a little local research. I've heard this building was once Plainfield's high school. Is that true?"

A brunette secretary stepped to the counter. "You're right. This building did used to be the high school, but that was eons ago."

Roger was ready with his best "I told you so" look, but she ignored him.

"The football team used to be called the Plainfield Quakers, right? Is there any way to find out the name of the man who coached the team in the late 1930s? My friend's family used to live here, and we're piecing together some family history."

The secretary brightened. "They still call the sports teams the Quakers. We don't keep high school records here, but I'm sure I could learn the name of the coach with a phone call." She stepped to her desk and placed the call.

Roger leaned close to Katherine's ear. "Got you curious, did I?"

"I'm a freelance editor, remember? This maneuver is what we call fact-checking."

Before long, the secretary covered the mouthpiece on the telephone. "The football coach in those days was named Scott Armstrong. Anything else you need to know?"

When Katherine merely stared at him, Roger answered. "No thank you. That's all we needed."

As he pushed open the exit door, Roger said, "Of course, those details don't prove anything, but I hope you're satisfied. Now, let's put more distance between us and Indianapolis."

With Katherine behind the steering wheel once more, Roger directed her north and eastward. When they reached the proper stretch of County Road 200 South, he asked her to slow a little, but not to stop. The Tucker farmhouse was gone. In fact, the entire farm had been replaced by a modern neighborhood of a hundred or more homes that glided past his passenger window. "I used to plow that land with a tractor. This whole detour has been disheartening. I knew things would be different, but I was sort of hoping . . ."

"Hoping what?"

Unsettling feelings of emptiness clouded his heart once more. Which words could describe his sense of purposelessness? After years of being caged like an animal and yearning to return home, he'd finally accomplished the impossible. Yet while he languished overseas, "home" had somehow packed up and moved away, leaving no forwarding address. Bits and pieces of it remained, like crushed paper cups on the ground after the circus leaves town. But nothing more. Plainfield no longer qualified as home, at least not for him.

"Okay with you if we get out of here for the night? Kokomo is north of Indianapolis. At least, it is if they didn't move it. We could drive a winding, unpredictable course there, spend the night at a motel, and then zip back to Indy in time for that veterans' ceremony tomorrow."

"I'll drive you to Kokomo on one condition. We get to eat supper in a decent sit-down restaurant. I'm getting sick of burgers and fries, but you'll have to pay. We can't use my credit card in case whoever is following us can use it to track us down."

Roger's jaw dropped. "Boy, life used to be so much easier. It's a deal. I'm not rich, but I've still got some cash."

◆　◆　◆

Suppertime found the pair ordering fettuccine Alfredo, bread sticks, and bottomless salad at the local Italian eatery they discovered along Highway 31 in Kokomo. A black wig and fake novelty-store glasses transformed Katherine's appearance. Roger felt conspicuous in his new wig and fake mustache, but Katherine had assured him he looked like a totally different person, especially with the denim jacket from Goodwill, so he maintained the disguise. As an extra precaution, though, Roger had requested a quiet booth in the back. He let the waitress assume they wanted the secluded corner for romantic purposes. The truth was, he wanted a seat where he could observe incoming patrons while not presenting snipers with an easy target through the window.

"Okay if I ask the blessing?"

Before each meal, his request sparked an expression of awkwardness in Katherine. As always, she wordlessly bowed her head with him. This time, however, she tacked on, "Amen to that!" when Roger finished with a request for divine protection.

She took the tongs and dished up their salad. "Did everybody in the 1940s pray all the time?"

"Nope. Some did, some didn't. Matter of fact, I never prayed seriously in the '40s. That didn't start until years later."

"Really? So what's the story?" She bit off the tip of a breadstick.

"When I was locked in the Methuselah bunker, I started going nuts. Stir-crazy from being underground so long. I asked Dr. Kossler to bring tons of books. English when he could find 'em, but German books when he couldn't. He even scrounged up grammar books in Dutch, Russian, French, and Finnish for me to puzzle over. Without reading material to keep my brain occupied, I'd be in a funny farm by now."

"Which explains why you're such an authority on classic literature."

He shook his head. "I'm no authority. Funny thing is, before my capture, I never read much at all, except aircraft technical manuals or maybe *Yank*, the army weekly magazine. Then, while I was a prisoner, I read millions of pages. One year—I think it was about 1959 or 1960—I memorized entire chapters of *Robinson Crusoe* just as a mental challenge. By the way, if you haven't read that one yet, stop at the point where Crusoe gets rescued. That final stuff about him sailing to Spain and getting attacked by wolves makes a crummy ending."

"That's when you started reading the Bible and praying?"

"Right. Of course, I'd heard about God all my life. Even back in Sunshine, an elderly lady named Hawkins used to tell us Bible stories and urged the orphans to pray. I did say a couple of desperate 'Help me' prayers right after my capture. Honestly, though, I never reflected much on God until the bunker. Suddenly the distractions of normal life disappeared. I had years and years of time to meditate on the universe, God, eternity, the meaning of life—"

"Are you convinced life has a meaning?" Katherine lanced a cherry tomato with her fork and popped it into her mouth.

"I'm sure. Yeah, I know all about Darwin and that crowd. I read his *Origin of Species*. Seven times, cover to cover. Despite all his talk about birds' beaks growing longer, et cetera, Darwin never comes close to explaining how earth could be a totally dead, lifeless planet one minute, and the next moment give birth to a living, functioning cell—complete with fast-working reproductive abilities to duplicate itself before the sterile environment killed it off again."

When she offered no comment, he continued. "Same thing for the whole universe. Only two possibilities exist: either God created the universe, or the universe created itself—out of absolutely nothing. If you cut God out of the equation, it makes no sense for anything physical to exist. Not even one molecule. I spent years dodging belief in God, but the more I dwelled on the subject, the harder it was to believe an enormous brainless universe popped itself into existence from empty space and started ticking like a Swiss watch. That's when I told Kossler to find me a Bible. The more I read it, the more the pieces fit together."

Katherine focused on her food, carefully plucking black olives from her salad rather than making eye contact. "I'll have to think about it. Maybe after this whole mess is over. My uncle raised me to think of religion as a crutch for weak minds."

He accepted her signal to change the subject. "I've been meaning to bring up another subject. Tonight."

"What about tonight?"

Now it was his turn to squirm with an uncomfortable topic. How did you talk to a woman about something like this? "Katherine, America has changed a lot. Even after only a couple of days I can tell people do a lot of things I've never done. At least some of them do."

"Meaning?"

Judging by her eyes, Katherine remained genuinely mystified. He would have to spell it out. "With killers on my six, I'd better not sleep in the car in a parking lot. On the other hand, well . . . Call me old-fashioned if you want, but the way I was raised, a man just doesn't go around checking into hotels with a pretty girl he's not married to."

Katherine burst into laughter. "Let me guess. You want to get married tonight?"

Roger felt his muscles relax as he joined in her laughter. "Don't put words in my mouth. What I mean is, it's like stepping into temptation. You know I'm serious about God. So let's take turns. Only one of us on the bed at a time. One sleeps while the other keeps watch at the window. Also, if I make so much as one suggestive move, I want you to slap me so hard it will knock some sense into me."

Her eyes twinkled. "Roger that, Captain," she said, borrowing his radio jargon. "I'll keep my slapping hand cocked and ready. But if any other Air Force vet had pulled a line like that, I wouldn't buy it for a million dollars!"

Roger chuckled and reached for a second breadstick. Good. The explanation was over and went pretty smoothly. Even after so many decades, he felt awkward broaching certain subjects with a girl. But Katherine was no ordinary girl. For once, he'd found a girl with whom he could bare his inner feelings. She was the down-home type you could go camping with, or sip cocoa with in front of a fireplace, the kind who might actually enjoy changing baby diapers.

Did he have a right to think such thoughts? He pushed the pasta around his plate.

Sure he looked young, but he was a lifetime older than she was, literally a geezer from a bygone era. Would a girl like Katherine be repulsed to learn he was developing feelings for her?

What do you have to offer a woman? You've got no job, no home, no money, no nothing. Worse, trained assassins are trying to rub you out. She might feel sorry for you, but why would any sensible girl want to love a dinosaur with a bull's-eye plastered on his back?

Katherine sipped her peach-raspberry iced tea. "You've grown awfully quiet. A penny for your thoughts."

He swallowed and plunged a fork into his fettuccine Alfredo. "I was thinking that this is, without a doubt, the fanciest spaghetti I've ever eaten!"

CHAPTER 41

The next morning after a simple breakfast in the lobby of the Comfort Inn, Roger and Katherine once again headed outside to her car. Their nighttime vigils by the window had ensured that no one had approached it, let alone planted a car bomb.

Roger inhaled the crisp spring air and smiled as his breath condensed visibly in front of him. As he scraped frost from the windshield, he wished for something a bit warmer than the fake hairpiece on his head. March in Indiana was colder than he recalled. Or maybe his body was just used to the constant temperature in his former cell. Rubbing his hands to warm them, he slipped behind the steering wheel and glanced at Katherine. In the passenger seat, she looked like a stranger in the wig. The disguise accomplished their goal, but he missed seeing her natural hair. She studied her portable phone.

"More messages from your uncle?" Roger put the car into gear.

She tossed the phone into her handbag. "Can't say. The battery died."

"I'll be glad if a battery is the only thing that dies today."

Her eyes weren't smiling when she returned his gaze. She appeared on the verge of tears.

"Sorry. I was trying to lighten the mood with grim humor."

"Roger, this pressure is getting to me. Even when it was my turn to sleep last night, I lay there wondering if bullets or a pipe bomb might smash through the window any second."

Roger's foot shifted to the brake pedal. He stopped the car before they left the parking lot. "The last thing I want is for you to get hurt. If you're frightened, I'll get out and walk. I won't blame you."

She shook her head. "You wouldn't stand a chance. They would run you over. Or do a drive-by shooting."

Roger searched his brain for an inspiring reply, but his mind hit rock bottom. "So what do you want to do? Your call."

"Let's compromise. We can still go to the veterans' ceremony, and our ad will be in today's paper. But if we don't find any leads by this evening, we'll stop running. We'll go to the police or the FBI and ask for protection. We'll tell the whole story."

Her suggestion led to the one course of action he'd been dodging all along. Couldn't she understand why? "They'll throw me into a loony bin, Katherine. I refuse to let anybody lock me up. I've experienced more than my share of being a zoo animal. Never again."

Tears welled in her eyes, overflowed onto her cheeks. Here she was, the most wonderful thing that had happened to him in seventy years, and she was crying—all because of him.

He snatched a tissue from the packet on the dashboard and dabbed her cheeks. "Okay. You've been more than swell through this whole crazy escapade. If we can't come up with one definite contact to pursue by six o'clock tonight, we'll go to the cops. One thing that might help is that photo of me in the Eighth Air Force Museum. I can't prove it's me, but it's one thread of evidence."

"Plus, if they contact the police in Georgia, there will be a report about the shootings in the museum. That redheaded woman and her son—"

Roger grunted. "Don't forget, only you and I know that that Griffin character did the shooting. The police might conclude that I—the madman with the nutty war story—am the maniac who shot them and fled from the scene. I'll admit I'm tired of running. I can't keep moving for the rest of my life."

She reached for his hand. "I'll stick with you. I'll vouch for your story."

The warmth and tenderness of her fingers felt so right. Before he could stop himself, he leaned over and hugged her. To his delight, her arms hugged back. "I appreciate your support. Only trouble is, you're too young to vouch for my story. The authorities won't believe a cute young lady who didn't know me during World War II."

Despite the teary glint in her eyes, Katherine returned a wry smile. "I believe that's the first time in my life a handsome bachelor has wished I was a wrinkled, old spinster."

He waggled a finger and grinned. "Now you're twisting my words. I'm sure you'll make a lovely old lady someday, but for now I like you just how you are." He gently nudged her with his elbow. "I do have one more strategy I'd like to apply, if you don't mind."

She cocked her head. "Strategy?"

"Remember the elderly woman at the orphanage I mentioned? She said always to pray. I was pretty slow catching on, but I pray pretty often these days. Join me?" He squeezed her hand.

When Katherine nodded, he could read in her eyes that she sincerely agreed, even if she wasn't accustomed to addressing the Almighty.

Roger bowed his head and prayed a from-the-gut request for God's guidance and protection. The words weren't flowery, just sincere and to the point. He finished with an "Amen," which Katherine repeated.

As he maneuvered the car onto Highway 31, Roger checked all directions for followers. His mind replayed Katherine's words referring to him as a handsome bachelor. Was she sending him a subtle message?

Don't waste your time getting confused about love. You're not out of the frying pan, Greene. Besides, her wording could've been totally innocent. He pushed Katherine's compliment from his mind for the moment. If she was sending a signal, he could interpret it later. Right now, he'd better concentrate on keeping both of them alive.

CHAPTER 42

THURSDAY, MARCH 12, 2015

NORTH KEYSTONE AVENUE, INDIANAPOLIS

Katherine pointed up the street. "Roger, pull into the shopping center. That electronic supply store should stock chargers for my cell phone."

Roger maneuvered into the lot. If she could telephone her uncle Kurt, Katherine might get some answers.

Five minutes later, she hopped back in the car, triumph on her beaming face. "Got one." She plugged the adaptor into the cigarette lighter. "Now, let's see if my uncle has his phone on." She keyed in the proper number.

"It's ringing." She flashed Roger an excited thumbs-up. "Uncle Kurt? Thank goodness you're back from Africa. Life has become a nightmare! Where are you?"

From the half conversation Roger heard, he guessed her uncle had spent the night at a hotel right in Indianapolis.

"Of course we can," Katherine said. "I need to talk to you as soon as possible." She explained their approximate location. "I know this sounds bizarre, but we were planning to attend a ceremony for military veterans downtown. I'll explain later."

Roger cringed. Although Katherine held her uncle in high esteem, the man remained a wild card. Surely someone who had spent years in this so-called organization couldn't be totally naive about it. An additional concern: could these portable telephone signals be traced with radio-finding equipment? If so, cunning people could be zeroing in on their location right now, even though he'd disposed of the chip from his arm.

Katherine balanced the road atlas on her knees while talking. "White River State Park? Yes, I see it. Just west of downtown. All right, we'll rendezvous there. Love you!"

"So he wants to meet at a park? Just like that?" Roger couldn't conceal the mistrust in his question.

Katherine swung to the defensive. "Roger, you can be suspicious of anybody else in the Heritage Organization, but please don't doubt Uncle Kurt. He's a compassionate man. He reared me from childhood and loves me."

"Sorry. Present company excluded, I haven't met many people I could trust lately. What's the shortest route to the park from here, navigator? We'll skip the veterans' ceremony and go see your uncle."

At 9:20 a.m., Roger steered into the parking lot of White River State Park. Only four other cars and one rusty pickup dotted the lot this early on a nippy morning.

"I wonder if any of these cars are his."

Katherine shook her head. "None of these looks like a rental. But there might be other entrances to the park."

Roger glanced in all directions. "Come on. Let's walk around. This parking lot makes me feel like a duck in a carnival shooting gallery."

The two locked the car and strolled to the park entrance.

"You'll see, Roger. Uncle Kurt is as clever as he is warmhearted. He'll know what to do once we explain the situation and convince him the HO is involved."

Roger held his tongue. His own knowledge of this HO and modern America were so sketchy that he simply didn't have enough information to develop a decisive plan of action. Could Uncle Kurt be insightful enough and trusted enough to advise a solid plan?

The two meandered in the park, both thinking their own thoughts without speaking.

"There you are, my sweetie."

"Uncle Kurt!"

Katherine ran into the embrace of a tall man with thinning gray hair. Kurt Mueller wore a double-breasted camel coat that reached nearly to his knees. His right arm hung in a sling. But the most striking feature about him just now was his blissful smile. A department store Santa with a cute tyke on his knee couldn't look less threatening. Maybe Roger had worried about this guy for nothing.

"Your arm. What happened?"

"Only a hairline fracture. I was running to get a second shot into a wildebeest when I tripped over a root and tumbled into a ravine. It'll be back to normal soon, but since I couldn't hold the rifle anymore, I decided to pack up and return home early."

"I'm so glad you're here."

Katherine quickly introduced Roger. Uncle Kurt shook with his left hand, smiling nearly as generously for Roger as he had for Katherine.

"Nice to meet you, sir, but this is no time for socializing. We have problems. Giant-sized problems. Katherine thinks you can help."

Uncle Kurt's face went serious. He motioned to one of the rectangular slabs of stone provided as benches for this park. "Let's have a seat. Tell me everything."

At first, Roger let Katherine do most of the talking. She explained about the communiqué she'd received from the HO and her supposed assignment of finding and trailing Roger. When she finished, Roger filled in parts of the story concerning himself, his background, his long captivity, and the escape. Periodically the man cocked his head or raised an eyebrow, but his eyes stayed fixed on Roger. Would the old gentleman believe Roger was who he said he was?

The presence of Uncle Kurt absorbed Katherine's attention, but not Roger's. While she recounted their cross-country trek, he scanned the park and the far side of the river to make sure no enemies with guns skulked about. He watched in vain. A middle-aged brunette walking a Scottish terrier sauntered past. In one hand she grasped an open paperback, and she appeared engrossed in its pages. Moments later, a thirtyish man with blond, curly hair jogged along in a navy-blue sweat suit and sunglasses. The man paid no heed. More important, he carried no weapons.

Jealousy bubbled in Roger's heart. *I've been an American for longer than these people have been alive. Yet they get to enjoy the fresh air and morning sunshine of a jaunt in the park, while I keep my head low for fear of thugs bearing guns. God, when will this end?*

Roger studied Kurt Mueller. What thoughts went through his head while Katherine poured out the rest of their story? The man owned a terrific poker face. Katherine's mention of Roger's remarkable recuperation after being shot elicited little more than a glance at Roger and lifted eyebrows.

Odd. He's barely showing any reaction. Then again, she says he's the analytical, intellectual type. Like a chess player . . .

When Katherine wound up the narrative, she concluded by saying, "We decided to go to the police tonight if we couldn't find any of Roger's old acquaintances. What do you think, Uncle? What would you do?"

Uncle Kurt clasped both her hands between his. "First, let me say again how very relieved I am you're all right, Katarina." Turning to Roger, he added, "Thank you for taking such good care of my little lady, Captain Greene. I can never repay you enough."

"Katherine has taken as much care of me as I have of her. She's a remarkable girl."

"Yes. That she is."

These last words rang with a slightly less cordial tone, almost as if other considerations were distracting Uncle Kurt. Then again, who wouldn't be distracted after hearing such a bizarre tale?

Still holding Katherine's hands, the elder Mueller turned his gray eyes to Roger. "I'll confess—everything I've just heard is extraordinary. It boggles the mind. So forgive me if I ask you bluntly: is everything you and my niece just recounted the absolute, total truth, so far as you know?" Those penetrating eyes bored into Roger and didn't let go.

"One hundred percent true, sir. I know it sounds incredible, but every word is accurate."

Uncle Kurt inhaled, as if he were coming to a decision but unsure how to express it. A skinny woman wearing tiny headphones marched along the sidewalk pumping her arms to an unheard rhythm. Katherine's uncle waited for her to pass.

"It's a fascinating saga, Captain Greene. No doubt about that. Since you declare it's the truth, I'm sure we can find ways to verify it—or at least the most important points. But let me clarify. You haven't gone to the authorities yet? Or to the news media?"

"No. I realized how absurd my testimony would sound without evidence of what the organization did to me. That's why we waited."

"That was wise." Kurt Mueller stood up. "It would be foolish of me to suggest a course of action immediately, right after learning the full scope of the situation. I need a few minutes to assimilate it all before I make my recommendation. Meanwhile, I wonder if you could excuse Katherine and me for just a few short moments? I have a vital matter I need to discuss with her."

"Uncle, I have no secrets from Roger."

"Of course not. However, this issue concerns me—it's personal. You know what a private man I am, Katarina. Will you excuse us for a couple of minutes, Captain?" He tugged his niece to her feet.

Roger stood too. Couldn't Kurt Mueller's personal "vital matter" wait a few minutes? What could he say, though? No, I don't give permission for you to talk to your niece outside my presence? "All right. I'll stroll around the park. With gun-toting goons hunting for me, I don't want to end up in someone's crosshairs. Please don't take too long."

"Thank you, Captain. Don't wander far. We'll be back shortly. Then the three of us can put our heads together and lay plans."

The blond jogger passed a second time as Kurt Mueller placed an arm around Katherine's shoulders and led her away. For some reason, Katherine seemed to give the curly blond head a prolonged stare as the figure trotted away. The glimpse became an invisible knife in Roger's heart. Just when he believed she might actually have feelings for him, she was giving other guys the eye. He stuffed his hands in his pockets and looked away. Maybe she did see him as an old fogey.

◆   ◆   ◆

"Uncle, please tell me you believe me about these men chasing us with guns. I'm not hallucinating."

"Of course you aren't. In fact, I knew something about it already. That's why I rushed here so urgently."

She halted in her tracks, stunned that he could know the organization was capable of such things. "You knew? Then, why?"

He hooked his elbow, the one not in a sling, around hers and tugged her into motion once more. "Katarina, until a short time ago, I'd heard nothing about this man you know as Roger Greene. Since my return from Namibia, I've learned a great deal about him. Now I need to tell you as gently as I can that his background isn't exactly the way he painted it to you. His real name isn't Roger Greene, and he's not an American pilot from the Second World War. Most of what he told you is a fabrication."

Katherine halted a second time and released her uncle's arm. His words made no sense in light of all she'd lived through the past several days. "What are you saying?"

Uncle Kurt's eyes flitted left and right. They were alone. "Nuts and bolts of the man's story are factual, but he has twisted them, rewritten the past to suit his purposes."

"How can that be? Yesterday morning I saw him take a bullet with my own eyes. Today you can barely see the wound."

"This will be difficult, *Schatz*," he said, employing his favorite German term of endearment for her. "Let me explain. As you know, the Heritage Organization exists to better mankind, to leave a better world as a heritage for the next generation. Some of our members are skilled physicians and brilliant scientists. Many years ago, HO scientists began experiments with cloning."

"Cloning?" Where was Uncle Kurt headed?

"Yes, and I don't refer to replicating a silly sheep or a pig. Back during the war years, men of science who first envisioned our organization were compelled by the politics of the day to feign loyalty to the Nazi regime.

They opted to make the best of a horrible situation in order to accomplish something beneficial for mankind. When an American bomb killed Allied prisoners on a train car, our early HO scientists requested and received some bodies for cloning experiments. They froze the corpses, intending to use them for research. One of those unfortunate victims was the original Roger Greene."

Katherine's mind reeled. The Captain Roger Greene who had flown for the Army Air Corps was dead? Did this mean the man she'd been traveling with was a genetic duplicate created from a frozen corpse?

"But the shooters? His recuperative powers? And I saw a photo of Roger in a World War II museum."

"As I told you, small chunks of his story are true, Katarina. Just not in the way he wants you to believe. You see, the organization scientists I mentioned weren't interested in merely recreating a living, breathing human who resembled the man from whose cells they fashioned him. Not at all. Rather, they hoped to improve human biological functions for the good of all mankind. You can't repeat what I'm telling you, but I need to let you know they were partially successful. The metabolism of their seventh subject proved remarkable, giving him near-miraculous recuperative abilities. They nicknamed their creation Roger Methuselah, partially in honor of the deceased American whose cells they harvested and partially in hopes of an improved species of human. In a top-secret experiment, they educated him and prepared him to conduct a responsible role, both in society and in the organization."

"But the HO sent him to Atlanta. They assigned me to trail him as a training exercise."

"Yes, they did. They intended for the excursion to be as much a training exercise for the clone as for you. This is his first trip outside Germany. But what his handlers didn't realize was their test-tube offspring was becoming mentally unstable. Evidently he now believes he truly is the original Captain Roger Greene. I saw as much in his eyes. Perhaps his twisted subconscious mind concocted that nonsense about being shot down and imprisoned to explain his youthful appearance. Worse, as soon as he got his hands on the airline ticket to fly to America, he murdered the HO member who drove him to the airport. A pleasant young scientist named Sophie, I'm told."

"Roger mentioned a woman named Sophie. He said the organization assassinated her for helping him."

Uncle Kurt sighed. "The clone is delusional. I suppose he actually believes everything he told you. As you can imagine, this whole affair has shaken the organization to its very core. Just think: we exist to benefit mankind, and here is a prototype of HO research committing murder! Of course, the scientists involved had to inform the authorities in Germany of this catastrophe. With the blessing and assistance of the American FBI, plainclothes lawmen have been dispatched to pull the plug on this inhuman menace once and for all."

"Pull the plug? You mean to kill Roger?" Katherine glanced behind her at the man she'd known as Roger Greene. The image of his stiff body, dumped on a stainless-steel table and adorned with a toe tag, sent a shiver down her spine.

"Please understand, Katarina, that creature is not a normal human being. It is a Frankenstein with faulty wiring. German and American authorities are working jointly to remove this dangerous mistake from society before anyone else gets hurt. They're doing it quietly, without panicking the population. It's best for you and me to step out of the way and let them carry out their duty."

Katherine's mind was swimming in new information as she allowed Uncle Kurt to pull her along. "This is all so hard to fathom. It's like reality turned inside-out."

"I agree. The news has been a nightmare for me ever since I received word of the situation. I was terribly worried about you, Katarina. Just knowing this artificial life form might go berserk at any moment and slay the light of my life . . ."

They had reached the parking lot. Uncle Kurt switched topics. He began recounting his hunting expedition in Namibia and a step-by-step description of how he'd hurt his arm. Katherine barely listened. She considered everything her uncle had said about Roger and a cloning experiment gone awry. The explanation sounded plausible, even if technologically spooky. She found it difficult to envision the multifaceted science needed to create a whole human being from the frozen cells of a dead pilot, but was that less likely than Roger's elaborate story of a Methuselah Project?

"Excuse me, Uncle, but can't I at least say goodbye to Roger? I mean, even if he's an android, or clone, or whatever, he does have feelings. I've seen them. It would only be proper to say goodbye before we drive into the sunset. You did promise to go back."

Uncle Kurt's eyes strayed to his Swiss-made Rolex. "We can't go back, my dear. I had to lie to the clone to move you out of danger. I didn't want him to become violent. The American authorities have all the details on the clone. The rest is up to them."

The light pressure of his hand descended onto her back, just between the shoulder blades. Always in the past, this endearing gesture had reassured or comforted Katherine. This time, however, she couldn't escape the uncomfortable impression Uncle Kurt was simply manipulating her in the direction he wished.

Her emotions clashed. She hated to doubt her only living relative, a man who had reared her from childhood. But something deep inside rebelled.

In rapid succession, Katherine reviewed snippets of scenes she'd lived through: Roger singing "Don't Sit Under the Apple Tree." The gunman who'd attacked her and threatened to hurt her until Roger had shot him first. Their marathon conversation on the interstate in which she'd recounted the twentieth century and Roger had described life in England during the Blitz. His demeanor and vocabulary—including quaint, old-fashioned words like *swell*—seemed consistent with an American who had been locked away for decades. She thought about Roger's chivalry, his wry grin and gentle sense of humor. She had truly liked him. Certainly more than any of the other men she had befriended or even dated. On the other hand, following her heart and believing in Roger could only make Uncle Kurt a world-class liar.

But Uncle Kurt did lie. Just now he deceived Roger when he promised we would come right back. Clearly Uncle had never intended to go back, but that deception had rolled off his tongue slicker than peanut oil.

When they reached her uncle's rented Cadillac, she stepped forward to block his path. "Uncle Kurt, do you know what a stirrup pump is?"

"A stirrup pump? I've never heard of such a thing."

"Do you know the name of the Plainfield High School football team? And how about the name of its coach back in the 1930s?"

He shot her a quizzical smile and held out a hand, inviting her closer. "Whatever are you talking about, Katarina?"

She ignored his hand. "Can you tell me the names of specific Hoosiers who once attended Plainfield High School, or the names of all the pilots in the Fourth Fighter Group in England?" Katherine was on a roll. "How about the Soldiers and Sailors Monument downtown—when was that built, and what was the first name of the German architect who designed it? I grew up in this country, and I didn't know any of these things until I learned them from Roger. How am I supposed to believe a clone who grew up in some secret laboratory on the other side of the Atlantic—a creature who has never been outside Germany before—can tell me things only a man who grew up in Indianapolis and fought in England would know? Worst of all, why would an undercover law officer shoot an innocent woman and child in a museum?"

Once again, the blond jogger approached. Despite his sunglasses, Katherine's earlier impression that she'd seen the face somewhere before overwhelmed her. He glanced toward them, and Uncle Kurt gave a barely perceptible nod as the man pounded along the edge of the parking lot. Those cheekbones . . . How could she possibly recognize someone in Indianapolis? Until this trip, she'd never set foot in Indiana. She saw nothing memorable about his navy sweats, but she noticed he wore the same new style in Reeboks that she did, black with white stripes.

Uncle Kurt's joviality vanished. "Katarina, you will speak to me with respect. I love you, but you may not challenge my words. If I say a thing is so, the matter is settled. *Punkt.*"

"But Uncle, how can you guarantee any portion of what you told me about Roger is factual? Think with me: maybe everything Roger said about the Methuselah Project is true. If the higher-ups in the organization are so ruthless they would send assassins after him, wouldn't they be willing to lie to you too? You admitted you weren't aware of Roger until recently. You know nothing more than what they told you."

Kurt Mueller set his jaw. His frowning face resembled chiseled marble. Never before had she seen such fury smolder in his eyes.

"Katarina, enough. You and I are washing our hands of this affair. We will trust the American authorities to end it as they see fit. And never again talk so lightly of the organization. They paid for my education. They set me up in my jewelry business. They've generously provided for you too. The organization is the guiding force that will someday ease this world through its birth pangs to initiate a new world order. Only by embracing the organization can you guarantee yourself a prize role in that order."

The organization. With those words, like the tumblers of a lock clicking into place, Katherine recalled where she'd seen the blond jogger's face. Her promotion to Leutnant in Florida. Not one but two blond males had sat at another table. They'd never reciprocated her glances, so she'd left without meeting them. Then another fact sharpened into crystal clarity: *The first time I noticed the jogger, he wore white running shoes. They matched the white stripe on his sweatpants.* She glanced at the figure now retreating around the bend. His running shoes were definitely black, like hers; only the stripes were white. These were two different men—the twins! They were heading in the direction where Katherine had left Roger.

Her head swiveled from the jogger to her uncle. "The organization— they're here! You told me the American authorities would handle Roger, but they aren't police or FBI. They're organization hit men."

"Get in the car."

Instead of obeying, Katherine turned and bolted. Unlike the blond men, however, she didn't merely jog, and she ignored the sidewalk. Like an arrow, Katherine sprinted across the grass with every ounce of speed she could muster.

"Roger, run! It's a trap!"

CHAPTER 43

Following the sidewalk and rail overlooking the White River, Roger glanced again in the direction Katherine and her uncle had disappeared. What was delaying them? He had promised they would be right back.

He turned and resumed walking. The direction didn't matter, just so he wasn't standing still. Without that transmitter, odds were against an unseen sniper trailing him, but in the unlikely chance one was, a moving body would make a trickier target.

An assassin tried to hurt her before. What if they try again? Her uncle didn't look spry enough to protect her. Besides, I'm the one with the gun.

More than ever, Roger regretted letting Katherine out of eyesight with a man who, at best, might be totally naive concerning the organization. Roger repositioned the uncomfortable pistol in his rear waistband as he trudged in the direction he'd last seen Katherine. When he saw the blond sportsman approaching in the distance, he was glad he hadn't pulled out the weapon. No reason to alarm the local citizenry.

A faint shout reached his ears: "Roger, run! It's a trap!"

Both Roger and the blond jogger spotted Katherine at the same time. She was speeding across the grass at a dead run, straight toward Roger. Directly behind her appeared another blond runner, an exact duplicate of the near one. The man trailing Katherine wasn't jogging; he charged right on her heels and, like her, pounded straight toward him at full throttle.

Two of them?

An eye blink later, the closer man's right hand slipped inside his sweat-shirt and reappeared brandishing a pistol.

Roger dove for cover behind the only object nearby—one of the stone park benches. The moment he did, a bullet whacked into its surface.

Roger peeked over the bench and sighted the Ruger on the nearest attacker. He squeezed off a shot, but the gunman continued closing the distance.

Missed. Keep calm. Aim. Do it right.

The attacker raised his weapon again. Roger saw no smoke and heard no report, but a whine like an angry hornet zinged past his ear.

Roger steadied the gun with both hands, held his breath. In quick succession, he pulled the trigger over and over.

The first several shots were obvious misses, but at last a bullet must have scored—the attacker stopped too abruptly for a planned maneuver and collapsed onto the brown grass. Roger straightened but kept his gun trained on his foe. He didn't want to kill; he only wanted to survive.

The panting man on the ground lifted himself onto one elbow. He hefted his weapon and swung the muzzle toward Roger.

Again, Roger squeezed the trigger. At this close range, he couldn't miss. The gunman crumpled.

"Roger!"

He looked up in time to see the second runner alter course and ram Katherine, bowling her over. Not slowing, he charged in Roger's direction with a weapon in his hand. Behind that man, yet another figure approached, but more slowly—Kurt Mueller.

How many bullets did he have left? Roger didn't want to run out of ammo in a firefight, but in the excitement of the moment, he couldn't recall how many rounds the pistol had started with, nor how many he'd just spent.

The second gunman halted and dropped to one knee, taking aim at Roger. Behind the stone slab, Roger aimed back. But now Katherine was on her feet again. Missing his target might kill her.

"Katherine, hit the deck!"

The instant she dove, a bullet whined over his head.

Roger squeezed off round after round toward the man—and missed every time. Grinning in imminent victory, the gunman leaped from his crouching position and ran a zigzag course as he closed in.

Roger adjusted for distance and raised his barrel higher. He aimed ahead of the target, as he would fire at a speeding fighter plane. *God, help.* He pulled the trigger. The blond man staggered back and fell. Both attackers now lay still. Approaching cautiously Roger kicked the pistol of the closer assassin away from the body, then picked it up and tucked it into the rear of his waistband. After retrieving the second man's matching weapon, he removed its bullets and dumped them into his pocket. Lastly Roger did what he longed to do most of all: he swept Katherine into his arms and kissed her.

"If not for you, I'd be dead."

Panting, she said, "Uncle Kurt—he knew."

The mention of her uncle reminded Roger that yet another organization insider lurked nearby. He looked up and saw Kurt Mueller standing not thirty feet away, regarding the couple.

"Katarina, it's true I haven't been fully truthful with you, but it's always been for your own good. A worthy end justifies lethal means. Please come with me. I'll explain everything. Don't throw away your future in exchange for this antique from the past." He reached out a hand toward Katherine.

Tears glistened on Katherine's cheeks.

Roger stepped in front of her. "Unbutton your overcoat, Herr Mueller. Do it slowly, please. Show me whether you have a gun in there."

Mueller sneered. "What if I don't? Will you play Lone Ranger and shoot me in cold blood? Right in front of my niece, whose affection you stole from me?"

Roger raised his handgun. "Thanks to you and your pals, both Katherine and I nearly got killed several times."

"She was never meant to be hurt. There was a mix up in communi—"

"Open your coat."

Mueller glared. But when Roger raised the Ruger, the man spat and unbuttoned the camel overcoat with his left, uninjured, hand. With exaggerated nonchalance, he sauntered closer as he plucked open both sides with a mocking, theatrical gesture. Roger patted the pockets. No bulges. "If not for this sling, I wouldn't have brought those amateur assistants. You've been luckier than you realize, Greene."

"Katherine and I are heading back to the parking lot. Don't follow until we're well out of sight."

Mueller ignored Roger, shifting his eyes instead to Katherine. "You're making a foolish mistake, Katarina. The old world is reaching a point where it must crumble under the weight of its own violence and ineptitude. But behind the scenes the organization has been carefully plotting, planning not just how to survive the coming storm but how to manipulate it, as well. We are forging a better world for better people. If that means some must perish, then so be it. Your parents were too sentimental to make the right choice, but you—I had hoped to usher at least one Mueller into the new order."

Katherine stiffened. "My parents? They died in a lab fire. They wanted to rid the world of diabetes."

"Only partly true. I had no choice but to adjust that tale because you were too tender to learn the truth. When the organization offered Frank and Ruth a furnished lab and all the resources they could imagine, they accepted because they wanted to cure diabetes. And they could have pursued that dream in their spare time. But eventually Frank learned of his actual assignment: to develop biological weapons—plus antidotes for all HO members. They could have received money, the privileges of rank. Instead they chose betrayal. They set fire to the lab to destroy their research. They would've betrayed us all, had I not intervened."

"What do you mean, *intervened*?" Katherine's voice trembled with fear.

"Don't think I wanted to shoot them. I didn't. But they wouldn't listen to reason. In the end, I made the hard decision. One bullet apiece. Then

I dragged their bodies back into the laboratory and torched it. Very sad, but necessary."

A choking gasp escaped Katherine.

"Ironic, isn't it? Your sentimental parents rejected the Heritage Organization, yet it was their beloved memory that enticed you to join and lend your many talents to it—until this interloper showed up."

Katherine grew limp in Roger's grasp. "He's stalling. This guy is no uncle to you. Let's leave him with his dead pals."

The pair had taken no more than a few steps when Kurt Mueller called, "Katherine, I beg you, don't go with him. If you do, I won't be able to protect you. By now more organization men are in the city. He has nowhere left to hide."

"Ignore him."

"You're finished, Greene. We're bigger than you can imagine. I vow, you'll be a corpse before sundown. Don't destroy my niece with you."

A camel-colored blur of motion yanked Roger's eyes back to Mueller. A miniscule pistol flashed into the man's left hand. Roger leaped clear of Katherine, lest a round meant for him strike her.

Mueller's gun popped, but the bullet missed. Lightning fast, Roger whipped up his own pistol, pulled the trigger—*click*. The Ruger's clip was empty.

Mueller cackled, his gold incisor glinting in the sunlight. "*Auf Wiedersehen*, Greene!"

Roger hurled the useless pistol into Mueller's face just as the man's weapon popped again. A hot scalpel-like pain seared Roger's left temple.

"No!" Katherine kicked and connected. Her uncle's hand flew up, discharging his third shot toward the sky.

Roger leaped onto Mueller, wrestled him to the ground, and ripped the concealed gun contraption from his wrist. He pressed the muzzle into Kurt Mueller's cheek. "I don't know if this dinky thing is still loaded or not, but even if it's not, one false move out of you, and my fist will ram your nose clear to the back side of your skull." He cocked his right arm back to dispel any doubt.

Kurt Mueller glared.

"Search him Katherine. Make sure he isn't hiding any more surprises."

She ran her fingers over her uncle's clothing and gasped when she extracted a glittering dagger from a leg sheath.

"So the snake had one more fang."

Katherine pressed a handkerchief to Roger's temple. When she pulled it away, only a little blood stained it. The wound would soon vanish.

"Roger, he meant what he said about organization men closing in. He never makes idle statements. We have to get out of here."

"One moment." Roger yanked Mueller's coat from him and, using Mueller's own razor-sharp dagger, effortlessly sliced it into several long strips. These he used to hogtie the man's hands and ankles behind him.

"You're fools, both of you! You don't know what you're up against!"

With a last band of camel-colored fabric, Roger tied a gag around his opponent's head, which he then patted as he might a child's. "Like you said, *auf Wiedersehen,* Herr Mueller."

Hand in hand, Roger and Katherine hustled back the way they had come. In the parking lot, a wine-colored Cadillac—no doubt Mueller's rental car—sat beside Katherine's Passat.

Roger tossed the confiscated weapons onto the rear seat of the Passat. His artificial hairpiece quickly joined them. He slid behind the steering wheel. Katherine climbed into the passenger seat and turned to Roger.

"Where are you going? We have no idea where the HO people are, or even how many there are."

Roger started the ignition and roared back onto Washington Street. "We're going to that awards ceremony. Keeping my mouth shut has played to the organization's advantage. Besides, I wasn't born to tiptoe around in disguises. If assassins want to gun me down, they'll have to try it with an audience watching. I refuse to crash and burn in silence."

The clock already showed 10:25 when Roger—again wearing his flight jacket—and Katherine dashed into the foyer of the War Memorial. Roger had no inkling how long such a ceremony might last. He hoped it wasn't already over.

A uniformed security guard rose from his stool and looked the pair up and down. Katherine, too, had ditched her wig, leaving her natural hair in desperate need of a brush. Roger assumed he looked equally haggard.

"Sorry we're late," Roger said. "We were delayed. Is this Pershing Auditorium?"

The guard pointed to a door. "That's it. You'll find empty seats in the back, but you have to be quiet. A TV crew is filming the ceremony."

This news about cameras lifted Roger's spirits. "Thanks." The guard eased the door open, and the two took empty seats in the last row.

Pershing Auditorium consisted of about five hundred red-fabric seats. On the wall behind the stage hung an enormous painting of a decorated officer Roger recognized as the famous general from the Great War. At the left side of the stage sat gray-headed men, evidently the veterans being honored. To the right was a handful of uniformed younger men and women, evidently representing branches of the military. In the middle aisle stood a man operating what Roger assumed to be a TV camera.

Standing center stage was an officer in a green uniform with a chest full of colorful decorations. He gripped a microphone and was apparently winding up a speech: "And so, fellow Hoosiers of this great nation, it is with great joy that we right the wrong of overlooking the commendable deeds of these veterans seated here today."

Roger squeezed Katherine's hand. "This is my chance. Say a prayer—and stay back. I don't want you hurt."

"Wait. Just for luck!" Without warning, she pulled him close and pressed her lips to his.

The kiss was quick. Still, it made Roger's heart race. It felt so right. Even more than right, it contained the tingle of—magic.

All he could do was wink before striding down the aisle. At the front, he mounted the steps and crossed the stage before anyone realized he wasn't part of the ceremony.

"Excuse me, sir. This is a matter of life and death." Roger pried the microphone from the grasp of the dumbfounded army officer. Addressing the audience, he launched into a presentation of his own, a speech with no script: "Ladies and gentlemen, I know this will sound crazy, but I'm a veteran too. A veteran of the Fourth Fighter Group of the Eighth Army Air Force in England. In 1943, I was flying a P-47 over the Third Reich when I was shot down. I've just escaped from Germany. Nazi goons with guns are chasing me. They're trying to kill me. I need your help!"

CHAPTER 44

When Adelle swept into his open doorway, he immediately noticed the new hair color. Overnight it had gone from dishwater blonde to strawberry blonde.

"Good afternoon, Mr. C. Did you have a nice checkup with the doctor this morning?"

From his wheelchair, "Mr. C." studied the artificial color. It was obviously from a bottle; anyone could tell that. But it matched Adelle's artificial cheerfulness. "Humph. Just a lot of poking and prodding and looking down my throat to tell me what I already know: I'm a run-down old-timer and getting older all the time."

"Aw, don't talk so gloomy. Here, you need a little sunlight to brighten your day." Without asking permission, she stepped to the window and twirled the plastic wand. Blinding sunshine cascaded into the room, forcing him to squint down at this lap. Couldn't she give him warning before taking over like that?

"Let's see, your family will be coming for a visit today, right? Would you rather see them here or down in the recreation hall?"

That's right, the family would be coming today. He'd forgotten. "The rec hall. This cubbyhole excuse for a room gets crowded with more than one person in it. For what this place costs every month, you would think it would offer bigger rooms."

"All righty, then. I'll wheel you down now." With her typical efficiency, Adelle slipped behind him and released the brake.

He folded his hands on his lap as he and his wheelchair started into the white-tiled corridor. Adelle must be in a good mood. The quick pace she struck with that blasted *squeech, squeech* of her gum-soled shoes caused a chilly breeze on his face. The sappy tune she hummed was another clue. She'd probably found a new boyfriend.

Ahead, Myrtle Van Johnson blocked the way as she stood motionless with her aluminum walker, but Adelle maneuvered expertly around her. Next came Murray who sat in his own wheelchair and pointed a shaking finger at the blank wall. Adelle steered around him as well. Poor Murray. Last month they had played checkers together. Since then, Murray had become just a shell.

A thought came to mind. "Did you remember to tape the news?"

Adelle's voice answered from behind him. "What, me, forget a thing like that? And risk you not speaking to me for the rest of the week? Of course, I remembered to tape the news. Everybody knows how much Mr. C. likes to keep up with current events."

Her excessive cheerfulness grated the nerves, but he let it slide. "Good. Anything special going on in the world?"

"That depends on what you call special. The stock market is down. A couple of policemen were shot in Ferguson, Missouri. The Secret Service is embarrassed because a couple of their agents got drunk and drove into a White House security barricade—"

He snorted. "Idiots. The whole world is being taken over by idiots."

The doors to the recreation hall swung into view. They stood open. A moment later, and he was rolling over the entrance.

In the middle of the room, four women huddled around a small table. Probably playing cards, although his eyes couldn't quite tell from this distance. He needed new glasses.

"Oh, one thing on the news might interest you, Mr. C., since you served in the war and all. In Indiana, they held some sort of military ceremony. A lunatic ran onto the stage, stood in front of the camera, and started shouting crazy things about fighting the Nazis in the war."

"What's so crazy about fighting Nazis? I fought the Germans too. Lots of people did. Push me over to the TV."

"Sure you fought. But you're old enough that people can believe it. No offense. The man who crashed the award ceremony looks young enough to be a college boy. Why, even my daughter Tammy in grad school looks older than that nut."

"Humph. Sounds like another idiot starving for attention. Fruitcakes like that disgrace the memory of men who sacrificed their lives." His hands automatically clenched into fists. *Somebody ought to punch out that faker.*

Adelle parked him squarely in front of the television. Picking up the remote, she let a playful twinkle appear in her eye. "Now, let's see . . . which one of those soap operas did you want to watch? Was it *Days of our Lives*, or *General Hospital*?"

Despite his resentful mood, Adelle's question caught him off guard and he accidentally smiled. "That'll be the day. Just play the news, please."

The television sprang to life. The familiar faces of two local news anchors appeared.

"Would you like something to drink, Mr. C.? Maybe some milk? Tomato juice?"

"Tomato juice?" He crinkled his nose. "You trying to poison me? How about orange juice? And an oatmeal cookie. That fool doctor keeps harping to add more fiber to my diet."

"OJ and a cookie. Got it. Be right back." Adelle strolled away, the familiar *squeech, squeech* receding in volume as she retreated.

He had just begun to follow the first news story, which concerned the latest violence in western Iraq, when an aged female voice sang out sweetly, "Oh, Mr. Crippen, would you like to join us for a game of euchre? Gladys Mae had to go powder her nose. You know how long it always takes her."

He kept his eyes on the television. "Not now. I'm watching the news. Besides, my daughter and her husband are supposed to show up any time."

He shook his head at the images on the screen. *Suicide bombers. Fanatics chopping off people's heads. Is the whole world going mad?*

Alice appeared beside him. "Hi, Dad." She bent to kiss his cheek. In her hands she carried a plastic cup of orange juice and a paper plate with two cookies. "These are for you. Adelle met me in the hallway and said you asked for them."

He accepted the juice and took a sip, alternating polite glances from the television to Alice.

On the screen, the male newsman addressed his co-anchor: "Right after the break, we have a curious story about a young man who got arrested for disrupting an awards ceremony in Indianapolis. Although he appears to be in his early twenties, he shouted claims that he is—get this—nearly one hundred years old."

The female newscaster picked up her cue: "All I can say is I hope I look like I'm still in my twenties when I hit the century mark." With a wink at the camera, she added, "We'll be back in a moment."

When the image cut to a commercial for triple-pane vinyl windows, he shifted his full attention to his daughter. "So how is everybody? Henry? The boys? All the grandkids?"

"Everybody is great. Henry would've come, but the office was throwing a retirement party for the vice president of marketing. He felt obligated to go. How are you? Still giving all the nurses a hard time, I bet."

His cracked lips parted in a good-natured grin. "It's a rough job, but somebody has to do it."

After showing him some cell phone photos of her grandkids—his great-grandchildren—in goofy poses, Alice rested a hand on her father's, which held half an oatmeal cookie. "Dad, you feel cold. Where's your lap blanket?"

"Must've forgot it. Probably on the chair in my room."

"I'll dash down and get it. Don't go 'way, now."

He lifted the glass of juice to his lips as the news broadcast resumed.

"And now, a story of stolen valor from Indianapolis, Indiana, where a wannabe World War II hero disrupted a ceremony in honor of veterans by claiming that he himself had been a P-47 pilot in the Fourth Fighter Group in England."

Crippen's left hand—which had been reaching for his second oatmeal cookie—froze in midair.

The Fourth Fighter Group?

The image flashed to a stage in an auditorium. Just as a uniformed army officer was delivering a speech, a young man wearing the old-style flight jacket dashed into view and snatched the microphone from his hand. "Ladies and gentlemen, I know this will sound crazy, but I'm a veteran too, a veteran of the Fourth Fighter Group of the Eighth Army Air Force in England. In 1943 I was flying a P-47 over the Third Reich when I was shot down. I've just escaped from Germany. Nazi goons with guns are chasing me. They're trying to kill me. I need your help!"

"Crazy upstart. But that voice . . . it sounds so . . ."

"Did you say something, Walter?" It was one of the ladies at the euchre table.

On the television screen, the intruder at the ceremony began talking faster, louder, as men in various military uniforms grappled with him. They struggled to separate the microphone from his hand. "German scientists performed experiments on me! They held me prisoner in an underground bunker for decades. They subjected me to a process that prevents my body from aging. I know I look young, but I'm closer to a hundred years old."

As the young man in the flight jacket continued to resist, the camera zoomed in for a close-up.

Now even Walt's failing vision could clearly make out the face—a face he never expected to see again. His heart lurched in his chest. He felt the plastic juice cup slip from his fingers. He tried to speak, but only a strangled gasp escaped his throat.

"Walter? Are you all right?"

Walt felt frozen, powerless to look away. There—even the name tag on the jacket said . . . "Greene."

He heard his own breathing switch to loud, staccato rasps. The hand that had held the orange juice now clutched his tightening chest.

The figure on TV continued to struggle. "Every word is true. My name is Captain Roger Greene, of the United States Army Air Corps. I grew up in Plainfield, Indiana. I've just escaped from Germany, and now assassins from a secret organization are trying to kill me. I need protection!"

Was this a ghost from the grave? Unable to take anymore, Walt uttered an unintelligible cross between a gurgle and a shout. His panicky breaths rasped faster, louder, but he couldn't control them.

"Mr. Crippen?" called one of the card players. "Nurse, help!"

In a final bid to escape the spectral image, Walter Crippen tilted his head back and strained to raise his voice. Between ragged breaths, he managed a broken shout. "In here . . . somebody . . . in here!"

CHAPTER 45

Once more, Roger kicked his bunk in the jail cell. "Stupid, stupid, stupid! How could you let them do this to you? You should've bolted while you had the chance!" He swung around and resumed pacing his miniature square of floor space. With every step, he saw the orange pant legs of his prison outfit. He was a jailbird. Caged again—in his own country.

Amidst the cacophony of noises echoing around the concrete and steel of the cell block sounded a mocking reply. "Don't sweat it, man. Yer gonna get used to it by yer third or fourth time in lockup."

Roger ignored the fool. *I escaped before. I can escape again. Nobody's going to keep Roger Greene locked up. Especially not inside the United States!*

He clenched his fist and drew it back, ready to punch the white wall in frustration. At the last second, he realized it was pointless. He was more likely to shatter the bones in his hand and wrist than to damage the wall. Instead he wheeled around and kicked the bunk once more, this time with the other foot.

"Hey, knock it off! Quit damaging taxpayer property."

Roger glared at the brown-uniformed deputy standing outside the bars.

"You've been raising a ruckus ever since they dragged you in here. I was sent over to escort you to a meeting with visitors, but if you keep up that stinking attitude, I'll tell 'em you got your visitation suspended. Can your thick skull understand that?"

The word *visitors* snared Roger's attention. How big and powerful was the organization? Could they sneak an armed assassin into the county jail and knock him off? Or maybe Katherine had returned with a lawyer. She'd shouted that she would try.

"What kind of visitors?"

The jailer crossed his arms. "We're not playing *Jeopardy*, so knock off the questions. All I know is it's more than one. The jail commander gave them permission to see you in a special room."

Suspicion flared. A meeting in a special room? Could this request mask an attempt to murder him? On the other hand, every chance to step out of the cell would give him the opportunity to size up the building, to look for escape routes.

He nodded. "Okay. Put the handcuffs on. Let's find out who wants to see me. But when we get there, stick around, okay? If I decide I don't like the company, I might skip the show and come back."

Once Roger's wrists were secured and his ankles in leg chains, he and his armed escort descended to the walkway that connected the cell block to the rest of the Marion County Jail. When they reached the room where his visit was to take place, Roger narrowed his eyes at the figure standing outside the door: a man with wavy black hair wearing a dark-blue blazer, gray pants, white shirt, and burgundy necktie. He held a cup, which Roger judged by the aroma to contain coffee. Question was, did he owe any allegiance to the so-called HO?

From an inside pocket, the man pulled out a leather wallet, which he flipped open to show the deputy. "I'll take over from here." He returned the wallet to his pocket and opened the door for Roger.

As Roger stepped closer, eyes alert, he spotted a bulge under the man's blazer that might indicate a concealed weapon. He stopped, uncertain whether to enter. "What's this all about? I don't know who you are."

"Then we're equal. I don't know who you are, either. But I intend to find out. I'm Special Agent McBride, with the FBI."

McBride's announcement took Roger by surprise, but he welcomed the chance to state his claims to a higher level of authority than the local police. The leg chains still restricting the length of his steps, Roger shuffled through the doorway. Inside, a number of men who were obviously waiting for him stood up. On a chair by itself sat a paper sack with his name printed on the side. The top item peeking from the sack was his flight jacket.

Another plainclothesman in a gray suit flashed his identification and introduced himself as Jaworski. He claimed association with some outfit called the CIA.

Roger shook his head. "CIA? Never heard of it."

To the right of Jaworski stood a man wearing a green uniform. "This is Colonel Davenport," Jaworski said. "You might recall wrestling a microphone out of his hand the other day. And beyond the colonel is General Overton."

Roger sized up Overton, a middle-aged man with gray flecks dotting his dark hair. Overton's blue uniform rendered the man an enigma. Could that be a new style of navy uniform? That wouldn't make sense. The navy has admirals, not generals. Could he be Royal Air Force? The RAF wore blue . . .

Before Roger could ask about Overton's branch of service, the door swung open again. The deputy who had escorted Roger ushered in Katherine and a stately looking gentleman in round-rimmed spectacles and a black suit.

"Roger!" Katherine threw her arms around him. "I found a lawyer to represent you."

She could say no more before Special Agent McBride stepped in. "No physical contact with the prisoner, please."

Roger looked over the group. "Quite a gathering you've got here. Is this how they conduct trials nowadays?"

Jaworski, who seemed to be officiating, shook his head and planted one foot on his chair. "No trial here. We're just going to talk. Have a seat, Mr. Greene."

Roger bristled even as he sat. "That's *Captain* Greene. I'm an officer in the United States Army Air Corps. I might be out of uniform, but I deserve to be addressed by my proper rank until officially discharged by Uncle Sam."

Jaworski motioned for the others to sit, although he remained standing. "Maybe you are, and maybe you aren't. But simply for the sake of a harmonious meeting . . ." He regarded the rest of the group. "For the moment, we will refer to the prisoner as Captain Greene."

General Overton, the man in the blue uniform, flipped a hand into the air to catch Jaworski's eye. "Just for the record, the supposed 'Captain Greene' has already contradicted the obvious. There *isn't* any U.S. Army Air Corps, and there hasn't been one for a very long time. The Air Force and the Army separated into distinct branches shortly after World War II."

At last Roger understood the blue uniform. "Then you're with one of the Air Forces?" Feeling a grin forcing its way onto his face despite Overton's skepticism, Roger stood. "Sorry, General. I didn't realize. Reporting for duty."

"Take your seat, Captain Greene," Jaworski said. "We won't be observing military protocol. Now I'm going to lay this on the line as bluntly as possible: every year the CIA and the FBI are called upon to deal with terrorists, murderers, serial killers, crackpot armed survivalists, doubly crackpot cult leaders, narcotics traffickers, sex traffickers, computer hackers, demented lunatics, and assorted other troublemakers on the national and international stages. Today we have a dilemma. This group needs to figure out which of those categories—if any—you fit into. Now it's possible you're a harmless eccentric who likes to run around in an antique flying jacket, making outlandish claims—"

"They're not outlandish," Katherine blurted. "They're true!"

Special Agent McBride crossed his legs with an air of impatience. "With all due respect, Miss Mueller, I find 'Captain' Greene's story approximately one notch below 'Jack and the Beanstalk' on the believability scale. In addition, there's been a spree of shootings connected with an individual matching his description. We have videotapes. If it weren't for some peculiar extenuating circumstances, we wouldn't be conducting this interview at all. The sooner we get on with this farce, the sooner we can sort out the facts and go our separate ways."

Indignation ballooned inside Roger's chest. "Mr. McBride, what you personally do or do not find believable will never change reality. If a fact is true, then it will remain true, regardless of your ability to accept it."

Jaworski laced his fingers behind his head and leaned back in his seat. "Exactly the point. If you're a crackpot or a dangerous mental case, that fact will remain true despite your wild claims or emotional outbursts. If, however, it turns out that, contrary to all logic and believability, any portion whatsoever of your claims can be substantiated, then yes, that also would remain true, despite our multitude of reasons to believe otherwise."

Words. Waste of time. The hours behind new bars had pumped Roger with anger, but also with fear. Was this the beginning of more decades in a cage? He folded his hands to keep them from trembling and forced himself to act calmer than he felt. "So this is some sort of test, is it? An interrogation? Shoot. Ask me anything."

McBride stepped to a device mounted on a tripod and pressed a button. "We would like to videotape your testimony, Captain Greene. For the most detailed record, please state your name, rank, unit, and whatever you want to say about yourself, your supposed military service, your time in Europe, and how you claim to have ended up in the United States. Please be sure to be as specific as possible, including your activities for the past several days. That is, if Miss Mueller's lawyer has no objections?"

The lawyer, whose name Roger didn't even know, cleared his throat. "Normally I prefer to confer with clients in advance. If he agrees to address the points you mentioned, he may do so, but I reserve the right to interrupt if I deem it advisable."

Roger couldn't keep the growl from his voice. "I've got nothing to hide. Let's get the show on the road already."

"No need to hurry," Jaworski said. "Take your time. Remember, include every pertinent detail you can."

For the next hour, Roger told them about himself, beginning with how he traveled from the United States to Canada and from there to England to fly with the RAF against German fighters and bombers. He explained how the Eagle Squadrons had reverted to American control when the United States entered the war, gave an overview of his flying career, and then explained how he was eventually shot down and taken prisoner. From there, he repeated everything he could recall concerning the other airmen forced to undergo the Methuselah experiment, the bombing, and his own survival and imprisonment down through the long, lonely years in the underground bunker.

The lawyer, who had begun doodling on his notepad and glancing at his wristwatch with increasing frequency abruptly stood up. "Gentlemen, I'm afraid I must excuse myself from this case. Miss Mueller, you didn't fully explain your situation. My law firm has an honorable, much-respected reputation to uphold. We don't handle insanity pleas, temporary or otherwise." With black leather attaché case in hand, the man marched to the door.

"Please wait," Katherine pleaded.

The lawyer had no intention of waiting. Without a backward glance, he opened the door and disappeared.

Roger stared at the door a moment. It was more or less the kind of response he might have expected. "Is that how the rest of you feel? You want me to clam up right now, so you can pack me off to a funny farm?"

"Keep talking, Roger," Katherine urged. "Tell them everything."

Despite the tension of the moment, Katherine's sincerity, the caring in her pleading eyes, caused a reaction even he didn't understand: tears welled in his eyes. The better he knew this woman, the more wonderful she became. Wasn't it to protect people like Katherine that he'd gone to war in the first place? Roger wished he could reach across the table and hold Katherine's hand just to stay in contact with one of the few people who had ever truly cared about him.

Jaworski nodded noncommittally. "Go on. We're listening."

Throughout Roger's account, each of the remaining men jotted notes onto pads or notebooks, although each one seemed interested in totally different portions of his story. As Roger spoke, he tried in vain to interpret their expressions. Katherine obviously believed him and hung on every word. Tears of empathy glistened in her eyes when he described the intense loneliness and near-suicidal depression he'd endured in the bunker.

Roger noticed Colonel Davenport rolling his eyes at one point. The other men, however, remained poker-faced, neither nodding nor shaking their heads. They simply watched, listened, and wrote down an occasional notation.

Roger completed his account by describing the events of the past several days: the museum incident in Georgia, the attack atop the Soldiers and Sailors Monument in Indianapolis, and the shootings in White River Park.

He paused and searched his memory for anything else worth mentioning. Thinking of nothing else earthshaking, he clasped his hands together. "That's about it. My whole life in a nutshell."

Special Agent McBride sat silently, contemplating his page of notes. The two men in uniform exchanged a look Roger couldn't decipher. Jaworski broke the silence: "Quite a tale. Do you offer any tangible proof concerning everything you've just told us?"

"I can verify all those last parts," Katherine said. "Plus, I can give a written statement about Uncle Kurt."

Roger jerked to his feet and began pacing despite the leg chains. "How can I prove it from this room? How would *you* prove it if those things happened to you? What? Do you want to shoot me and watch me heal in front of your eyes?"

Katherine's head jerked up. "He does have a bullet in his chest. It came from the gunman at the Soldiers and Sailors Monument. That should prove something."

Colonel Davenport leaned back in his seat and fiddled with his ink pen. "These days, people perform all kinds of piercings and insertions on their bodies. Even if he does have a bullet or something embedded inside him, it won't corroborate his story. A bullet might be evidence of a robbery attempt gone bad. For all we know, he could be the survivor of gang violence."

Roger glared at him. "So you agree with that snooty lawyer? You think I've lost my marbles? Listen, all I've ever wanted to do is to fly airplanes, serve my country, and find the perfect woman to share life with. Why is the whole world conspiring to stop me? I was serving the United States by fighting fascism before America woke up and jumped into the battle. It's not my fault I got caught by a gang of mad scientists on the other side of the pond. I tell you, I am Captain Roger Greene!"

"I've heard enough," McBride stated to Jaworski. "Are you ready to bring him in?"

Confused, Roger looked from man to man. Bring him in? Was this modern lingo for "lock him up and throw away the key"? When Jaworski nodded, McBride strode from the room, shutting the door behind him. Heavy silence ensued.

"What's happening?" Katherine's voice was tremulous. "Where did he go?"

Jaworski pulled a cell phone from his pocket, glanced at it, then put it away again. "Don't be alarmed. While we've been conducting this interview, another witness who wished to remain unseen has been observing via closed-circuit TV in the next room. That witness is one of the extenuating circumstances I mentioned earlier. Our panel would like to hear his assessment of the prisoner's testimony."

A moment later the door reopened, and Special Agent McBride held it while the deputy rolled a wheelchair into the room. In the chair sat a wrinkled man who had little more than a half-circle of wispy, white hair around his bald pate. His sky-blue eyes were rimmed in red. Those eyes locked onto Roger and didn't let go.

To Roger's surprise, it was General Davenport, who had sat in silence throughout most of the proceedings, who approached the old gent in the wheelchair. "Well, sir, you've heard and seen the prisoner's whole testimony. Would you please tell us your opinion?"

Eyes still fixed on Roger with a glare that could have melted cast iron, the elderly fellow wiped a handkerchief across each cheek. Something about the man's eyes stirred vague recollections. Lately Roger had spent so much time dredging up memories of classmates from Plainfield High. Could this be someone from his school days?

The man pointed a quavering, bony finger in Roger's direction. "Young punk, you are a scandal. That is the most impressive impersonation I've ever seen. Your plastic surgeon must be a real doozy, because you even look like Roger Greene. But any student of history could research everything you just said about the Eagle Squadrons, the Fourth Fighter Group, Debden, the whole kit and kaboodle." The man's voice became shriller. "If an imposter wanted to, it wouldn't be hard to find the names of fighter pilots who flew over Germany and never returned. So I'm going to prove you're a faker by asking three questions only the honest-to-goodness Roger Greene would know. I warn you, if you don't know all three answers, I'll come out of this chair and tear you limb from limb for besmirching the memory of a great American patriot."

The truth dawned on Roger. This old codger served in the war! Had he flown with the Fourth Fighter Group?

The elderly man cleared his throat. "First, what was the name of the pilot who flew as Roger Greene's wingman on his final mission?"

"Easy. He was a swell guy and my best pal in the army, Walt Crippen."

The man in the chair maintained eye contact. Clearly the old boy was searching for the slightest trace of a deception. But Roger also detected just a hint of shock in those blue eyes. His mind raced. *Could this old-timer be—?*

"Next question. Before Roger Greene was shot down, he did something special for Walt Crippen. What was it?"

Roger groped through his memory. He and Walt had done thousands of things together, but those events had happened so long ago. He might've bought Walt a beer at the Rose and Crown pub. He might've carried a letter for Betsy to the censor. As each possibility occurred to him, he discarded it as not the sort of event this elderly fellow would consider significant. Then his mind locked onto it. "Walt and I did a lot of favors for each other. Like I said, we were buddies. But if you're asking about the very last thing I ever did for Walt Crippen, it happened in the sky over Germany. He had an Me 109 hot on his tail, and I was fighting for my own life. I broke out of my dogfight just long enough to flame the Hun gunning for Walt. It was a pure luck shot. The bad part was, that action used up the last of my ammo. Then two Me 109s pounced on me and shot up my plane. I bellied into the Third Reich."

With trembling fingers, the old man dabbed his red eyes with the handkerchief, but maintained an air of disbelief. Roger ignored the others. He could practically feel electrical tension in the room. Were they all holding their breath? Did they realize they were witnessing the most extraordinary interrogation of their lives?

Roger couldn't bear not knowing any longer. He softened his tone. "Are you . . . are you Walt Crippen?"

The elderly fellow didn't answer directly. "I have to be sure," he said with a quaking voice. "I have to be dead positive. Last question: Roger Greene and Walt Crippen had an ongoing private bet between them. Only those two knew about it. What was the bet?"

Roger immediately grasped the allusion. More importantly, the very question revealed that this frail figure before him was, indeed, his former wingman. Roger laid both of his cuffed hands on the man's shoulder. "Walt, each time you and I flew on a mission together, we renewed a wager about who would be first to take out an enemy airplane. It was our private game. None of the other boys knew about it. The prize was a ten-dollar bill."

The man in the wheelchair emitted an astonished gasp. His eyes couldn't have registered more terror than if he'd spotted a skeleton clawing its way out of a grave.

Awkwardly, because of the handcuffs, Roger dug into the sack of his clothing and removed the leather jacket. He unsnapped the right-hand pocket flap. "Walt, I've been waiting an awful long time to pay my debt. You scored the first kill in our last mission together. This belongs to you."

Out came the ten-dollar bill that had lain in that pocket, practically untouched, throughout most of his captivity. Roger unfolded it. He held the banknote up so his old friend could see his own printing and then read aloud the words jotted along the edge in blue ink: "To my good buddy, Roger Greene. On loan until I bag the next German fighter! Walt."

"It's him! It's really him! I don't know how it's possible, but this really is Roger Greene." Walt Crippen dropped his head and broke into sobs.

Roger eased down to crouch beside the wheelchair. "Walt, buddy. You don't know how I've missed you." He embraced the hand of his old friend, the man who had once flown side by side with him through deadly skies— the man who'd probably spent most of his years believing that Captain Roger Greene had paid the ultimate price for saving his wingman's life.

With Walt's weeping face buried in his shoulder, Roger looked at Katherine. Tears ran down her cheeks and got caught in the corners of her huge smile. He lifted his eyes to the open-mouthed officials. "Well, gentlemen? Any more questions?"

CHAPTER 46

Roger's new suitcase lay on the bed, halfway packed, when a knock sounded on the door. A quick check through the peephole revealed Katherine's cheery face in the hotel corridor. He yanked the door open.

"Katherine! I was beginning to worry you weren't going to—"

Before he could finish, she had her arms around him and was delivering a kiss. "Who me, miss a chance to say farewell to my favorite old geezer? You can't get me off your six that easy. By the way, how is the patient recovering after surgery?" She pulled away to gently touch the spot where the surgeons had removed the bullet from his chest.

"All healed. No side effects. Same as when I cut out that GPS chip. The CIA docs were flabbergasted. Said they've never seen a body functioning at peak efficiency like mine. Of course, they asked to keep me around 'for observation,' but I told 'em to jump in a lake. Sounded like a medical excuse to keep me prisoner in a hospital."

"Good. What about Jaworski? Did he agree to your terms?"

"Yup, even though I had to do some heavy-duty negotiating. He wasn't thrilled about pulling strings to get me into the Air Force Academy. But I stuck to my guns. I wouldn't play Captain Midnight and help him track down organization big wigs unless I could fly for Uncle Sam. The cloak-and-dagger stuff will stay a sideline. For now, I'll just be on-call for the CIA."

"So the CIA knew about the HO? I still can't wrap my mind around Uncle Kurt's involvement in all this." Moisture filled her eyes, and Roger gently wiped away the stray tear that rolled down her cheek.

"I know he meant a lot to you. But the Heritage Organization is a nasty group, and I, for one, am glad you're free of it. The CIA agents haven't told me specific details. But I do know that some organization agents have been caught stealing high-tech information, equipment, and classified research. Mostly military and scientific applications. If they're likely to be caught, their agents have put bullets in their own brains instead of being taken alive. Or blown up themselves along with their captors. That Schneider guy from Florida you mentioned killed himself. What little the CIA knows has been pieced together through clues left on bodies or by intercepted snippets of messages. Jaworski thinks they're infiltrating modern societies. What exactly they're up to, no one seems to know. My guess is that they're trying to gain control of the world's major governments and manipulate things for their own agenda."

Katherine's eyes sparkled. "I'm proud of you, Roger. Even after all you've been through, you landed right-side up. You get to follow your dreams, flying and serving your country."

He took her hand and pulled her closer to him. "I never could've done it without you." He rubbed his thumb across her knuckles. "But I'm worried about you. Do you know what happened to your uncle?"

She shook her head. "It still feels strange to think about what he really is and that he's out there somewhere. But he vanished without a trace. The official, public explanation is that a natural gas leak blew up the house. Of course, you and I know better. He's covered his tracks."

"What about you? Where have you been all week? You've been more secretive than the G-men who work under Jaworski."

"I've been away on a secret mission. I didn't tell you about it because I didn't want to get your hopes up if I failed."

"Secret mission? I thought it was only a desk job Jaworski offered you."

She laughed. "This mission was personal. I drove back to Indianapolis.

I wanted to see if I could track down anything about your past."

Roger blinked involuntarily. Was there any shred of his early life still out there to be uncovered? "Okay, Detective Tracy, was your fact-finding mission successful?"

"Far beyond my hopes. You'd better sit."

A lump settled in his stomach. She'd found out something about his origins? He eased down to the bed, unsure whether he wanted to hear it.

"I finally tracked down Sunshine Children's Home. It changed its name and location in the late 1930s, then merged with another orphanage in the 1950s. In the '70s, they were absorbed by an association of Christian ministries. In the end, though, I discovered they still had all the old records from Sunshine stashed away in cardboard cartons in a basement."

"No fooling?"

"No fooling. And believe it or not, I discovered something that belongs to you." Katherine held up a tattered manila folder.

Roger swallowed. He had no clue how old he'd been when he entered Sunshine Children's Home. His earliest memories had taken place there. What had Katherine dug up? Evidence that he was illegitimate? That he had a prostitute for a mother?

"You wouldn't believe the rummaging I had to do in order to locate the case file on little Roger Greene. Like I said, all the old records were transferred to the new association, but years and years' worth of files were boxed up and stored away willy-nilly, in no particular order. I reckon no one expected they would be needed again."

Whether the news was good or bad, Roger decided to dive straight toward the target. "Okay, I can't stand the suspense. What did you find out?"

"They left something for you. You were supposed to receive it from the woman who directed the orphanage when you were old enough."

"A woman director?" Roger thought back. The orphans didn't normally have direct contact with the administration. Yet in the haziest recesses of his memory, he did recall something about a woman.

"The director I remember was a man named Fettler. But yeah, before Fettler, the workers took instructions from some lady. She wore her hair in a bun."

"I don't know about Fettler, but this belongs to you." She opened the file folder and handed him a yellowed envelope. Rather than being sealed, it had a length of pink lace tied around it. "I've already read it, to make sure it was something you would want to know. Now it's your turn."

Roger sat on the edge of the bed, slid off the lace, and read aloud the hand-printed words: "For Roger Greene. To be given to him on his sixteenth birthday." What? His eyes met Katherine's. "My sixteenth birthday? The Tuckers yanked me out of there when I was twelve."

Katherine nodded, and he noticed more than the usual amount of moisture glistening in her eyes. "Somebody goofed. They forgot about the letter. Read it, Roger."

He attempted to swallow but found his mouth had gone dry. He extracted the ancient sheet from the envelope and silently began to decipher the faded lines, which a quivering hand had written with a fountain pen:

August 21, 1922

Dear Roger Greene,

Since you are reading this letter, I assume you are now sixteen years old. I asked Mrs. Kline of Sunshine Children's Home not to give this to you earlier, because I didn't want the news of your parents' death to shock a young child.

Kline! The lady with the hair bun. So they really did hold back information. And this writer had known his mother and father? Indescribable emotions welled up as he focused his eyes on each word, one at a time:

Let me start at the beginning. My name is Harriet Ficke. I was landlord to your mother and father. Because my husband had

*passed away and I had time on my hands, the Greenes sometimes
hired me to babysit you.*

*You see, your father loved to fly aeroplanes. He learned to fly in the
Great War. He was a pilot for one of the aerosquadrons in France.
(Your mother, Laura, told me he shot down at least three enemy
aeroplanes, so he must have been a skilled pilot indeed!) When
Anthony came home from the Great War, he married your mother,
whom he had met at a church social somewhere. As soon as he could
afford it, Anthony bought his own biplane, and he used to take your
mother flying every Saturday morning.*

*After a while, he sold his plane and bought a different one. The
first time he planned to take your mother up in it, I rode with
them to the field to watch you. You were three years old, and I held
you while we waved goodbye. But something went wrong with the
plane. Witnesses say part of the tail broke off. The plane crashed,
killing both your parents. They are now buried in Danville South
Cemetery. I'm afraid I had to sell all their belongings to pay for the
funeral.*

*I tried to find relatives. I asked around. No one seemed to know
where your parents came from. I am 71—much too old to raise a
baby. Besides, it breaks my heart to see you look at the sky and say,
"Momma? Dadda?" every time an aeroplane flies over. I have no
choice but to take you to the orphanage. Very possibly, I will be dead
and gone by the time you receive this letter. In case not, though, here
is my address. If I'm still alive, I would be happy to tell you a little
more about your parents.*

*Very sincerely yours,
Mrs. Harriet Ficke
101 South Indiana Street, Danville, Indiana*

P.S. Just so you know—your birthdate is December 16, 1920. Your
daddy said you were "the finest Christmas gift" he'd ever received.
Anthony and Laura loved you with all their hearts, Roger. Enclosed
is a picture I found among their belongings.

Roger slipped two fingers back into the envelope and pulled out not one, but two brown-tinted photographs. One was a wedding picture showing a proud groom and an embarrassed-looking bride. The second photo looked a year or two newer. The wife's wavy hair was longer, and the couple posed beside the fuselage of an old tandem-cockpit biplane. A Curtiss JN4D.

"That's a Jenny," he said, using the nickname for the aircraft. He struggled to keep his emotions under control. Maybe if he concentrated on the plane, the tears wouldn't start. "Because of the number produced and its popularity, military-surplus Jennies became the aircraft of choice for American pilots after the Great War. I took my first flying lesson in one of these."

Katherine sat beside Roger and slid her arm around his shoulders. "You have your father's eyes."

He kept staring at the brown-tinted images. His throat grew tighter. "I can't believe it. My own mom and dad."

At last. He wasn't a throwaway child. Not the unwanted castoff of some illegitimate union or other unhappy event. His mom was no floozy, and his dad—unexpectedly—turned out to be a pilot. A veteran of the Great War, at that.

"I think I understand why you always felt born to fly, Roger. You saw your parents soar into the sky but never saw them come back. Even as a child, you must have yearned to follow them, but you no longer remembered why when you grew up."

Roger let Katherine's words sink in. She made sense. He remembered that back in Sunshine he'd stared upward whenever an aircraft chanced to putter overhead.

She stood and pulled him up with her. "I didn't have time to drive out to the cemetery. But on the map, Danville looks about twenty miles west of Indianapolis. I thought you might like to visit their gravesite."

He nodded. "I've been to Danville. The Plainfield Quakers played football against the Danville Warriors. I never dreamed I could find my parents just by wandering through their cemetery." Against his wishes, a lump formed in his throat. He looked at Katherine, who smiled through tears. "I don't know how to thank you."

"I can't claim all the credit. Mostly I was hitting dead ends until I tried what you do. I prayed for God to help me. You know what? I believe He did."

Before Roger knew it, his arms wrapped around Katherine and pulled her in. He could feel her heart beating against his chest as he leaned down and kissed her. His hands tangled into her hair, and he felt her smile under his lips.

"I've wanted to do that for a long time, but maybe—"

She pressed into him again. When his lips met hers, he let the kiss stretch into the longest of his life.

At last, Katherine pulled away with a giggle. "You really know how to rob the cradle, Captain Greene. You're four times my age!"

"Aw, admit it. You have a hankering for older men."

As she swatted his arm, a newspaper caught her eye. "Say, what's that in your suitcase? An *Indianapolis Star*? Still looking for old classmates?"

"Nope. Just decided it might be fun to keep a copy of my obituary." He released her and flipped the paper open to a small news item on page nine: "'Correction officers of the Marion County Jail report the suicide of a Caucasian male recently arrested in the state capital. The actual identity of the deceased remains unknown. The individual was arrested for disrupting a military awards ceremony and physically assaulting law-enforcement officers. Witnesses state the man claimed to be a veteran from World War II. Authorities, however, concluded the deceased was a mentally unbalanced individual. The unidentified male was a suspect in a spree of shootings. . .' Et cetera, et cetera." Roger tossed the paper back into the suitcase. "The bottom line is I'm officially cremated, along with all cell samples. Think the HO bosses will swallow Jaworski's handiwork?"

"Maybe, but maybe not. They'll still wonder where I disappeared to. The G-men, as you call them, promise my new name under the Federal Witness Protection Act will keep them off my trail. But that won't stop them from wondering or searching for me. By the way, I've been so busy tracking down your roots that I never heard how you'll be getting to the Air Force Academy. I assume you're flying?"

He couldn't stop the grin. Now he could show her. "You know how the government owed me a bundle of back pay for all those decades I spent locked up as a POW? I used part of the money to buy something I really wanted—a Mustang."

Katherine's eyebrows went up. "You bought an antique fighter plane? When you could afford a much newer—"

His laugh cut her off. "Come here." Taking her hand in his, he led her to the window of the hotel room and pulled aside the curtain. "Isn't she a beauty?"

In the parking lot stood a product of the Ford Motor Company, a gleaming silver Mustang convertible with black pinstripes.

"Sitting there with the top down, she looks eager to hit the road, doesn't she? Sure, I was tempted to buy a plane right away. But the way I see it, I need to get reacquainted with the United States. Before going to the academy, I want to visit big cities and small towns. I need to get a feel for what America really is now. I want to visit churches, too, and worship God with grassroots Americans. First, though, I'm heading to Michigan to spend a couple of days with Walt."

"Sounds like a fun road trip."

"Are you sure I can't talk you into coming along?"

"I'd love to, but I need to get resettled. It was easy for the government to issue me a new name and social security number, but I still need to find a permanent place to live before I start the new job."

"It was nice of Jaworski to find you a writing spot in his clandestine services."

"Or maybe he just wanted me nearby. After all, outside of you, I'm the only person he has who can recognize HO members. Who knows, though? Maybe I really will accept his offer to train as an operations officer."

"You'd make a beautiful spy."

"Say, you won't forget about me, will you? I mean, visiting all those small towns, a handsome, swashbuckling pilot like yourself is bound to turn the heads of a few farmers' daughters."

Roger pulled her close again and pressed his lips to hers in another long kiss. "Does that answer the question?"

"Yes, sir, Captain. But are you sure your vocabulary is up to speed for the modern world? You know, ATMs, CDs, DVDs, HD TVs, kilobytes, megabytes . . . You haven't exactly been flying with a full vocabulary since you got back in business."

"Oh, I think I've learned enough to stay airborne. Besides, to update my vocabulary, Jaworski encouraged me to start watching movies on Netflix. I don't want to brag, but I think my education is coming along pretty groovy."

Katherine burst into laughter. "*Groovy*? That's worse than *swell*. What movie did you get that from? On second thought, I don't even want to know. But don't repeat *groovy* unless you're trying to be funny."

Roger didn't understand her amusement, but he chuckled and gave a shrug. "All right, so this pilot still has to adjust the trim-tabs on his vocab. I'm getting there."

Katherine slipped her arms around him again. "And even before your time at the academy is finished, I'll be there to help you put some distinctive vocabulary into practice—words like date, dinner, candlelight, romance . . ."

"Mmm. Sounds like my kind of lingo."

"Now, that's my romantic pilot."

"Roger that." He tapped the tip of her nose with his finger. As she wrinkled her nose, Roger couldn't help recalling how wrinkled Walt had become. "Katherine, before we grow closer than we already are, I just have to warn you. I don't know what's going to happen to me. I mean, the whole Methuselah thing. I'm flying over uncharted territory here. I could fall down from a heart attack ten seconds from now, or I might live for hundreds of years. I just don't know what to expect."

She tightened her embrace and whispered, "Sign me aboard anyway, Captain. I'm not expecting a milk run. Intuition tells me that life with you promises to be one remarkable ride."

Their lips met again. In the warmth of Katherine's arms, the realization truly sank in. *I'm home!*